CODEX
A Psychological Thriller

Copyright © 2024 by Lisa Towles

First Publication June 2024
Indies United Publishing House, LLC

This is a work of fiction. Any references to historical events, real people, or real places are used fictitiously. Other names, characters, places and events are products of the author's imagination, and any resemblances to actual events or places or persons, living or dead, is entirely coincidental.

All rights reserved worldwide. No part of this publication may be replicated, redistributed, or given away in any form without the prior written consent of the author/publisher or the terms relayed to you herein, except in the case of brief quotations embodied in critical reviews and certain other noncommercial uses permitted by copyright law.

ISBN: 978-1-64456-712-8 [Hardcover]
ISBN: 978-1-64456-713-5 [paperback]
ISBN: 978-1-64456-714-2 [Kindle]
ISBN: 978-1-64456-715-9 [ePub]

Library of Congress Control Number: 2024902248

INDIES UNITED PUBLISHING HOUSE, LLC
P.O. BOX 3071
QUINCY, IL 62305-3071
indiesunited.net

The mind can calculate, but the spirit yearns, and the heart knows what the heart knows.

- Stephen King

To Lee – my love, my North Star, and my home

Other books by Lisa Towles

Terror Bay
Salt Island (E&A Series)
The Ridders
Hot House (E&A Series)
Ninety-Five
The Unseen
Choke

And published under the name Lisa Polisar:

Escape: Dark Mystery Tales
The Ghost of Mary Prairie
Blackwater Tango
Knee Deep

Codex
A Psychological Thriller

Lisa Towles

INDIES UNITED PUBLISHING HOUSE, LLC

Chapter 1

Present

I shouldn't be here. I know I shouldn't. But sometimes the decisions of the heart immobilize the brain and body. While my conscious intentions might challenge the tenets of logic, a more wicked part of me decided long before today that Wendell Peters must die. Exhausting all possible alternatives, in some twisted full circle, I'd been chosen for this karmic payback. Or maybe I chose myself.

Of course to those closest to him, those who reported the incident, he was already dead. I knew differently.

To see a billionaire like him living in this smelly shack filled with dying spider plants and moldy bread reminded me of all the glossy trappings I'd been avoiding. Shiny cars, new clothes, ideas that gleamed with promise at first, then faded into one of those hinged boxes we keep in the basements of our minds, dusty reminders that we've forgotten how to live. But as my favorite singer Sam Tinnesz says, the things you avoid have a way of hunting you down. Truth, he calls it. So be it.

"Hey, tighten up. Twenty seconds."

The house technically belonged to his mother, and my associate determined that she'd be gone today, all day, at a medical appointment. Bad for her, good for us. Fat beads of perspiration slid down my forehead from too many layers of clothes, or maybe too much adrenaline. The low humidity of this part of California, most parts for that matter, meant nothing inside the confines of this stagnant sweat box. Only mid-May, it had to be close to a hundred by now. Blame everything on climate change, right? Counting down, twenty seconds till we busted through Wendell Peters' tri-level encryption. I heard the click of the front entry door, which looked like you could blow it over with one breath. But he was like that, wasn't he? A broken stereotype full of surprises. A sheep and wolf all at once—you just never knew which.

"Copy that," I said into the earpiece. I touched the side of the house and crept under the eaves to the back, ready for the escape my partner said would happen. But no, I knew him. Wendell Peters looked like a street waif but that was his con. "You know he's not here, right? E? You hear me?"

"I hear something coming out of your mouth, just never quite sure what it is."

Even her snippy British elitism still appealed to me, funny in a demeaning sort of way that I'd never minded. How could we be so different and emerge from the same womb? E - Elaine Mariner, born and raised in England and me, two years later, born right here in Northern California. Same father, different mothers.

The floorboards creaked under our weight as we moved through the dark interior now, informed by the night goggles and a spill of moonlight outside in the grassy yard. I took the back half of the house, rummaging through cabinets and stacks of papers, palming the undersides of kitchen drawers.

"We're never gonna find it here," I said.

I heard the weight of her heavy sigh in my earpiece. "And why not? You said yourself it was the last place anyone would look. Wouldn't that make a clever hiding spot?"

"Reverse psychology, then. The old man lived twenty minutes ahead of everybody else."

Elaine's silhouette darkened the kitchen doorway. "Meaning what?"

"He was a finance guy." I shrugged like she would get it. "He dealt in futures."

"I thought you said he was a doctor."

"Dr. Mengele, maybe. He spent his career forecasting the future. Studying trends, statistics, history, to make predictions. I'm sure he knew we'd be coming."

I watched her roll her backpack off her shoulder and onto the floor, one hand on her hip. "Do you know how many hours it took me to get here? Yesterday, Heathrow at bloody four o'clock in the morning, emergency landing in Gatwick, boarded a different plane to JFK, then Atlanta, and I flew into LA, not SFO. That's a five-hour drive."

"E, listen…"

"You asked for my help, Angus. What are we doing here? And why's it so bloody hot? Northern California's supposed to be cold."

"You're whining. I hate that."

"I'm here. We're looking."

"I know," I said. "But we're not gonna find it here. Or him."

"You never used to be like this. Do you believe in conspiracy theories now too? Flat earth, fake moon landing?"

"I'm ignoring you."

"Angus, I know what this is." Her know-it-all voice. "Refusing to acknowledge one death points to a larger inability to—"

"Stop analyzing me. We're on a mission."

"I'm trying to help you."

I widened my eyes, visually telling her to fuck off.

"Fine." She heard me. Jessica was the last thing I wanted to think about right now, but that was so like Elaine, wasn't it, bringing up the past to avoid the present, or future.

"How's Miguel?" I asked of her drug-dealing love interest, knowing at any given point they were likely "amicably separated." See how she liked it.

"No comment."

We completed the task and searched each room of the abandoned safe house, wasting almost thirty minutes. Putting my night vision binoculars to use, I took pictures of random files and pieces of mail with the camera feature, while sliding my hands under mattresses, the pockets of jackets in a bedroom closet. Nothing so far labeled ADS or even BA-Vi, if those letters were actually a code. In my haste, something stopped me—my reflection in a full-length wardrobe mirror. I slid the goggles up to my forehead and took a step towards it like on a dare, an inch at a time to meet the reflection I'd so cleverly avoided for the past year. It was dark but my pupils had dilated. Same ragged crop of hair, mostly brown, lighter during summer. Same pointy nose, which Jess used to call my singular British feature, meaning the rest were Scottish from my mother's side. It wasn't a bad face, all things considered, and probably not so necessary to have hidden it from view all this time, except for the ugly truths your eyes can't help but tell you.

"Are we done now?" my sister asked with the patience of a toddler. "This isn't my idea of a good time."

"Almost. One more thing."

She moved beside me and swiveled the mouthpiece up to her left ear so we could talk quietly. I liked how her fairy blonde hair kicked up at the ends, an almost friendly gesture on an otherwise rigid exterior. I was staring at it and pointed.

"What?"

"I like it, your hair. It's a nice look for you," I said, careful with my tone, knowing she always cut her hair when a relationship ended. At least she didn't shave her head like last time. I couldn't help wondering what she was really doing here. Maybe she was running. Again.

"I don't feel like talking about—"

"I didn't ask you to. Touchy a bit?"

"Finish up. I want to get out of here," she clipped, and stood guard inside the window from behind a tweed curtain.

I moved past her to the back bedroom. "Can you hear me?" I whispered.

"Unfortunately, yes."

"Remember *The Second Stain*?"

"The second what?"

She'd heard me. It was her condescending way of repeating things to make it seem like you were talking out of your ass, wasting her time and irritating her more than usual. We'd grown up watching those episodes together, each of us living in different countries but spending every summer in enchanted Half Moon Bay, staying up late watching the BBC Granada versions of Sherlock Holmes with Jeremy Brett in the title role. Favorite Holmes conversations were as polarizing as James Bond but it was the one thing we always agreed on. As a ten-year-old boy, I thought he epitomized human intelligence in a way that indelibly shaped my conception of the world. Dig dig dig. And even if something seems like it fits, keep digging.

Imagining Holmes in his Dorchester tailcoat and pipe, I remembered the TV episode and the short story on which it was based. Dying to flip the light switch, I carefully moved two small tables to the hallway, then gently slid the bed over a few inches. A square rug remained on the floor—undetectable under the bed and too small to be considered decor. What the hell? I stared down at it feeling Elaine's prickly presence in the doorway. Her arms were probably crossed, one finger tapping the outside of her arm.

"Looking for blood on the floor, are you?" she asked.

"Ha, you do remember." The episode, and the story, referenced Sherlock Holmes noticing a blood stain on the floor without any blood on the underside of the rug that covered it. I pulled up the rug and tossed it onto the bed, then spread myself on all fours with my hands grasping for anything out of place. There could be a floorboard that wasn't nailed down, a trip wire, or a trap door. The heavy varnish on the boards surprised me, slick to the touch. Was that… Wait. I stopped moving.

"What is it?"

"I thought it was something…wet." I pulled back my hand and rubbed my fingers together, then touched them on the inside of my wrist. "Not wet. Cold."

Elaine crept down beside me, palming the spot I'd felt, one small patch of floor that felt at least ten degrees colder than the rest.

"Get me my—"

I heard breaking glass first, then the "pop" of a bullet hitting the wall of the bedroom six feet above my head. Jesus.

"Shit," she hissed. "How could he have found—"

"Get down." I waited a full ten seconds before moving again. I thought I'd heard the door after the shot was fired but wasn't certain. "Quick, help me get the room back together."

We fumbled getting the rug on the floor, dragging the bed back over it, then we each took one of the small tables from the hall and put them back, careful to keep our heads below the window. She'd said "he". Who...and found what? Found her? There was no time. God Elaine, who are you running from now?

I motioned for her to follow me to the next bedroom, which had a tree outside the window.

"And how do you suppose we might get out of here?" she asked.

"Alive you mean?"

As we slipped into the bedroom, the "chi-chick" of a round chambered into a semi-automatic handgun in the hallway reached our ears just before the voice boomed. "You won't."

CODEX

Chapter 2

Elaine's legs were already out the window when I turned back to see the origin of the voice in the hallway. I watched her turn her head and pause. The voice wasn't familiar to me, but she knew him. Miguel?

"Follow me. Hurry," she said.

But the man was gone. I could hear the heavy footsteps heading toward the first bedroom, no doubt searching for whatever he thought we'd gotten first. That would hopefully give us enough time for a fast exit. Still, why was he hanging back now? Waiting for something?

I found myself in this mystical limbo, Elaine's swift retreat with the help of a sycamore tree, and me desperate to stop our visitor from discovering the dirty little secrets Wendell Peters had been hiding from the world. In those tense seconds, it all fell into place. Wendell, my beloved Jessica, and a whole world I'd known nothing about until now...until it was too late.

I climbed out the window, still monitoring the man's movements. I could tell he hadn't moved the bed or any furniture. Maybe he was looking for Wendell Peters himself, or maybe like us, for evidence of his research—the million-dollar missing piece. As for me, I wouldn't rest until I'd found every last detail. And only now did I know where he'd been hiding it.

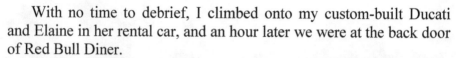

With no time to debrief, I climbed onto my custom-built Ducati and Elaine in her rental car, and an hour later we were at the back door of Red Bull Diner.

The last booth, the *Angus booth* as Rudy called it, was empty and as inviting as always. I pulled a menu out of the holder, set it in front of her and we sat.

Elaine scowled in her impractical clothes, arms crossed tightly across her chest. "You've memorized the menu or you're not eating?" she asked.

"Not hungry right now."

She weighed ninety-five pounds and could eat more than a body builder. Rudy, my best friend since our Air Force days, brought two waters to the table, his dark eyes glaring.

"Don't ogle my sister," I said.

A wide grin lifted his face. "Glamorous as ever. How are you doing, sweetie?"

Elaine rose and kissed his cheek. "Better now. Banana pancakes please."

"Coming right up." Rudy Richards, owner of Red Bull Diner, nodded and lumbered off with his six-foot-four, bulky frame. Elaine put her sunglasses in her purse, elbows on the table.

"What's that brain of yours concocting?" Her finger rolled around in the air pointing at my forehead. "I see it. What's going on in there? You know, don't you, about the cold floor?"

My phone buzzed with a text. From Rudy, who was six feet away from us. *Your other best friend's pulling in the lot.*

Dekker? I wrote back. *Shit.*

Get out of here, I'll cover you.

"Hello?" she said. "Need I remind you of the time and expense I incurred flying here at a moment's notice?"

"I think it's his laboratory, where the whole nightmare started," I said, my eyes on the door.

Rudy set a plate in front of Elaine. "Four minutes," he said to me.

"What?"

He raised his brow.

"No."

"I can see his car from here," he argued. "You know what he—"

"I'm not leaving," I said.

"He's pulling into the lot now. Come on, man, you could still leave through the back door and he'd never see you."

I looked at Elaine because, with her, there was no such thing as decisions. Act now with no remorse. It was one of her more enviable traits. Stuffing banana pancakes in her mouth, she side-glanced at Rudy and me. The glass door swung open with a flourish. Here we go.

"Angus Mariner..." the man announced, as if anyone else would care.

"You can't arrest me, Dekker."

"Who said anything about that?" Palms up.

Asshole. He'd been following me for days, bordering on harassment. I pointed to the cuffs dangling from his belt loop. "I haven't done anything wrong."

"Today you mean? Last time I checked, breaking and entering was still a felony in California. I'm within my rights to bring you in for..."

"Breaking and entering where?"

"You know where. Property owned by a Mr. Wendell Peters."

How could he have known this? "What evidence do you have? None." Now I wished I'd ordered food. I sipped Elaine's water instead.

Detective Walt Dekker with the San Mateo Police Department sat on one of the red swivel stools at the bar six feet from our table, arms crossed, Cheshire cat grin. "We're gonna bring a sofa into the jail with your name on it, you know, give you someplace more comfortable to sit every time we drag you in there."

"Fuck off. We're eating breakfast."

"You're coming with me."

"You have no proof that I entered any such property. Besides, it's not like it's a crime scene."

"The man's found dead under suspicious circumstances so it most certainly is a crime scene." Dekker looked at Elaine. "That's your blue rental car, Miss? You drove that because it would be less conspicuous than Mr. Mariner's motorcycle, I'm guessing."

"Don't answer that," I told her.

"I don't think it was a question," she said.

"And the probable cause to warrant my surveillance would be... what?"

Dekker moved from the elevated swivel chair at the bar to stand in front of the table. And with the agility of a cat, he gently crouched, angled his head into Elaine's neck, said "'Scuse me" and shoved her body to the left, where he settled in beside her. Elbows and shoulders touching, Elaine handled the intrusion with the comedy and grace of everything else: she sniffed loudly and wrinkled her nose, then fanned the air in front of her face. I made a point to watch her, laugh, then stifle that laugh just as Dekker caught my reaction. It was perfect, actually. Why? Because Elaine looked like a runway model and now she'd just humiliated Dekker, changing the balance of power. I silently counted. One...two...there, he rose and stood in front of the table again.

"Sorry to crowd you," he said to her.

"Just back from the gym? Or perhaps they turned the water off in your apartment?"

I shot her a 'that's enough' look. She caught it and nodded.

Dekker needed to save face, whether he was going to arrest us or not. "How's the search and rescue business going?" he asked with a smirk.

And how could he have known about that as well? I hadn't told anyone, and I'd only been out on two rescues so far. The law enforcement community in Half Moon Bay and San Mateo was small. Even still, I'd asked to keep my name out of it. And that was the crux of it, wasn't it? If I wanted to help search and rescue anonymously, why hadn't I used a fake name? The old me, pre-accident me, would have done that and not given it a second thought. I still wasn't back on my game yet, the game of life, the game of negotiation. I was still operating from reptilian brain survival mode. I hung my head and sighed, not caring that Dekker saw me.

"Fine. It's going fine." I looked up. "Kind of you to ask."

"Oh I'm not asking to be kind, believe me."

"No?" I asked. Elaine watched him like a firecracker waiting for a

CODEX

fuse.

"I know why you're doing it," Dekker said, back on the swivel stool, leaning against the counter. He crossed his legs, swiveled left and almost fell off the stool. But nothing fazed this guy. He could fall on the floor in front of us without his ego bruising, like he never had one in the first place.

He was baiting me to start a fight so he'd have witnesses and a more viable reason for arresting us. That way it wouldn't be only on suspicion of a felony, but he was betting on padding it with assault and battery. I tried to remember the way my grief counselor described yoga breathing in our sessions—four second inhale, eight second exhale, something like that. I felt like pulling a blanket over my head, because that was what trauma did to you—pulled apart your coping mechanisms so you'd go from zero to sixty in an instant. Dekker was more than just watching me. He was studying me, and seemed to understand where I was at. Still, he'd started it and had to run it through.

"I think you joined search and rescue so some part of you could rescue the wife you weren't able to save in that accident." His voice was venomous, but his face told me he was sorry for treading on sacred ground. I could tell.

Before he even got to the word accident, Elaine popped up and would have reached Dekker's throat had I not grabbed her skinny waist. At least my reactive instincts were in good form. Dekker put up his hands in front of his face to swat her away and take a victim stance in front of the other customers in view. Bastard. And me, where was my reaction to this affront? It worried me that she was so volatile and I'd lost my ability to be wounded. Which one of those made you more human? I wondered about this, about so many things.

"Get up, Angus. You're both coming with me."

Chapter 3

One Year Ago

May

The sky looked strange, and I'd been hearing weird noises for the past hour. Footsteps. Sure, I could have been dreaming. But thuds, too, and the shuddering tremor that vibrated the floating deck I slept on every night. I'd built it myself from repurposed, pressure-treated lumber and attached it to my Airstream trailer. That way I could sleep outside with the stars and the surf, protected by the wall of dunes. In other words, free.

There, again. Footsteps.

Running this time, and the sound of heavy breathing. Where, though? It was all rocks down by the water, too dangerous for running even in daylight. My fingers fumbled for the crumpled pack and pulled out my last cigarette, a nasty habit that kept me from nastier ones. I leaned over to light it and moaned at the same creak in my lower back, exacerbated no doubt by sleeping on a hard surface with nothing but a thin sleeping bag. In some strange way, my self-imposed discomfort

CODEX

right now was a form of comfort. Or maybe penance.

I jerked upright, ears peeled for my frantic runner. I felt the thump of his steps on the sand heading away from me down the beach, but something was behind him nearer to the parking lot.

My posh Airstream was parked in the back of Rudy's property facing the water. I'd declined his invitations to stay in his house, so of course he didn't understand why I wouldn't want to sleep *inside* the trailer. At the same time, he knew how claustrophobic I'd become, since the night that changed my life forever, observing the peculiar vices that were keeping me sane.

I heard a voice, a word repeated or maybe a moan that resembled the word no. I reached under my pillow for my gun, remembering Rudy took it from me for safekeeping. Owning things, anything, seemed so pointless now.

The footsteps were higher up, at the top of the dunes. I could hear two people running. Someone was being chased in the dark along a treacherous path - a thirty-foot cliff drop to the beach below. I stubbed out the cancer stick and shook myself awake, willing myself to care about something. Anything. This stranger might die out there in the dark tonight. But how could I stop it?

Fine, I'd go wander around in the dark stalking a potential murderer and his intended prey. I heard the word "No" again, followed by "Leave me alone." The voice was thin and strained, with a desperation I recognized all too well. I didn't seem to care much about my own life lately. Was I really willing to save somebody else's?

I jammed my feet into the tennis shoes on the ground under the platform, they were freezing cold. My own fault for sleeping outside like a teenager. My leather jacket was draped over my bike, but I didn't want to risk being seen. I pulled a hoodie over my head and took off on foot, away from the beach toward the dune path that ran the length of Ferry Road to Highway 1 and Pillar Point. A pickup roared down the street, masking the sound of my runner, dammit. Now where were they? Rudy kept binoculars in his truck, which was locked. There, another *No*, I caught it. Further down the beach now, it still sounded like he was in the rockier part of the bluff.

I turned back to grab my phone from its hiding place and took off again down the sandy beach path, the moon watching me, judging me,

13

waiting. Two new sounds now, layered on top of each other, a metallic poof followed by a guttural moan, likely the sound of my runner taken out by a pistol with a silencer. I knew that sound. Think, Angus. Order of operations. Call the cops with my phone right now? The shooter could see the light from my screen if they're down on the beach. Or I could slip back to the trailer first. But if the runner's not dead, he could be by the time an ambulance gets here.

Care about something, goddamnit. Save him. Do it.

The old me, the before version would be halfway down the beach by now, following the shooter with the cops behind me. But things change when your heart falls out of your chest. That invisible symbiosis with the brain is unerringly stunted, like neurons that stop growing, cells that stop replicating.

I hadn't heard any footsteps running away from the beach, but a car sped off just now, no tires screeching but obviously someone was in a hurry to get out of here. I kept my iPhone light off and didn't bring a flashlight. I'd trained my eyes, after sleeping outdoors every night for a year, to adjust to pitch darkness in seconds. I jogged in and out of the rocky ledge that overlooked the north side of the Half Moon Bay jetty, knowing somewhere down there was a man whose light was dimming. There, just ahead, I caught sight of a dark mound, but when I approached, it was a coat that felt like a summer weight wool suit jacket. Old me, FBI-me had known about such things, had nice clothes and a place to wear them.

It would be an hour, still, before the sky was light enough to see anything. By then, he could be dead. So I did the next best thing.

"911, what is your emergency?" said a female operator after making me hold for thirty seconds.

"I just heard a gunshot fired near where I live, and before that a man was being chased."

I provided a few more details, none of which were the ones they really needed, like a description of the victim or the assailant. How far away was I from the shooter when I heard the shot? Hard to tell, at night, in the dark, under the roar of ocean waves. I estimated one

CODEX

hundred and fifty feet. I asked them to send an ambulance and said the man might still be alive, but I couldn't see him.

"Do you know for sure the victim is a man, sir? You didn't see him, correct?"

"No, I didn't see him. But I heard him. He said *no, no*, over and over, as he was running down the beach."

"And an assailant was chasing him at that point?"

"It sounded like two people running," I said.

"An officer will need to take a statement from you. Are you at home right now sir?"

The dispatcher used the word home. That was the problem, wasn't it? I got triggered easily these days. At the sound of the word, I found myself fumbling for keys, changing out of sneakers to put on boots, and crunching over Rudy's gravel walkway to my motorcycle. It was the same morning ride I took every morning, ostensibly to find myself. Forever looking.

But today's ride was to escape.

Chapter 4

I killed her. I did. Officially it was deemed an accident, but since it was my event and my idea to go, of course I was to blame for the bluest eyes I'd ever seen ceasing to open again. She had this special way of rolling her long, red mane into a bun at the crown of her head —all in the span of two seconds. I don't know how she did it, but there was so much I didn't know about her. She once said, in passing, that keeping secrets was her superpower.

I remember the day she announced her rebellion from the most prestigious law firm in San Francisco, launching an eponymous private practice after stealing half her old clients. They'd always seemed shady to me - Worthington, Pendleton, Bradbury and Burnes with an e. They'd promised to make her a partner after another year if she stayed, but she never believed them and left the next morning. After a week they called her in, offered her instant partnership, and demanded she bring her clients back. This new offer also included a 40% salary increase, which she'd never cared about in the first place. In true Don Draper style, she brought her insouciant swagger to their conference room and reluctantly accepted their offer. The woman belonged on Wall Street. So if she wasn't looking for more money, why did she return? Just to humiliate them? "I don't like bullies," was her answer.

CODEX

But hadn't she been the one to bully them? I asked her, of course, to which she answered with her same sideways smile, always a trick up her sleeve.

My brain hadn't been quite right since the accident, and not from any traumatic brain injury. I'd read about grief and recovery as part of my FBI training in Quantico, intellectually understanding the different stages and typical blockers. As for me, you can't recover when you haven't yet grieved. My broken heart was a lump of coal and my soft tissue injuries, well, that might take even longer. My body was sore every morning after sleeping on a wooden plank. I still liked it that way, using the pain and discomfort to remind me that at least some part of me was still alive.

I took off on my typical loop, east on Highway 92 to Upper Crystal Springs Reservoir, stopping to smoke one cigarette and drink in the serenity of that still, always-blue water. It was a fifteen-minute ride and, if stretched out, took the better part of an hour. I redirected my brain away from that word—*home*, with its painful connotations of the life I'd lost and sucked in fresh air to clear my head and lungs. Almost light now, I turned the corner on Princeton Avenue toward Rudy's waterfront property and saw flashing blue lights. Good, they made it. I wondered about the body, realizing the height of that drop from the rocky bluff.

I slowed my speed, noticing three—no, four—squad cars and an ambulance parked on the grassy shoulder of Columbia Avenue with barely enough room to walk my bike down the gravel driveway. I hadn't yet mentioned anything to Rudy, because when I left the incident still had nothing to do with me. I suspected that was no longer true.

Hey, I texted him, still in the street. *Are you home?*

Nope, Fridays are busy so I got here early. Noticed your bike was gone. Everything ok?

Cops are here, I heard a shot fired down the beach a ways about an hour ago. Called it in then went for a ride.

Let me know if you need help, I can slip out if needed.

Will do.

17

A female officer, early thirties with long, reddish-brown hair, watched me park my bike. I nodded at her, eyes wide. The place crawling with cops. Jesus.

"Angus Mariner," I said, approaching the officer. She looked down at my hand a moment before shaking it.

"Do you live here, sir?"

Her name tag read "Lopez." She had a long, sculpted nose and a high forehead, which together gave her an authoritarian air that I didn't appreciate this early in the morning. "Yeah, I called it in." I crossed my arms. "Did you find the guy who fell?" I asked, remembering my own law enforcement training, reminding myself to be careful with my words.

Raised brow. "Can you tell me why you decided to leave the premises after calling in a possible homicide?"

"I never used that word, Ma'am. I just said I heard someone running, then a shot fired, and a heavy thump that sounded like someone had gone over the bluff."

"You didn't check it out?" she asked.

"I didn't want to get shot," I pinged back and waited.

"I just find it curious that you'd witness something like this and pick that moment to go riding around on your motorcycle."

I looked at the sand under my feet, humbled suddenly by the emotions in my chest and throat. "Morning tradition, I guess. Since my wife died."

"Sorry to hear that, sir," her voice lower in pitch. "When was this?"

I looked up now into her dark eyes, desperate to veer the conversation away from Jessica but knowing the hazards of redirects to a police officer. "A year ago," I said, one year, three months, twenty-seven days, two hours. Now I wished I'd asked Rudy to come back.

"Do you own a gun, Mr. Mariner?" Officer Lopez asked.

"Yes. I mean yes I own one but my friend Rudy keeps it for me." I lifted my chin toward Rudy's beach house. "It's registered to me, though."

"Transferring a firearm is a violation of your gun permit in

CODEX

California. Are you in the habit of lending firearms to your friends?" she asked, but this wasn't a real shakedown. She seemed to arrive at the answer on her own.

Again, out of practice with the psychological games of law enforcement, I wondered how much to say and if I should answer at all. "I haven't touched that gun in over a year. I think that's what you need to know for this investigation anyway. Rudy will corroborate that."

She nodded, pinching her lips. "I need you to come down to the station today and give us a statement about exactly what you heard." I blinked back without answering. "It's not really optional," she added, tilting her head to the side.

"Fine. Whenever you want. I'm ready."

Officer Lopez turned to watch two crews positioning a body on a canvas stretcher on the beach and wrestling it up the treacherous slope to the top of the bluff. I normally only allowed myself one or two cigarettes a day. I took out a new pack and burned through three, wearing the soles off my boots pacing on the gravel drive. Rudy asked for status reports about every thirty minutes. I'd ignored his last few texts.

"What's going on over there?" he asked.

"I'm headed to the precinct—"

"San Mateo?"

"No, Half Moon Bay, to give a statement about the body they found."

"Christ. I can't leave you alone for a minute, can I?"

"Yeah, good times."

"Do I need to call your lawyer or what?"

"You might." I hung up.

Lopez stood down on the beach with her hands on her hips, supervising the extraction of the body, looking like a badass boss and a woman of authority. I didn't want to but I liked her, seeing a few sparks of warmth under her rigid exterior. She loped back up to Rudy's yard after another thirty minutes of discussion with two younger officers. I stubbed out another cancer stick when she approached, ready with my pitch.

"And I'm guessing I can't provide a statement here and now

because there are tactical advantages to getting a potential suspect alone in a room with nothing but their thoughts."

She blinked her long lashes. "Exactly. You a cop?"

"No."

"FBI?" she pressed.

"Not relevant."

"Retired then," she decided, pleased with herself.

"Need to know, Ma'am."

She broke into a full smile. "I do need to know. Look—"

"No longer FBI. Not retired," I said, the dark dread returning to my chest like a storm cloud that lived inside you.

"Involuntarily separated?"

I was tired of this hapless, non-interview. "Voluntary."

She was watching my every move, those eyes like chess pieces on an invisible board, decisions being made. "After the accident?" she asked.

I was sure I hadn't used the word accident. So she knew. She knew what happened, to me and to Jess. What a faker. The wind speed had increased to about twenty miles per hour in the past thirty minutes. Officer Lopez zipped her jacket to the neck.

"Don't you miss it?" she asked.

"Yeah. But the fact is, I'm not capable of working right now. Not at that capacity."

She turned away to check the status of the crews. "Too bad you're not a pilot," she mumbled.

"Why's that?"

"We're down a couple air support officers right now. Sit tight a minute. I'll take your statement here."

"Appreciate it."

Chapter 5

Something in that conversation obviously changed her mind, maybe realizing I was likely more skilled at witness interrogation than she was. I was older than her, but not by much. Beautiful eyes, and not lacking in compassion. Always good to have allies.

Another text from Rudy buzzed my phone. *What's happening over there? They'd better not be messing up my succulents. They're very fussy you know.*

Your ice plants are fine, I typed back without looking at them. *They're not even yours.*

I saw the little dots blinking back and laughed to myself. Rudy and his ice plants. *Not those*, he corrected. *Ice plants are indestructible. The smaller ones on the left.*

The little orange things? Sorry, someone stepped on them. I think they're done.

Don't even try it. Any word on the victim?

I wrote back about the crews taking the body to the Medical Examiner's Office in San Mateo and said I'd stay in touch. Rudy could have asked if I was a suspect, if they'd questioned me or arrested me, but that wasn't his way. One of our many shared traits, he assumed I was okay unless I said otherwise, appreciating that verbal communication worked best when it was tactical and transactional. The wind came up stronger now. Thick, dark clouds hovered over the white capped water. Someone had died on this beach today. The sky knows all our secrets.

Lopez said it was too windy to get a written statement here, despite her original invitation. I ended up riding with her to the newly renovated police substation on Kelly Avenue. Half Moon Bay used to have its own police department and separate substation, but three years ago it was torn down and the city began contracting with San Mateo County law enforcement. Now the new substation functioned as local Half Moon Bay policing but with county-level resources and staffing. Best of both worlds, in theory.

I'd been here four times in the past year. Once for speeding on my motorcycle, when the ticketing process resulted in angry outbursts. Next was drunken and disorderly behavior in a public venue at the Old Princeton Landing, one of the oldest bars here and by far my favorite. A third time for assault...for repeatedly sleeping on a public bench. Not just any bench either. A special bench that in some way still smelled like Jess' favorite fragrance. A San Mateo Detective relegated to work at the new Half Moon Bay station found me sleeping there first thing in the morning every day for a while. When he demanded I find somewhere else to sleep, threatening to remove the bench if I didn't, let's just say it triggered a reaction resulting in a bloody nose. The detective seemed sturdy enough and wasn't badly injured, but his huge ego was poised for revenge. I'd managed to avoid the precinct for the past few months. Maybe today was my reckoning.

Officer Lopez seemed surprised when I asked to ride in the back of the squad car. "Long story," I said as a sort of blanket response to uncomfortable questions. The new building smell had faded since my last visit, with a new Community Policing banner hanging over the dispatch area in the front.

I ended up in one of the four interrogation rooms. Jarring fluorescent lights and one chair on one side of a rectangular table. I knew the routine, so I sat there and let the interrogation unfold. Fighting took too much energy. Besides, pushing back meant acknowledging something was wrong, and I knew I wasn't stable enough to open Pandora's box—right now or ever.

CODEX

Lopez opened the door and gently set it closed, an apology on her face.

"Someone else joining us?" I asked.

Eyebrow raise.

"God no."

Lopez stood aside and grinned as Detective Walt Dekker pushed open the door. Lopez leaned against the wall behind the door, arms crossed, eyes and nose contracted like she'd smelled something bad. Good, I could use a friend right now.

Dekker slammed the door. His jacket was unbuttoned, his brown, wavy hair matted on one side like he'd been napping. Hilarious. "Mr. Mariner," he said, like Agent Smith greeting Neo in "The Matrix". I should have been afraid of him, but I wasn't. Risk is nothing when you've got nothing to lose. "Pleasure to see you again."

"How's your nose?" I winked at Officer Lopez. She closed her eyes and tried not to laugh.

"Lopez, please bring Mr. Mariner—"

"Coffee? Yeah I'd love some."

"A pen and paper."

There were no windows in the room; the requisite two-way glass window was on the left wall. I suspected no one was watching today, and it was just Dekker and me volleying animosity across the table.

"Appreciate you coming in today."

"Didn't realize it was optional."

"Well, it isn't really."

Lopez returned, set a pen, two pages, and a cup of water in front of me. She didn't look at Dekker because I suspected she didn't care what he thought about the water or anything else. I picked up the pen and narrated my words as I wrote them.

"Okay here we go," I said. "Angus Mariner." Dekker rolled his eyes. This was gonna be fun. "I was sleeping outside," I wrote and said aloud, "I heard someone running down the beach, I heard them say *no* over and over. Twenty minutes later, I heard a shot fired and I called 911. The—End." I set the pen down and pushed the page toward Dekker.

"Nice," Lopez replied with a snicker.

"Is that what he told you on the beach?" Dekker asked her.

"Yes, sir."

Dekker snatched the pages from the table. "Sleeping outside. Are you...camping or something?"

"No. I just sleep outside."

Dekker moved an inch further into the room, eyes squinted. "Why?"

"Personal preference."

"Like...on the bare ground? Are you a Navy Seal or something?"

Lopez and I exchanged looks, and Dekker saw this. He was rattled and desperate to change the balance of power in the room. Now, suddenly, I cared about something.

"Where exactly do you sleep, Mr. Mariner?"

"A wooden platform I built onto my Airstream. I put a sleeping bag on it. It's perfect. Officer Lopez saw it, didn't you?" I asked her.

"Yep, saw it," she said.

"Why not sleep in your trailer?" Dekker made a lemon face.

"Why do you care?"

"Is it possible you were waiting for the victim, and being outside gave you easier access to him?"

I shrugged. "Who's the victim?"

"You tell me!" Dekker said, more animated now, losing what little composure he had to begin with. Omg, I had a new reason to live.

"You don't know, do you?" I said.

Dekker crossed his arms again.

"Well you're the police, aren't you supposed to be investigating these things? I was awakened by the sound of footsteps, and someone was chasing him."

"That wasn't in your thirty-five-word statement. Guess you left a few things out."

"Yeah, I guess so. Sorry about that. I'd be happy to add it if you'd like." I was being ingratiating and it was ungluing him. Lopez was frozen but I could tell she was on my side.

Dekker tossed the pages back on the table. "Anything else you forgot? Like maybe what the hell you were really doing out there and why you fled the crime scene?"

"I did nothing of the sort," I said, calmly. "There was no crime scene when I went for my morning ride. I heard a shot fired and I

CODEX

immediately called it in. Was that not the right thing to do?"

Dekker dragged his fingers through his hair. "Lopez, what was that about a gun you mentioned?"

"Mr. Mariner said he owns a gun and it's kept at the home of his friend, who lives in the house on the beach property. A Mr. Rudy Richards."

They pinged this topic back and forth a few minutes, me determined to share as little as possible with Dekker and liking the fact that my new ally, Officer Lopez, knew things about me that he didn't. So far anyway, they had nothing on me, and until we all found out who the victim was, they couldn't reasonably consider me a suspect. Sure, I was at the crime scene, but only because I lived there. I knew it was possible Lopez would tell him about my wife, and what I'd shared about Rudy taking my gun. But for now, I knew I'd won this round so I didn't care what happened, and Dekker hated that. Mariner 1, Dekker 0. Nice.

Rudy picked me up from the station and brought me back to his house, even though he'd already clocked in at the diner. I saw my reflection in the passenger window of his car as I got out.

"Cops asked about my gun," I told him on his front porch.

He was in the doorway, still wearing a dirty apron. "Do they consider you a suspect?"

"Nah. Not yet, I don't think, or they wouldn't have let me go. But they'll probably—no, certainly—ask you about my gun."

"That's fine. I haven't touched it. Better hope the rifling doesn't match the gun that killed that guy on the beach."

"No kidding," I said, distracted by a noise behind me. A small fishing boat slowed its engine heading toward the harbor pier. I turned back and saw concern in my friend's eyes. "I know."

"What?" he squinted his eyes.

"I know what I look like. It's bad. Worse than last time."

"You off?" he asked after a pause.

"Off the wagon? Hell no. That's why I sleep outside, man."

Eyeroll. "What's one got to do with the other? Sleeping outside keeps you from drinking?"

25

"No, smoking keeps me from drinking. Most of the time."

"You just said—"

"I don't know, man, I don't know. Stop grilling me."

"I'm sorry. Sleep wherever you want." Rudy was half in the doorway, awkwardly holding the door open with one arm, his bad arm, the one that got injured and always hurt.

I let time slow down a moment while I thought about it. I turned, knowing the ocean always gave me answers, sometimes to questions I hadn't yet asked.

"Come in the house, Angus. God made coffee for mornings like this."

Chapter 6

Unfortunately Rudy knew nothing about good coffee and wasn't even qualified to make it. I was a purist, but that wasn't the point. He was my best friend in the world and my shattered heart still had space for gratitude. We talked about my two part time jobs—deliveries for his diner and search and rescue work I did because the after-hours work paid well. Maybe that's not the only reason. Maybe I liked the risk and danger of it, or liked being peripherally involved in law enforcement because it was all I really knew.

He drove us to the diner after that, then I took his white van to do four supply pickups for him. I walked home from the diner, not even a mile, and the fresh air always felt so good to my soul. A flock of hungry gulls swirled over my head gaming for dinner as I noticed a squad car parked in front of Rudy's house.

Carl Deakins, once a Hell's Angel, went through the police academy and was later promoted to Human Resources because the previous HR Director left one day for lunch and never came back. I could see his beefy forearm out the driver's side window, finger tapping the side mirror. I approached the car giving him a wide berth.

"Hey Carl," I said with a curious smile, pretending to be glad to see him.

Single nod. "Angus."

His neck tattoos seeped out over his shirt collar, and I knew he had a 1% tattoo on his left forearm, covered up by his uniform. "You lost? Substation's that way." I pointed behind him.

"Came to talk to you, actually," he said, emphasis on the you. I felt a pitch hanging in the air.

"What about?"

"Could we talk somewhere?" He squinted behind me at the tiny Airstream parked precariously close to the dune cliff. I could've jerked him around but, after the encounter with Dekker, I was all out of bullshit.

"Yeah. Come on in."

I fumbled in my pocket for the trailer key. The sixteen-foot Airstream, just a few years old, was a ridiculously overindulgent space for someone with Spartan taste. After the accident, Elaine insisted on buying it for me, and I was too afraid to ask where she got the money to pay for not only the rig but the lavish customizations. Dark walnut cabinets, bamboo floors, quartz counters, stainless drawer pulls, a full-sized fridge. And the walnut carried over to the walls. It looked more like the captain's quarters of a luxury ship. Half the time, I felt like giving it away to a homeless person, and I still might. But the other half liked the creature comforts even if I never touched them. I also knew someday the dam would break and I'd need a place to hide. I reluctantly unlocked the door and stood aside so Carl could enter.

"Damn, man. You live here?"

"Sort of," I mumbled, gesturing toward the small dining table with cushioned, bench seats. "Something to drink?" Carl lowered himself to the edge of the seat gazing around the place. It always happened this way, the oooh and ahhhs whenever I had occasion to bring someone back here.

"Water no ice."

"Icemaker's not hooked up in the fridge anyway."

"Cold water's bad for your gut. Apparently, according to my ex-wife."

The ex-wife that he'd recently remarried, that is. Small towns had their advantages.

CODEX

He grabbed the water I'd set in front of him. "I'm sorry," he said. "For what?"

"I know what happened to your wife. To both of you. I'm just— sorry. I should've said it up front."

"It's alright Carl, thanks for mentioning it. We've all lost something, right?"

He was still looking around. "This place looks like it was designed by Architectural Digest."

I doubted Carl Deakins had ever read that magazine. "It was, sort of. My sister's a designer and she customized everything for me. What are we doing here, Carl? I don't like it in here."

"You live here, don't you?"

"I live on my bike. I ride around. Occasionally sleep." I stared back now, starting to get annoyed by the intrusion. He had that sales pitch look on his face, like he was about to offer me an opportunity he knew I wouldn't want. I wondered if Carl worked in the local station here in Half Moon Bay, or if he'd driven all the way from San Mateo, and that made me wonder if he worked with Officer Lopez, what her first name was, and when it might feel okay to think about a woman again. Maybe never.

"So you're a pilot!" he said, breaking into game show host mode, showing his straight but yellowed teeth.

"Used to be. Why?"

"Do you, well, did you enjoy flying?"

"You kidding? Rudy and I…" I angled my head toward the house. "Air Force. Before I joined the bureau." The memory made my stomach queasy. Most memories did.

"You must miss it then," he said, still fishing.

"Carl—" I sighed.

He put up his hands. "Alright, sorry to beat around the bush. As you can imagine, we've got some supply chain problems here, also in San Mateo, really everywhere."

I assumed he meant post-pandemic, which by now was a while ago. "What's in short supply?"

"Pilots."

I remembered what Officer Lopez said about air support. "You need an Air Marshal?" I nodded. "Officer Lopez mentioned it when she was out here this morning, interrogating me. You know her?"

"Regina, yeah. I know her."

Regina, nice. I liked that name. I watched his face for signs, a slick smile that might tell me how he felt about her, or an eyeroll that might betray he thought she was a drama queen. His face was blank.

"Anyway, we're down two air support officers."

As a kid, I'd always loved the idea of bad guys being chased down by helicopters. The little kid inside me who never grew up was wide awake now. Carl took two sips of water, watching my face for the signs I wasn't giving him. He kept talking.

"As you know, an Air Marshal is a covert, federal, counter-terrorist role, flying undercover on commercial flights to investigate possible terrorists. But they also work with local law enforcement. We've got none of that right now. I'm in Human Resources trying to rebuild staffing after a lot of attrition due to Covid, federal legislation, budget cuts, fucking politics. And we've got a shortage of pilots, and someone told me you had your pilot's license." He sat back and smiled, end of pitch. "So here I am. Interested? The pay's good."

I didn't care about money, and no I wasn't interested. "I'll think about it."

Understanding human nature, he seemed to know the conversation was over. He took a minute to wrangle his large frame out from behind the dining table and took one last look around the place. "Beautiful home. You ever want to sell it, let me know."

I opened the door and stepped down to the gravel.

He eyed me hard when I shook his meaty paw, almost like he'd had another reason for coming. We stood there a moment while waves crashed onto the beach below.

"Later," he said and took off down the driveway.

I replayed Carl's last comments and the word *home* felt so alien. Not that a mobile home couldn't be a home, but for me the word was still indelibly linked to my house in San Carlos, twenty-five minutes away on the other side of Highway 280. I locked the trailer door behind me and stood at the edge of the bluff watching the sky darken to midnight blue. Time for a ride, and then dinner.

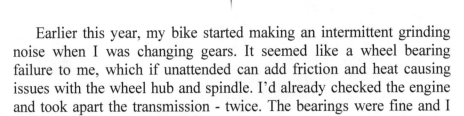

Earlier this year, my bike started making an intermittent grinding noise when I was changing gears. It seemed like a wheel bearing failure to me, which if unattended can add friction and heat causing issues with the wheel hub and spindle. I'd already checked the engine and took apart the transmission - twice. The bearings were fine and I hadn't had time to continue the investigation.

Weird day, I didn't feel like my typical ride into the hills tonight. I found an empty road so I could listen to the engine when it changed from fourth to fifth. Still that same scraping noise, which could be something as simple as insufficient transmission fluid or something more complicated, and expensive, like a dragging clutch.

I landed where I usually ended up this time of night—Half Moon Bay Brewing Company. The patio looked over the water and was a great place to smoke and think while my burger was cooking. The pretty, dark-haired girl wasn't there tonight, so I gave my order to a younger, skinny guy, the kind who belonged on that TV show Below Deck. Spikey, blond hair, hyper movements, looked like a cocaine user. Hard to tell, and who was I to judge someone else, right? The guy said twenty minutes, same as the dark-haired girl always said. I didn't bother asking where she was, because I didn't know her name, and if I asked, that would be seen as interest.

I could tell myself that I didn't really care that much, but I'd gotten used to seeing the same face every night I came in here. Not a bad face, as far as faces go, and I liked her hair. That self-confession came at a price, though, a slippery slope down the path of self-loathing and guilt. Sure, it had been over a year and I knew Jess would want me to be happy. Thing is, loathing might be a more comfortable place.

Chapter 7

A few stars blinked back, peeking through layers of overlapping blues and grays. I felt tomorrow's incoming rain in the air while the scent of low tide crept up the bluffs.

"How 'ya doin' on this nice night?" someone asked behind me, not from one of the patio chairs but perched on the edge of a railroad tie under the doorway. I turned away from the water and leaned on the railing to get a look at him. Scruffy beard, wrinkled, my dad would say he looked like fifty miles of bad road. I don't know why I thought he was a biker. The only bike in sight was mine, thirty feet away.

"Doing well. How about you, sir?" I said, lapsing back into rapport-building mode, a vestige of the former me. As a federal investigator, I'd been trained on how to use social and psychology skills to get close to people, pretending that I cared about them to extract the necessary intel. I always hated the duplicity. How was that any different from a con man? It seemed like such pointless theater, useful for sussing out criminals from underground but left you with a hole in your heart.

"I saw you in there," the man said, pointing to the bar and dining room.

I tried to find the meaning in that phrase, wondering if he'd emphasized one word over another. I didn't move from my spot against the railing, almost too far away to hear him. I liked it that way.

I stood there like I didn't have a care in the world. Sure, I came here three, four times a week and ordered the same burger and side salad, most times eating right here standing up under the stars, silently talking to Jessica. I liked how the chef always put two thick, ripe orange slices on my salad, like a garnish of hope that toppled over as it was being carried in the to-go box. I ate every bite of it, every time, like I knew it was the sustenance that would repair the holes in my heart and fortify my body for whatever new version of me was emerging. So yeah, I was comfortable here at this bar. Right now, lately, this seemed like home, as much as I was capable.

I came back to the man's comment, watching his face as he watched me.

"I think there might be more interesting people to watch."

"Her name's Jordan," he said.

"Who?"

"The girl bartender, you were looking for her."

"No, I wasn't."

The man's wrinkled finger shot up, and a smile broke out on his face, showing teeth that looked too white for his age and condition. "But you know who I mean." He nodded once, deciding something. Who the hell was this guy?

Right on cue, the dark-haired girl walked out with a to-go box that I knew was my dinner, with real silverware rolled in one of their large, white linen napkins. It made eating out of a box a bit more ceremonial. She handed it to me and I set it on one of the patio tables behind me.

"Thanks." I'd already paid inside.

"I told him your name, Jordan," the old man bellowed. "I could tell he was wondering."

"Stop causing trouble, Wendell. Go inside and eat your dinner. I've got you set up at your favorite table in the back."

So she knew him. That made the encounter a little less odd. Every bar had one, right?

"Yes, Ma'am," the man said, struggled to his feet and retreated inside like a student to the principal's office.

She came out to the railing, palms up, eyes wide. "Sorry about that," she said, a little sheepish. "Hope he didn't say anything embarrassing about me. He does that, or he did last night."

"Is he a regular or something? I've never seen him before."

"Not like you, you're here every other night," she said, looked up, then quickly down into the water. I guess that meant she'd noticed me. "He showed up a couple days ago, comes in the morning and hangs out till closing."

"What does he want?" I asked.

She shook her head. "A handout maybe? I don't know, there's more to him than meets the eye, I'm sure of it." She looked back at the patio doors and wiped her hands on her pants. "We might as well be civilized. I'm Jordan, nice to meet you." She held out her hand and I grabbed it without shaking it, unsure what to do next. Her skin felt warm and I could feel the pulse of her energy with my index finger on her wrist. After releasing it, I thrust mine into the pocket of my jacket, shamed by my lack of social grace. "Angus," I said.

"Nice name."

"I never thought so." I pulled out a cigarette and lit it. "Oh sorry, do you mind?"

She stared at me, then at the cigarette between my fingers.

"You don't look like a smoker," I said. "Would you like one?"

"I'm not, anymore." She closed her eyes and drew the toxic smoke into her nose.

"Still trying to quit?" I held my hand out over the banister to let the ocean pull away the smoke. "Sorry about that."

"No problem," she said. "Temptation shows you how strong you are, right?"

"Ironic."

"What?" she asked.

"You're a bartender trying to quit smoking, and I'm an alcoholic talking to a bartender." I hadn't been to a meeting in a long time. It felt funny saying that word now.

A small, polite nod and smile. I could tell she wanted to say I'm sorry and was so glad she didn't. "Sort of poetic in a way."

"More like a Greek tragedy," I mumbled, to which she laughed out loud, an accidental, apologetic laugh.

The moon slid above the dark clouds to observe our awkward

CODEX

moment, shining a white line on the tips of the tiny waves. We stayed like that for a good thirty seconds, waiting to see who would break the silence, who would make it okay to move on from our pain.

"Well, the Raiders won today. That's something." She leaned hard on the railing, hanging her head toward the water sloshing below.

"Considering their record this season. Las Vegas, I'm still not used to that."

"No kidding," she said. "That move was tough on diehard fans like me."

"Football fan?"

"Football family," she said. "Four brothers, and my dad and *his* four brothers all watched football together growing up. Way too many men in that house."

"Four brothers probably meant four bodyguards."

"They barely let me leave the yard till I was eighteen." She stifled a yawn, reminding me that this was probably the end of a long shift. "I'm closing tonight so I gotta clean up."

I can't say why, but something made me want to ask her if she needed help. Even in the awkwardness, there was something here, on this patio and in her presence that felt almost comfortable. I watched her walk back toward the glass doors, take out the stoppers and, before closing them all the way, she poked her head between them. "Goodnight. Angus."

Chapter 8

I thought about how cold that burger would be by the time I got home, the compostable cardboard box stowed in the open cage on the back of my bike. I had a microwave in the trailer, and of course I wouldn't use that to reheat my dinner. That would make too much sense.

Through the branches of a large oak growing smack in the middle of the parking lot, I caught sight of the moon again, this time slipping back behind the clouds. My tacit cue to return to the safety of my little hobo camp.

"She's not married, you know."

The familiar voice, gravelly, taunting now, and he'd already interrupted me once tonight. In the parking lot twenty steps from my bike, I could have easily ignored him, pretended like I hadn't heard him, and drove off. So she wasn't married. So what?

"Neither are you. Anymore," he added.

Obviously baiting me, ohhh the temptation. I could crouch low and set my dinner box on the ground, clasp my hands behind my back, and approach slowly, unleashing my years of human behavior expertise to dismantle his composure and twist the power out of him thread by thread. I'd done it, many times. The gray mask of dusk covered the

CODEX

whole waterfront now except for a narrow slice of orange, which lit up the man's crooked teeth and stubbly face.

"What do you want from me?" My tone was curious but neutral, monotone but not disinterested. He'd gone in the restaurant at the woman's request, yet here he was again, this time on a mound of dirt under some tall shrubs between two railroad ties. Had he walked in the back and come out the front? It was a great spot, actually, with a perfect view of sea and sky. But I'd gotten here first and he was the infiltrator. Now I needed to find out why.

"I have something for you." The man slid down, planted his feet and wobbled, regained his footing and wobbled again when he took a step. Drunk. Great. I stayed put and waited, drawing the clean, salty air in my lungs. He pulled something out of one pocket of his fleece-lined denim jacket. Keys, I heard them jingle under his grip.

"You're giving me a car? Great, I need one." I pointed to my bike.

Up close, I could see that the two weeks' worth of stubble on his face made him look older than he probably was. The smell told me he hadn't bathed in a while, but his jacket looked new. This guy wasn't homeless. Behind him, Jordan looked out from the back door shaking her head.

The man held the ring out to me. "Here. Take it."

Jordan had angled her head to get a look at us.

It was a single key that looked too small for either a car or a house.

I put my palms up. "I don't need anything from you. Why don't you move on and I'll do the same." I turned away and took three steps toward my bike.

"It's not a car," he shouted, a smoker's cough tangled what he intended as a laugh. "Bigger than one, though."

"A house? Don't need one." My back still to him, I set the food carton in my bin and zipped my leather jacket.

"A helicopter."

I learned a long time ago to never ask if things could get any weirder. Alright fine, he'd gotten my attention. I turned around and came within a foot of him, but I didn't touch the key dangling from his finger, swirling around and around as if the situation needed even more spectacle.

"I heard Jordan call you Wendell."

"She calls me WP for short. I let some people, special people, call me that. You can call me Wendell."

Whatever. "What are you doing here? Getting drunk, sitting alone in the parking lot harassing people, giving away helicopters. What's your scam?"

"No scam. It's exactly what it looks like."

"It looks like a waste of my time, and my dinner's getting cold." I crossed my arms and turned my back to the ocean, where the wind had come up, just like last night, the night a man got shot not fifty feet from where I sleep. A free helicopter. Again I reminded myself not to ask the universe questions that shouldn't be asked. "For one thing, most newer helicopters have a starter button ignition. Besides that, my mother told me there's no such thing as a free lunch."

"She still alive?" he asked, suddenly interested, his face changed even, like that piece of information could have some bearing on this slapdash transaction.

"Yeah, she's alive. I'll introduce you to her next time she drives up the coast."

"Where does she live?"

"Cut the crap, Wendell, or WP, or whatever your name is. I'm tired, it's been a strange day and I've had enough. You have ten seconds. What do you want from me?"

"I have a helicopter, it's mine, and I'm gifting it to you."

I shook my head.

"You don't believe me?"

"Why me?"

"You're a pilot, aren't you?"

"How would you know that?"

"That's irrelevant," he struggled the words out. Another gust blew him off balance, but he didn't fall. Just sort of swayed with his arms out at his sides. He took two steps toward me, picked up my hand, and placed the keys in it.

"Where is this magic helicopter? Does it even run?"

"You'll find out, won't you?"

He turned and walked down the other side of the parking lot near Capistrano, laughing. "There's noooooo hope for you, Mr. Mariner."

He was probably right.

CODEX

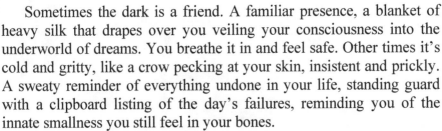

Sometimes the dark is a friend. A familiar presence, a blanket of heavy silk that drapes over you veiling your consciousness into the underworld of dreams. You breathe it in and feel safe. Other times it's cold and gritty, like a crow pecking at your skin, insistent and prickly. A sweaty reminder of everything undone in your life, standing guard with a clipboard listing of the day's failures, reminding you of the innate smallness you still feel in your bones.

I knew it was too cold to sleep outside this time of year. There's a doctor I saw post-accident who insisted on seeing me every three months, not just to remind me of the obvious—no drinking, stop smoking, eat, hydrate—but to give me a pair of eyes to reckon with a few times a year since I obviously wasn't doing that for myself. He's a backpacker, who understood the allure of seeing stars over your head as you drift off. I knew better, though. My immune system wasn't just weak; it was thready. I'd ignored it long enough. My weather app said it would get down into the thirties tonight. Elaine designed me a bedroom fit for royalty with its queen-sized pillow top mattress. I might never find my way out of it and so far, I'd never tried. Maybe tonight was the night.

Fine. Change is good, right? I rolled up the sleeping bag, sniffed the salt air once more and unlocked the door to the Airstream, seeing the old man's key dangling from my ring. Who the fuck gifts someone a helicopter? I had no idea what type it was, but they're not cheap—more than a car, some of them more than a house. Had to be a story there but I'm not sure I cared enough to find out. This bed felt ridiculous, literally swallowing me into his belly, I could barely move. But the dark prickled less in here. And as I slid toward sleep, it wasn't the image of old man Wendell with his outstretched key in my mind. It was the outline of Jordan, the bartender, watching out for me from the back door.

Chapter 9

The Pilot Light Café had a cheery, yellow sign that brightened my dark mood. It beckoned me into its naturally lit interior walled with floor to ceiling windows. A two-seater in the back gave me perfect observation cover where I could eat a breakfast burrito, guzzle down more coffee and people-watch.

I didn't really think I'd see Wendell Peters here, but the café was attached to the southern part of the airport, and the facility was small so anything was possible. I needed to find out how serious he was about his offer and, more importantly, understand the why-me. Andreini Airfield, locally known as the Half Moon Bay Airport, was one of San Mateo County's smaller airports and accommodated eighty aircraft and up to 137 short flights a day.

The café server's uniform matched the bright yellow signage but did nothing for her disposition. The older woman clunked down my burrito platter so loud the table wobbled and coffee spilled over the edge of my cup. I remembered my rule about maintaining structure when things got weird. Just chill and eat your breakfast, Angus.

The tortilla on my burrito was a bit charred and overcooked, a rare treat that gave it more flavor. I pretended to immerse myself in the feeding frenzy, eyes peeled for any sight of my asset amid the normal morning traffic from both entrances.

After I ate, I rode around the airport facility and saw two aircraft hangars side by side in the west field. Maybe a ten-minute walk from here, my gut told me now wasn't the right time. I'd be exposed, and honestly what would I say that would make sense to anybody? I didn't understand it myself.

After a good breakfast and short recon, I returned to the scene of the, what would I even call it, incident—the brewery. I knew whoever managed the place got there early because most mornings on my ride into the hills, there were lights on inside. At 8:15am, when I rolled into the lot, I saw the same Volkswagen as last night. It had to be hers.

The back doors were propped open by plastic trash bins. The pungent scent of stale beer spilled into the parking lot where I parked my bike under the same oak tree as last night.

"Is that a Ducati?"

I recognized Jordan's voice and willed my mouth not to smile. It wasn't working. There was something flirty in her delivery, like she thought I was keeping it from her. She came up to me as I turned, her arms full of folded towels.

"Parts of it," I said, apologetically. "Your football-loving brothers ride motorcycles too?" I asked, realizing I'd hung on her every word last night.

She stood a foot away with her smarty pants grin and perfect posture, the morning sun lighting up the right side of her face. Guilt vibrated in my chest, the part of me that still blamed myself for her death. Jessica Mariner, brilliant lawyer, twenty-eight years old. There were accidents in life, and then there were other things that just weren't meant to go down the way they did. And as we stood there under the lone tree in the parking lot, talking about towels and sick staff, something happened inside—in my mind and heart, something growing out of the ashes of sorrow. A theory, but more than that. No, more like a knowing spoken by a small deep voice that the accident that killed my wife wasn't an accident at all.

I told Jordan about my encounter with the old man last night, and she agreed to ride with me to his condo so I could revisit the topic of his generous gift.

"My shift doesn't start till six tonight," she said. "So I'm free for a while anyway."

It was a chilly morning and she wore no jacket, explaining that she rarely got cold. I was glad I put the longer seat on the bike now that I had my first passenger in a long time. I'd changed out that seat just last weekend. Maybe the heart knows things before the mind is informed.

Feeling the weight of her on the bike behind me, her arms around my waist, it occurred to me that we barely knew each other. We'd seen each other nearly every night for the past year but I'd never taken the time to introduce myself. So much for social skills. Maybe I could make up for lost time.

"Is he expecting you?" she shouted at a red light.

I shook my head and continued north on Highway 1 toward El Granada. I'd looked up his name online and found an address to a luxury apartment complex on Avenue Alhambra.

"Left here and right at the stop sign," she said.

"How do you know where he lives?"

She smirked. "I told you, he has a crush on me. He's been coming to the brewery a lot lately, sweet talking me out of free food, almost like he's hiding out or something."

After I parked at the curb, Jordan climbed off and I wondered who Wendell Peters could be hiding from.

"Wait here," she said. "He knows me."

"He was also shitfaced last night," I said. "So who knows what he'll remember."

She disappeared into the exterior stairwell and went up one flight. From the parking lot, I heard three knocks, a pause, then three more.

"Wendell, it's Jordan." She waited, then looked down over the railing. "Want me to keep trying?"

"I've got another idea."

She came downstairs and approached the bike, but I didn't start the engine. "I'd like to head back to Andreini Airfield and see what I can find there."

CODEX

"Well if you're looking for a chopper, I think that's a logical place."

"Look, you barely know me and you've already come with me on one errand. I can't ask you to give up even more hours of your afternoon for me."

She crossed her arms. "I've been sort of taking WP under my wing, you know, trying to help the guy. He seems a bit lost."

Lost wasn't the half of it.

"I'd like to know what's going on with him. Besides, it's not like we're complete strangers."

I hated this uncomfortable moment, the flirting, lilting innuendos so inherent in early stage relationships. "I'm sorry I didn't talk to you sooner. I regret that."

"You're grieving."

"Is it that obvious?"

"To someone who's been there, yeah." She climbed back on the bike and for the second time today I rode to Andreini Airfield. We entered through the café to get to the hangars on the west side.

"What are you looking for?" she asked as we were walking.

"A story. Why me?" I stopped and looked so she'd understand the urgency. "He knew things about me."

She narrowed her eyes. "Had you met him before last night?"

"No." I looked up at wispy, cirrus cloud rushing across the sky. It seemed too windy to fly today.

"What things?" she pressed.

"He knew about my wife. He knew she was dead."

"Greek tragedy," she whispered. "Last night, I was saying there was something poetic about my cigarette addiction and your…"

I nodded. I remembered.

"So that's what you meant. I'm so sorry."

I still hadn't learned how to respond to that comment. "I can't explain why, but I feel like he knows something about what happened that night. The night she died."

"WP?" she asked.

"Wendell Peters." I said his name aloud now, with more lines and color appearing on the invisible picture that was slowly coming into view.

It's amazing how small you feel in the presence of aircraft. We stood in the doorway, scanning the array of single and twin-engine planes. The helicopters must be in a different hangar. A man with neatly trimmed hair and a gray sport coat came out of a door with a clipboard.

"Excuse me," I said. "We're looking for Wendell Peters. He owns a helicopter and keeps it here." I honestly had no idea if that was true.

The man lifted his chin. "Next hangar over you'll find helicopters, I don't know that name though. You can cut through here," he said, pointing. The place was made for giants—huge and cavernous with what seemed like forty-foot ceilings. It took a full five minutes to get to the next staging area, this one dotted with several small choppers and a collection of larger law enforcement aircraft.

"Help you folks?" A younger man this time wearing a yellow reflective vest. He was probably an aviation safety inspector who knew we didn't belong here.

"Wendell Peters?" I said the name to gauge his face.

"Haven't seen him today."

"I was looking for his helicopter." I held out the key.

Now the man looked more intently at me, then Jordan, then me again. "I can show you his hangar. Is that his key?"

"Look," I said. "He gave it to me last night in a bar. He was drunk. I'm just here to give it back to him, and to make sure it really is his key."

The man didn't move. "He gave you the keys to his chopper, or gave you the chopper?"

Jordan snickered. "WP. He'd definitely pull a stunt like this."

"Like what, Miss?"

"Giving away a helicopter. Just saying that sounds like him. He's prone to grandiose behavior."

"Follow me."

Chapter 10

The man took us across the back of the hangar and down the other side where there were three large, police helicopters parked in a row. He stopped at a lacquered, bright blue aircraft at the end of the line. I could hardly breathe.

"Is that a Bell? A Jet Ranger?" Metallic blue with gold accent stripes, it looked brand new. The eight-year-old boy part of my heart swelled. I'd read about how law enforcement agencies snagged all the supply and now the waiting period for one of these was two years or more. Gorgeous.

The man pinched his lips and nodded in approval. "You're right. A 2014. You fly?"

"Not for a year or two."

His eyes rose to examine my hair. "Ex-military? Airman?"

The buzz cut always gave me away. "Yes, sir."

His face softened. I'd pushed past one gate anyway.

"This is a $3M aircraft," I said, now even more wary of the old man's gesture.

"At least," he confirmed, and looked at the key in my hand. "You a friend of Mr. Peters?"

It was an honest question, and there were too many possible angles from which to play it. I gave Jordan a look, and her dark, earnest eyes reminded me of my first rule—tell the truth. I tried, but it sounded today even more absurd than it had been last night.

"Gave it to you?" the man began. "Take it for a spin, or transferring ownership?"

"I don't know. I'm really not interested in either but I think he intended to transfer ownership. He didn't have any paperwork on him, just these keys."

The man peered down to examine then. "Looks like a helo key alright, though this one's got a push ignition. Why don't you take a look inside. See if that sheds any light on why someone would do something like this."

"Is there a way that I could find out when he last flew? I mean, if it's something he wasn't using, that's one thing. But if he used it regularly..." My voice trailed off. "I don't know what to think, and I'm really not that interested."

The man raised his brows. "You're asking a lot of questions for someone who's not interested. Besides that, you're here."

He posed his mouth in a gotcha half-grin. It felt like all the air had been sucked out of the room.

Jordan touched my back as she approached and joined our little semicircle. "Jordan Reid," she said and offered her hand to the man.

"Mason," he replied.

"I've actually known WP, Mr. Peters I mean, for a few weeks as he's been spending a lot of time at the bar where I work."

"Can't say I blame him," Mason replied, looking at me.

"Oh, he's just lonely is all. He comes for the beer and some company, I assume after work though I'm not sure what he actually does." Jordan shrugged and looked at me. "I asked him," she said. "He didn't answer."

"Sure, I'll take a look inside," I said. "Who knows?"

The heavy wind whistled outside, but all I felt in the hangar was the cold.

Mason opened the door to by far the most beautiful aircraft I'd ever seen, climbed in to grab the logbook, then jumped down and stood beside Jordan. He flipped to the most recent entries. "The log shows he took this up early last week."

CODEX

"Oh?" I asked. "Where?"

Head still trained on the logbook, he raised just his eyes to mine. "Texas."

"That's a long way. How many fuel stops would be needed for that?"

"Several, at least."

So Wendell Peters flew to Texas last week and then decided to give away his helicopter. I climbed into the cockpit, wowed by the slick console, and scanned through the standard controls – collective pitch, throttle, antitorque, cyclic pitch, still wondering what I was really doing here.

It moved around in my head, this new epiphany about the night of our accident. Not completely new, it was like it had been implanted in my brain and somehow became activated today as I was talking to Jordan about something unrelated. The mind just worked that way, didn't it? Topically engineering the activities of your day, all the while a background program sucking up all your waking energy, using your resources to make connections and decisions. And then you suddenly just understood, somehow, that your life as you've known it has been a lie. This thought was just now waking up, stretching its limbs, making me aware. The accident that killed my wife was no accident. And now everything was going to change.

I climbed out and clicked the door closed, Jordan watching me.

"What do you think?" the man asked.

"I think it's time for some answers."

"Couldn't agree more." Mason and I turned toward the voice of Detective Walt Dekker.

"Are you following me? This is harassment." Even his name made my teeth vibrate. His dark, wavy hair spilled down onto his sweaty forehead, rumpled jacket with sleeves an inch too short, threads hanging off the bottom. Class act.

"It could be considered hazardous to your freedom and liberty to talk to the police that way. Ms. Reid, nice to see you." He tipped his head toward Jordan.

"Do I know you?" she asked with a tone.

"Mason," Dekker said, and nodded. "Sorry to interrupt the party. I need a word with Mr. Mariner if you don't mind."

So Dekker knew Jordan and Mason. Great. "Thank you," I said to Mason and shook his hand before following Dekker outside. He didn't talk on the way out, just strode in his wrinkled clothes past a line of small choppers. Jordan caught up but I didn't want her with me right now. This was humiliating enough.

Dekker brought his smug grin inside the hangar and hovered with his back to the entrance, a breeze shifting the back flap of his jacket.

"What do want, Dekker?"

"Ms. Reid, my question has nothing to do with you," he said, looking at me. "You're free to go if you wish."

Jordan didn't move. I loved that about her.

"What are you doing here, Mr. Mariner?"

I couldn't stop the eyeroll. "I'm a pilot. This is an airport. What's the issue? Am I being blamed for the death of that body found on the beach yesterday?"

Jordan's eyes widened.

"That's still under investigation and I would say that while you're not in the clear, we do have another lead we're tracking."

"Then what? Why are you following me?"

"I received a report today that I thought might be of interest to you."

"Oh yeah? What's that?"

"Wendell Peters is dead."

Dekker hadn't arrested me yet and I willingly agreed to go with him to the HMB substation, Jordan in the backseat as my hapless accomplice to this strange turn of events. Dead? How could this be? Dekker provided no details, nor was he obligated to. Jordan and I might have been the last people to see him alive last night. Jesus.

My hands buzzed with the shock of this news, my brain replaying the odd bits of conversation with WP, as Jordan called him. I couldn't help feeling like a rat in a maze. Of course I felt played, WP lurking in the shadows of the brewery patio. He knew where to find me because he'd obviously been surveilling me. My working theory right now was that Wendell Peters gave me his helicopter because he had something

CODEX

to hide—something he wanted me, for some reason, to find.

The reason police put witnesses to the same crime in different interrogation rooms is because they believe there's strength in numbers. When they're separated, they'll feel vulnerable, and fear is a powerful influence for making people blurt out their secret truths. Jordan was in the room adjacent to mine, Dekker pacing in the hallway plotting his approach.

I didn't mind being here in this semi-dark room alone, still uncuffed and free to move about the cabin if I wanted. I liked the idea of a few minutes of breathing space. Every day, it seemed, the world grew more complicated. Just a few days ago, I was a grieving widower purposely cut off from the world, riding around California on my motorcycle, avoiding the world, biding my time. Ride the wave, Jessica would say. She believed when things got complicated it was because you'd been chosen to simplify them. That was her strength, though. As a lawyer her job was to advocate in the interest of justice, but her superpower was bringing order to chaos. She was not only good at it—she loved it. Where are you right now, Jess? Is there heaven and are you there? I'm ashamed of what's become of me lately. You'd be so disappointed. I could almost hear her voice hidden in the air, in the ether. There's a truth, she's saying, and that truth chose me to reveal it. Okay. I'll try.

Chapter 11

Dekker's footsteps in the hall were an indication of his emotions. Nervousness? No. Frustration? Absolutely. I watched the door handle open from the back wall where I stood. Go ahead, bring it.

"Mr. Mariner." It was Officer Lopez, a nice surprise. "You get around, don't you?"

"Do you work out of this substation?" I asked.

She shrugged, closed the door behind her and leaned against it. "I work where I'm needed." Long pause, awkward silence. "So. Anything you want to tell me?"

I let the question go unaddressed. As a measure of compliance, maybe even gratitude, I pulled out the chair and sat at the long table. Unmoved, she was still dressed in uniform, her long, curly dark hair pulled back from her face.

"Were you one of those kids on the playground who got in trouble every day, causing fights, getting bloody noses? Because I've seen you twice in twenty-four hours and, as I've just discovered, it's for completely different crimes."

I shook my head. "I was the smartest one in the class, which means the one who ate alone in the cafeteria every day."

"The reason I ask is, I see a lot of parallels in adult life to what we

CODEX

see on the elementary school playground."

Smart, insightful, beautiful. A deadly combination. "Oh?" I watched her uncross her arms, though I was much more curious about her relationship with Dekker than her human behavior instincts.

"You have bullies," she began and reached back to adjust something in her hair. "Their victims, kids who stick up for the victims, the Karens who pretty much tell on everyone, and loners who sit off to the side torturing bugs and drawing circles in the dirt with sticks."

She'd make a good profiler someday. "That's me, the latter," I said, though it wasn't true.

She joined me at the table but kept the chair pulled out to get some distance. I always loved the nuances of interrogation room seating. As an FBI agent, I'd had interrogation training that was part of the core curriculum of the FBI academy, but there was more to it than pulling information out of an unwilling witness. Psychology and Police Interrogation had been one of my favorite courses and I went on for deeper study on it later, which caught the eye of IB—the FBI's intelligence branch.

Wondering about Jordan, I kept my eye on the door handle, waiting for the inevitable. "Where's your buddy?" I asked, with a bite to my words.

"You mean my asshole boss?"

I laughed. "Yes, he is."

"In his line of work, that personality trait can be useful."

"Officer, meaning no disrespect, what am I doing here? I didn't even know the guy."

"Sit tight. Dekker will be right in."

Now it was me who smiled, because I could tell Dekker didn't know she was in here. It's not that I minded being attended to by an attractive woman—more like the appreciation of a friendly contact. God knows I needed one.

I heard a clanging noise and the vibration of thuds from the front of the building. Then the door to the next room, Jordan's interrogation room, slammed against the frame breaking the silence. Dekker opened the door, skidded in with a breathless flourish and left it wide open.

"Mr. Mariner," he said, like a disappointed school principal, then jerked his head to the right. "Lopez. What are you doing here?" Brows contracted. OMG funny.

"Loitering." She smiled at me, not him. Small triumph. "It's a free country. Sir."

Lopez hated Dekker, I had proof now, which was all the better for me. She looked at the floor, moved awkwardly past him and hovered in the doorway.

"You're like a bad penny, Dekker," I said.

"Well if that isn't the pot calling the kettle black. You've been here twice in the past week."

"I think that's my cue." Lopez got up, looked back at me and slipped out.

"Don't go," I called out. "The fun's just getting started."

She left and Dekker slammed the door behind her. I pictured her laughing on the other side. He lingered just inside the door, shoved his hands in his pockets then pulled them out. I knew Dekker's ego didn't like when his typical intimidation tactics didn't work.

"I don't know anything, Dekker. I didn't even know the guy." I was getting tired of saying it.

Dekker showed his palms and took the seat across from me. "We'll find out whether you knew him or not, but you might know more than nothing. The point I need you to understand is that a man is dead, and you may have had the last conversation with him that he had with anybody. That's worth looking into, don't you think?"

"Do what you need to do. I'll do the same."

The detective shifted in his chair, which made me wonder if he had a bad back. He probably never exercised. Then again, neither did I lately. "I get the feeling you don't appreciate the seriousness of your predicament, Mr. Mariner. You're not only a person of interest in this investigation but I'll just say I am very interested in learning more about your connection to Wendell Peters."

I took a moment to think, carefully planning my reply. "I suspect you're not going to ask me where I was when Peters died because it's too early to have gotten a confirmed time of death stamp from the coroner. Am I right?"

He looked down at the table with a smirk. "Where were you last

CODEX

night, Mr. Mariner?"

"Half Moon Bay Brewery."

"Anyone see you there besides the deceased?"

"Ms. Reid," I said.

"Seeing as she's also a person of interest, anybody else?"

"Another bartender was there, I don't know his name. Young, skinny dude." So. I'd answered all of his questions so far, and quickly enough to not appear cagey or false.

"I wouldn't plan any trips. And I need you to leave a statement. Meaning today."

"So you're letting me go?"

"You're not handcuffed, and so far I'm not charging you with a crime. But like I said, we're looking into everything."

Now seemed as good a time as any to ask my question, knowing he wouldn't likely answer. "Did he die of natural causes or do you suspect foul play?"

Dekker played with the collar on his shirt, yanking it in and out. "Natural causes is such an interesting phrase."

"He was older," I said, maybe with too much snark. "I only talked to the guy for a few minutes but he seemed like seventies or so. Natural causes wouldn't be unreasonable."

Dekker crossed his arms and leaned back against the hard chair back. "I don't know what the history is between you and Wendell Peters yet but—"

"History?" Anger buzzed in my palms. "There is no history. How many times do I have to say it? I literally met the guy once."

"So you said," Dekker replied. "And you met him because he was targeting you for some unknown reason. I'd like to know why."

"Me too," I admitted.

"Here's the problem. People seem to die around you, Mr. Mariner. One just a few feet from your trailer, and—"

He stopped talking when he saw my face, and I suspect it looked stone-white. There was no way I could hear those words and not think of Jessica, instantly pulled back to the chain of guilt that had suffocated me all this time. He was right, and now there were three. Three deaths, none of which were directly my fault, but three deaths with which I was somehow entangled. Were they all accidents? There wasn't enough data yet about the second two to know. Then again, were any of them?

"I'm sorry," Dekker said. "That was insensitive. I know about your —"

My phone rang, ruining Dekker's apology. Rudy. Not caring that I was in a police interrogation, I answered it. "Hey," I said, giving nothing away.

"Where've you been lately?"

I knew Dekker could hear the conversation. "Around," I said, with an impish grin. "Can I call you later? Kinda busy right now."

"Yep. Later." I disconnected the call, leaving the phone on the table. "Sorry, I'm popular I guess."

"Rudy?" Dekker asked.

"Rudy Richards. Owner of Red Bull Diner."

He nodded. "Great burgers. Good cigars."

Rudy had lung cancer on both sides of his family. "Cigars, huh. Rudy's never smoked a day in his life."

"Not with you, apparently."

I just hate this guy. "Alright Dekker. Are you charging me with a crime or not? If not, I'm outta here."

He rose, towering over the table. "You're 'outta here' when I say you are."

"This is harassment." I was trying to recall the Internal Affairs contact I used to have at the Bureau.

Despite our venomous standoff, I could tell Dekker liked me, and that the irritation he displayed was topical and maybe more related to other irritations in his life. Rudy and cigars—was that even true?

He inhaled hard, like he'd just made some decision about me. "You were CIA, I mean before the...sorry. I don't mean to keep bringing that up."

I believed he meant it, this time anyway. I ignored his apology by shaking my head. "FBI. IB."

"Intelligence Bureau." He nodded slowly. "They're an elite group. Surprised you weren't recruited for the CIA."

"Who says I wasn't?" I asked, with a raised brow, but there was no point in hiding anything from Dekker. I'd known people like him before, trained investigators, even informants. He was hungry and reckless, like a dog who lost his bone. That made him dangerous. Noted.

"What a waste." He walked out, like he had some personal stake in my career success. A minute later he returned, tossing a form and pen onto the conference table. "Your statement. If it's filled out to my satisfaction, you can go, but we'll likely have more questions for you later."

"Understood." It was all so strange, and somehow I felt in my bones that I was indeed to blame for that man's untimely death. Now that would be two.

Chapter 12

Dekker left but another officer came in to pick up my statement and process me out. Jordan was still being detained... I thought she'd just met the guy a few weeks ago.

The small precinct had a clear view of the Half Moon Bay jetty. I stood on the edge of a sandy mound and took in the wide vista. A man in a hoodie sat below me on the sand with his eyes closed. When I stepped left, I could see he was wearing some kind of metal band around his head. My stomach felt suddenly queasy.

"Hey," Jordan said, beside me. I hadn't heard her approach. "Are you okay?"

"Yeah, fine," I said, not sure it was true. "How'd it go in there?"

"Same as you, I suspect. I barely knew the guy. I wrote a short statement and that's it. Do they know how he died?"

"Dekker's gunning for trouble so that's the last thing I'd ask him at this point. I suspect we'll hear more after the body reaches the Medical Examiner." My phone vibrated in my pocket, a text from Officer Lopez. *Call me when you have a minute.* "Then again..." I said and smiled.

"What?"

"I might have another channel open." I showed Jordan the text.

CODEX

"Friends in high places?"

"I'll let you know if I ever have any. Is someone picking you up?" I asked, suddenly aware of how that must have sounded. "I mean, I didn't mean—"

"No, but it's not far. I'll walk back to the bar."

I followed her around the building and out to the street, deciding whether to clarify what I meant. Did I even know?

The air had cooled. Jordan had on a short-sleeved t-shirt that showed toned and slightly tanned arms. We walked in silence in the middle of the empty street, mid-afternoon before rush hour. I could tell we were both enjoying the comfortable silence between us, devoid of anxious chatter and small talk. At one point, our bodies veered close together and our fingers touched at our sides. We both said sorry at the same time, then laughed. What was this, eighth grade for God's sake? I felt no more equipped to deal with a mature friendship as I had back then.

This time of day in late spring, the sky could turn from day to dusk in fifteen minutes, it seemed. Orange streaks almost instantly grayed, leaving only a faint shadow of vibrance to ornament the empty expanse.

"Can I ask you something?" she asked, after a while.

I nodded, turning to catch a glimpse of her. Her arms had goosebumps on them. I took off my leather jacket and draped it over her shoulders. I knew what it would look like to someone watching, and how it probably felt to her. I felt shame, in that moment, more than anything. Shame that Jessica would be looking down at me from wherever she was, thinking I'd forgotten her, thinking my love had died. Never, I said in my mind.

"How are you getting through it?" she asked, reading my thoughts. I could play dumb but I knew what she meant, and I liked the question. Or maybe I just liked the way she asked it.

"My wife? I don't know. I feel like my life's been this series of *befores*, except I keep waiting for *after* to happen and it never does. After college and before I joined the FBI academy, I enlisted in the Air Force. They said Air Force Intelligence was the most obvious fit for my skills and talents. What were those exactly? I never did get that answer, but the military is more about questions anyway. Knowing

57

what to ask, to whom, when. And in the intelligence community, answers can be the most dangerous thing of all."

She drew a quick breath and slid her arms through the sleeves of my jacket. I knew it would look good on her. "That's sort of an answer," she smirked, somehow knowing I'd allowed her to push me in this way.

"I can't think about it too much because I don't know how to think about it. Process grief, you know? I have no fucking idea what to do with that."

Now she turned and stopped walking. We'd just passed Oceano Hotel and stood looking out at the water next to Barbara's Fish Shack.

"I can't think about it because I'm scared."

"Of what?" she asked.

"I feel…nothing. And that terrifies me." I hadn't even acknowledged these things to myself, let alone to my sister, or Rudy. "When I'm out riding in the early mornings, I sometimes think about crashing my bike into the rocks, or riding over a cliff. Not because I want to end my life but to crash myself back into it. To feel something, finally, instead of nothing."

She pointed at my right eye.

"What?" But I knew as soon as I blinked. My eye felt cold because it was wet. Maybe I had a heart in here after all.

I left Jordan at the brewery and didn't feel like waiting for my nightly burger. It was a half mile from here to the trailer, but after that talk I didn't feel like being alone either. So I walked up to Rudy's diner. The booth he'd let me sleep in, right after the accident, was empty, with only a few couples sitting at tables and no one at the counter. He saw me when he strode out of the kitchen holding two large plates.

"Bro." He smiled. "Be right there. How was your afternoon?" he bellowed from the other side of the room. I saw him stifle a laugh.

"Do you have spies at the police station or something? How could you know—"

"I own a diner. I know everything about this town." He plopped down across from me at my special booth. "Where's your jacket? It's cold out."

"I let Jordan wear it, Jordan from the—"

"Did you now?"

"Cut it out, she was cold."

He sat back and crossed his arms, stretched out his legs under the table, and crossed his ankles, watching me.

"Now what?"

"Nothing, you're just funny is all."

"That's a compliment. Thank you."

"Funny in the way you hide from yourself. I'll be right back."

The comment was intended to sting but he wasn't wrong either. Rudy knew all my tricks. I'd been hiding from myself, from everyone, for too long now. He returned a minute later carrying one of his red baskets containing a cheeseburger and fries and a large Coke, like they'd been sitting there waiting for me.

"Where'd this come from?"

"Odd thing, someone ordered it and the guy just ran out and left it. Go ahead if you want it."

I didn't think I was hungry but the burger smelled savory, though not as good as the ones from the brewery. Then again, I might have to start admitting to myself that burgers weren't the reason I kept going there. I ate in silence, humbled by the truths I was somehow willing to speak tonight—to Jordan who was still essentially a stranger. I checked some things on my phone, remembering the text from Officer Lopez. Rudy came back after waiting on a few more tables and talking to Eduardo, his chef. He sat down again with a look of appraisal.

"Something's off about you tonight," he said, shaking his head.

"What now?"

"I don't know. Something. You feeling okay?"

"What are you, my mother? Where's your jacket? Are you feeling okay? For God's sake."

"What are you yelling for? Just answer the question."

I put the burger back in the basket, wiped my mouth, and leaned forward. "No, Rudy, I'm not okay. Okay? I spent the fucking afternoon in jail, that was today. Two days ago, a guy was shot on the beach fifty yards from the trailer. And yesterday a rich, old dude gave me a fucking helicopter, then apparently died this morning. That's how I'm doing."

"First of all, you weren't in jail, as you put it. You were brought in for questioning. I don't think they even cuffed you, did they?"

"So you do have spies in the PD. Who was it? By the way, Dekker likes your cigars." I picked up the burger again and took another bite, glowering.

He laughed. "Cops like diners. What can I say? Dekker..." He shook his head.

"He's not gonna sleep until he arrests me for something."

"Don't worry about him. He's just another lonely dream-crusher with nothing to live for except his job."

I didn't disagree, but he didn't seem to appreciate the gravity of my situation. I kept eating and drank the cold Coke. It started to revive me.

"Come on, man, I know you. What's going on?"

"Aside from everything I just told you?"

He cocked his head to the side.

"I think there's some kind of connection between Wendell Peters, the helicopter dude, and Jessica, and lately I can't shake this gut feeling." I leaned forward and stopped chewing.

"What?"

"Maybe it wasn't an accident."

Rudy widened his already large eyes just as the door opened, ringing the bells he hung on the handle.

"Oh shit." He looked at my plate. "That guy's back and you're eating his dinner."

CODEX

Chapter 13

Another cold night forced me inside the Taj Mahal of trailers surrounded by lacquered wood and something Elaine called antique brushed nickel. Like sleeping in a factory showroom, without even fingerprints to show signs of habitation.

It was becoming harder and harder to not feel targeted by all of these recent events, like some mastermind was playing a game and I was the pawn. No, not pawn—pawn implies chess. This felt more like monopoly, except so far I didn't know any of the other players. Where was that Get Out of Jail Free card when you needed it?

I went over it again in my mind as I typed some notes on my laptop: a guy dies on the beach fifty feet from me. That night at the brewery, another guy interrupts my oceanfront vigil with some song and dance, gives me a $3M aircraft...then dies the next morning. I mean, come on. No sane person could blame Dekker for his harassment. It looked bad from every angle.

I set aside the laptop to gaze out the window. A light from a passing car illuminated my luxurious interior, causing my eyes to land on something on one of the built-in shelves Elaine had custom-built across from my bed...an official Staunton chess game. Sometimes the universe talks to you like this. Fine, I eased it down, pulled out the board and set up the pieces. It was too dark to really see anything, but my eyes didn't want artificial light right now. A bit of glow shined in from the half-moon hovering over the trees.

Clearly I was a pawn, right now anyway. I was twisting one of them around with my thumb and index finger as if it might miraculously start spinning. The serfs, only moving one square at a time but with a biting diagonal sting venomous enough to attack even a queen. Their secret superpower, unique only to pawns, was in their numbers—eight on each side. Rooks, of course, were the military police of the board, a never-sleeps security team doing continuous perimeter checks. Bishops had the ordered universe of their single-shade binary world, able to make swooping lunges as quiet vigilantes cloaked under the veil of clergy. The knight, every boy's favorite, was at once a powerful adversary and a wildcard trickster capable of invisibility, obstructionism, and overt brutality. Unlike real royalty, the king and queen's dysfunctional dynamic was on display for all to see. She's a conspicuous assassin singularly obsessed with her prime directive and the king cowering behind a thin line of pawns, everybody's victim.

I picked up my laptop again and plugged it into the wall. Finally the trailer was useful for something. I typed 'Wendell Peters' into Google sensing I was at the beginning of a very long path. Too many options came up. A lawyer, a DJ, @Willybwilly on TikTok, a Snapchat profile, and a Facebook page. This guy was too old for social media, certainly for Snap and TikTok.

Saving those results, I opened another browser tab and tried LinkedIn. The Wendell Peters I'd met last night was a scruffy, drunken old-timer, the kind of guy you'd expect to see hanging around a bus station late at night scheming for whiskey money. Here's one—a LinkedIn profile of a ginger-haired fellow with mid-fifties wrinkles, thick mustache, short hair though. Could be him. The profile was titled Willy P. Could this be the Willy from TikTok and was Willy even a nickname for Wendell? I'd heard Dell as a shortened version of Wendell, not Willy. But it looked like it could be the same face I'd seen. I scanned down through his career content—a company called ADS, which he'd apparently founded in 2006 and was the current CEO. I returned to Google and did an image search on the phrase

CODEX

'Wendell Peters ADS'. A picture came up of the same guy from the LinkedIn profile, this time looking off-center, wearing a shirt and tie and flanked by two other men almost like in a police lineup. Then again, everything about the guy was odd so far. I had a feeling I'd barely touched the surface.

In the before-days at the bureau, I'd had access to almost every law enforcement agency in the country. Aside from NCIS, the FBI shared database access to the Terrorist Threat Interrogation Center and Joint Terrorism Task Forces. I'd been gone eighteen months and now had access to nothing. I knew I couldn't do this alone; I had to tread carefully. There was one person who might be not only qualified but willing to help.

I fell asleep right there on top of the bed, my face inches from the chessboard and laptop. The sky was lighter when I woke to a squawking of gulls circling overhead. Better than vultures.

Elaine's crystal desk clock, which she'd set on the lowest bedroom shelf, showed 5:55 am. My phone chirped, the notification sound I'd set for WhatsApp messages. Since I had no other regular contacts overseas right now, it had to be Elaine, my cosmopolitan, globe-trotting half-sister. WhatsApp didn't have voicemail, so she always recorded an audio message.

"Hey, big brother, ha! Cracking myself up over here. I'm in town and I'd like to see how you're enjoying your lux living space. I'm in San Francisco and should be free tomorrow afternoon. Let me know if you're free. Bye!"

Right. I knew her. Elaine loved surprise visits and her version of tomorrow afternoon could mean she was standing outside my door right now. I set aside the chess board, rubbed sleep from my eyes and swung my legs to the floor, put on my boots, and remembered I'd left my jacket with Jordan. Normally I would have grabbed a hoodie, but this morning's errand required more strategic attire. I chose jeans, a dark t-shirt and a suit jacket, slightly wrinkled. I sent Rudy a quick text to let him know Elaine might show up and peered out the windows. No sign of her yet, what a relief. It wasn't that I didn't want to see her. Just not in the mood for any more surprises. Besides, I had more important business. I got on my bike and hit Highway 101 to San Francisco.

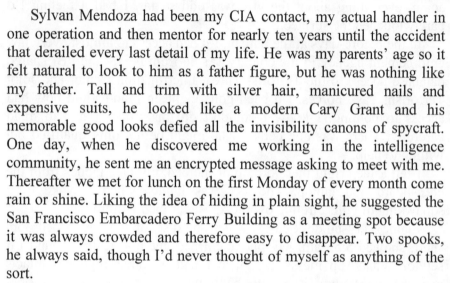

Sylvan Mendoza had been my CIA contact, my actual handler in one operation and then mentor for nearly ten years until the accident that derailed every last detail of my life. He was my parents' age so it felt natural to look to him as a father figure, but he was nothing like my father. Tall and trim with silver hair, manicured nails and expensive suits, he looked like a modern Cary Grant and his memorable good looks defied all the invisibility canons of spycraft. One day, when he discovered me working in the intelligence community, he sent me an encrypted message asking to meet with me. Thereafter we met for lunch on the first Monday of every month come rain or shine. Liking the idea of hiding in plain sight, he suggested the San Francisco Embarcadero Ferry Building as a meeting spot because it was always crowded and therefore easy to disappear. Two spooks, he always said, though I'd never thought of myself as anything of the sort.

He made it clear I was never to contact him outside of our monthly meetup. That meant any calls or emails, even within our established channels, would be a direct breach of our customary agreement, and I'd risk never seeing him again. I also knew from the return address label on his annual Christmas cards that he still maintained a residence in San Francisco. Last year's card was postmarked Twin Peaks.

I'd been there once for a reception my first year with the bureau. Maybe I'd remember it, but I also knew his car.

I grabbed a coffee from Mezza Luna Café as soon as they opened, and in fifty minutes I got to San Francisco. Sylvan Mendoza's midnight blue Lexus was parked in the driveway of a modern, two-story mansion with a remarkable view of the whole city. This was the house I'd been to before. Grandiose bordering on ridiculous, it definitely matched his ego. Beautiful car, never more than a week away from a wash and wax.

I took the newspaper I'd picked up at a 7-Eleven, folded it in thirds and dog-eared the third page to signify that I wanted to meet at the Embarcadero at 3pm tomorrow. That was the schtick, per his own instructions. Hopefully he'd remember, maybe he'd care.

CODEX

I parked down the street, then set the newspaper on one of the lacquered flagstones between two landscape solar lights with a large rock holding it down. A beautiful home; a sad reminder of the life I'd lost.

I didn't hear the front door open but felt Mendoza's eyes on me, watching me retreat in that way he had of smiling and sneering all at once. I stopped but didn't turn. I'd left my sign, now it was his move.

"You don't look much like a birdwatcher."

Birdwatcher, British spy slang, delivered in his typical tone of irritation. "Hey," I said, eyeing his dark slacks and starched shirt with the sleeves rolled up. That meant he was cooking breakfast. I knew this man. I knew his wife, Bekah, and his deadbeat son. Why hadn't I been in touch for so long? Maybe he knew. Of course he knew. Guys like Sylvan Mendoza knew everything.

Chapter 14

Thirty minutes later, we were seated in his glassed-in terrace overlooking the most stunning panoramic view of the city, the bay, and the ocean.

"I remember this. Amazing."

"It's why I bought this place. I need to see the water." He sipped coffee. "Your heart is the size of an ocean. Go find yourself in its hidden depths." Then he looked out at the expanse and smiled. "Rumi."

He told me how Bekah, his wife, had apparently moved out a month ago in a trial separation that he said had been long overdue, resulting from legal trouble their son had, which Sylvan refused to fix.

"I'm sorry to hear it," I said. "He's a good kid."

He sat back and chuckled. "He's a punk and you know it. You said so yourself once."

"I don't think—"

"You can't fool me, Angus." Two more sips. "But that's not to say I can't be fooled." He set his cup on the table, crossed his legs and then his arms, waiting for me to speak first. Spies and all their tricks. I knew he thought of me as an asset, so why couldn't I think of him the same way? It was me who needed something anyway.

CODEX

"I'm sorry it's been–"

"No," he stopped me, palm up. "I'm the one who's sorry. I should have reached out a long time ago, to check on you. You've gone through something unthinkable. I followed every detail of that night, too. Your car went off a cliff. Christ, you're lucky to be alive."

I blinked back at some solid silver bird sculptures set on a table by the glass doors. "Is that what I am right now?"

"Aren't you?" He leaned forward with his elbows on his knees.

"Biologically maybe."

"You haven't gone back?" he asked.

"Back? The bureau?" As if he didn't know every detail of my life. I shook my head and lost myself in the deep blue Persian carpet under our white leather Barcelona chairs. His wife told me about that rug, Oushak from Western Turkey hand made out of wool and silk.

"How are you doing lately?"

"Like you don't know." I winced as I sipped the last of my coffee. Cold and bitter. Fitting. I guess I hadn't planned on talking about Jessica. How could we not, though? I assumed he meant how was I doing with my connection to the two recent deaths. "Wrong place at the wrong time maybe?"

"If that were true, I don't think you'd be here. You'd be calling a lawyer. What do you need?"

I gave him the quick and dirty version, knowing he'd put his own spin on things. "I'm sort of in the middle of something and I need to know what, but I've got a very narrow passage through which I can move without making myself even more of a police target."

"You need intel? On who? Sounds like you've got not one but two problems."

I shook my head. "The first one, the guy on the beach, has nothing to do with—"

"How do you know? Nothing to do with you, or nothing to do with the old drunk?"

So he knew about Wendell Peters. I shouldn't be surprised. "Okay," I acknowledged the flaw in my assumptions, an old trait. "Can you…"

"I'll see," he said, but his face told me he already had his suspicions. "Who's investigating the old man?"

"Dekker. Detective Walt Dekker. An asshole."

"Aren't they all." He got up and opened the sliding glass doors to his living room. That meant we were done. "You know the Peets Coffee next to New Leaf Market?"

I knew it. San Mateo Road in Half Moon Bay, I shopped there every week and got coffee at Peets on the way out.

"Nine o'clock tomorrow morning."

"You have time to drive to Half Moon Bay? I can—"

"Angus, my friend, you can't just knock on my door here. I mean, you can, but then again I don't exist. Remember?"

Just after 9am now, I saw the tangled knots of rush hour traffic as I hiked down the hill to my bike.

The whole ride back south I had this terrible image of Elaine rummaging around my fridge, looking through the laundry hamper, checking for signs of habitation that of course didn't exist, other than last night. I'd slept in there, but not more than once or twice. She designed the place for me so of course she'd have kept a key, maybe pretending to call it a spare in case I lost mine. I knew her. What was she doing back here? Had to be a reason.

Two could play at that game. I pulled over and drove into an empty parking lot to call her. I turned the engine off before dialing her number. Two rings, three. Was she searching my underwear drawer?

"Ahoy, mate!" Her typical greeting.

"Are you in my house?"

"Fine thanks, and you? Nice manners."

"What are you doing here, Elaine?"

Long sigh, nervous laugh. "Where are you right now?"

"San Francisco," I lied. "I'll be home in about an hour. And don't touch anything, okay? Please don't Sherlock Holmes your way around my living space and—"

She hung up, but I was two minutes away and could see a car parked on the street next to Rudy's house from Main Street. She'd recognize the sound of my bike motor, so I parked it in the street and walked up Rudy's driveway. I caught sight of her platinum hair through the bedroom window. I tiptoed around the trailer and banged on the door with both fists, then yanked it open.

"Oh my God you startled me! Bastard." She'd been lying on my bed and jumped to attention. "Forgive me, I do apologize. Jet lag, you know."

"Make yourself at home."

I kissed her check and wrapped my arms around her wiry frame, thinner than the last time I saw her, but there was a pirate packed into that delicate package. "Nice to see you."

"Do you mean that?" she asked.

"Of course I do. What are you doing across the pond?"

"Can't I visit family from time to time?"

"What can I get you?" I asked.

"A vodka tonic would be nice, two ice cubes."

I stared her down. "Seriously?"

She covered her mouth and closed her eyes. "Sorry. Of course. Water would be fine."

"It's ten in the morning. I don't mind people drinking around me. I've got my problem under control." I didn't, but it sounded good.

"Still going to meetings?"

"You can have a drink if you want. But fix it yourself."

She pursed her lips and sat on the edge of my bed, no doubt noticing I hadn't answered her question. I sat at the kitchen table, which was too far away for a normal conversation.

"What are you doing here, Elaine?"

"Why are you so suspicious?"

"You hate Americans," I argued. "You hate American food—no wait, you said Americans have no food of their own and they culturally misappropriated everything. Kind of ironic."

She lowered her head and giggled. "I did say that, yes."

"Look, I'm up to my eyeballs in something here and really don't have time right now for entertaining." I raised my brow and looked around the interior.

"And that means…"

"You can't stay here. Not right now, anyway."

"Oh for God's sake, why not? You sure as hell don't live here. There's not a single shred of evidence that you've so much as eaten a meal here. Ever."

"I'm tidy, what can I say?"

She laughed, wide-mouthed, head tilted back. "You're nothing of the sort. Would you believe me if I said I'd been worried about you? Because I have. You haven't returned a single one of my calls, emails, or texts. I mean, I know why." She came to the table, sat across from me and grabbed my hand. "I just wanted to check in on you."

It was a good pitch. Well-rehearsed, perfectly executed. I wasn't buying it. "What are you running from, Elaine? Or should I say who? What millionaire did you run out on, and will he be coming here to look for you?"

Slight nod. "He might. That's fine, I don't need to invade your space. Rudy already said I could stay with him."

"What?"

"I stopped in at the diner, knowing you probably didn't want anyone in your space." She touched the glass of water I set in front of her, then slid into a long, black leather coat draped across the kitchen table.

I walked her twenty steps to Rudy's front door, then got my bike and parked it in its spot next to the trailer.

Thanks for telling me, I texted him about Elaine.

Sorry. You know I'm defenseless around blondes.

Growing up apart, Elaine and I met when I was a teenager and she was twenty, the year my father remarried. Funny the way you can think you understand the world and then bam, one day you inherit a sibling and the balance of your life is irrevocably changed. Like waking up one day with three arms, not quite knowing what to do with the extra one but feeling like it could come in handy someday, in some unconventional circumstance. The fact that she and my stepmom were British had a sort of regal appeal at first. They taught my dad and I how to make tea, not for our own benefit but theirs. Of course a little brother meant a free servant. I didn't mind, except when I'd gotten used to having them around, Elaine took off on one of her jaunts. Italy. India. What I realized only in her absence was that I'd never dealt with the loss of my mother, and now I'd be stuck with her as a surrogate and a daily reminder of the hole in my heart. One of many.

CODEX

Chapter 15

Soft shoes on a tiled floor. Muted earth tones. A small handful of us seated individually, not randomly but assigned. Special, custom-fitted chairs made per strict specifications. Lower, higher, raise your arm, not that high, turn your head ten degrees to the right, like I could approximate ten degrees or any degrees for that matter. The man's voice was low and thin, so maybe he was older, but I can't see him from here. I can't see anyone because our eyes are covered, but I feel them. And I know they can feel me. It smells like disinfectant in here, in this small laboratory with windows up near the ceiling. I don't mind the smell as much as I mind the tin clangs of metal as they're carried from the back room onto the floor, to each of us. I hear it. He's coming. Not again.

I woke sweating, confused by the ghost images stuck in my head post-dream. At least I knew it was a dream. Wasn't it?

I'd spent the whole afternoon riding, all the way down to Santa Cruz, and by the time I came back it was rush hour. I loved those slow rides on the coast road with the ocean bearing witness to my mania. Dead man #1, dead man #2, now my sister shows up out of nowhere and she seems like a bundle of nerves. I felt like putting her on a leash, or surgically implanting a tracking device in her wrist so I could monitor her movements. I had to do something. The good thing was, whenever I didn't know what to do, the right answer was always my bike. I went to bed early and barely slept, churning through the meeting with Mendoza, anticipating what he might come up with by morning, and wondering how to find my way through this fog.

Again, I woke with my face mashed down on the chessboard, a rook and knight looming over me. The pawn was about to make a move. It might not be the right one, but I'd been standing still for long enough.

I made a full pot of French press coffee and brought two mugs to Rudy's. It was eight already and he'd be at the diner. Elaine was at his kitchen table eating a bowl of cereal in sweatpants and a heavy sweater. Her eyes brightened at the sight of mugs in my hand.

"Thank you, Jesus. All I found here was ground coffee stored in a large can. What is this, 1980?"

I set the mugs on the table and turned back toward the door.

"Join me for breakfast?"

I felt bad, after she'd asked me so politely. But until I understood what she was really doing here, I'd keep my distance. "Sorry no, I've got an errand I need to do this morning. I shouldn't be too long, though. Back by ten-ish. Will you still be here?"

"I can be," she said, with a lilt to her voice.

I waited, watching her from just inside the door, sipping my delicious coffee with the perfect one-click each of cream and sugar.

"When are you gonna tell me how you're doing?"

"You didn't ask. I would've told you," I said.

"No you wouldn't. Watch—how are you doing lately?"

"Great," I said.

"See?"

We stared at one another for a few seconds. Without makeup on, I could see the depth in her face, the dark circles under her eyes. "What are you doing here, Elaine?"

"Would you believe me if I said I missed you and wanted to be with family for a while?"

"You tried that one yesterday. It didn't work." There was no sense asking her questions she had no intention of answering. Maybe the same was true of me.

I sucked down the rest of the coffee and left my mug on the bookcase inside Rudy's front door, then paused realizing I hadn't locked the door to the trailer.

New Leaf Market was a half mile away, which gave me time to consider Elaine's most recent trip abroad. She inherited half of her biological grandfather's estate when she turned eighteen and was essentially a billionaire, with a small allowance she got from my stepmom every month. Not that she needed it. Last I heard, she was soaking up luxury in a five-star hotel in Rome three blocks from Chigi Palace, home of the Italian prime minister. I'd ask her about it later, and she'd answer a different question, like always. Which chess piece was she, then?

I parked my bike on the side of New Leaf Market closest to Rite-Aid because there was an arrangement of tall shrubs I could use as a vantage point. I scanned for Sylvan Mendoza's Lexus and knew I wouldn't find it because of course he'd never make a drop like this himself. He had a team of assets he could use for menial jobs, probably some printed pages sealed in a small, white envelope with heavy paper. I wondered if he'd come up with anything about Wendell Peters, but more than that I wondered how much he'd be able, or willing, to share with me. Guys like Mendoza did nothing by accident, were never caught in an awkward moment, never had a shoe untied or parsley in their teeth. Every second of his life was pre-planned and expertly calculated to fit into a larger whole.

I decided I needed to be visible, so I walked in a straight line from Rite-Aid across the lot to the main entrance of the market. I faced outward and crossed my arms, staring up at the sky long enough to be seen by Mendoza or his team, then hit the men's room in the corridor just inside the front door. I took the opportunity to wash my hands, and laughed again at the same old trope, almost hearing Jessica's taunting in my ears. "Men never wash their hands of their own accord, not even to cook." We'd go round and round like that. Her biting humor was dependent on sarcasm, generalizations, unfair stereotypes, and exaggeration, but always with the smirky smile that promised affection behind her quips.

I heard a hiss behind me and jerked back toward the men's room door. Sure enough, an envelope—white, sealed, nothing written on the outside. Showtime.

Before I even picked it up, I tore open the door and ran outside, scanning the parking lot only to realize my mistake too late. But of course. Mendoza's courier slipped the envelope under the crack in the door, assumed I'd run outside, and then tactically disappeared into the store's bakery aisle or, even better, the narrower wellness aisles with essential oils and homeopathics. There was no sense walking through the store, because the courier could just as easily be an old lady in a crocheted hat as a twenty-five-year-old jogger. I knew better than this. At least I used to.

The envelope was still there, its thick paper absorbing some moisture from the floor. I picked it up and used my fingers to assess the contents. It felt empty. I closed the restroom door before opening the envelope and found nothing inside. No folded sheets, no coded dossier typed in courier font on airmail onion skin paper. But handwritten in blue ink was a single word on the inside of the envelope under the point of the flap: *Alice*. Fucking Mendoza.

Elaine was expecting me back by 10am. That gave me thirty minutes to think like an FBI agent, if I could even remember how after all this time. Dead, that's what it felt like. I'd been dead for the past year and a half. Seeing Jessica's body crumped-beyond-repair, her death had been mine, too, and I did it willingly. Sylvan Mendoza knew about the accident; he mentioned it last night saying he'd followed every detail. Had he been keeping tabs on me all this time?

I was riding now but not toward the trailer, not even toward Rudy's Diner, but into the hills. The high hills over Pillar Point. I can see up here, the valley, the water, and from the very top I can see the cliff our car went over that night. I knew if I lived to be a hundred, I would never forget opening my eyes in that upside down car and seeing the blood covering that luminous face.

CODEX

Pawn, that's what Mendoza was doing. Moving me involuntarily around the chessboard of his career, watching me panic, curl up, and retreat. He knew how to do it, too. He'd been my mentor, a family friend. And right now he was doing it again, inciting me into action. Alice, at first, was where I'd felt the most alive, the very top of my game until it all went bad and I left there running for my life. Mendoza was trying to wake up that old part of me, the fire that burned for justice and revenge. By refusing my request, refusing to enable me, he was re-igniting the part of my brain I'd used as an FBI intelligence officer, the version of me that solved an eight-year-old cold case and pulled together three victims under one umbrella. Alice. I'll be damned.

Closer to Mexico than either Dallas or Houston, you could find a nice hotel room there for forty dollars, all within the twelve square miles of its borders. Lush trees, wide streets, despite most residents living at the poverty level. I didn't mind it there because as a green FBI agent, I wanted to see places. Any place, really. My unit was brought in to investigate a string of unsolved embezzlement cases involving three suspected federal district court judges near Alice, Texas. An accidental informant, Nigella, led me to evidence linking the three cases to a drug smuggling ring, and I risked my job and reputation promoting that theory. I successfully found the perp at the center of multiple crimes, but it was never only about drugs. It was risky, anything involving federal officials would be, and especially in a small rural town where there was nowhere to hide. I hadn't yet met Jessica and I was alone trying to find my way, swimming in a sea of sharks. Sometimes crimes had a way of redefining your code of ethics, making almost binary clarity out of the grays in life. I staked everything I had on a tenuous notion, standing on thin ice and trying not to drown. I got lucky. So it seemed at the time.

Then as things started closing in, paperwork filed to the DA's office, subpoenas issued, i's dotted, t's crossed, the three judges— Drumm, Sykes, and Lockhart—vanished. All on the same day, homes emptied, bank accounts cleared, gone without a trace. I'd been told by my informant that their cars were each left in their respective driveways, keys in the ignitions, and completely sanitized of all DNA residue. A typically incorrect assumption which, in this case, turned out to be true. No forensic evidence was found in any of the cars. It was like *The Leftovers* all over again.

Though they were never found, Alice was still the case that pulled me into the most exciting track of my law enforcement career—the FBI's coveted Intelligence Branch, and I realized only now that Mendoza had hand-picked me for that post and probably bribed someone with a dirty secret to do it. Wasn't that the currency nowadays? They didn't know me back then; I'd done nothing of consequence other than my job—investigating conventional leads the conventional way, eventually uncovering three corrupt federal officials who were never brought to justice. Even so, something about that case made me stand out to Mendoza. Did he, like Jessica, see something in me that I didn't see myself? Some hidden talent worthy of the trust needed for a post like that, or was it my six-month tenure in Air Force Intelligence?

I hovered at the top of Pillar Point looking down at a world I'd been avoiding for too long. Somebody was setting me up, and I had a feeling Wendell Peters wasn't the only player on this new chessboard of my life.

CODEX

Chapter 16

I didn't go home to meet up with Elaine like I said I would. I didn't text her either, which made me guilty of her same crimes of evasion. The temperature had dropped, and I needed my jacket back. I'm not saying I didn't want to see Jordan Reid anyway, but I did have an ulterior motive. Really, I just had a lot to think about and Elaine's melodrama was simply further down the list.

I knew she typically got there early, but her VW wasn't in the lot. I got out anyway to look at the waves and draw in the cold sea air. It felt almost wet on my face. *Alice.* The question was whether I would leverage Mendoza's little game to mobilize my thoughts and start moving forward in my life. I thought back to my cramped, gray desk in the J. Edgar Hoover Building in D.C. with its wall of whiteboards around the main room. What did I do back then? I remembered the way it was, the way I was. I didn't trust anybody or anything, what people told me, what they wrote in reports. I ran down facts and researched evidence like Dustin Hoffman in *All the President's Men*, one of my favorite political thrillers about the labyrinth of secrets and lies that protected the truth about Watergate. I imagined being in that room again, part of that culture surrounded by other Intelligence Branch agents working on other cases. What would I write on the whiteboard right now?

"Morning," someone said behind me. Dekker. Just kill me now.

"Did you miss me, Detective? You're welcome to sleep in my trailer if you're afraid I'm gonna skip town."

He was coming through the back entrance of the brewery with a white mug in his hand. Why would he be here this time of day? He looked like he was about to walk out to his car. "Am I under arrest?" I asked, but knew I wasn't.

Dekker swigged the last sips of his coffee. "Local punks, you know. Need something to do after they're all liquored up."

"What, a robbery? Here?" I asked.

He turned and looked back at Jordan behind him. She was moving around the bar to arrange some paperwork. "Come on in," she said, when she saw me. "Got a fresh pot and I've got your jacket."

"I hope no one was hurt," I said to her, working to decipher a look I hadn't seen before.

"Nah," Dekker said, then closed his mouth, reminding me it was a crime scene and therefore none of my business.

"No one was here," Jordan said with squinted eyes. The coffee smelled fresh and so did the orange-scented fragrance she was wearing. There was something else in the air here: fear, and some nonverbal communication between she and Dekker. I don't know why I felt jealous, possessive almost. I barely knew her. Could she and Dekker...God no. No way. I settled onto a barstool and sipped, turning away to gaze at the water. I heard them mumbling behind me. She handed him some paperwork, probably an official statement that would be added to the incident report.

"Nothing missing?" Dekker asked her. "Unusual, don't you think? Nothing from the cash register?"

"Nope," I heard her say.

"No alcohol? Nothing from storage?"

She snapped her fingers. "Wait a minute, I knew I noticed something, just couldn't put my finger on it until now." She disappeared into the kitchen area, leaving Dekker and me to deal with our mutual contempt. She returned and handed me my jacket, then motioned Dekker to the back room. I followed him because I knew he wouldn't want me to. He purposely stood in front of me blocking my view. Asshole.

"There's a key missing," she said, pointing to the wall. "An old key tied to a long piece of dirty string. I think it's been there since before I started working here. No one ever touches it."

"What does it unlock?" Dekker asked, scanning the room.

"A storage shed out back, there." She motioned toward the rear door of the place. I'd parked my bike in that spot before, thankfully not today. All I needed was another crime Dekker could tie me to.

"What kind of storage?" Dekker asked, running through the typical list of questions I would have asked myself, had I been assigned to the case.

"That's the thing." She laughed. "It's empty, and has been for a long time."

"Apparently not everyone thinks so," I added.

What I needed was a whiteboard and a place to work. I thought about my trailer, thought about converting it to a workable office, then remembered the presence of Elaine and wondered again about her ulterior motive for being here because she always had one. Something told me she'd be more likely to tell Rudy than me. Note to self—check with him later.

In the meantime, my heart hungered again for the open road. Overcast in the west with blue peeking out from the north, I left the bar and followed my freedom impulse past Sam's Chowder House toward Montara. I loved the Montara Mountain Trail, but today was a there-and-back. A quick ride, then I had work to do.

Almost noon now, I felt my phone buzz with a text and resisted the urge to pull it out of my back pocket. Maybe only now did I no longer feel the need to take unreasonable risks like that. All this time, there'd been something unspeakably comfortable about the numbness—the post-trauma don't-give-a-fuck mode. Right now, though, it felt familiar but no longer comfortable. Something had shifted. Maybe Sylvan Mendoza's little trick, maybe enough time had elapsed. Or maybe pain gets tired and just gives up eventually.

I paused at a little overlook at the corner of Cabrillo Highway and

Capistrano, deciding to coffee-up again at Mezza Luna because their cappuccinos were the best. I took two sips and checked my phone again. The text was from Officer Lopez, reminding me of her previous text, which I'd forgotten about. I called her back right away.

"Lopez," she answered, and waited for me to speak.

"It's Angus. Sorry. I've had a busy morning."

"I know," she said. "You've had about five cups of coffee so far, and it's not even lunchtime."

I closed my eyes and recalled Dekker's smirk at the brewery earlier, like he and Jordan had some kind of secret. And now obviously Lopez was tailing me. I felt watched, tracked, and on display. Small town was one thing, but this was more than that. "If I'm not mistaken, you still need a warrant to put someone under surveillance," I said. "Not to mention probable cause, which you clearly don't have." I gave her a second to think about it. "I have a bug detector at home. I'll be scanning my bike when I get back there today."

"Wasn't my idea," she said, of course referring to Dekker. "I'm sure he could argue there's probable cause but hopefully it won't come to wiretapping. As for a bug on your motorcycle, not likely. That's not his style."

I wondered where she was right now, maybe in the breezeway attached to Oceano Hotel, which was about ten steps from here. I got up and started walking, keeping my eyes peeled. Besides her memorable hair color, she walked with a sort of swagger, digging her body weight into her hips with each step. Distinctive, to say the least.

I'd walked the length of the breezeway now and came out through the glass doors on the other side, no sign of her. The parking lot to the hotel emptied into a walkway leading to the other side of Capistrano at Barbara's Fish Shack, a greasy dive with lines down the block that probably net $5M a month. Can't go wrong with fried food.

"I don't suppose there's been any word about Mr. Peters' death."

She didn't answer but she cleared her throat.

"You're not at liberty to share any information, especially with a potential suspect."

"Person of interest, for now," she corrected. "And I might, actually. But I need something in return."

She asked to meet me somewhere. I thought about the lobby of

CODEX

Oceano, but the acoustics of their high ceilings could prevent privacy. The one room, standalone gift shop next to the hotel had a small sitting area in the front, which no one ever used. I suggested it.

"See you in five minutes," she said.

Aha. So she'd been here all along. I moved quickly down the sidewalk and planted myself in one of the wrought iron chairs at a matching table with plants on it. I saw her walk out of Barbara's across the street, the smell of salt and grease trailing behind her.

"All you need is a bone china cup and a plate of scones and you've got yourself a tea party." She stifled a laugh.

Her hair was pulled back into a bun today, a more severe look that showed off her high cheekbones. Serious, smart, no-nonsense, trying hard not to be pretty. It wasn't working. "What, you think I look out of place? I like tea." I turned and pointed. "And Mezza Luna Café's got black current scones right now. A little dry but tasty."

"They're supposed to be dry. They're scones." She sat beside me and set her sunglasses on the table. Her eyes looked tired and puffy, like she'd been up all night. I knew enough about women to not ask.

"So…Wendell Peters," I started.

"Right. I can't tell you anything officially, of course—"

"You do know I had nothing to do with whatever happened to him. Right? Do you believe me? At least tell me that."

"Are you asking me if I think you're capable of murder, Mr. Mariner? Because the answer's yes."

Chapter 17

There was a gap in the almost constant line of traffic on Capistrano, an easy cut through from Highway 1 to Pillar Point Harbor Boulevard. I closed my eyes and, for a split second, forgot Officer Lopez's comment and vanished into the sound of waves hitting the shore.

"This is going well so far," I said.

Her right cheek pinched upward with a smirk. "I think everyone's capable of it if the circumstances are right. If you were smart, you'd volunteer to give us your fingerprints and a blood sample for a DNA test. If you're not, Dekker can get them from you anyway. And if you want to make things worse for yourself, you could get a lawyer."

"A lawyer? For fuck's safe, are you serious?"

"Keep your voice down."

"You know as well as I do that no judge would see probable cause for that."

"Not at the moment."

"What could possibly be my motive? I didn't even know the guy."

"Well, he apparently knew you."

I took a few long breaths. "I have no idea where the guy died, how he died, and there's no way you'd find any of my forensic material anywhere near him. He was old. Maybe he died of natural causes, or

CODEX

an accident."

"Read the paper lately?" she asked, brow raised.

"As in newspaper? What century are you from?" I usually did scan the news online every night before going to sleep. Bad habit.

She looked up, her dark eyes blinking back some kind of secret message.

"What, not an accident?" I asked.

"Look, my advice is to cooperate with Dekker. If he thinks you're hiding something, I'll just say that won't be fun for you."

"Because I'm having so much fun now you mean?" I inched toward her. "I believe you. But I'm at the center of two murders in one week and I had nothing to do with either of them. Try to appreciate what that feels like from my perspective. I need to find out what this is all about."

"No one's stopping you," she said. "Just don't cross any lines. I don't want to have to lie for you."

"Fair enough," I said. "Thanks for the advice. You said there was something you needed from me."

Officer Lopez put on her sunglasses and slid them to the top of her head. "I think I mentioned that we've got a shortage of pilots. I checked and you do have an active commercial license."

"Sorta sounds like blackmail to me."

"No need to get defensive, I'm just asking."

"What about it? I'm no longer a law enforcement agent. I left the bureau after the car accident and have been out of commission for a while."

She paused. "Were you...injured?" she asked, careful in her approach, a sensitivity that Dekker obviously lacked.

It was a difficult question, one I'd gone through repeatedly with two grief therapists at the insistence of Jess's family. The accident that killed my wife left me completely intact without anything more than a mild concussion and a few bruised ribs. Guilt wasn't the half of it. "Not on the outside."

I thought back to my training, my history, to who I was when the Alice investigation went down. What I needed was a whiteboard and about a dozen questions answered, like the cause of Peters' death, time of death, location of death, identity of who discovered him. Only after those initial questions were clear could I begin to form a picture of why he died and how on earth I was involved. Not only that, every investigation needed allies and informants. Lopez had made it clear that she was far from either, but I sensed she wouldn't stand in my way. First things first, a reckoning with my sister was overdue.

I left Lopez with a handshake, which she held one second too long. I turned back after walking away, though, remembering something Jess said to me once, one of those prophetic wisdom bytes executed between shifting pans on the stove. Sometimes asking for what you want, she said, is the most courageous thing you can do.

"Any chance you've got a spare whiteboard?" I asked her, blocking a laser of sunlight with one hand.

"We've actually got two extra boards in a closet that nobody uses. Where do you want it?"

Elaine's rental car was gone. Her sudden disappearances unnerved me historically, especially now with so much in flux. She was close to Rudy and I suspected they'd maintained contact while she was abroad. But there was something else going on, I could feel it.

I don't know how she did it but an hour later Lopez showed up with a pickup truck and a large white board on rollers. We managed to haul it into the trailer, but not without a few visible dings in the doorway and two bleeding knuckles. When I came out of the bathroom, she was drinking a glass of water that she'd helped herself to.

"Do you need a doctor?" she asked, laughing.

Skinned knuckles would heal, everything did eventually. "Hey, thank you for this. I mean it."

She nodded and pulled open the door, then turned back and dropped a square package on the table. "Might need these."

Dry erase markers. She'd thought of everything.

"And don't get any ideas. I don't date cops."

She slammed the trailer door to give her comment more punch. I should be flattered, really. Smart, pretty, a spitfire, and there was no mistaking the innuendo, which of course meant she did date cops.

CODEX

Fine. She liked me, that could come in handy. This was the new me, wasn't it? Hard, dispassionate, calculating. That's what you get when you have an icicle in the center of your chest.

I made quick work of the large, white surface, dividing the board into three columns. The left was the shooting victim on the beach, the right was Wendell Peters, with a toddler's rendition of a helicopter in the corner. The center column was the accident, our accident, with a big question mark under it signifying my uncertainty that it even was an accident now. I drew stick figures of Jess and I, the car, even the cliff. I moved in this sort of trance changing markers from black to blue, writing down everything I knew so far. Every fact, days, times, addresses. Something caught my eye finally, drawing me out. A car— headlights. When had it gotten dark? I checked my phone—8pm? How could that be? I hadn't been at it for more than an hour or so—but that was four hours ago, and now the whiteboard was filled with content.

I drank some water, paced on the gravel walkway outside the trailer, then plopped onto the kitchen bench seat. My phone buzzed— Rudy.

"Hey, brother. What's up? Where's my sister?"

"Yeah, that's what I was calling about."

"She at the diner?"

"Nope, and we are dead here tonight. Like three customers. I might close up early. You busy?"

I was, actually, busy trying to understand my life. Rudy was my best friend and I could tell when he needed to talk. The fact that he changed the subject quickly when I asked about Elaine told me it had something to do with her. I knew her; she was more calculating than I was. I eyed the square in the bottom right quadrant of the board with her name on it, then drove to the diner.

I entered through the back and heard Rudy's jolly voice booming from the dining room. He kept chilled soda back here in a spare fridge. I took one and poked my head into the kitchen to wave to Eduardo, who was forming dough on a wooden board.

"Eduardo, what's up?"

"Angus, how you doing?" he asked, without turning around. I watched his bare, thickly muscled arms kneading the dough, and

85

remembered tomorrow was gourmet sandwich day.

"You making roast beef sandwiches tomorrow?"

Now he turned, flashing his bright, toothy grin. "That's classified, bro. Need to know."

"Aren't you funny now. See ya."

I sat back there on a wooden crate and sipped, then ran it over my forehead. The cold was waking me up and something told me I was gonna need it. I heard Rudy's heavy footsteps. He moved a duffel bag out of the way and sat across from me on another box.

"What's going on?" He didn't look okay.

He kept his head still but widened his eyes and looked up.

"What?"

"You talk to Elaine since she's been back?"

My palms went up in defense. "Bro, I tried. It's hard to get anything out of her."

"What do you think she's doing here?"

I took another sip and considered the question. "She seems nervous to me, like she's running."

"Yep."

"Am I right?" I asked.

Rudy nodded.

"From Miguel?"

He answered with just his eyes. Miguel was a former meth dealer she'd supposedly cleaned up, but not before he beat her a few times too many and she eventually ran out on him.

Rudy shook his head then looked down.

"What happened?" I asked.

Long sigh. "She apparently hustled him out of what she says is a large sum of money."

"Shit." I set the can on the floor by my feet. "Why didn't she tell me about this?"

"Come on, bro. Why do you think? She's ashamed. She's afraid. You're family; she doesn't want you to worry."

"How much money are we talking about?"

"Hundred thou."

"Jesus," I whispered. "Did she say why?"

"All's I know is someone made her do it. She said she couldn't tell me any more than that."

I felt bad, now, for all the bad things I'd said about the trailer, avoiding her for the past two days. My sister needed me. Finally, I got to the most important question. "Who else knows she's here right now?"

Chapter 18

Instead of answering, Rudy got Eduardo to feed me a grilled chicken sandwich with his signature creamy sriracha sauce. It was a crime to leave any of Eduardo's food uneaten. I ate three bites, thanked him, then escaped out the back. How could I possibly eat right now? Without explicitly saying so, Rudy's silence implied Elaine's drug pusher ex knew she'd fled to California. A hundred thousand dollars is a lot of bacon. I might need to get my gun back from Rudy.

I went home and added "Elaine/Miguel/$100k" to that section of the board, knowing she had her own key and cared nothing about personal privacy. Likewise I had to assume, by now, that she also knew about Wendell Peters and all the other chaos I'd been party to lately. I remembered, only now, bits and pieces of details she'd shared when she and Miguel first moved in together. Three dozen roses, diamond bracelets, and a black eye every few months. Maybe to her it seemed like a small price for sexual compatibility and companionship. The mental image of him with his lanky frame and tattoo sleeves made me flinch. I'd be on blood pressure medicine over this eventually.

I collapsed on the bed from mental exhaustion, secretly glad for the pillow-top mattress. My laptop still mostly charged from its last usage, I returned to the pages I'd bookmarked on WP: his name shown in

Google search results in an entry about his company ADS—Alternative Design Solutions, a lawsuit in the state of New York, an academic paper on Google Scholar, and a commercial bio that mentioned four patents. I hadn't yet been able to cross reference each entry with the image I'd seen on LinkedIn, and Wendell and Peters were not wholly uncommon names. I sat back against the overstuffed pillows, setting the laptop on my right side. The chessboard was still on my left under the window, and I could see that Elaine had made the first move, her standard Italian Game opening, when she was snooping around here. A creature of habit.

I checked Wendell Peters' LinkedIn profile one more time for any mention of patents, scrolling to the bottom in the Honors and Awards section, where one patent was listed. I copied and pasted the name of it into patents.google.com and the same title came up as a link. Next, I did a WP name search on Google Patents and four came up—all with the same Wendell S. Peters. Okay. WP was a scientist—in particular, an ear, nose, and throat surgeon. ENT wasn't what I would have guessed of the drunken waif outside the brewery.

His ADS company website specialized in edge-case ENT research and also the manufacturing of specialized devices. Were those the same as hearing aids? I called the number and asked for Dr. Peters, just to see, then quickly disconnected. It might be too late and the firm might have logged my phone number.

I had to step outside for a view of the sky over the water, something I'd come to call medicine. I climbed up the slope of the grassy dune and sat on the cold sand. Empty and silent, just how I liked it. Why was I thinking about Jordan Reid every time I looked at the sky lately? My stomach still felt knotted up but I was hungry again. I locked the trailer and stood over my bike, knowing it needed an oil change, new air filter, and a chain and cables check. Maybe next weekend.

I found Jordan wearing a dark red apron behind the bar at the brewery. The tie on it was wrapped around her waist and joined in the front. Dinnertime now, the crowd was thick for a weeknight. I shouldered my way onto the only open barstool.

"He-ey," Jordan said, in what must be her bar voice. She was shy, bookish, intellectual. She could fake it alright, I'd seen it, but I was starting to understand her nature. I smiled and waved. "Why do I always want to call you detective?" she asked. "Were you—"

I leaned forward so she could hear me over the din of heavy drinkers. "I left the military and applied to the FBI Academy, and it went from there."

"Went where?"

"Various places." I took in the almond-shape of her eyes, feeling slightly less ashamed than I had before.

"The usual?"

"Yep," I confirmed.

She pointed to the end of the bar to pay. Where had this wall of suits come from? There must be a conference that just let out. I think Oceano Hotel had some meeting event spaces. Come to think of it, I'd seen a sign out front when I walked past the lobby on my way to see Officer Lopez. The brewery was literally twenty steps from the hotel and my dinner would take at least twenty minutes. I told Jordan I'd be right back, then escaped the crowd, passing the forty-foot queue outside Barbara's Fish Shack to the front steps toward the hotel lobby. An easel had a printed 18 x 24 glossy sign that read, "ENT and Audiology Masterclass". ENT, audiology. And our friend Wendell Peters was one of the country's foremost experts. Coincidence? Doubt it.

No sign of Jordan when I got back, I picked up my burger, stood out by the water nibbling a few fries, feeling the weight of the darkening sky. A system was supposed to be moving in tonight, something they call an atmospheric river. So much for my morning ride into the hills tomorrow.

Before I left, I got a text from Rudy that Elaine was asleep in his guest room safe and sound. Thank God. I took another quick scan for Jordan, then rode back to the trailer and sat at my kitchen table to eat my burger and fries. So this was how it was done, I laughed to myself, laptop beside me as I prepared a list of potential assets from ADS to contact tomorrow. My hands were buzzing with energy, while the rest of my body struggled to stay awake. I nodded off mid-sentence still sitting upright. It was too early but I laid back and closed my eyes. Maybe that was enough for one day.

Officer, over here—I can't move him—miracle he's even alive—

died on impact—smoke—I can't move my legs—I'm trapped. Can you hear me—she's not breathing...get a medevac out here...

    I woke at 6:15am after waking up every two hours. I felt like I'd just gone to sleep. Dreaming of the accident had become typical for me, even after all this time. Usually just bits and pieces of conversation my unconscious mind played back in its surreal mishmash. It didn't unravel me the way it used to, which in itself showed some signs of recovery. Recovering inevitably meant moving away from my deepest longing. Love, at some point, becomes like heroin. Maybe now it was time to quit.

    But there was something different in last night's dream medley. A man, thick brows, stern eyes was all I could remember. And a gun he pressed hard into the right side of my ribcage. I reached my hand up my shirt to see if it still hurt. Three ribs on the right side felt sensitive. With nothing but a fleeting image, I could still see that one as clearly as the French press looking back at me from the counter. Coffee had never failed me yet.

    I boiled enough water to make a full pot, so I could have some now and drink more later. I inhaled the intoxicating scent deep into my nose, repeating with a few more deep breaths. The before-me used to do yoga—Jess and I did it together—when my body was flexible, fast, and strong. Maybe it was time to get back to that, too. I probably still had a mat somewhere, maybe at the house in San Carlos.

    I took another trip to Andreini Airfield to poke around WP's chopper, knowing that guy Mason might have something to say about it. I had my spiel prepared about being released by the PD and my obvious vested interest in the aircraft. No one was in there yet except an older, biker-type woman who opened the door for me and then left. I walked out onto the main floor and could see right away that WP's chopper was gone. What the hell? I spent a few minutes looking around, checking all the vessels on the floor, then I went back into the hallway.

Listen to the signs, Elaine always tells me, based on her overuse of astrology and twenty-five other new-age fringe sciences. Theories, really, but who was I to judge something I knew nothing about? The signs today were telling me to come back to the hangar later this afternoon, and to go home and start over again.

Still barely awake, I got halfway through coffee #2 before I realized Elaine's rental car was gone—again. I looked out the window to verify and found nothing but my bike parked by the fence in its usual place. Maybe Rudy borrowed her car. And maybe an alien spaceship was going to land at the Half Moon Bay jetty today.

I pulled open Rudy's front door and thundered through the house. "Elaine, you here?" I shouted, knowing she wasn't and realizing in a sudden shake of fear that the man I'd dreamt about was Miguel. My stomach churned and I lost my balance, grabbing onto the sofa. What's happening to me?

Chapter 19

My hands were shaking. No, not my hands—my arms, my chest. My knees wobbled. The room seemed to be spinning, and my stomach felt swimmy. My face was cold and wet. Tears? Me? What the fuck was going on?

I hadn't seen him at first. The room was dark, his skin was dark, and my eyes weren't working right. My face, my eyes seemed to be tearing up but my heart felt still and solid. My trembling hand reached for the corner of the sofa and instead found another hand, larger than mine. It grabbed me and pulled me to the couch where I collapsed into the soft, gray cushions. This wasn't trembling. Trembling comes from fear, trepidation, anticipation. I didn't feel any of those things. I was thinking of Elaine and Miguel, if he had taken her and where he might go. That's what my brain was thinking of. But my mind, my deeper, higher consciousness was thinking of someone else.

Standing over my coiled-up self, I felt Rudy drape himself over my shuddering form, bear-hugging me from behind with his arms clasped at my chest, providing structure to this terrible moment, whatever it was. Elaine, I kept seeing her light blonde hair muddied by ash and soot and blood, hanging back with her mouth open in a grotesque lopsided shape, teeth bared. I stood over this dream-image of her, my sister, and then I knew. It wasn't Elaine. It was Jess. Rudy was holding both of my hands in one of his, gripping my body closed as if all my insides might spray out across the room if he let go.

I started coughing into the couch pillows, retching like I might cough up my lungs—whole and slimy. It felt like a sort of sudden purge, like you see in religious purification rituals after drinking ayahuasca. But the sickness didn't seem to be coming from my stomach. How had this happened, and why did it happen so suddenly? Elaine's car was gone, she wasn't inside Rudy's house, and something just snapped.

"What's happening?" I said into the couch pillow. "Rudy—"

"I'm here, bro," he whispered.

"What's wrong with me? I'm all fucked up."

"Not wrong. Right. It's time."

"What?" More coughing. "Time for what? What is this?"

"Grief, bro. That stranger who's been livin' in your bones. You've been hiding him for a long time, and I suspect he's got a lot to say."

An hour later, my nerves had calmed and a more subdued, rational version of me supplanted the vulnerable me. I heard Rudy puttering around in the kitchen. He was always cooking something and he did it in stages. Stirring something on the stove, marinating something in the fridge, while he prepped something to be cooked tomorrow. He was right. I'd hidden this part of me from the world, and from myself by staying busy with projects. Fixing my bike, roaming around foggy hillsides, perfecting the armor of anger.

"Where is she?" I asked him finally. He came to the doorway.

"Who?"

"Cut it out."

"We're not talking about Elaine right now, Angus."

"Where—is—she?" The sound bellowed through the whole house springing from my knees and hips. A new desperation, unfamiliar. God help me. "I'm sorry," I said.

"It's alright. It's not you talking right now."

I looked up at him, my eyes begging him to answer this time.

"Where's my sister?"

"Her car was gone when I got here." He shook his head like all was lost.

My tears surprised me, more like shock. But intellectually I could understand how my missing sister had in some way triggered the loss of Jessica. I finally got up from Rudy's sofa and went to the kitchen. I wanted brandy but he gave me water instead. "Drink it."

I sat at the kitchen table, wondering what he was simmering in his stew pot. "What do we know about him—Miguel Santos?" I mumbled, only then remembering his last name. "Did she say they broke up?" I asked, ironic that I was asking Rudy about my own sister.

"Michael Santos. He only goes by Miguel to his drug buddies."

"Figures."

"She said he disappeared, and a week later someone contacted her telling her that he stole $100k and she needed to return it if she wanted him to stay alive."

I nodded, taking it all in. "So she didn't steal his money, she stole back money he stole from someone else? Is that it?" Rudy stared back. "Last night—"

He raised his palms. "I know what I said, and that's all I knew at the time. Okay? She told me someone made her steal the money but she wouldn't elaborate."

"And then?" I pushed.

He turned off the gas burner, pulled the large pot to a back burner, and sat at the round table. "She was asleep when I got home last night from the diner. I woke her up and asked her if she wanted some protection."

"My God, please tell me you didn't give her my gun. I know Dekker's gonna be looking for that."

"I offered her mine but she wouldn't take it. She said she gave them what they wanted, she followed directions."

"And then she flew here? From London?" I asked. It didn't make any sense. "Wouldn't she stay to make sure they held up their end and returned him to her?"

Rudy shrugged. "I don't know. Maybe she didn't want him back. That's all she told me so far. I left super-early this morning, while she was still asleep. When I came back to check on her, the rental car was gone."

I returned to the comfort of the gray couch and curled up on my side, feeling suddenly sick. I told Rudy what I'd learned about WP's company so far. "I'm heading over there today to see what I can find out."

"Fine, but stop using my name when you go under cover."

"I only did that once," I said. "You should be flattered."

"This is a small town and everyone knows me."

"Yes, as you're constantly reminding me." I liked the lighter vibe in the room, but it didn't last long. Rudy took the chair across from the couch and leaned in.

"What's that look?" I asked.

"You've been avoiding grief for a long time. Do you think I don't know?"

I exhaled. "Know what?" I watched him pinch the corner of his mouth and shake his head, a scorn. Disapproval. "I know I haven't talked about it." My voice was a whisper, like I was ashamed. "I guess I can't."

"You have nightmares. I can hear you all the way in the house. You scream in your sleep. You're reliving it, aren't you?"

"Reliving what?" I asked, but I knew of course.

"Are you ready to talk about it now? About her?"

"Nothing to talk about," I said, before I'd even planned the words. "Wait…" I caught myself. I knew better than this. Everything slowed to a quiet pulse. "Maybe there's a lot to talk about. Maybe I just don't know how."

"And maybe you blame yourself for her death because it was your event you were going to. That's irrational, but natural."

"She didn't want to go." I laughed a little too loud, a little too false. I clinched my eyes closed and balled my hands into fists to keep the sobs from rolling out, the grief I'd kept carefully stored, folded neatly into a tiny box in my chest all this time. "I went to therapy, Rudy, for six goddamn months."

His eyes widened. "You went three times, showed up late, left early, and cancelled at the last minute. And there's nothing wrong with your memory."

I was trying hard not to hate him right now. "Sitting in that hard chair in a cold room with chipped paint on the walls, like some kind of karmic penance. It seemed fitting at the time, cognitive behavior therapy. It's all fucking psychobabble."

"Don't knock it." He shook his head in that slow way he had, a way that's at once critical and supportive, questioning but understanding at the same time. I'd never known anyone else like him.

"I don't. It might have saved my life, had I gone every time. It was supposed to keep me connected to daily structure like eating, hydrating, regulating sleep."

"Have you looked in the mirror lately?"

"Not when I can avoid it."

"If you did, you'd see that you've lost about twenty-five pounds. It's alarming to folks who haven't seen you in a while. People talk. They ask me about it all the time."

"At the diner?" I laughed. "Okay, Mom."

"Dude, what's the matter with you?"

"I'm broken! Do you hear me? I'm broken for fuck's sake. That's what's the matter with me."

"Alright, alright. I hear you. For the record, I love your mom. If she were here, she'd say the same thing. I think you blame yourself for Jessica's death and for Elaine's predicament. I also think that's bringing up the grief and guilt you've been carrying about the accident."

I watched Rudy sit back in the chair as I swung my legs to the floor, tired of laying down, and even more tired of talking about grief. It was time for action. "Thanks for looking after me," I said, immediately feeling the inadequacy of those words. "I've got some investigating to do."

"It's Saturday," he said.

"Betcha someone will be there."

The headquarters of Advanced Diagnostic Services, WP's company, took up the whole third floor of a building adjacent to the Hyatt on the corner of Drumm Street and Embarcadero in San Francisco. It drizzled the whole ride north; the coolness felt good on my body, though it felt so wrong to be driving away from Half Moon Bay with my sister missing. And my stomach still felt queasy from my sudden outpouring. My mind concocted all kinds of fairy tales about where she could be. Manicure, haircut, shopping, sightseeing— possible, but not likely. She didn't fly five thousand miles to get a manicure. She found money that Miguel stole, gave it back to save his life, skipped town to avoid his wrath and now he was here for revenge. Could it be as simple as that? Probably not.

Drizzle turned to near flooding as I got off the freeway, so I found a parking garage to take cover, using the time to dry off and get my thoughts in order. I kept a folded towel in the zippered pack inside my seat, which did nothing for the bags under my eyes and two days' worth of razor stubble. Twenty-five pounds, really? It couldn't be that much.

I went through the details as I climbed the gray-tiled, circular staircase. WP had a Ph.D. in otolaryngology, I reminded myself. My Google search earlier showed he got his degree at Stanford and did his residency at UC Irvine. Not sure why that mattered but I'd made note of it. I'd be asking for Dr. Peters, not Wendell Peters.

I smelled soy and soba noodles from the sushi restaurant Sens on my way up the stairs, oh my God. I'd be stopping there for lunch. ADS was down a curved hallway on the other side of the staircase. A woman in workout clothes sat behind a reception desk in a lobby that looked more appropriate for a law firm. What was this place? If it was medical research, wouldn't it be in a lab? Or was this research academic only? Those soba noodles were calling to me.

"Can I help you?" the woman asked, her eyes on her large screen monitor.

"Yeah, thank you. I'm here to see Dr. Peters." I watched her closely.

Her eyes widened, she looked left and right, then seemed to shake herself back to office decorum. "I'm sorry, he's not in but I'd be happy to take a message, Mr.—"

"Wright. Mr. Wright."

She stared, waiting.

"I saw Dr. Peters was speaking at that conference down in Half Moon Bay, and I was looking forward to meeting him but I had to

CODEX

miss it at the last minute." Great pitch. It wasn't working.

"Are you a journalist?" she asked.

"No. My mom's hearing impaired and I wanted to consult with him."

I knew she wasn't buying it but she played the part, picking up a pen and notepad. "What's your number, Mr. Wright? Where can he reach you?"

"(650) 726-6657." Rudy's spare cell phone, on which he never checked the voicemails.

"Very good, then. I'll give him the message." She stared at the door.

I walked away, conscious that I was excited about food for the first time since the accident. My phone buzzed with a text. I pulled it out of my pocket so fast it fell on the floor and skated across the rough-cut tiles. I grabbed it, praying it was from Elaine. It was a number I didn't recognize.

Mr. Mariner, you don't know me. My name is Michael Wise. We need to talk.

I didn't recognize the name and didn't feel like online research right now. I was dreaming about those soba noodles. *What about?* I wrote back.

Your wife.

Chapter 20

June

I agreed to meet Michael Wise at the noodle house the following night, so I'd have time to go back to HMB. Of course nothing back from the message I'd left for Wendell Peters at ADS, still no sign of Elaine's rental car, and Rudy hadn't heard from her. I was one click away from filing a missing person's report. But that would undoubtedly involve Dekker and he would undoubtedly blame me for her disappearance.

The man replied later to say that Sens was way too public for *this conversation*. Slightly intriguing, I had to admit. Still, I was sure he was some kind of muckraker looking for an exclusive.

The man suggested the second-floor lobby of the Hyatt Embarcadero across the courtyard from Sens and back down Drumm Street. I knew the hotel. I'd stayed there with Jess, where we'd spent hours talking over drinks in their cozy lobby alcoves. He was right, it was perfect for private or maybe even controversial conversations. But what was there to say, really? Jessica was a brilliant lawyer and a shining star who died at twenty-eight years old, pretty much because of me. The worst short story ever told.

CODEX

We agreed to meet at 8pm. That still gave me plenty of time to ride up to San Francisco. I parked in the underground lot and strolled through the Hyatt lobby, past a C-shaped nook with orange pillows, covered two-seaters more appropriate for date night, and then a long row of booths that seemed like one of them might work. I'd no sooner dropped my jacket on the seat when a man cleared his throat behind me.

"Mr. Mariner."

Clean shaven, dark brown skin, large eyes framed by thick brows, mid-thirties. Handsome, I couldn't help but notice. He held out his hand. I could've been a dick and left him standing there like that, reminding him that no widower wants to talk about his dead wife to a stranger, or anybody else for that matter. I grabbed the hand quickly, let go, and sat with my arms folded. It was body language intended to display impatience.

"What can I do for you, Mr.—?"

"Wise. Get you a drink?" He had a quick, insistent way of talking that so far supported my idea of a journalist, but mainly I watched his eyes because I'd learned what people did with their eyes during tense situations betrayed emotions and motivation. His eyes were stone, penetrating and emotionless.

"I don't have much time." I took out my phone. "I'm good."

"This should take five minutes."

"Well, in that case, couldn't this have been a text?" I shot back.

The man shook his head, soberly. He sat across from me, body-matching with his hands folded on the table. It was an old tradecraft trick for rapport-building. The fact that he knew it told me something else about him.

"You wanted to talk. About my wife. So talk."

Single nod, then he shook his head and got up. "I'm sorry. I think I do need a drink for this conversation. I'll be back in a minute."

"Sure," I said, deciding whether I was gonna just take off or wait. No text from Elaine so far. A tennis player walked past the table in shorts, baggy shirt, and one of those vintage terrycloth headbands carrying a tennis racquet. The north waterfront of the Embarcadero had courts. I moaned softly, my stomach once again a sudden pool of acid. I held my hand over it and closed my eyes, remembering that man meditating on the hill outside the police station wearing some kind of metal band around his head. Maybe I could use a drink after all.

I opened Chrome on my iPhone and typed *Michael Wise Journalist* into Google. A Michael Wise was associated with the Pasadena Star News and the Santa Cruz Sentinel. It was a common name, so more research was required. I changed to a Google Image search, scrolling, more scrolling, there. Michael Wise. Three images came up matching the description of the African American man wiping his palms on his pants at the bar across the room from me: one wearing a suit shaking the hand of what looked like a politician, another with his hands cuffed behind his back. The third image was him standing on a podium holding up an award. Interesting mix. As he approached, I zoomed into the second picture and held out my phone.

"What were you arrested for?" I asked.

He froze in his tracks, let out a nervous chuckle and sat with his hands curled around a tall glass of clear liquid, probably a G&T. This can't be good.

"Breaking and entering," he said in a clear voice, eyes wide, face animated.

"Where?"

"Your house."

"Come again—"

"You heard me right."

Another staring contest, me wondering if he was full of shit and what his agenda might be, him watching my next move. How could he be telling the truth? "Then why don't I know you? I still own that house, so obviously it wasn't recently."

"You don't live there. No one does right now."

I shook my head and sat back, resenting the fact that this stranger was making me think about the San Carlos house and all the memories I'd trapped in there when I closed it up. Work it, Angus. Think. "You're saying you got arrested for breaking into my house that I haven't lived in for over a year?"

One nod. "Yes."

"Okay. Why wouldn't I have been notified?"

"Your real estate agent, Ginger. She—"

CODEX

"Ah," I said. "She's in Hawaii, she just got married." This was getting more interesting by the minute. "How'd you get through the lock box on the front door?"

The man twisted his drink back and forth on the table. "The alarm's not on. I got in through a window in the back."

"Sorry, I don't get it. Why go through that trouble? What's the urgency?" None of this answered the question of why the alarm was off. Now I'd need to either bother Ginger on her honeymoon or drive down there. I don't know which was worse.

About sixty people came up the escalator and were hanging out in front of Eclipse, the Hyatt restaurant. Must be a convention from downstairs breaking for dinner. I eyed the man's drink, suddenly desperate for fortification.

"Help yourself," he said, pushing the glass toward me. Did he know about that, too? Was he taunting me? Didn't seem like the type.

"Doesn't agree with me," I said, which I'd used as my canned response to any invitations to alcohol. So far, he'd supplied a logical scenario by which he could have potentially broken into the house Jessica and I owned together. "So just to be clear, we're talking Elm Street in San Carlos, right?"

The man sighed. "Built in 1937, worth about three mill right now on Zillow."

"It was in my name originally. After Jess and I got married, I filed a Quit Claim Deed and added her to it so it would be in both our names." I had no idea why I told him that detail.

Michael Wise leaned forward. "Is it still?"

"Still what?"

"In both your names?"

The man's insistent staring and solid composure rattled me. "I haven't changed anything, so yeah. What about it?"

"Jessica had a lot of secrets."

"She was a lawyer. A lot of her work was confidential," I argued, suddenly dreading what would come next. My brain spooled backward in time, trying to recall any history of deception or concealment. I didn't ask her about her work, generally. If I did, she usually told me what I wanted to know, but it was a confidentiality breach and was disrespectful of me to put her in that position, so I didn't do it often.

Had I ever, come to think of it? Now, looking at this ambitious hot shot, I needed to know how they knew each other.

Michael Wise sighed and sat back, crossing an ankle on his knee. "Look, maybe this was a bad idea."

"Oh right," I eyerolled. "Like you hadn't thought through this conversation a hundred times before texting me. You're a muckraker, a journalist. You want a juicy story to make you look good to your editor, maybe get you a promotion? A raise? What are your aspirations and how do I fit into them, Mr. Wise?"

"First of all, I'm not a journalist," he said. "I'm a podcaster."

"Is there a difference?"

"Do you care?"

"No, not really."

"And I do have an editor. But whatever."

Well, we were off to a great start. The room got louder, and a man with an apron approached us holding what looked like a credit card. "I believe you left this, sir, when you purchased your drink."

"Thank you." Podcaster tucked it in his wallet. "Look," he said after the server stepped a safe distance away. "Jessica came to me, not vice versa."

"When?" I asked. "Why? How did you know each other, and how did I not know about it?" I felt ashamed hearing those words out loud, like I was some jealous husband. I was never jealous with her. She never gave me reason to be. I felt as loved by her as I'm sure she felt by me. But maybe I wasn't sure of anything right now. I needed to hold it together and keep listening to get to the point of this charade.

He leaned in further. "Six months before your accident, she contacted me. And let me just say, Mr. Mariner, that I'm deeply sorry for your loss. I was very fond of Jessica."

"Fond? Fond. Think maybe you're just sorry for *your* loss? Maybe you wish it was me who died in that accident." Now I really wished I'd ordered that drink. The last thing I needed right now was an assault and battery charge. I mentally counted back from twenty and took in a few deep breaths. "Okay," I said. "I'm sorry. Keep going. Why did she contact you?"

"She was working on a case that she felt pushed the limits of ethical business practices."

"I think she would have been more likely to go to one of the other partners in the firm than to contact a journalist." I knew the word journalist would get a response.

He shook his head sharply.

"You're saying not if her concerns involved someone from the firm?"

"Getting warm."

"So she suspected the firm was doing something illegal and—"

"No," he stopped me, his index finger pointed up. "Not the firm."

Chapter 21

I still didn't get it and this was taking more time than I wanted to spend. I needed to track down Elaine. I pulled out my phone and texted her again right in front of Podcaster.

Call me, I wrote, set my phone aside, and took a long look at Michael Wise. A picture began to form in my head, sort of a delayed response to this unlikely story.

"Did she or didn't she talk to anyone at the firm about her concerns?"

He shook his head. "She did. It went nowhere."

"Meaning they didn't believe her?"

"They apparently told her to keep her head down and stop making waves."

I exhaled all the stress that had been trapped in my body. "Alright, Mr. Wise. You've got my attention. What's really going on here?"

He stared back with his large, dark eyes, brow raised, lips clenched tight.

"Was Jess some kind of whistleblower? Is that the word you're avoiding?"

"That's a good word. I like that word. I'm sure you've got a number of questions—"

CODEX

"Questions? Why would I have questions? A stranger contacts me and tells me I essentially knew nothing about my own wife."

"Verify my story then," he shrugged.

"Believe me, I will definitely do my own research. But you seem to know a lot here, so I want to hear it from you."

He stared back. I was willing my heartrate to slow down.

"Did you love her? Did you love my wife, Mr. Wise? Because if the answer's—"

"No." Palms up, but head down. "I admired her," he explained. "She was brave. Crazy, actually. I wanted to help her. I'm sorry I couldn't."

Gratefully, a throng of people flooded the lobby from one of the second-floor conference rooms, giving us a nice breather.

"Alright," I sighed, making some sort of tacit agreement with myself. "What was she onto?"

He leaned forward an inch and put his arms on the table. "Faked clinical trials, for starters."

Was that even all that uncommon at this point? "I didn't think her firm took pharma cases," I said.

"They don't. They were doing the legal due diligence for a merger one of their clients was involved with."

"I still don't recall hearing your answer about why you felt the need to break into my empty house."

He didn't answer. And why did I have this sudden feeling that WP was somehow involved in this discussion?

"Who was the client?" I asked. "You probably can't tell me."

"I don't know, and that's the truth. Jessica knew but she hadn't yet given me that detail. She was about to when…sorry. She was, um." He lowered his eyes onto the table. His voice trailed and I knew why when I saw the emotion in his face. This man had loved her, had loved my wife. I felt sick.

"She was about to tell you before the accident?" I asked, surprised I could get the words out.

"We were scheduled to meet after your event, later that night."

I got up without ceremony or explanation, walked to the end of the lobby, down the long concrete staircase to the rear courtyard, but remembered the exterior access from that door required a guest

107

keycard. I came back up the stairs and circumambulated the lobby a few times, doing perimeter laps to get my heart rate up and my blood moving, Michael Wise glancing up every few minutes from his phone. Anything to calm the ocean of rage I felt at this brazen interloper. All this time, all the agony I'd inflicted upon myself, blaming myself for her death when all the while it was probably him who had gotten her killed.

If someone had Jessica's or Podcaster's cars or phones bugged, they likely would have known about their scheduled meeting, and the formidable breach Jessica was about to inflict on her firm and their client. I needed to know the name of that company, what they were doing, and why. While I waited for a fresh round at the bar, I moved to viewing distance of the table, zoomed in and snapped a photo of him that showed the basic shape of him. Could be useful later.

I returned with a Coke and another G&T. After I sat, Michael Wise looked at the table giving me a minute to collect myself. He seemed more thoughtful than annoyed. That was something.

"Look," he said. "I probably could have done a better job preparing you for this information. I'm sorry."

I two took large gulps of Coke, honestly not caring about his lack of sensitivity. Would it have mattered? Probably not. "Why didn't she tell me?"

"I suggested it, more than once," he said. "She said no way."

I stared, asking for the rest of it with my eyes.

"At this point, I'm willing to share everything I know with you, but this is not the place."

"Where then?"

"Hold on, there's another piece of the puzzle I need to mention. Jessica kept a journal, which she said she would bring to me when we met after the FBI event."

"So she had it with her in the car, when—" I couldn't get through the sentence. I tried to recall what kind of purse she'd brought with her that night, so much of it was still blocked out. Besides, she owned about fifty purses.

Michael Wise nodded. "Supposedly, yes, though I would have no idea what became of her possessions that night."

He wasn't telling. He was asking, and I honestly had no idea. After

CODEX

the accident, I still couldn't remember much, other than Elaine, Rudy, and Jessica's mother hovering, force feeding me soup and vitamins, constant reminders about grief therapy. I drew in a long breath and exhaled slowly through my nose. "Probably still in San Carlos somewhere."

The man raised his eyebrows.

"Okay, which is what you were looking for when you broke into my house."

He said nothing.

"I assume you didn't find it?"

"No. Feel up to taking a ride?"

The Coke was sweet and fizzy and cold, and just what I needed. I knew what he was asking, but there was no way. He said nothing while watching me work through it. "You're asking me to go to the house to dig around in Jessica's things to find a journal that may or may not exist, and may or may not contain dangerous information?"

"Pretty much."

"I haven't been there yet. Not since the accident."

He waited.

I crossed my arms. "Why now? She's been dead more than a year."

"I can't tell you that."

"But you're not a journalist?"

"Right."

"Mr. Wise, meaning no disrespect, I think you're full of shit and I'm not willing to engage any further down this painful path. You're obviously not willing to share relevant details that could influence my decision-making on the matter, so I don't see that there's anything more to talk about."

Geez, I sounded like a lawyer. Had Jess rubbed off on me finally? If she were here, she would have laughed at that delivery. I loved her laugh. She was stingy with it, but when it erupted involuntarily, it was like a light turning on in the sky. My heart wasn't ready for this, whatever it was.

He rubbed his nose, did a quick eyebrow raise, and got up. "Look, I—"

"We're done." I rubbed my face and stretched out my legs on the bench seat of the booth. Michael Wise wriggled his muscley limbs into

109

what looked like a $1500 leather jacket, probably lambskin if I was right. I don't know what outcome he intended from this meeting, but it hadn't gone well. No parting handshake, at least it hadn't come to blows. Things were left somewhere in between. He walked away from our booth sullen, hands dug low in his pockets, and I had a feeling it wasn't an act to inspire guilt, assuming I was watching him. Which of course I was.

I had to time it exactly right, or else he'd see me behind him. The gods were in my favor, for once, and I managed to tail him. Out on the street, I stayed half a block back. Luckily it was already dark and I was wearing a dark jacket. I knew from experience that if I planned to keep this up for a while, I'd need a change of clothes, or at least a baseball cap to keep from being recognized.

He headed out the main doors of the hotel and turned left on Market, past Philz Coffee and around the back side of the hotel, which was great for me. It was dark back here, with no streetlights and lots of tall trees. It was always packed there late at night with folks looking for last minute supplies, and food before finding a place to sleep. San Francisco's homeless problem seemed to get worse every year. I'd done my part in Alice, TX with Nigella Lawson, with a rescue that supposedly gave her enough money to find an apartment. It didn't last long, she was soon back on the street, but her endearment to me meant I forever had an informant. And in this city, that was like gold. Before the accident, she'd moved back to California and maybe she was still here. Who knows, Nigella Dawson might be able to help me with my Michael Wise problem.

He was still on the east side of Embarcadero but closer to the street under the lights, where it would be safer for him, more visible, in case anyone thought the value of his fine leather jacket might be worth the risk of violence. He'd only looked back once so far and to the right, which could mean he didn't spot me tailing him. It could also mean he was smarter than I thought, knew I was here and was playing it cool. I don't think so. Michael Wise had an agenda tonight. And I needed to find out what it was.

I liked the feel of the post-rain night air on my face, everything smelled fresh. Past Starbucks, the Exploratorium, Pier 23, we were almost to the Aquarium of the Bay when he stopped, checked his

CODEX

watch, and turned around heading back toward me now. Where the hell was he going?

Chapter 22

I hung low in the tree line till he moved past me, him on the bay side of Embarcadero, me on the other. It looked like he was heading back toward the Ferry Building, but this time I watched him cross the street. Shit. There was no one else was around so I'd be visible if I crossed behind him, but it was otherwise impossible to see. Wait, he stood in the median waiting to cross to the Ferry Building, stooped over with his hands on his knees for some reason. Was he sick or something? I hiked to the other side of Drumm Street to get a better look, wishing I had my binoculars. Luckily a throng of people came out of the Hyatt, maybe from that same conference. Concealed by the mob now, I moved closer with my eyes glued to Michael Wise. He was waiting for someone. I watched him turn to his right just as a dark blue car slowed, the car's driver's side window opened, and someone passed him something—some kind of book. Wise stuffed it in his zipped-up jacket and crossed the street toward me.

I'd just witnessed a drop, but it wasn't drugs that were transferred.

I was sure it was my dead wife's journal.

With my eyes still glued to that black lambskin jacket, I couldn't tear my thoughts away from Elaine. I texted Rudy to see if he'd heard from her. Still within my sights after sliding my phone back in my pocket, Wise headed toward the Hyatt again. I'd love to know where he lived; I had a feeling it wasn't San Francisco. So where would he be staying? He moved down Market Street at a nice clip, turned right on Drumm like he was about to enter the Hyatt's main doors but he kept walking. I was still a comfortable half-block behind him, and though he moved quickly, he didn't act like he knew he was being tailed. I went through our conversation, his preposterous story and the unsettling point about San Carlos. There wasn't time to assess the veracity of his claim yet; I'd need to do that later when I was back at my laptop. Gut reaction? No way. Jessica wouldn't have kept something that important from me. So, if I was right, what motivation would Michael Wise the Podcaster have to deceive me? And what secrets were buried in that journal?

He walked two blocks up from Market and turned left on Sacramento. If he turned right on Battery Street, that meant he was probably staying at the Le Meridien Hotel. Sort of high profile for a muckraker like him. He was working on a story, he planned to capitalize on that story, and unfortunately for me that story involved my wife. He turned right and slipped through the entrance to Le Meridien. Got you now, Michael Wise.

Rudy texted back. *Nothing. You? I'm getting worried.*

Me too, I wrote back, then cruelly turned down the phone volume knowing he'd be calling me any minute to discuss a tactical plan. Unfortunately, I was working on another one.

Le Meridien was the ultimate in modern luxury hospitality. Even better was the Embarcadero Center Landmark Cinema building directly across the street with its dark windows in the front, tables with umbrellas, and a line of trees providing lots of available cover. I entered the cinema and hovered by the front windows catching my breath. I was wet from the drizzle, and I sensed something waking up inside me. Even the mention of our home in San Carlos, though it rattled me at first, was a reminder of the death cocoon that had kept me from acknowledging guilt and pain. I felt a sensation in my chest as a new challenge flashed through me. *Time to wake up, Angus. Find the truth that Jessica died for.*

My next call would have been better as an in-person conversation, but there was no way I was letting this smooth-talking punk out of my sight. The old number, from my pre-accident FBI life, was still stored in my contacts—Nigella Dawson. Ringing, more ringing, please pick up. Voicemail, dammit.

"This is Nella, leave a message."

"Hey Nella. Angus Mariner. Remember me? I think you're still in California and I'm in San Francisco. Not sure if you're nearby and available tonight, but if so I've got a job for you."

The thing about informants is that most of them were accidental. They don't have business cards, don't market their skills or try to get gigs. If they're good, they're invisible to the world of commerce by paying cash for everything, mostly because they can't get a bank account, and if they're really good, they're invisible to law enforcement. Nigella had somehow mastered enough visibility to get work but not enough to get noticed. She'd watched me along with my team investigate the abandoned homes and cars of the three judges in Alice, Texas. Probably looking like a bunch of bunglers, she stepped in, sidling up to me from behind an oak tree in the side yard of one of their homes.

"I saw them wiping down that car," she'd said, and so started a long friendship and fruitful exchange of favors. Information for food, information for a safe place to sleep, use of my bathroom, money when I had some to spare. She was just too young and too smart to be caught up in that slice of life. And sometimes you've got to save someone to make the world feel right again.

I'd seen her once in a silk dress with her dark afro teased out to frame her face in an eight-inch round halo, enough beauty to stop traffic. Tonight required stealth mode, though. Without even texting me back, I knew she'd probably used the fact that I enabled my location to be visible to trace me. I laughed out loud when I caught sight of her sitting on the pillared steps next to Le Meridien. Barely more than five feet tall, she could disappear in the shadows or look like a movie star. She knew it, and she worked it when it was needed. Tonight's attire was a long, hip-length black hoodie, zipped to her neck, hair combed straight back covered by a hood, dark-rinse jeans and short black boots. I left the cinema through the side entrance, out of view of the hotel lobby, and crossed the street to her. I knew she'd be expecting me, so I sat facing the cinema on one of the front steps, a few feet to her right.

"You were in a dress last time I saw you," I said. "And your hair was, wow."

"Wig. I've got lots of them, for all kinds of jobs." She winked.

"Is that so?"

"Don't butter me up. You still gotta pay me."

"I'm not trying to stiff you, for God's sake."

"How are you holding up?" she asked.

We hadn't spoken since the accident but she obviously kept up with law enforcement news. I appreciated the question but there was no time for that. "Hanging in there."

"What do you need?"

There was no one else around, but it was risky to be out in the open like this. I got up and moved a few feet closer, so we could speak quietly amid the traffic noise. "Surveillance."

"Of?"

"You're looking at it."

She leaned back and put her hands on the concrete behind her and crossed one leg over the other. "Nice hotel," she said. "Who's the mark?"

I texted her the picture I'd taken of Michael Wise, along with his name.

She pulled out her phone, lowered her head to take a quick look, then turned directly to me. A no-makeup look tonight, her intelligent eyes always trying to figure me out.

I never knew what brought Nigella to Texas, and history had told me she didn't like personal questions. For me, it was the smuggling case I'd been assigned as a fresh FBI recruit. I met her a second time again by accident, waiting at an Amtrak station in San Francisco for a meetup with another informant, back in the days of profiling and deep cover assignments with FBI's Intelligence Branch. I was still new to the bureau so that meant I was hungry to build my resumé with short term, completed, successful projects. My informant, an old drunk not unlike WP, never showed and Nigella was just there, maybe at the right time, maybe camped out for the night, just like in Alice, TX. I never knew if maybe she was the mark they'd arranged for me, and I still wondered if she was a skilled operative or just a wily opportunist. Either would work for my purposes, so tonight I paid her up front, a hundred bucks cash, which I knew would be more than she was expecting. She pulled the bill from my fingers and folded it twice, then stuck it in the front pocket of her dark jeans.

"Classy," she said. "Legend?"

Legend, in tradecraft, usually meant a cover story. She was asking about Michael Wise, again revealing herself as a trained operative. The Michael Wise story? I hadn't had a chance to think about that yet. I lowered my head between my knees and rubbed the back of it the way I often did in times of stress.

"I don't think he's local. I think he's staying here to keep an eye on —"

"Keep looking down." Nigella tapped a finger on my knee. "He's on the move."

"Already? Where?" I asked, almost impossible to keep from looking.

"Other way, back down Sacramento. You want me to pursue?"

"Yes."

"How long?" She rose, keeping him in her sights. "Hundred bucks will get you till breakfast. Then if I'm still needed, we'll renegotiate."

"Fine," I said, the weight of the past week coming down a few clicks. "I'll let you take it from here. Keep an eye on him but—"

Now she turned and grabbed my arm. "Don't tell me how to work, okay? I got this."

"Fair enough, but I'll be asking for status," I said to the back of her head.

CODEX

Chapter 23

I made my way back to the Hyatt and booked a room there, not to ride the super-fun glass elevators or eat from the awesome menu at Eclipse. I needed a change of venue and a quiet place to think. I didn't ask for it, but they gave me an oceanfront Presidential Suite room for the price of a Standard King because it was a weeknight and it was available. Or maybe I just looked as pathetic as I felt. Fine, I'd take it. I liked the sitting room area with the long couch that had a full view of the Bay Bridge, skyline and, even better, the neighborhood. A tall table with stools in the corner next to a wet bar had a perfect view of Drumm Street and a partial view of the waterfront. Somehow the idea of sleeping indoors, here anyway, didn't bother me so much.

I was always amazed at the activity in San Francisco, day or night without reprieve. The Ferry Building was a tourist destination during the day, but why go there at night if all the inside venues were closed? Because of the view, I reminded myself, the lulling sound of water meeting the wharf. I did it too, in my own little quiet hamlet. There were no clock towers in Half Moon Bay, no open seating, chic eateries. Just a jetty with occasionally good waves, a brewery with the best burgers ever, and a diner open late. Diner. Rudy. That's the one thing I needed right now. I dialed his mobile.

"Hey."

"What time is it?" he moaned.

"How old are you, anyway?" I joked. "It's barely past dinner."

I knew he went to bed early when he worked a fourteen-hour shift, 6am till 8:00pm when he left Eduardo to close up. I gave him a minute to put on the bathrobe he always kept at the bottom of his bed and to find the slippers that he always left in the bathroom. Sad, isn't it, that I knew this about him, both of us bachelors now. By some definitions we were probably almost married.

The clink of a glass on his counter, the sound of a faucet. Please, please don't take your phone in the bathroom, Rudy.

"Now," he said, big sigh. "What's up?"

"What's up?" I laughed and repeated the question. "I was just wondering where my sister went, and why she seems to only be talking to you."

Another sigh. "I don't know, man, I don't know. Alright? I'm sorry. I meant to call you before I went to bed but my body had other plans. Where you at right now?"

I didn't want to tell him because that would just raise more questions. What I really wanted was for him to meet me down here, walk along Embarcadero and help me hash it all out. That wasn't gonna happen, not tonight.

"Go back to bed, buddy. I'm okay. Was just checking in."

I went downstairs and did a few more laps through the vast, second-floor lobby. I eventually waited at the crowded bar watching women's soccer, dreaming of the taste of beer, then remembering tomorrow would make 115 days sober.

There were a lot of people like me, I'd learned, who measured the passage of time by the length of their sobriety, BC and AD, a rebirth before which they had never even existed. I'd been to 12-step programs a few months after the accident, with Rudy as my sponsor, even though I hadn't been drinking enough to warrant it. That lasted a sum total of two weeks because of the perspective that nothing leading up to the breakdown was of value. Alcohol had helped me cope with Jessica's death—at a time when I also considered myself dead. Things had changed during those eighteen months, and I needed integration now. Not more separation.

"Sorry about that, we got slammed all at once. What can I get you?" The bartender reminded me of Jordan, dark hair, laughing eyes, same build. I kept finding myself in bars. Maybe that was no accident.

"Coke, please."

I was dying to hear back from Nigella, but reaching out to her would defy the laws of delegating, wouldn't it? Trust someone. She'd lived on the street for probably most of her life and knew what she was doing. More than I could say for myself.

I took the Coke with me and roamed around the first two floors of the Hyatt—the bottom street level with conference spaces and a fitness room, second floor offices, searching for a dark, empty room, preferably with a white board.

The concierge who'd checked me in seemed cooperative, more than what was required to do his job. Reginald, according to his nametag. I took the glass elevator back down to the lobby, descending on the gigantic Charles Perry sculpture and about thirty random people looking for respite. Dark ginger hair, head down, Reginald was writing something.

"Hey, sorry to—"

"Yes, Mr. Mariner. Everything okay?" No smile this time but still friendly.

I explained the problem.

"Wow, must be an important work project."

"It is," I explained of my fictitious project management job and my laptop that wasn't working, another lie. "A whiteboard and an empty room for like an hour would really help."

"Give me a minute."

I drained the last of the Coke and watched the crowd ebb and flow. Reginald hung up his phone.

"Follow me," he said.

All these years coming here, I'd never seen the conference rooms on the back side of the restaurant. We were behind the kitchen in a hallway, when Reginald pulled a single card from his pocket. He stopped at a door that read, "BAV2".

"Business...Admin..." I started to decode the acronym.

"Business audio visual," he said, touching a card to the door to unlock it. "It's one of our multimedia-equipped rooms. There's a white board that won't be used till tomorrow morning." He turned back toward the lobby. "Help yourself."

I shook Reginald's hand and gave him my most deferential smile, because those were the rules of rapport-building, and that's how you got access to the resources you needed—for a mission as an operative, or as a hapless civilian. Sylvan Mendoza mentioned Alice, Texas. I'd been an operative once, and according to him, that work was one of my special gifts. Maybe he was right. And there I stood on another threshold, another layer, deeper down this rabbit hole, looking forward and back, wondering which was the life I was destined for.

The room was dark; I liked it that way. I propped the door open and kept the lights off, with enough ambient light from the hallway to see the whiteboard. I recorded bullet points for the threads in my head, as if pulling them out, one by one, to see them in a different way, or maybe see how they might be related. But journaling, even on a dry erase board, was no substitute from the intuition I innately possessed. Even before meeting Michael Wise, I'd felt my way to the truth—our accident was no accident and, worse, I now knew that Jess was the intended target. I imagined her sitting across from me at the dark table. What did you learn in those files that threatened the natural order of our life together?

I left the conference room from time to time, restlessly walking the halls, gazing out the long windows at a sky that looked like madness. As I sauntered back, hands low in my pockets and preparing to erase my notes from the board, something clicked in my head. BAV, the Hyatt Embarcadero's Business Audio Visual room. Something about those letters, all caps standing side by side, reminded me of something only a distant part of my brain had noticed before.

CODEX

Chapter 24

I'd seen it before. The brain maintains these holding cells for dormant information, with only very specific triggers, keys maybe, that prompt the release of it allowing the machine to do its magic. The association, in this case, triggered by the BAV conference room sign, led me to two things. The second time I saw it, they appeared as a set of letters and numbers on the tail of Wendell Peters' helicopter. The first time was on some paperwork Jess had spread out all over the dining room table, a file stamped with something—BA-Vi on the cover. Where had that paperwork gone, and was that what Michael Wise had been looking for at the San Carlos House?

Another detail bothered me, too. Who passed something to Michael Wise through the open window in front of the Ferry Building? I tried to remember the car—fairly small and low to the ground, dark gray. Was it an employee, an employer, or an associate? The way Wise carried himself, I suspected it was an associate, another podcast producer maybe or, if my original inclination was correct, another journalist.

Back upstairs in the presidential suite, I called Andreini Airfield and asked for the helicopter hanger. It was late, almost midnight, so I expected to leave a message. A woman answered, raspy voice, probably the older woman I saw the last time I went. I asked to speak with Mason, the man who'd shown Jordan and me the Jet Ranger.

Long pause, during which I swear I heard her snoring.

"Ma'am?" I said. "I apologize, I know it's very late. I planned on leaving a message."

"We don't have voicemail on this phone, Mr. Mariner. Most people here don't even have cell phones."

I had no idea what century she was from, but I was sure that wasn't true. Nonetheless, I needed information and she was in a unique position to give it to me.

"I understand Miss...Ms..."

"Is there something you need?" she asked. No nonsense. Fine, I would be too then.

"Yeah, actually there is. I need to know the call letters on the tail of Wendell Peters' helicopter, it's a dark blue—"

"Yep Bell Ranger I've seen it hold on," she said, jumbling the words together.

Two seconds later, I heard another voice. Mason. He must have been sitting beside her the whole time. His wife? Mother? "Don't sleep much, Mr. Mariner. Do you?" the man said.

"Not lately, sir," I said. I made my request.

"I'll give you the information you need, and I'll do even better than that and not ask you why you want it."

I felt a question coming. "And—"

"Well, I feel it would be irresponsible of me to not inform you that Detective Walt Dekker wants me to call him as soon as I hear from you."

Give me strength. "Are you inclined to help Dekker, Mr. Mason, or help me? I suspect you'll need to choose one side or the other."

I heard a snicker in the background. "Are you at home right now, Mr. Mariner?"

"No."

"Well, that simplifies things then. If Dekker asks me whether I've talked to you, I can honestly say yes, and when he asks where you were when you called, I honestly don't know. That works for both of us, I think."

"Much as I appreciate that, the question is whether you'll tell him what information I asked for."

"Would it matter if I did?" he asked.

So far, I suspected Dekker knew less about WP and his dealings than I did. Plus Dekker already knew that WP gave me a helicopter, so it would be natural for me to be inquiring about it. "I guess not. Get the number for me, and if Dekker asks why I called, go ahead and tell him."

"Right. You looking for the serial numbers?" he asked. "Those I've got right here. Any other vanity numbers the owners put on there for identification, we'll need to—"

"There were some other numbers, in green, on the tail."

He muffled the phone, said something to the woman. I heard keyboard clicks. "The only green letters are on the very bottom of the tail and they're small. Looks like BA-Vi."

Though I'm not sure why, my new best friend Mason said he'd text me if he heard from Dekker instead of calling him like he'd originally agreed. That meant one down. Now I just needed to get to the storage area to rifle through Jess's office contents and match that number with her paperwork, if she'd even kept it. I'd been in a daze the weeks and months following the accident, so I had no idea what was or wasn't moved into storage. Luckily, I still had a key to the storage facility in San Carlos. I would have loved to have my sister with me when I opened that unit for the first time in over a year. After texting her, I tried calling her mobile again, five rings, no voicemail. Naturally. Where the fuck are you hiding?

By 3am I'd been dozing on and off, and now the sofa felt too hard under my hips. Recalling my conversation with Michael Wise, I connected the BA-Vi with the clinical trials he mentioned. Could that be a Clinical Trials Identifier, or an FDA serial number for an approved substance? The midnight skyline over the lights of the bridge woke up my tired eyes. What a beautiful view. Time to check in with Nigella.

Hey, how's it going? I wrote while brewing coffee in the mini-coffeemaker. I waited for a response.

Five minutes later: *Yr gonna owe me bigtime for this.*

I knew calling would be breaking the rules of surveillance. She picked up on the first ring. "Hey," I said. "Where are you?"

"In an Uber heading to San Carlos."

My body froze, standing half in front of a long wall mirror outside the bathroom, cup of coffee in my hand. My hair was longer than a crew cut now, two days' worth of stubble on my face and chin, bags under my eyes. The coffee was bringing me up, while the truth of the moment nailed me again to my past. I looked at the man in that mirror and Rudy was right. A man on the verge of something looking like death.

"Still there?" Nigella asked. I felt her impatience but also knew she cared about me. She knew my history, so she knew the significance of San Carlos.

"Yeah." I sipped the last of the weak brew.

"You okay, boss?"

God, Nigella. There was nobody like her in the world. I loved her for that question, three words that made me feel seen and known.

"What's the word? You want me to keep going?" she asked when I didn't answer.

"Stay on him," I said. "I'm gonna meet you down there."

"Down where?"

"Where I think he's going."

I had no proof, but I felt someone tailing me. You can feel it sometimes, walking in the dark. I'd felt their presence on my way back to the hotel earlier tonight. No shadows darting, no noises behind me. Even still, there was someone interested in the details I was running down. Watching me, investigating what I was investigating. Could be Dekker, my relentless shadow, or someone working for him. That meant from now on, I'd have to be more than smart. Being the wily sort anyway, I left my bike parked at the Hyatt. I'd paid for the Presidential Suite and, besides, the motor would be too conspicuous. Again, relying on the conveniences of our modern world, I booked an Uber.

This wasn't how I'd planned to spend the night. Fact is, I had no plan. I'd been drifting, like a plastic bag stuck in the sand on the beach. It gets pulled out to sea, swirls around a while in the waves, then ends up back in the same spot, under the clouds, under the pier, still tangled, half-filled with water and debris. Me at the helm of a lonely ship in troubled waters.

"Hey stranger," someone said when I picked up my buzzing phone in the back of the Uber. Not Nigella like I expected, it was Jordan. My start started pounding.

"Oh, hey, Jordan. You're up late. Sorry I've been sort of, um—"

She did her flirty, muffled laugh that she does. I was getting to know those quirks. It scared me a little. "Are you on a date?" she asked. "I don't want to interrupt you if you're busy. I'll see ya when I see ya."

"Wait!" My wait came out a little too loud, or maybe desperate. The Uber driver's eyes widened in the rear view. "Not you," I said to him in the mirror. "Jordan, you still there?"

"I'm here. I've been here since the beginning."

Chapter 25

Not completely sure I'd heard her correctly, I think I hung up without saying goodbye, or maybe she hung up first. It was an odd comment, the kind of thing you hear as the last line in a movie. Not a pretty bartender checking in on a potential hookup. Maybe she thought of me as more than that, something potentially longer term. I wasn't even sure my machinery still worked after this long of non-use. What could she possibly mean by this? The beginning...of what? There was a yellow sticky note now on the Jordan file in my head.

Once we got onto the South San Francisco Bay peninsula, I texted Nigella. *I'm in San Mateo heading south—where r u?* I wrote.

Near Lucky's on Old County Road. Your man's three cars ahead of us. Is he going to your house?

Nigella knew where Jess and I had lived in San Carlos. I explained the relevance of the storage unit, let her know it was just over a mile from our house and told her how Michael Wise was arrested for breaking in there.

Got it, she replied. *I'll stay on him and will report back if he stops. This will cost extra.*

I had no problem paying a professional for quality work. Nigella started as charity, then became a good investment. Now, she felt like a

CODEX

trusted member of my team. I just wish I knew what game we were all playing.

Something else bothered me. The logic of Wise's behavior didn't add up. If he'd already broken into the house and found Jessica's journal, what was handed to him from that car on Embarcadero? Maybe he hadn't broken in after all. The more likely scenario was that Wise got an associate to break into the house, he got caught, Wise bailed him out, and his contact was simply making the drop when I saw the transaction from across the street. But I'd seen a picture of Wise in handcuffs online—maybe that was a prior arrest. How many did he have, and then why was he headed back down there tonight? Clearly there were a few details he'd left out.

He's pulled over, Nigella wrote. *We're in a wooded area east of San Carlos, it might be Arguello Park. I'm about a quarter mile behind him and on foot now. My Uber's parked and waiting for me. Look for a Hyundai when you get here, pull up behind it and wait.*

I pointed out the red car and told my driver to park ten car-lengths behind it. I didn't like the sound of her being on foot, but as I started stepping out of my Uber, she texted again.

Something's happening.

Jesus, where are you?

Looks like a rendezvous point. Another guy, taller and skinnier than Mr. Wise, is stopped on the shoulder across the street. They're outside and talking.

In the middle of the street? I asked, surprised to see any after-dark activity in a sleepy little billionaire's village.

Keep listening. They're arguing now. I'll try to capture it. Hold on.

Maybe she was taking a video or using a recording app. Meanwhile my driver was a capitalist who said he'd be more than happy to cart me around all night. Good, I might need it. I might also need to open another bank account just for surveillance. I waited outside behind Nigella's Uber, wondering what those two Uber drivers were thinking.

"I delivered. Now where's the rest of my money?" I heard one of them say.

"It's not there." That was Michael Wise's voice. I peered over the car to see them but it was too dark.

"Hey, I delivered the fucking journal as agreed. You owe me for the rest."

"Nah, man. You delivered a journal but it's not there. You owe me." Wise was trying to sound like a badass, but I knew he wasn't one.

"What do you mean it's not there? I handed it to you, you grabbed it. I saw you," the other man said.

"The map, the map's not there. I paid you $30k to get it."

Thirty thousand dollars? I gulped hard. There was a five-second pause. It was cold out here. Where the hell was Nigella?

"I don't know nothing about no map. You said it was in a journal, and I found the fucking journal. We agreed thirty-k up front, another thirty on delivery. I delivered."

Sixty thousand dollars for a journal with a map inside it, a journal Jessica put together. I was starting to see the impact and the danger she had been in and couldn't help thinking that if she'd just trusted me, I could've helped her and maybe prevented all this.

"Where's the fucking map, bro?" Wise again, clearly upset. "Thought you'd take it for yourself, sell it maybe to the highest bidder?"

Both voices escalating, I had to get Nigella out of there. Map to what, and where the hell did Michael Wise get sixty g's to throw around? The question made me think about his fine leather jacket again.

The other guy got in his car, slammed the door hard, and sped off. Wise didn't follow. He got in his car and just sat there, his interior light dimming, staring out. I could see the back of his head from here. I texted Nigella to stay put. A few seconds later we heard his car motor, and he took off in the same direction as his associate.

I held up my index finger to my Uber driver and jogged across the dark street under a broken streetlight. I found Nigella coming toward me. "Let your driver go and come with me," I said.

I grabbed her hand and pulled her into the back of my Uber. My

CODEX

driver took off down Highway 82 after Michael Wise's car.

"What kind of car am I following?" the driver asked.

"Dark red Camry," Nigella said, with a sigh. "I'm so sick of watching that car I'm going blind."

A little further and I recognized where we were. God, I hadn't been down this road since right after the accident. For many years it had been my daily commute. We'd just passed a sign for Laureola Park, where Jess and I used to walk on weekends. Something tightened in my chest. I couldn't deal with that right now.

"You got too close over there," I told her. "Who knows what that could have turned into."

"Or could still," she added.

I opened the Uber app on my phone and tipped my driver fifty bucks before we got too far down the road, to let him know his patience was being rewarded. I loved how he was just barely following the car. We were only able to glimpse it going around curves. This guy was a pro.

We'd just passed what would have been the logical turnoff to get to my house on Elm Street, in the block between Arroyo and Morse, so I had to assume Wise was either headed out of town and back to Highway 101...or he knew about the storage area. Bay Area Self Storage had a branch in south San Carlos almost to Redwood City. He exited Highway 82 at Brittan Avenue. Smart. That told me Michael Wise was a local. It was a crafty shortcut to the frontage road that gave easy access to 101 where you could get to the storage area easily.

Map...the word kept knocking around in my brain. Map of what, or where?

"I think he knows we're on him," Nigella whispered.

I turned to see her face. She had sparkly purple eye shadow on her lids that I'd only noticed now under the shine of a streetlight. "Why do you say that?"

"His speed," she said. "He's not in a hurry but not going too slow either. Just fast enough to get to where he's going but still see who's behind him." I watched her pull her hand out of her jacket pocket. She formed her hand into the shape of a gun and looked up, brows raised.

"Hell no." I shook my head, unsure if she was asking or telling. Yeah, of course I wished I had my gun on this kind of crazy-ass errand.

She patted her pocket.

I hung my head. Jesus. That brought in a whole other variable to our pursuit. "What the hell for?" I asked her.

"Tools of the trade, brother."

And somehow, in the span of one minute, we lost him. "Fuck, where is he now?" I asked the driver.

"He disappeared, like, somewhere on this street," the driver said.

"Maybe he made us and ducked into someone's driveway," Nigella said.

"Loop around," I said.

The driver took a quick right down a short street, another, and another until he got back to the same street but a quarter of a mile back.

"Dark red Camry," Nigella reminded us as the driver moved ahead slowly, our eyes peeled left and right.

I shook my head in my typical shut-down mode. We'd lost him and wasted a night of surveillance coming to a place I least wanted to visit.

We had the driver stop in the empty parking lot beside Bay Area Self Storage and wait there. I was gonna owe the equivalent of a mortgage payment to him and Nigella before we were done here, but I needed to know the truth and we'd need a ride back north.

"Still got your key card?" Nigella asked.

"I don't know why but I kept it in my wallet." We were huddled under a large tree with a wide canopy.

She turned to check my expression. "Are we going in?" she asked at the same time a metal clang sounded from inside the gated compound. Was he already in there? Nella and I climbed out of the car and walked around to the front entrance. I used my key and the arm of the gate lifted.

Not twenty steps in we could see it - Michael Wise's red Camry parked at the end of the second row.

CODEX

Chapter 26

The back of the storage lot looked out onto the freeway. The steady road noise made for a perfect sound-camouflage for whatever was about to go down.

"How do you wanna play this?" Nigella asked.

"View or stealth you mean?"

She nodded and held up her phone. I grabbed it and leaned down to see what she'd brought up—a picture of a finely suited Michael Wise on the company masthead of a pharmaceutical company.

"Where the hell is this?" I asked. That guy, Jesus. What now?

"Dallas. Long way from home."

I zoomed in to see his job title. "Public Relations Director?"

"Former PR Director. This is an archived webpage. Looks like he was ousted."

That's right, Nigella the hacker. Handy, I suppose. "So he had an in with pharma." Interesting. Had Jess known this when she went to him?

"What's he doing down here?" she asked.

"I'm still trying to figure that out. Follow me."

We left the Uber driver in the lot next to the storage area and went on foot under the boom of the second entry gate. The red Camry was gone but it would be easy to find this time of night, especially because there was only one entrance to the place.

"There." I pointed, heading to the right. At the end of the third row, the Camry was parked on the right side of the aisle, driver's side door wide open, dark inside. Most interior dome lights went off automatically after fifteen minutes, so the car had likely been there for at least that long. Fast getaway or something? I found my unit, second to last in the row, assuming Wise had somehow gotten inside. We listened at the bay door and heard nothing.

We'd seen him, tailed him, and now his car was parked in front of us - empty. Maybe Michael Wise wasn't just a podcaster and a former pharmaceutical executive.

"Where the hell is he?" she asked.

The ground vibrated, we both felt it, a thump inside my unit. Something heavy dropped from a higher surface. I had no memory of the contents or arrangement of the interior, only having gone there once after the accident to retrieve a first aid kit I'd always kept in my motorcycle seat. How would Wise have even known which unit it was? Jessica, most likely, or he'd found something about it in her journals.

"Wait here," I said to Nigella and walked around the building to see the back side, but it only had more units on the next row. So that meant the only entry into the units was through the front. Michael Wise, a working theory anyway, was inside my unit right now with the bay door closed. I came back around and gestured to the unit beside mine. Nigella nodded.

"You don't have a key to this other unit, do you?"

"No, but in the absence of an underground tunnel, he's gonna need to come out of there sometime."

I tried my front gate keycard in front of the card reader on the door of my unit. It didn't work. So how had Wise gotten in?

I stayed beside the unit door listening. Nigella hung back at his car, rifling through the glove box. We needed to smoke him out somehow. I dialed 911 and moved toward Nigella.

"How's your acting ability?" I asked her, during the hold. Chances are, if Wise heard a siren coming into this lot, he'd hightail it out of my unit to move his car before being seen.

"Try me."

I explained to the 911 operator that my girlfriend passed out and wasn't breathing while on an errand to pick up a box from a storage unit. I gave the address, adding that her lips were turning blue. I knew the penalty for fraud and misuse of official emergency resources. Balancing that was the new truth that Jessica Mariner was murdered and Michael Wise might be the only person who knew why.

While we waited for either Wise or the ambulance, whichever came first, I had Nigella take iPhone photos of everything in his glove box, including a bag on the floor of the backseat.

"Yep, it's his name on the registration and insurance cards. What's AAA?" she asked.

"Emergency Road Service," I said. Good for him, he was a planner. Well, I too was a planner, and it was time for the next step. I moved to the metal bay door of my unit and put my ear to it. I heard rustling sounds, like hands shifting boxes around. Positioning my mouth in the crease of the door hinge, I drew a deep breath and readied my bar voice.

"We know you're in there, Wise. The police have been called."

Something inside the unit slammed, maybe his hand, maybe a box. I'd gotten his attention at least. "You-have-no-idea!" The volume of his words echoed against the metal of the doors. I glanced back at Nigella, she'd heard it too.

"No, I don't," I admitted. "So fucking tell me what's going on and quit hiding for God's sake."

I knew guys like Michael Wise. The word *hiding* wouldn't go down well. Three seconds later, the bay door rolled upward. He stood there in the middle of the space surrounded by open boxes. I took two steps toward him, now wishing I hadn't called 911. A deep crease above his nose wrinkled his whole forehead showing me a sense of frustration. Who was putting pressure on him? The man in the woods, whoever he was.

"What are you doing here?" I asked in my normal voice now.

He sneered and shook his head, looking away. "You have no idea who these people are." He looked up again. "And what they will do, to all of us."

"Tell me about the map," I said, coming one step closer.

133

His single head shake told me no way. Who was he protecting? Himself?

"Okay, let me see if I can pull it together. Jessica was a lawyer with Worthington, Pendleton, Bradbury, and Burnes assigned to work with a company on a potential merger. Right so far?"

Staring and silence, no siren yet. Good thing Nigella wasn't actually dying. I had little time. "You said she found something, evidence of something. Corruption, right?"

Another sneer. An understatement? "You could say that."

"Evidence of faked clinical trials, you said, from Wendell Peters' company. She told her bosses about it and they told her to keep her mouth shut. Am I right?"

"Pretty much."

"I assume, for obvious reasons, that she didn't. So what happened?"

"I can't—"

"You will!" The volume of my voice startled me. An old voice, that older me waking up maybe. "Mr. Wise—she's dead. Whatever she found in those files, you and I both know that her death is directly because of it. You can tell me and you will tell me. It might as well be now."

Nella was standing at his car, arms on the hood watching us. Wise angled his head left to see her and shifted his feet on the concrete floor. That leather jacket was getting dirty in there. I don't know why that pleased me. He either wouldn't or couldn't talk, so I kept going.

"She went to you to investigate the company she was assigned to look into. Why? So you'd produce a podcast exposing the corruption she found? Why take that kind of risk?"

"She couldn't do it," he mumbled, eyes on the ground.

"Couldn't do what? Betray that company? She obviously wanted to or she wouldn't have gone to you in the first place." What I wasn't asking was how Jess even knew about Michael Wise. She'd never been into podcasts; she said they were too long, usually, and she was too impatient. We'd talked about it.

"They were real trials. Some of the results were faked, so she said, to get through the FDA approval process faster." His lips barely moved and he avoided my eyes. Was that shame or fear?

CODEX

"Were you preparing a podcast episode about it, to expose them?"

Single nod. "I was." Then a long sigh. "Until they killed my roommate."

"Sorry, what? I'm not following."

I could see he was holding something in his left hand, but it was concealed by a box on a table. I had to assume it was a gun. I'd never stored a gun in any of those boxes, so it had to be his. "Black guy, same build as me too, so I guess we looked alike. I came home and found my studio torn up and my roommate lying dead on the floor."

"And you think you were the intended victim?" I asked.

"Yeah."

"I'm sorry," I said, trying to be. "When was this?"

"Before your car accident."

I blinked back at him, thinking a terrible thought, about how if they'd gotten to Wise, Jessica might still be alive now. "How long before?"

"A week."

"Whoever did this was looking for, what, the files Jess had been investigating, or evidence she'd compiled in her notes?"

Single nod.

"Her journal."

"That and some other paperwork she'd been storing in the journal. Do you remember her briefcase?" he asked.

It was a birthday gift when she became a partner in the firm, their youngest ever. I had it engraved with her initials on the gold flap of the lock mechanism.

"It had a false bottom, a secret compartment."

"Not when I bought it for her it didn't." Jess installed a false bottom to hide documents? It just didn't sound like her. She hated anything to do with white-collar crime. We watched movies about it and talked about them for hours after. What it sounded like was desperation. My God, Jess.

"Who knew about the briefcase?" I asked.

"No one."

"No one besides you, you mean." There was a bite to my words. I still couldn't stand the idea of her sharing so much with him.

"It's not about the briefcase anyway. It's about the map."

135

"Look, we need to trust each other, and I need to know what we're talking about here. Is that map—"

"I didn't choose this!" His head shook as the words thundered out. "I didn't choose any of this. She came to me. I was trying to help her." He backed up a few steps and started pacing inside my unit.

"If whatever she found was so controversial, why did she even have access to it? You'd think the firm would have been covering it up."

"Well…" He tipped his head. "Ultimately they did, right?"

CODEX

Chapter 27

The sky was starting to lighten. Why was there no siren? I jerked my head back to check on Nigella. She looked at me with her WTF face. The air felt still and magnetic, like sitting in the eye of a massive storm. My palms buzzed with a weird energy. Nigella nodded back as if she felt it too, always ready for anything.

I played his words back in my head. Why would Jessica have known where to look for buried evidence of corruption at a tech company? ADS, WP's company, did research and development on assistive listening devices for the hearing impaired. Where did corruption fit into something as innocuous as hearing aids?

"WP's company, ADS," I said to Wise. "They manufactured hearing aids, right? Did research into new technologies to make them work better."

"Maybe that's how it started," Wise said, staring now, asking me to fill in the blanks to avoid having to say it out loud, like he'd done at the Hyatt.

"Jessica wasn't hearing impaired, and I don't think she knew anyone who was. So are you saying she was somehow connected to that company, and that's how she was able to access evidence about clinical trial data?"

He shook his head. I was missing something.

"Okay…maybe that's not all they were manufacturing? Was there another business segment she found out about? I want to help you here, but you gotta give me something. Am I warm? Maybe they weren't hearing aids at all?"

"They were hearing aids. Sure, in a way," he said.

I watched him dig his hands in his pockets after putting whatever he'd been holding on the table. A gun? He looked up, eyes wide with fear.

"They just weren't being used as hearing aids?" I asked, the words coming out slowly, to which Michael Wise nodded, lowering his chin with a deep stare.

"Jessica knew about this because…"

"She worked for them."

The words hit my chest like BB gun pellets. Before I got a chance to consider this, I heard Nigella. "Hey," she said. "Incoming," her head turned toward the entrance.

"A car?" I asked.

"No, a woman."

"Angus! Are you here? I'm so sorry I couldn't get away."

Elaine? Thank God. I felt something loosen in my chest at the sound of her voice. But I'd told her in one of my texts I'd be at the San Carlos house, not storage. She helped me pack the boxes we put in this storage unit, but how could she have known I was here now in the middle of the night?

"Stay where you are." It was a new voice coming from my right. A man's voice, deep, with a British accent. I saw Wise's forehead as he looked left and right, searching for egress. "Step out of the unit," the other man said. "And you'd better have that map with you." Map again. Map…of what? What did you find, Jess? Help me here. I can't do this alone.

The next sound was the siren, finally, a few blocks away. Nigella popped out of Wise's car and headed up the driveway, no doubt to check on our Uber driver, who was hopefully still in the adjacent parking lot.

"Elaine, stay there," I said, but I couldn't see her from here and I needed to keep my eye on Wise and what had been in his hand. I could

CODEX

take cover behind his car if needed, but I suspected I wasn't the intended target. I looked at Wise. "What map?" I whispered. A twitch of his lips said he'd heard it. I watched him pull his left hand out of his pocket, pick up what I thought was a gun on the table, then he shifted the table so it scuffed on the floor at the same time that he chambered back a round like a pro. Podcaster? Right.

"I want to help you," I whispered, as he moved to the right wall of the unit.

"In the Ranger," he mumbled.

WP's helicopter, the Jet Ranger. "The journal, or the map?"

His head moved left and right, then I saw his eyes dart left.

"Angus, listen to me." Elaine, I could see her now, was coming toward me, her hair covered by a watch cap. It barely looked like her.

"Where the hell have you been?"

"I need to—"

"Step away!" The booming voice again from my right. Now the man held a large semi-automatic pistol with a silencer screwed onto the end. Jesus. "Give me the map and no one needs to get hurt." He was aiming at Michael Wise's head.

"You know you have it," Wise replied calmly. "You found her journal, gave it to me, but you pulled the map out first. I should be asking you the same—"

"I have no time for games," the man said.

"Miguel, no!" Elaine screamed as the other man lifted the gun to his eye level. Miguel? Wait a minute. This was *her* Miguel Santos? The drug dealer? If that was even true, was he abducting her or protecting her?

I looked back at Nigella as she was climbing over the wall separating the storage facility grounds from the empty parking lot. Elaine was three steps to my right. Out of instinct, I lunged right to cover her body from whatever hell was about to be unleashed, knowing whatever was going on here was ultimately between Michael Wise and the other man. I heard four, quick shots behind me and jumped onto Elaine's body, both of us crashing to the hard ground.

"Don't move," I told her, my hand covering her head as we lay flat on the concrete.

Two more shots. I could see from here that Wise was still in the

139

unit. I needed to get Nigella and Elaine out of there; hopefully Wise could take care of himself. I had a feeling he was used to this type of thing. The man Elaine had called Miguel moved near Wise's car, the driver's side door still open. When the next shot was fired, from Wise this time, I grabbed Elaine and tossed her thin frame into an outcrop of pea gravel in front of the short, cinderblock wall. I hoisted her up and pushed her over the edge to the empty lot. "Nigella," I shouted.

"I got her," she said from the other side, now crouched beside Elaine. "Our driver's ready over here. You okay?"

"Hand's bleeding is all."

Amazing how strong you become during times of duress, like a shootout. I climbed over the wall, straddled it at the top, hopped down and ran around to the front passenger seat of the Uber. Nigella pushed Elaine into the backseat then joined her.

"Wait," I said. "Nigella, switch places with me."

She opened her door without a second's hesitation, understanding, it seemed, the need for careful planning of these next steps. We switched seats, I closed my door and leaned forward to put my head down. "You okay up there?" I asked my driver, certain he was anything but.

"I will be when we get out of here."

"Go now, quickly," I told him.

"Then what?" he asked.

"Turn right, then left, and loop around the block. Come up on the other side of the facility and park someplace where we can see who's coming and going. Slowly though."

"Right." The driver got a good screech from the tires, then another when he peeled out the back entry to the parking lot.

Wise would recognize me, so it was safer with Nigella up front. I took a deep breath, finally, crouched under the backseat. I motioned for Elaine to do the same. She looked stoic, eyes wide, waiting.

"My legs will fall asleep," she said. "I hate that."

"For fuck's sake, just do it."

She did, glowering through squinted eyes. "What's the matter with you?" she asked.

"Miguel? That was Miguel? Your Miguel?"

She looked at the floor.

CODEX

"What's he doing here?" I asked, the driver slowing while he scoped out a parking spot. There were none. He drove around the next block.

"We need to see the entrance," I shouted.

"I know."

"Trying to kill me, I suspect," Elaine answered.

"No," I corrected her. "I mean what's he—and you—doing here in San Carlos, at my storage unit? I don't get the connection."

"Neither do I."

I saw the emotion in her face, confusion, maybe a bit of guilt. This was a man she'd lived with, bonded with for three years, I think, maybe longer. But there was something else, something new this time: she was lying to me.

We were now parked across the street from the storage entrance with only a partial view but enough to catch Wise's red car. It had to come out sometime.

"I can't wait here all night," the driver said, which meant it was time to pay him again.

Nigella pulled cash out of her jacket and handed him two twenties. "We good?"

"Thanks."

Though only in her early twenties, Nigella seemed like the only grownup among us. Elaine, avoiding my eyes, caused a shadow to grow in the center of my chest. What the fuck was her gangster boyfriend doing in California? She could be right. I mean, she did steal his money, but I thought she gave it back in exchange for his life. But if he'd been the one interrogated by Michael Wise, that gave him a connection to more than just Elaine. He must also have some connection to Jessica as well. The sick feeling returned to the pit of my belly.

"Any sign of it?" I asked the driver of Wise's car.

"No, nothing. Wait, it's coming out now."

"Don't move," I told him. "Not yet." My phone buzzed. I pulled it out of my pocket; it was from Nigella in the front seat. "I'm right here."

"Open the link," she said. It was some kind of Lojack app. A map came up on the screen when I opened it with a red dot in the middle.

141

I grinned. "You put a tracker on Wise's car?"

"Bloody genius," Elaine said.

"I have my moments."

"Okay, driver. Sorry, what's your name?"

"Isaac."

"Okay, Isaac. How many people were in the car? The red Camry?"

"Just one," he said.

"What'd the driver look like?"

"Black guy, young, clean shaven."

Michael Wise. "Okay, get back on Industrial Parkway and turn left on...one second." I squinted down at the tiny map. "Taylor. Right on Taylor."

"Can I please get up now?" Elaine stretched back onto the seat and strapped herself in. "Jesus, I'll be walking funny for the next week."

"Left on Old County Road, Isaac," I said, ignoring her.

"Got it."

"Then right on Holly and left on Camino Real."

"You know where he's going." Elaine now. "If he didn't find what he was looking for in storage, he must think it's at the house."

"He's already looked in my house," I said a few clicks too loud. "Michael Wise said he got arrested for breaking and entering there. But maybe he didn't complete his search."

"What on earth's he looking for?" Elaine asked me.

I let it play out a few more minutes, watching Isaac steer us into my old hood, St. Francis Way, and the signature gigantic elm tree on the corner of our street, the street I'd managed to avoid for the past eighteen months.

"We're getting close," Elaine whispered. "Are you okay with this?"

CODEX

Chapter 28

"Wait a minute." I gazed down at the map on my phone. The red dot wasn't moving. "Looks like he's parked but not on Elm Street. He's on the corner on Elm and El Sereno."

"What's there?" Nigella asked.

We saw the car before I had a chance to answer. The red Camry stopped on the shoulder, motor off.

"Up here," I said to the driver, trying to puzzle it out. "Drive around the car slowly." He did while I rubbernecked. No one was in the front seat. If I was being honest with myself, I'd admit that Elm Street was the last place I wanted to go, but logic told me whatever Michael Wise was looking for was in that storage unit, not in the house.

A text notification showed up with a message from Jordan, but the timestamp was two hours ago. *Check voicemail* was the only message. I touched the voicemail in the list but the transcript wasn't showing up. "Hey, it's Jordan," it started. I loved her voice. "Had a visitor at the bar tonight asking for you, an older woman who said the helicopter given to you by WP was not the one you saw in the hangar. No idea what that means. Anyway call me when you get a chance, and hope we see you around here soon. Bye."

143

"Who was that?" Elaine asked in a taunting voice.

"No one." I hadn't shared anything about WP with Elaine yet and there was no sense getting her involved in yet another tangled mess. We were a half mile from the on-ramp to Highway 92.

"Isaac, can you take us over the bridge to Half Moon Bay?" I asked our driver.

"Yeah, but that'll be the last stop."

"No problem. You'll be able to buy yourself a new car after tonight."

A shooter and an unsuccessful pursuit—our chase was simply played out. We weren't finding any answers, not here and now.

Nigella stayed in my trailer and got settled in my pillow-top bed, while I took Elaine to Rudy's. It was late, and we were both too tired to get into it. But clearly we had a lot to work out. I felt pretty sure we hadn't been followed, but if Miguel found the storage facility, he had to know where I lived. She reached to grab me in the doorway. I backed away, studying her inscrutable face, searching for everything she was hiding from me.

"He's looking for you," I said, shaking my head. "Aren't you—"

"I'm sorry I don't live the kind of life you wish I did."

"Where's that coming from?" I asked, though I honestly couldn't think of a thing to say in response. "I just wish I understood you better," I managed as she turned away.

"That's something, I guess."

"We'll talk more in the morning," I said, praying she'd still be there.

The outside air froze me, despite the many layers of weather protection in my $400 REI sleeping bag that I slept in most nights. It wasn't that sleeping outside was getting old—maybe I was. So I slept on Rudy's couch, leaving Elaine in his guest bedroom with a brand new bed.

I was a light sleeper, but I'll be damned if she hadn't done it again. I woke up and immediately checked the guest room – empty. And this was Rudy's early day, so he left the house at 5am. Nigella and I sat in his warm kitchen, drinking his terrible coffee. She didn't mind it, unlike Elaine who was high maintenance and impossible to please.

"I said I'd drive you," I argued with her. The ride to San Francisco wasn't that far.

"Appreciate you putting me up. Luther's coming," she said, like I should know who that was. I just stared. "My Dad. You never met him?"

It was an interesting question that you'd think she would be able to answer herself, but those days, back when we first met, she was strung out on whatever she could afford to buy, usually meth. I'd definitely never met her Dad. I made us two egg sandwiches, using up the last of Rudy's butter. A criminal offense in his opinion, and I had better remember to replace it with exactly the right kind or else.

I saw a bright blue pickup pull up in the street behind Rudy's house. "Blue truck?" I asked.

"Maybe," she nodded, then laughed. "With him, you never know."

After she walked outside to meet him, I called Jordan to ask her about the woman who'd come into the bar about. The old woman had apparently left an address and Jordan was eager to go out there with me. I cleaned up Rudy's kitchen and retreated to the trailer, dying for a cigarette and realizing, suddenly, that I hadn't smoked in the past two days. Wow, an accidental but noteworthy achievement. Did that mean I was quitting again? Then again, had I even bought cigarettes since I met Jordan Reid? Also noteworthy.

Two knocks on the trailer door startled me. Probably Nigella forgetting something she'd left here or at Rudy's. What would her father think of—

"Open the door."

Definitely not Nigella, and it didn't sound like Dekker either. I opened it to find a basketball-player-tall man, forties, caramel-colored skin. A handsome face with what looked like mixed-race features, the same shaped nose as Nella. God knows what he'd be thinking. "You must be Mr. Dawson. I—"

"Step outside, please."

Jesus. Did he think we'd slept together? Did I even remember how to do that? I obliged, closing the door behind me. But he stood with his hands in the pockets of a long jacket. That wasn't a threatening pose.

His face looked like a tangle of emotions.

"I'm Angus Mar—"

"I know who you are," he cut me off, then glanced behind him. Meanwhile, I positioned my feet in fight-stance as a precaution. Nigella walked towards the blue truck. "I wanted to thank you, sir," the man said. He called me sir. I stared back in disbelief, ready to get my ass kicked.

"Sorry?"

"When Nigella was..." He looked at the ground. "Alice, Texas. Remember?" Head shaking, eyes closed. "She was living on the street for two years, lost to us. I wasn't sure she'd make it to her next birthday. You supported her, she told me. She was a stranger and you took care of her, way more than anybody else would have."

"I might have—"

The man put up his palm, then wiped his eyes and pinched the bridge of his nose, holding back tears. "You bought her meals, gave her a place to sleep, but she told me you also sat with her, looked right at her instead of averting your eyes like everybody else did back then. You asked her about her life, about her story, her dreams. She told me. You saw her bright light, even when it was almost out."

Well, this was the farthest thing from the moment I was expecting from this formidable man, Luther Dawson. He pulled a business card out of his pocket.

"You respected my daughter at a time when nobody else did, when she probably didn't deserve respect. The way she says it, you saved her life. And I think it's because of you that she came back to California." He handed me the card. "If you ever find yourself in a bad place, I hope you'll give me the chance to repay your kindness." Instead of shaking my hand, he came toward me and wrapped his long arms around me, then wiped his eyes again. Nella waved before they took off.

The encounter left me feeling like I'd just inherited two new family members. More than that, though, Jessica was a part of that story, so it seemed right that Nigella had helped me last night. Who knows, maybe I'd need Luther Dawson someday.

I showered and cleaned up before heading to the brewery, looking over my shoulder intermittently for Miguel and secretly hoping Jordan was working today. The engine on my bike was running loud again, and not the same muffler problem I'd already fixed. Rudy liked offering to buy me a new bike just so he could see my face and mimic me saying, "You just don't get it."

My mind drifted back to Luther, something else about that encounter still needling me. Of course I felt uncomfortable and unworthy of his praise; wouldn't anyone in that situation? But more than that, was I still even that same person? If I met Nigella now, and she was strung out, desperate and near death, did my heart still have the same capacity for compassion? I'd felt dead inside for so long, I've wondered if I could ever feel anything again. Jessica was always up for a humanitarian mission, especially rescues. But my heart was fed and full back then. I wasn't sure it was even still beating in my chest, until my eyes detected the shape of Jordan Reid in a yellow blouse outside the back door of the patio, waiting for me.

Jordan and I hadn't had time to discuss a specific game plan on the way here. It was too cold for my motorcycle so she drove taking a phone call from her boss the whole ride.

An hour later, she and I sat on a hideous floral sofa in the dark den of someone named Vera. Not WP's wife, as I originally thought, but his mother. Large, brown eyes framed with oily, puffy skin, straight, gray hair and a mouth I was sure hadn't smiled in decades. But she wasn't frail, five-foot-six with a self-assured stature. The old woman vanished into a back bedroom.

Jordan leaned in and lowered her head, her face inches from mine. "What are we doing here?" she whispered.

"I don't know yet. Is this Burleigh Murray?" I asked of the historic ranch-turned state park 15 miles from the Half Moon Bay jetty.

"Outskirts," she said. "I think we're just north of Purisima Creek Woods."

"How do you two know each other?"

She shrugged. "WP liked me. He must have told his mother about me and she came to see me at the bar."

The woman returned to the flowered chair that matched the

flowered sofa and plunked down with a squint to her eyes, her right hand gripping the arm. "Got a bad hip."

"Mrs. Peters –" Jordan started.

"Madigan," the woman said, and shook her head. "Vera Madigan."

"And you're Wendell's...mother?"

"That's me," she confirmed, but only after a slight pause, which told me we might be here a while.

"We understand you know something about a helicopter that belongs to –"

"Apparently to you," she said, looking at me. "So I've been told." The woman removed a cloth from her pocket and dabbed at her nose.

Jordan and I took a second to silently negotiate the next few questions. "I guess I'm trying to find out why your son would give me a helicopter. We don't—didn't—know each other."

"Maybe not directly, no. But your lives have most certainly been entangled," she said, brows high.

No one spoke for a long minute. The air in here smelled like sawdust. I gripped my knees, breathing through the awkwardness. Our lives entangled, mine and WP's? I'd never met the guy before I saw him in Jordan's parking lot. At least I don't think I had.

"I know why you're really here." Vera Madigan gazed up at the ceiling. "You'll never find them, you know."

"Who?"

She rolled her eyes down and met mine with another hard stare. "The Primes."

CODEX

Chapter 29

"**The Primes.**" **I repeated the word, seeing how** it sounded coming out of my mouth, like it had some importance. She was watching me. "What is that?"

"Don't go pretending, doc. That won't work on me." She had a habit of clamping her jaw tight after speaking, lips pointed into a tiny dot.

Doc? I had no idea what she was talking about. I thought back to the era of my life I'd so carefully blocked out, my day-to-day with Jessica, working all day, weekends together, both of us up late at night embroiled in careers we cared about. And her work on ADS, WP's company. I'd never heard her mention the phrase *primes.*

Vera Madigan resettled her wide frame within the confines of the chair. "There's four primes. There were anyway. You received a call from one of 'em, or you're going to."

"Called by who?" I felt like I'd stepped into someone else's conversation midstream.

She turned her chair to face me. "I don't see how you couldn't know. It was your wife who –" She cut it off before finishing whatever blame game she was planning. Michael Wise said she'd been working for them, in some capacity. I guess I felt like if I didn't think about it,

149

LISA TOWLES

the whole thing might go away. Life doesn't work that way, does it? Jessica, what have you done?

I got up, opened the door, and stood on the cold porch. The wind blew right through me but I barely felt it.

"It was his wife who tracked 'em down!" she said to Jordan, loud enough for me to hear with the door open.

The cold air nipped at my cheeks and ears. But it was like some other part of me was shut off. I heard them talking inside, Jordan doing her magic to try to pull something useful out of Wendell Peters' mother. I knew about the medical company Jessica's firm was investigating, and knew she'd come across something shady, told her partners about it and got nowhere. Had she gone somewhere else, then? Gotten someone else involved, someone besides Michael Wise? She contacted him to get on his podcast, I guess to expose what she discovered in the BA-Vi files. But what did that have to do with Vera Madigan and her drafty shack and accusing eyes?

"No smoking," the woman bellowed from inside when I lit up.

They helped me think, and right now I needed all the help I could get. Maybe that habit was coming to an end now, too. What would I substitute this time? Mud water, adaptogenic mushrooms, microdosed LSD? I sucked the nicotine deep in my lungs, held it there a minute too long then coughed like an amateur. Funny.

I came back into the house, and this time leaned against the wall of what should have been the living room, except for the lack of any furnishings. No rug on the worn, gapped wooden slats, no heat, nothing on the walls, scant mismatched furniture. Probably no electricity either.

"Vera," I said. "You came to us, to Jordan. Help me out, here. I need some background."

Jordan glared, like I'd interrupted her trust-building exercise. My patience had just run out. I crossed my arms and waited.

"Vera, would you tell Angus what you just told me?" Jordan said, still staring me down.

The woman scratched the side of her scalp, then combed back her wily, curled mop with her fingers.

"You said four primes," Jordan said. "What – is that?"

"Originally four but they lost one," Vera said, gesturing toward me like I would understand.

So *primes* were people. Patients maybe? "Lost one," I said. "Like died?"

"Well, let's just say now it's three." Vera cleared her throat. "Three patients, identified as three prime numbers."

"That's what they were called?" I asked.

One nod.

"By whom? And in what context?"

She shrugged. "The staff. The doctors."

"Hospital?" Jordan asked, turning back to me.

"Wendell's company, ADS, is a medical research company. Right?" I asked Vera.

"Well, he alone might have called them by their names, but no one else knew that information. It was secret. Never in their meetings, not in their meeting minutes and certainly never during the clinical trials. Their identities were –" She stopped to laugh. It came out as a gurgly cough, a smoker's cough.

"What?" I probed.

"Wendell. One time he said their identities were a matter of national security. But I'm sure that was an exaggeration. He was like that, everything grandiose. Life or death."

Maybe it was. "Which prime numbers, Vera?" Jordan asked.

"One, five, and thirteen. Number seven's the one they lost. Died, escaped…who knows." Again that stare like I'd been the one who killed him.

"You saw them? You met them?" I asked her, but she shook her head. Everything she said had the same inflection, like we should of course know this already. "They were patients of Wendell? Was he treating them, or were they a part of his research?"

Another cackle. "A part? They were all of it. The whole company was based on them."

Jordan cleared her throat. "Vera, who's taking over Wendell's company now that he's passed on?"

"He's got two partners but he never trusted them." Her head turned left and right. "Always thought they were gonna kill him. And look what happened. Maybe they did."

"Why would Wendell's business partners want to kill him?"

Vera liked Jordan, I could tell. She took a long drag of air through her nose and exhaled with a sag to her shoulders. This woman was made for the stage. "He said one of them disagreed with the application of the research and was trying to stop the experiments. Then his other partner said there wasn't enough money to continue funding the project."

"Who were their funding sources?" I asked, still stuck on the word experiments. Clinical trials were common for testing out new medical advances. *Experiments* put a different spin on it. "Is the company a nonprofit?"

"Are you kidding?"

"Grants? Investors?"

"Wendell was the money guy and didn't much like sharing, if you know what I mean. It started out fine, but over the years it got bad. I can't remember the last time they were all on speaking terms."

Jordan this time. "So how did they communicate and work together?"

"For the past year or so, all communication was done through their lawyers. Before that, they had directors and senior staff. There used to be two hundred employees, before...anyway. Then after the merger, they resized, changed the focus, and scaled everything down."

"Down to what?" I asked. "They manufactured specialized hearing aids. Is that right?"

The woman tipped her head to the side and moved to the fireplace.

"Whatever they've been doing is probably why your son is dead. What are we talking about here?"

"Mind control," she said, with her back to us.

The room had darkened. I moved to the front windows, wondering if what Vera said could actually be true. If so, who could be listening to this conversation, and who might feel threatened by us knowing?

"Where?" I asked, teasing one question out of the hundred possible responses. "Not in the main ADS offices, I assume. Right?"

"And certainly not here," Jordan added, glancing around the shack.

Vera shook her head, eyeing the floor. "In his labs."

"Where's his lab, Vera?" I asked, my frayed nerves becoming more obvious.

"Well, if I knew that, you wouldn't be here right now, would

CODEX

you?" She plopped against the back of the sofa, arms crossed.

So that was her silent request to find WP's secret lab. I moved around the right side of the sofa and rickety coffee table. I circled the sofa and landed two feet from her. How could she live in a place like this if her son was so wealthy? None of it made sense. I paused to draw a few breaths, hoping the oxygen in my brain would help me synthesize the swarm of competing thoughts.

"Wendell gave me his helicopter, and then he died of suspicious circumstances the next day."

Vera stared, unblinking.

"Then you called Jordan this morning to let me know we had the wrong helicopter. Do you confirm that you made that call?"

Vera laughed. Jordan squirmed in her seat, unsure what I would do next.

"Did Wendall even own a helicopter?" I asked.

"I can tell you this. It's how he got to his lab," Vera said.

I hung my head and Jordan got up to stand by the door. She was right, we were going nowhere. "Where's his chopper?" I asked.

"Same hanger you were in before. But it's not that right-shiny blue jobber, I'll tell you that much."

"Then why —"

Vera shook her head. "That one belongs to the firm, you know, the new firm that acquired Wendell's company. Wendell's helicopter's an old, vintage thing."

"Where are his logbooks?"

Vera's thick brows rose. "I'd be surprised if he kept them anywhere visible." She glared at me with some kind of intended telepathy. I wasn't getting it, and this was feeling like a wasted trip to the Twilight Zone. I looked at Jordan and headed for the front door hoping we wouldn't step through any busted floorboards on the way out.

Vera followed us, leaning out through the doorway watching us head down the steps.

"You don't sound like you're from California, Vera," Jordan said, when we were almost to the car.

It came across as a back-handed remark, something Detective Columbo might do on his way out of a witness interview. *Just one more thing...* I don't know why she asked it, or at that particular time. But I was starting to feel like there were no accidents, not where Wendell Peters was concerned.

"Well, I'm from Texas, of course. It's where Angus and I first met."

Chapter 30

***He's dead. No, give him time. Doctor, he's** not breathing!*
I'm in the same room as before but separate, somehow. I hear their agitated voices, trying to revive one of them, one of us, an injection that had an unexpected result. Words like trembling, seizure, reverse the procedure, saline drip. They'll come for me eventually. Usually I'm last. Am I the youngest, or maybe the oldest? Strongest, the least likely to die on them before they extract their data? I feel their energy from twenty feet away, clustered around one patient, their angry, nervous energy, frustrated that all their knowledge can't accurately predict human behavior in response to stimuli. That's what they call it, I've heard them mumbling in the far-left corner of the lab where they think we can't hear. But their voices are near a heating grate in the floor. Under my feet, I feel the vibration of their words—not actual words but the energy of them, the fury of them. They're experimenting on us, and some of us are dying. I'm about to be next.

"Hey." I felt Jordan's hand on my shoulder before her silky voice registered, her lips precipitously close to my face. "You okay?" she asked, but clearly I wasn't. It had happened again, how many times was this now that I'd checked out in broad daylight, even mid-conversation?

"Uh, sorry." I blinked a few times, coming back to Jordan's car outside Vera Madigan's shack.

"What do you make of –"

"She's gaslighting me," I quipped as Jordan drove us away from the freak shack toward civilization.

"So you've never met her before today?"

"Hell no," I said. "And I've only been to Texas once, years ago, for a case I was working on," I added, hoping to leave it at that.

I felt Jordan's energy, reading me, recalibrating her planned barrage of questions. "So what do we know now?"

"I know that place, that shack made me feel rank."

"By the look of the ceiling, I'm surprised the walls didn't fall down," she said.

"I mean sick," I said. "I still feel it."

"Do you want me to stop somewhere? Do you need something?"

I didn't answer, and not because I didn't want to. My eyes on the woody, dirt path, I felt like we'd stepped into another dimension somehow, like Vera Madigan didn't live in the 21st century and we'd somehow found our way back to the past.

I texted Nigella when we were close to Half Moon Bay with an assignment to track down the new owners of WP's company, principals only. She said she'd reach out tonight with details. Meanwhile, nausea had spread through my entire body, the bumps and potholes in the dirt road making it worse. I closed my eyes and surrendered. Something, somewhere was pulling me. Down, down, all the way down.

"Why are you driving like that?" I heard myself ask. It was my voice but not words I would ever use, at least not to her.

Jordan didn't answer, and I was learning that this was her way, slow to react but deep in her observations. My mood turned edgy, grumbly about everything suddenly. It was too cold in the car. My jacket felt scratchy on my skin, and the back of my throat seemed thick and fuzzy.

CODEX

"Look," I said, turning my head to see Jordan's reaction. "You might wanna slow down." Why was I saying this? I was sitting close enough to see she was going forty on a freeway on-ramp, which was the right speed.

"Are you okay?" she asked again, staring at the road.

"Just ignore me. I don't know what's wrong."

After a short pause and a quick adjustment of her seatbelt, Jordan gave me a quick glance. "Do you remember her?"

"Who?" I shot back, instantly irritated.

"Vera. She said you guys met in Texas."

The thickness in my throat seemed to double. I made a gurgling sound to clear it, then coughed, and rubbed the front of it. My skin felt hot. Was this what it meant to go crazy, like what happened on Rudy's couch recently? My palms were clammy and my breathing shallow. Get a grip, Angus. We were still a ways from Half Moon Bay, and eventually Jordan would be looking for an answer to her very simple question. It was simple, wasn't it? Then why did I feel like I couldn't breathe?

Alice. Alice, Texas.

Breathe. In, out. Again. The cold air cooled my throat, which made it feel even worse. I knew Jordan could tell something was happening, and I loved how she wasn't panicking. She would have made a good ER nurse, or maybe an operative. She could be one for all I know.

"Vera seemed to know you. You don't remember meeting her before today?"

"No! I don't fucking remember her, and I never lived there."

"What's wrong with your voice?" was her response to my sudden, explosive outburst. Not the volume, not how unglued I'd become, but the vocal quality. What the fuck was wrong with me? I felt like texting Rudy but I also felt nervous riding in someone else's car. I'd never felt that way in my life. Good God, what was next?

Jordan slowed as we approached the intersection of Highway 1. There was a turnoff before the freeway to the Purissima Cemetery overlooking a vast field. She parked and turned off the motor, her hands clenched around the steering wheel. I loved this countryside out here, or I used to. Today it felt hollow and threatening, leaving me wondering who might be hiding out in the tall grass.

It occurred to me that Vera could have slipped me something, like poison. But we hadn't drank anything in her house. I couldn't remember the last time I felt fear like this, except for the night of the accident when the police restrained me while they took Jessica's body away on a stretcher. Was this some kind of PTSD episode? But triggered by what?

Michael Wise had answers to my questions. I pulled my phone from my pocket and felt Jordan staring.

I need to talk to you, I wrote to Wise. *No guns, no car chase this time. Can you meet?*

Where? He wrote back right away.

Rudy's Red Bull, HMB.

OK, tomorrow night, he wrote back.

"What's going on, Angus? Why are you unglued suddenly?"

"I don't know," I whispered, jerking my head left and right.

The pre-dusk sky looked surreal—ordered, beautiful, serene. Too serene. And honestly there was nothing sudden about it. Had I been paying closer attention to myself, I would have realized it's been happening gradually, more and more, almost daily now.

"Something about Texas?" she asked. "When were you there?"

"Years ago, one of my first cases."

"Vera?"

I shook my head honestly having no recollection of ever meeting her before.

"Do you believe her? Do you believe anything she said?"

I watched Jordan's face soften back into its usual shape, but a hard line still showed between her eyebrows. I'd scared her today. Dammit.

"That story, The Primes as she called them?" she went on. "It seemed a bit too complex to make up. I thought she seemed pretty credible, actually."

"Credible?" I asked, working to keep my raw emotions intact. It wasn't working. "Vera Madigan seemed the opposite of credible to me. What was her agenda feeding us that line of crap? We got some additional details today, no question about it. I've definitely got some things to follow up."

"Like?"

I drew in a quick breath and blew it out my mouth to steady my

CODEX

nerves. "The other helicopter for one thing. I need to see it, see if it even starts, look into the key he gave me and find the logbook to see where the fuck he's been going."

"She wants you to find his lab. You heard her, didn't you?" Jordan asked.

I heard her mention it but she hadn't specifically asked me to find it. Though, reading between the lines, she was probably right. "I don't know what to do about that yet but I've got someone helping me track down WP's company. It's a starting point anyway."

Jordan restarted the engine, shaking her head. "She didn't seem to be grieving his loss. And that whole thing about mind control. When I think of WP rambling into the bar half in the bag, and then hear Vera talking like he's some evil mastermind, something doesn't fit. Maybe he has a twin. Or maybe Vera Madigan's crazy."

I was only half listening, my brain replaying the image of Vera in her flowered nightgown on the front porch, telling me that Texas was where we'd first met. What if she was right? Why couldn't I remember? I knew of memory wipe drugs, technologies and practices used in covert military interrogations. The uncertainty felt like lightning crackling through my veins.

I couldn't bear to be around Jordan right now, unstable as I was knowing my erratic behavior was upsetting her. She dropped me at the brewery where I rode my bike to Rudy's and parked in one of his two reserved parking spots in the back. It was our code. No one dared park in Rudy's special spots. If my bike was there, it meant shit was going down.

Tomorrow, if Jordan was still talking to me, I'd pick her up and find the vintage helicopter owned by WP. Hopefully, if the logbook was still inside, I'd have an opportunity to develop a picture of his latest movements, which could explain, well, so many things. I'd sent a text to Officer Lopez asking if there were any developments on WP's cause of death. No response yet. Wendell Peters was dead, presumably at the hands of the principals of his newly acquired firm. So far there were no details of a memorial and his mother didn't appear to be grieving, not in the least. After parking my bike, I pulled out my phone and added to the Notes file:

- WP's cause of death

- WP's acquired company, check back with Nigella on their executive team
- His helicopter logbook, Andreini Airfield
- His secret lab if it even exists

For now, I needed to search Vera Madigan's fishing shack, knowing if there was a secret lab anywhere, it was most likely in or near that house. Whatever he was hiding, whatever he was doing in there, I knew in my bones it had something to do with Jessica and why she was dead.

Chapter 31

Present

Dekker never did arrest us, maybe because he had no actual proof that Elaine and I had broken into Vera Madigan's house. But he did drag us out of Rudy's diner in handcuffs for all the world to see. That was his game, wasn't it? Abusing his power.

We'd seen no evidence there of any ADS paperwork from WP's illicit company or anything related to BA-Vi, the supposed name of his secret project. On the surface, Elaine and I had found nothing in that rickety shack, other than a few of Vera Madigan's flowered dresses slung on the backs of chairs. What we did find, though, was a cold spot on the floor under the bed in one of the guest rooms, something you'd never see in another house unless it had a root cellar. This was a rural area so I guess that was possible, but I had a feeling WP was keeping more than roots down there.

I brought Elaine back to Rudy's house after Dekker released us. She sat stiffly in one of his kitchen chairs.

"You need to tell me about Miguel. Right now."

"There's nothing to tell," she said folding her hands. "We broke up."

That's how she was gonna play it? Fine. "The way I see it, Miguel stole money from his associates, they picked him up and contacted you to return it to them in exchange for his life. You found his stash, returned it per their instructions, they let him go and you skipped town. Right so far?"

She was tapping her fingers on the table.

"But there's one problem." She looked up. "You saw them, you probably saw their faces, maybe their cars, heard their voices and now you can identify them. So even though you returned what he stole, you're a liability, and Miguel's associates are probably here to silence you."

The chair she sat on wobbled because of Rudy's expensive hand-scraped wood floors. She moved, crossed her legs, then re-crossed them the other way.

"Look," I said, taking the chair across from her. "I can get you protection or protect you myself. Is that what you want? What went down with the two of you before you left London? You've got to tell me something, Elaine, or else why are you even here?"

"To help you break into old ladies' houses apparently. You never found what you were looking for anyway, did you?"

"Answer the question."

"So two interrogations then? Dekker and now you?" She rose and slapped her palm on the table. "I'm laying down for a while, I'm tired." She left the kitchen, limping toward the bedroom, probably having injured her leg crawling out the window of Vera's house. I never should have brought her there, that sinister shack in the woods protecting God knows what. I'd put my sister in harm's way. Another problem I'd need to fix.

I'd asked Michael Wise to meet me at the diner. I texted him that I was on my way and replaced my phone in my pocket. A wave of dizziness washed over me and I detected an odd, metallic taste in the back of my throat. The air smelled sour.

After a five-minute ride, I turned off the engine and sat on an asphalt curb lining the edges of Rudy's parking lot to steady myself. My hands felt trembly, like I might not be able to hold a cup of coffee. The metal taste in my mouth was more pungent now, and something still smelled odd—maybe the problem was my nose and not the air. I was outdoors, a cool night with a slight breeze. Why would I smell chemicals here and at the trailer?

I texted Elaine. *I'm at a quick meeting. Will you be there when I get back?* But I knew smothering her was the best way to never hear from her again. I couldn't help it.

From this vantage point, I could see into the rear of Rudy's diner, heads bobbing past the window, Eduardo the head chef, another temp who worked a few nights a week, and Rudy's large, square-shaped buzz cut.

The cold asphalt penetrated through my clothes. For just a second my lids fell, not out of fatigue but out of something pulling me in. An air-conditioned room with a few other people, a buzzing sound overhead, and some kind of metal band around my head. It was me in there, this ghostly image that appeared out of nowhere. Where was I and what happened to me?

With no response from Elaine, the sound of breaking glass pulled me back to the dark parking lot. One of the servers must have dropped a tray. My bike was right beside me. I reached up and touched the seat, reassured in a way.

I rode to the back lot in this sort of daze, still not sure where the images had come from, though more certain than ever it was me sitting in that chair.

I found Michael Wise at an empty booth in the middle of the diner. His hair looked shorter, and strain showed on in his forehead and eyes. We needed a more private place to talk, but I hadn't yet decided what I would reveal or, more importantly, what I needed from him right now.

"Hey man, how's it going?" I asked from the back door. I could see Eduardo leaning over a butcher block kneading dough. I waved.

"Angus. What 'chu need today, brother?" He looked up from the dough pan with a smile as big as the sun. Love that guy.

"Nah, I'm good." I pointed to the dining room and stood in front of the table, but Wise looked deep in thought, eyes glazed over.

"Hey," I said, quietly and waited.

When he looked up, I jerked my head toward the kitchen. He got up and followed. I led him to the parking lot and stood beside my bike, arms crossed, feet spread apart.

LISA TOWLES

"I'm here."

"I see that," I said and half-smiled, because at least some part of me liked him. "Did your associate find what he was looking for in my storage unit in San Carlos?" My delivery of the question was completely neutral, like I was asking how his day went. I watched his eyes as his brain worked through all the different ways of answering.

He signed, finally. "No and yes. I mean – yes and no."

So he was trusting me with the truth. Now it was my turn. "I know you were down there. I saw your car. And you already have Jessica's journal because I was watching when your associate passed it to you at the Ferry Building." I didn't mention the possibility of his associate being Miguel, Elaine's ex-boyfriend yet. I had to keep a few tricks up my sleeve.

Michael nodded. "He's looking for the map that was in the journal."

"He's looking?"

He shrugged. "Okay, I'm looking for it."

"A map to what?" I asked, but I already knew. Vera said as much. It had to be a map to WP's secret laboratory. I could tell by the blank look on Michael's face that he had no idea what was on that map or why it was important. This could be to my advantage and I logged it in the back of my brain for future use.

"Look –"

"It's not in my storage area, is it?" I asked. I knew my wife. If there was a map she put in that journal, and she knew she was being pursued because of it, the map had to be a fake, or a decoy. Jessica must have known where WP's lab was, and there was no way the real location was anywhere near her journal. The only way of finding it was to uncover WP's helicopter logbook. Even before Wise answered, I started making moves toward my bike.

"What are you doing?" he asked.

"I've got research to do."

"You dragged me down here because you said you had information."

"No, I said I wanted to talk to you about some information."

"Quit stalling and tell me what you know. Or maybe you know nothing, and that's the problem."

CODEX

I turned on him; he stepped back two paces. "I'll tell you what I know, Michael. I know your gunman-associate passed you my dead wife's journal at the Ferry Building the other night. And aside from all the other objections I have to that breach, I also know that you have no fucking idea what the relevance of that journal really is. Do you?"

Blank stare, jaw set. He didn't respond, but he wasn't walking away either. There were a couple of ways I could work this right now. He'd been playing me for sure, but he did come to the Hyatt to give me information, introducing a hundred questions. And now my body was starting to answer those questions in the form of nausea and dizziness – the same kind of sickness I felt on Vera Madigan's porch a few hours ago, Rudy's house, and on the curb out back with a vision of a place I'd never been to. Something was changing, something in my world but something in my head, too - details, experiences were shifting around beyond my control and according to someone else's plan. I felt, somehow, tampered with. But the last thing I needed right now was another enemy.

I looked at the man and nodded. "Alright," I said. "Ever hear of Vera Madigan?"

"No. Who is she?"

I believed him. "She's Wendell Peters' mother. I went to see her today, a –"

"Wait, you, how did you –"

"Shut up and I'll tell you," I said. "She summoned me through a friend, and we went to her house out in the hills earlier today. She had some, let's just say…interesting things to say."

"About?" He followed me outside to the back lot.

I was already half down the path. "She mentioned something called The Primes," I said and waited for signs of recognition.

He nodded. "The journal made reference to that word, not plural but singular. I didn't know what it meant, but from the context it didn't seem like it was referring to math or numbers."

I hated how I'd never even seen that journal but he had. It didn't seem fair. Michael Wise had spent time with my wife behind my back, the week, maybe even the very day she died. I tried to be angry, I wanted to be angry. But instead it was a wound growing in the soft patch of grief in my heart. One wound on top of another.

"No." I shook my head and glanced around the lot to make sure we were alone. "They were people, subjects. A control group. Apparently Jessica found them, though I don't have any other details. Like I don't know if they were missing or—"

Michael had put a hand over his mouth and walked toward the diner. He turned back a moment later, thinking, hands clasped behind his neck. "So that's what it was. She never told me the details, just that she was bringing me something. I assumed it was her journal, which she'd told me about and said she was worried someone was trying to steal it. Maybe it was…them. So where are they now?"

I needed sleep, hydration, my stomach was feeling worse and worse. I could use a partner right now. I told him what Vera told Jordan and me about the acquiring company and how I was gathering data on them.

"Look. Trust begets trust. You've shared this with me, so I'll share some background with you tomorrow."

"The journal," I said, and not as a question. "That's all the background I need."

He nodded. Hopefully that meant he would bring it. "Are they still open in there?" he asked pointing to Rudy's. "Want to join me?"

My phone buzzed. "Sure. See you inside." I watched Michael Wise walk back around the building, presumably to enter through the main doors in front. A slight limp showed him favoring his left leg. Another logged detail. I looked in through the back window as he was opening the front door. I pulled my phone from my pocket and saw a text from an unrecognized number.

CODEX

Chapter 32

Mr. Mariner.

Who is this? I wrote back.

A friend.

I have enough friends.

Really? Doesn't seem like it.

Who are you? Mendoza?

That's a name I don't hear often, not in civilized circles. Friends in low places?

So whoever it was knew Sylvan Mendoza. That narrowed the scope slightly to those in the intelligence field, possibly military. *Who are you then?* I asked.

You have to go back there.

Where? I wrote, but the sudden sick feeling in my stomach told me the answer. Not this again.

You know where. Alice.

Alice, Texas. I knew, somehow, that's what this person meant. From Mendoza's note. This person must be one of his minions. *WTF is it about that place? I went there once 12 years ago. What do you want?*

To help you.

167

I don't need help.

You're sick lately, aren't you? Stomach, you can't sleep, dizzy, constant headaches.

How could they possibly know this? I panic-scanned the perimeter of the parking lot, like some kind of thought-police agents would be visible, tall and lurking in special suits. Ridiculous.

Do you know why? the stranger asked.

I'm putting my phone away.

You're remembering.

I'm asking you one last time: who are you?

I'm Five.

I hadn't told Michael anything about Alice, Texas, the case I'd worked on back then, and I had no intention of sharing anything extra with him because it was his turn. I went to the back door of the diner, told him I was taking off after all, and asked Eduardo to comp his meal, then hid out in the men's room to think. The room was too small, I'd said it a hundred times to Rudy. His argument was that it was a staff bathroom only, and the larger one was on other side of the building. Tonight I liked how small it was in here, feeling contained and protected, somehow, by the four dingy walls.

My phone was back in my pocket; there were no further texts, but the bait had been set and my stomach told me the truth of his words. Maybe I was remembering something. A cold room on an otherwise hot, sunny day. Seated in special chairs, four of us, not talking or maybe just unable to talk with metal plates or some kind of apparatus on our heads.

I leaned over the sink and wretched, turned on the water slurping up a few handfuls, hoping to neutralize the pool of acid that had gathered in my stomach. It didn't help. I leaned my head down and drank from the faucet. Again, my throat felt like metal. All of these odd symptoms reminded me of a PTSD episode brought on by some kind of trigger. I'd read about them, soldier stories, case studies. The only PTSD I'd had was that stretch of Highway 1 where our car had gone over the edge.

You're remembering, the texter wrote. Maybe something I'd buried was revealing itself. Now I had to know what that was.

CODEX

After texting Elaine for the tenth time tonight with no response, I slept for a few hours in the actual bed in my trailer, curled up fetal under the thick covers. The idea of sleep scared me after the dream I'd had, and another sort of daydream at Vera Madigan's house. Was it considered a recurring dream even if it was different every time? Like someone was showing me bits and pieces of a story in sequential order. Maybe Jess was sending me a message, and this was the only way she could communicate with me. Was that crazy? Hell yeah, it was crazy. I'd seen movies about it before, but they were movies, not documentaries. Dead people can't send messages to the family members they leave behind. Can they? I so desperately wanted to pick up my phone and text my new friend, Five, to demand more information. But that's the snag with Pandora's box, isn't it? The lid never fully closes again once it's been pried open.

I slept fitfully, scraps of like thirty minutes at a time all night. I got up in the dark and opened all the windows, desperate to freshen the air in the trailer. I made an egg sandwich and called Nigella—no answer and her voicemail inbox was full. Great. Elaine, now Nigella. I added both their names to the upper right corner of the whiteboard. I sent Nigella a text, wondering if maybe her ringer was just turned off and she didn't see my call. Okay, yes I was growing paranoid now. I could call Luther, her dad, but that would only worry him. No, stop. I can figure this out.

I opened my laptop. A search for 'ADS acquired by' turned up five companies called ADS, and none were WP's company. Next, I tried 'Advanced Diagnostic Services acquired by' and this brought up two articles referencing a hostile takeover by the acquiring company purchasing a large percentage of shares to gain access to company revenue and decision-making power over the future direction of the company. Kroger Management Partners, in another browser tab, was run by A. Acosta, Anthony Acosta of Rolling Hills Estates in Los Angeles. Bingo.

I checked Anthony Acosta's LinkedIn profile, found his list of connections, searched for anyone named Acosta and found Rhonda Acosta. Next, another Google search, this time for Anthony and Rhonda Acosta, Rolling Hills Estates—nothing. I went back to LinkedIn where Rhonda's picture looked much older than the picture

169

of Anthony. Mother maybe? I kept searching, scrolling, then found Debra Reese-Acosta, who looked younger. First I tried Debra's name on Facebook and found an account with the same picture as LinkedIn, here we go. I clicked her profile and scrolled for images of her and Anthony Acosta, vacation pictures, dog pictures, a Shelty. I loved those. There, last Christmas, a family photo of Debra and Anthony Acosta, with Rhonda Acosta standing behind a row of teenaged children. Rhonda was Grandma. Now the last step—a property search. I typed in both of their names along with Rolling Hills Estates, and a whitepages.com page showed 17 Crest Road East. The property was deeded to Anthony and Debra Acosta and was currently off market. Hello Anthony. I got you.

I texted the information to Nigella, hoping for a text back, a single word, something. Frustration buzzed in my hands. I tapped the keyboard. Nigella's fine, I told myself. So was Elaine. Gotta love those fairy tales.

I always liked long rides, alone with my bike on an empty stretch of road with nothing but a jug of water and an empty sky. I liked how this felt, even now, striking off in the middle of the night on a research mission. Jess would have liked my spirit, my passion, as she called it. It felt a bit like the old me. The before-me.

I kept a spare toothbrush, an extra iPhone charger and a set of keys locked in the console under my seat, but this was a quick strike mission. Truth is, I needed the solitude, but more than just peace and quiet. My mind needed space to help me think. It was all too much lately, the past, present, and future all converging into a big mess, mimicked by the tapestry of brooding clouds over my head.

I heard something, I couldn't put my finger on it. Was it a tapping? Some kind of chime? No, nothing audible. But I felt its presence more and more lately. A change, that's it, something that's different from what I've thought, challenging my version of reality. Something was coming. Maybe it was already here.

I kept my eyes lasered on Interstate 280 knowing I'd be merging onto 17 in a few minutes, then 101 to the dreaded I-5, an endless, forgotten shell of a road that always felt like purgatory. Maybe that's where I belonged.

By the time the iconic IHOP sign became visible outside of Bakersfield, where I stopped for gas a second time, I'd formulated my plan for the Acostas, and my pitch. I felt a pull in the engine with my foot on the gas when I should have been going faster. I knew it was an old bike, part of it vintage, custom built. But every single part in that engine was new. I-5 became 405 just outside the LA city limits. I stopped to gas up again in Culver City. Instead of Elaine or Nigella, there were two texts from Officer Lopez in Half Moon Bay. What now?

Are you ever gonna call me back? And a second one that read, *Need to talk to you.* Helmet on and about to take off again, the phone rang. No caller ID, a bad sign. I pulled off the helmet and put the call on speaker.

"Yeah, Angus here."

I heard a man clear his throat.

"Mendoza? That you?"

"No Mr. Mariner, this is Luther. Luther Dawson."

Despite the authority in his voice, my chest relaxed at the sound of him. "Hey Luther," I said. "What's up?" My tone denoted friendliness; I liked Luther. Why would he be calling me though?

"It's Nella."

Nigella, shit. "Is she okay?"

"I wish I knew. I can't reach her and wondered if she was working for you tonight."

God. Would Nigella Dawson be another woman I'd put in harm's way? "I had her on a research assignment," I admitted. "But just internet work to try to track somebody down. I thought she'd be doing that at home."

There was a pause. I needed to get back on the road. Maybe there was another reason now for this call.

"May I ask what kind of research?"

I told Luther about the Acostas and their possible connection to a case I was working on.

"They live in LA?"

"Yeah, Rolling Hills Estates. You're thinking Nella went down

LISA TOWLES

there?"

"She doesn't have a car," he said, though that had never stopped her before. I'd seen her break into a car and hotwire the engine in the time it took to sneeze.

After Luther and I agreed to contact the other if either of us heard from her, I angled my bike back onto what had quickly turned into a long line of steady traffic. I also knew Luther Dawson would likely be getting in his car right now to head down here.

A mile from the turnoff to Palos Verdes Drive off of 107, my phone buzzed in my pocket. If it was Luther, he might have information about Nigella. It also could be Elaine. Tired, sore butt from five hours on I-5, I pulled to the shoulder and grabbed the phone from my pocket. I'd just missed a call from Officer Lopez.

I checked the time—1:35am. I texted instead of calling her. *Angus here, what's up? Sorry I missed you.*

Dekker needs to see you tomorrow morning. Said to say it's not a request this time.

Copy that, I wrote back. Shit.

Chapter 33

Copy that, **of course, meant fuck Dekker and** his idle threats. So far, he's been investigating a shooting on a beach, the death of an old man and he'd been able to produce no evidence tying me to either of those crimes. Now I had another reason to hang out in LA.

I'd copied the Acosta's address from my Google search onto my phone and used Waze to get me within a block of the home. Castle was more like it, I could see from my quick drive-by to park on an adjacent street. Tall, modern, vertical windows lining the front, and landscaping that likely cost as much as the monthly mortgage payments.

A car out here would have provided more privacy, but bikes had more agility. I had no idea what to expect from Anthony Acosta and needed to be ready for anything. I found a dog park two streets over and was able to stop under a curtain of weeping willow branches. It was cold but smelled fresh. I stretched out my arms and neck, sitting back on the padded seat while my brain rifled through a fresh set of stimuli. We were no longer looking for Jess's journal, nor were we looking for the missing map, or even for WP's secret lab. My new directive was to establish what he was doing in that lab and find the four missing patients Vera referred to as The Primes.

Luther texted me as the sky started to lighten. He was an hour away. Problem is, he very likely thought I was down here looking for Nella. I tried texting her again, and re-sent the same text to Elaine with no response yet from either of them. The universe must be punishing me for something, my past sins coming back to haunt me in the form of fear and uncertainty. Maybe I was a bad husband to Jess, not as attentive as she needed. No, I was the farthest thing from inattentive. I adored the ground she walked on, smelled the pillow she'd slept on, made an inventory in my head of her shoes. The strappy ones, sparkly flats, ankle boots, and heels. No, dammit, I did not fail you. My lips moved as I said it out loud, there alone in the grassy dawn in an alien neighborhood. The reminder about Luther's text blinked again on my phone, lighting up the shadowy trees as a tiny moment of hope.

I dozed for a few minutes, dreaming again of the cold room with the strange chairs. My body shook itself awake with an odd sensation in my left ear. Woozy on my feet, I struggled to pull my bike back a few inches deeper under the trees and out of view of any early risers heading to work. I climbed off the bike and sat, feeling the solid cold of the morning ground. My palms flattened on clumps of wet grass. I grabbed them, they slipped through my fingers. I leaned forward onto my knees, the toes of my boots digging into a few inches of soft mud.

Forehead cold. Buzzing sound. A low tide smell. Metal clangs.

Something was happening. My lids closed again.

I don't know where I am, yet I still felt the chilled, wet ground under my knees. There's a sensation above my left ear, like an itch or irritation but inside my head. Could that even be possible? My heart's pounding but in an irregular rhythm. I'm clutching wet clumps of grass, which gives me a tangible place to anchor my mind while it spins into this other place and time. I sniff the grassy air but it fails to calm me. In. Out. Again. Was this what a breakdown felt like? You see it on TV, you read about it, other people's breakdowns. They can't take another thread and they crack and lose control. I know I'm dangerously close to an abyss; I can almost see down into it, a shimmer of water at the bottom. If only Jess was down there, then there would be no question. But she died because of what she knew. That information, data, evidence made her someone's liability. She died protecting something, someone, four test subjects, and she was about to expose their team of abusers. Get up, Angus. Get the fuck up. You owe it to her to find her truth and make her death mean something. Then maybe that abyss can wait a while.

My eyes blinked in more of the morning light and when I opened them all the way, I knew I had to find The Primes. They were now my salvation, and maybe I'd be theirs too. I fumbled for my phone, found the message from my mystery-texter and re-read the message. He said his name was Five. You're remembering, he'd written. Yes, I was. I knew that's why my left ear hurt, that there was some connection.

What am I remembering? What does it mean? Need to know, I typed back to him.

I'll tell you, in time.
No, now. When can we meet?
I'll be in touch. You're being tracked.

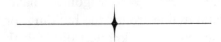

I had to get to the San Carlos house because I had one advantage over Michael Wise and whoever else he was working with: I knew Jessica Mariner. I knew her when she was still a teenager, I knew her when she was a lawyer and I knew how her mind worked. If she died to protect The Primes, she had to know I'd be the one to take over if anything happened to her. That means she left me something in that house, some way of finding them. She had to.

But the reality was that I was six hours away from San Carlos at the moment, and now Anthony Acosta was getting in his car, probably going to his Kroger Management Partners office in Riverside. I'd already saved a route and directions in Waze for that trip. I just hoped I could get there first. As I weaved in and out of traffic, I remembered the text from Lopez, Dekker's messenger. Sure, I'd go see him when I got back north, when I had time. Maybe when hell froze over.

Anthony Acosta parked his silver Lexus out front of a slim, three story, modern building with small windows and no visible front door. Was that clandestine by design? I drove past it and found a space on a side street, arranging the play in my head. Not ideal, of course, my going in there myself in broad daylight. I tried my one last option for backup - Rudy.

"Yeah man, where the fuck are you?"

I closed my eyes hearing the familiar voice. Rudy, thank God. He sounded angry. "How's it going? I'm around."

"Where? You haven't been home, and it's not just Dekker out looking for you. I'm worried about you."

"Come on, I'm fine."

"Look, people look out for each other. Just sayin'. And you're on the edge right now. Don't try and tell me otherwise."

"I know, I'm sorry. I'm researching something. To be honest, I could use backup right now."

"Where you at?" he asked.

"Rolling Hills Estates."

"LA? Shit. I can, but it'll be a while. I could send Eduardo."

Awww. My heart melted hearing Rudy offer up his star chef on his busiest day of the week. "Who's gonna make his pulled pork sandwich? They stand in line around the building for that."

Long sigh. "I can cook, you know. I did start this business on my own with –"

"– five dollars in your pocket, I know. No worries, I'll be back by tonight. Keep Eduardo in your kitchen where he belongs."

"I better see you soon, man. Not kidding."

Another threat, I'd add it to the list. Hearing his concern calmed my nerves a bit. At least until I pulled up the website of Kroger Management Partners on my phone and read their description:

Specializing in consultation, full life-cycle management and advocacy for research firms seeking FDA approval of science and technology projects. Areas of experience: ENT (Ear, Nose, and Throat) innovations, cochlear implants, BCI (brain-computer interface).

I swear my ear tingled again after reading this, the part of my ear that was sore, or maybe the right word was activated during my half-dream under the willow trees across from Anthony Acosta's house. BCI? Oh my God, WP. What have you done?

Chapter 34

I headed north at that point because Kroger Management Partners didn't have a front door. That told me they had no impetus to welcome new clients off the street and, instead, their clients were Big Pharma, venture capital funds, and probably corrupt white-collar criminals looking for short cuts through a tangled process. I suspected Sylvan Mendoza likely knew about Kroger and, if so, that pretty much meant Kroger was a front for an intelligence operation. CIA. State Department. Why was my left ear aching right now?

I took Highway 91 heading East and picked up I-5 northwest of Anaheim. The scant sensation, which I thought at first was psychosomatic, had turned into actual pain by that time and my ear and temple throbbed at Bakersfield. After a second fuel stop, I managed through the long stretch north and stopped, finally, at a drug store once I got onto 101 toward San Carlos. I was almost there. Keep going.

A cold gust swept up from the ground and pulled me two steps to the right as I stumbled down the driveway of my home in San Carlos, almost as if the house itself was rejecting my presence. How long had it been? Eighteen months, with only a cleaning crew coming up once a month to vacuum and make sure sheets were covering the furniture, and Ginger to check the lockbox. I still needed to call her. Michael Wise had broken in, at his own admission, to look for the journal and the mysterious map. But Jessica was smart. She had secret hiding places all over the house – for birthday surprises and for staging special projects. But the house had its own hiding place – something we'd discovered but never accessed. No one knew about it—that is, unless she shared it with Michael Wise. I'd know in a minute.

I turned back to regard my bike parked in the driveway, remembering parties where cars had lined the street on both sides, lights and music spilling out through the front door and windows. On second thought, I moved it to the side yard so my presence wouldn't be so obvious. My key still worked on the kitchen door on the right side of the house, which we'd used as in-law quarters, with the larger, main kitchen in the center of the house. Someone must have aired it out because it smelled fresh as I pushed open the door, fresher than it would have smelled being closed up all this time. Maybe a window had been left open. My boots made an odd echo on the tiled floors as I moved through the back corridor. That same cold wind from outside was coming from a guest bedroom on the right.

My phone chimed in my pocket; it never did that. I must have accidentally turned up the volume. It was a text from my mystery caller, the one called Five.

Are you ready? he wrote. I had no idea what this meant.

For what?

Is it time?

I watched the words light up on my phone while my eyes scanned the interior of a place I'd called home. I had no time for this. *Stop playing games*, I wrote. *I'm busy.*

Not a game, not to me.

To who then?

You don't remember everything yet, it's okay. You will.

Let me know when you're ready to meet and have a real conversation.

Not yet. It's not safe.

I sent back a *W*, which I assumed he'd know meant *whatever.*

I kept the phone face-up in my palm as I made my way into the living room. The velvet curtains were still bunched together, with

CODEX

sheers hanging in front of the long windows. I peered out behind the sheer through the bare glass. Almost 4pm by now, the sky had turned gray with a slight tinge of orange. One car though, back and forth, up and down. Gray. No...silver. A silver Lexus.

Anthony Acosta had a silver Lexus.

I jerked back, wondering if he'd seen the movement of the curtain in a house that should be empty, had been empty for a long time now, a roof and walls holding up secrets and ghosts. I toggled off Wi-Fi and did a quick Google image search for Anthony Acosta, resuming my surveillance spot at the window. There it went again, about twenty miles per hour past the house, about to turn around at the next intersection and come back the other way, which should give me a view of the driver. If it was him, he would have had to head north from Rolling Hills Estates to San Carlos as soon as I did, yet I hadn't noticed the silver Lexus en route. I hadn't checked the license plate, but what were the chances the same make and model car was stalking the house, my house, after I'd entered? That pretty much confirmed that he'd seen me outside his house in the park across the street or stalking his office. But I was concealed by trees, even my bike was out of view from the street. My mystery texter told me I was being tracked. Maybe he was right.

I stared down at the phone exchange we'd been having and wondered. He professed to know things about my experience, so maybe he also knew about Acosta. The front grill of the Lexus emerged from the trees on the right side of the lot. The driver looked middle-aged, tanned skin, prominent features, dark hair slicked back, brown shades and a gray suit. At least my observation skills were still intact. I checked the image search on my phone but nothing specifically for Anthony Acosta. I tried the name in combination with Kroger Management Partners, then checked the website for a list of principals, but there were no pictures, only bios. That was noteworthy. So there was no way of knowing for sure whether that was Anthony Acosta at all, let alone the right one. I went back to the text exchange. Worth a try.

Who are you? I asked him.

I told you. An interested party.

You said your name was Five. What kind of a name is that?

Not a name. A designation.

I knew what he meant, the four primes Vera Madigan mentioned on the strangest day of my life. So if this was five, where were the other three? *Look,* I wrote. *Someone's tailing me.*

He didn't respond, and at the same time I heard a thump and felt a vibration on the floor under my feet. It was coming from the back of the house by the garage.

Not just one.

Clarify, I typed.

You said someone is tailing you. You've got a few pursuers, and they're all after you for the same reason.

The journal?

No.

The map?

No.

I knew it! Jess, that's my girl. *Is it a decoy?*

It's you they want.

Why? And who's they?

I can't say anymore right now. I'm taking a huge risk as-is.

What am I supposed to do? I felt stupid writing it, expressing vulnerability to a stranger. But whoever they were and whatever their motivations, this person was trying to help me.

Doesn't matter. You've got nine lives. Or at least seven.

Question was, how many did I have left?

I stowed the phone in my back pocket again and heard a third thump coming from the rear of the house. Someone was trying to get in the back door. Maybe Acosta, but he wouldn't have had time to park and get inside. Regardless, that meant I had two minutes at most to find Jess' hiding spot.

The house was dark inside even though the sky was still light. I knew the electricity was still on because cleaning crews were coming in, but lights were out of the question right now. I stepped carefully down the main hallway toward the living room. The mantel looked just as grand: white marble with a thick slab of polished granite as the

CODEX

pedestal.

Another thump, this time accompanied by two short knocks. I'm being pursued, according to Five, by more than one person, which reminded me that I'd need to add Dekker to that list. Officer Lopez had now given me two warnings, which meant Dekker would come himself the next time. Tick tock.

The pair of club chairs in the living room had no sheet over them, which made it easy to lift and up-end them, displaying the undersides. A thin piece of gritty fabric was velcro'd on all four sides but pulled right off. It was just as I remembered, the same way we'd done it when Jess and I first discovered it. These two chairs and a few other old pieces: a maple credenza and a grandfather clock, came with the house. The old man, who owned and built it, apparently told Jess the house had a lot of secrets. I'd watched her face that day as she spoke of him, noticing he'd made a deep impression on her. She'd thought at first that he was flirting, saying things to try to impress her. Bring the chair into the fire, the old man told her when she asked how to find his hiding spot. She mentioned this to me in passing but I forgot about it as we settled into our first home together, our only home. Then one night she woke me and asked me to follow her downstairs. Her face glowed, eyes wide and she couldn't stand still. So long ago now and I remembered every detail.

"The chair," she'd said, though I was still half asleep, irritated but curious. "It's a clue."

"The old man with the bad teeth? Did you figure it out?"

A smile curled one side of her mouth while she lifted the front of one of the club chairs, tore off the Velcro fabric underneath and reached her hand upward. From that dark crevice she withdrew a key small enough to fit a padlock.

"Angus...do you realize what this is?"

Chapter 35

She was quizzing me. Of course I knew. We'd spent entire weekends looking for something that could lead us to an empty room or cubbyhole. God only knows what we'd find in there.

"Bring the chair into the fire," she'd said, repeating the old man's clue, mumbling all the while about her one meeting with him and his crooked front teeth.

"So, there must be a lock somewhere in the fireplace," I said, moving closer.

I pulled the key from her fingers and examined it, then ran my hand over the top surface of the mantel. It was solid marble, smooth, and even. Jess ran her hands down the sides, the beveled edges, even the granite on the floor. We never found anything that night, other than the key the old man had hidden under the chair.

I hadn't heard anymore thuds from the back of the house, which could mean my pursuer had gotten in, or maybe they'd gone. I should have gone to check but the power of that key was calling me. On all fours, I crawled to the chair and reached underneath, my fingers fumbling around the wood, nail heads, more fabric. There! Taped, like last time, to a piece of backing.

I sat in the chair with the key between my fingers. That clue the old man had given her—*chair to the fire*. Why that? It occurred to me to stand on the chair to get a different perspective of the fireplace. I climbed out of its thick cushions and stood behind it, then shoved it forward with my hip, hoping it wouldn't screech. A few more inches, three more shoves, and the foot of the chair was against the granite slab. Shoes still on for additional height, I stood on the seat looking down at the mantel, ran my hands over the smooth surfaces, imagining Jess behind me, eyes wide with excitement, but tonight it was me alone in a dark shell of a house looking for somebody else's secrets. Fitting, it seemed.

I stayed like that, gazing at marble and wood, listening for sounds of intrusion, wishing the mantel could somehow transform itself into a magical wardrobe or portal. I grabbed onto the cold edge about to jump down when I saw something I hadn't seen before—a gap. The backsplash attached to the mantel, forming a low L, was gaping about a half-inch, like you could stick a finger in there. This wasn't like the ninety-year-old house I grew up in, where there wasn't a single ninety-degree angle in the whole place. This house was built in 1970. Why would there be a space between the mantel and the back wall? Palms flat on the cold surface, I hoisted myself up an inch to see how long the gap was—no more than about seven inches. So, a six-inch marble backsplash to a fireplace mantel had a half-inch gap that was about seven inches long. I shined my iPhone light into the crevice, but it showed nothing. I pressed on it, pushing it forward to try to close the gap. And I heard something click. I glanced behind me as a reflex, seeing nothing but shadows and ghosts. In front of me was a part of the backsplash that had flipped down and lay flat against the mantel. And behind it, a piece of wood with a tiny lock in the center.

I fingered the chair key in the ring pocket of my jeans, when another sound pulled my attention to the back of the house. I closed up the backsplash, jumped off the chair, carefully moved it back to its original position, then made sure the Velcro underside was flattened the way I'd found it. Next, I checked out the front windows for the gray Lexus, but there was no sign of it. Two more thuds behind me, and now the Lexus was parking out front. Sounds out back, a car in front. What is this? Behind the curtains, I watched the same man in a gray suit and dark glasses exit the driver's side and walk slowly down the left side of the house.

The front door seemed as good an idea as any other, at this point. I closed the door behind me, locked it, and slipped across the front grass. It was soggy. Someone must have been watering it—maybe the property managers were showing up after all. I moved around the Lexus, which now looked more silver than gray, and tried the passenger door. Unlocked. I stood tall, breathed, opened the door and plopped into the passenger seat like I belonged there. With the door still wide, I pulled down the glove box. Would they really be stupid enough to keep the registration in here?

I looked down to quickly scan for a name or address: Jaspar Holding Company, LLC with an address in Texas, which reminded me I hadn't checked the license plate. I walked around back – California plates.

I felt brazen, secretly hoping the driver might come out and confront me. This change told me I was coming to the end of something, like pain. I didn't trust this confidence, though. Less than an hour ago under the willow trees across from Acosta's mansion, I could barely stand up. I was an emotional rollercoaster lately and this wasn't like me, not even broken-me. Dead wife aside, there had to be another explanation.

I wasn't sure if Anthony Acosta or his operatives were monitoring my movements or not. I closed the car door after snapping a photo of the registration and insurance card and walked my bike out of the driveway around the next corner to see into the back yard. Time to wait and watch.

I desperately needed coffee and felt just as desperate about using my chair key to unlock whatever was accessed through the fireplace. It still seemed preposterous that we'd never discovered this secret while actually living in the house. But right now my biggest priority was making sure no one else got access to that lock, and waiting till the house was empty to try again.

Two new epiphanies came to me sitting there waiting for operatives to finish ransacking my house: this is what Michael Wise and his operative had been looking for in the house—not the journal, and not the map—if there ever was a map. The other epiphany was that Jasper Holdings was likely the parent company of Anthony

CODEX

Acosta's Kroger Management Partners, and they'd likely killed WP. This also meant Jasper was likely a CIA front organization, probably run by Mendoza. Parent-subsidiary relationships in this country came with a lot of rules, which meant more research and no time to do it.

A flash of something at the back of the house drew my attention away from the front yard, some kind of reflection. Maybe they'd found a way in through the back door, and the metal screen reflected against the last bits of sunlight when they opened it. But that door always squeaked and I'd heard no such sound. No matter who was in the house, and for what reason, now was not the right time to use that secret key. But I needed to know who was in my house.

My bike was in full view on the side street cul-de-sac that connected with Elm Street. I climbed off and stooped low to move around to the backyard, still with its endless overgrown brush by the brick wall lining the rear property boundary. I could never keep up with that. Stay focused, I reminded myself moving over the slate pavers toward the back door. Sure enough, the screen was propped open with a rock, and the inside door was ajar. Looking in the windows gave me an instant view of the bottom floor, which showed no one inside. Upstairs was another matter. I would wait them out.

First, I moved around the right side of the structure, and peered between tree branches at the Lexus still parked in the same spot. Anthony Acosta had been here almost an hour now, and though I'd watched him leave the Acosta residence, his name was not on the car registration. Assumptions were dangerous. I'd stored some of Jessica's things in the detached garage. The door was still locked. What were they looking for, if it wasn't in the garage or the fireplace? Something in my gut told me Sylvan Mendoza had answers to the world's thorniest questions. Why not play the elimination game?

Chapter 36

Where are you right now? **I wrote.**

I tapped my thumb on the handlebars while I waited for Mendoza to psyche me out. Of course a guy like him had my number saved. He'd probably cloned my phone.

Don't pretend you don't know who this is, I added.

Salty. Wrong side of bed? That's right, you don't sleep in one, so I've been told. Looks like you've gone a full week without getting arrested. Nice work. He sent a photo of a cocktail glass with a white sand beach in the background. I lowered my sunglasses and ignored the jab.

Nice beach. How do I know you're there?

Another photo arrived, same background but with his face in the foreground, brows raised. Fine, it was him in some tropical paradise. I was deciding how to play it when his inevitable call came in. I let my phone ring three times before picking up.

"What's the matter, Angus?" he asked in a whiny tone.

"I can't really talk right—"

"No, of course you can't. You're at the wrong place at the wrong time and you call me when all of your other avenues are blocked. You should be with a priest confessing your sins."

CODEX

"Kind of the pot calling the kettle black." A large raptor, probably a hawk, screeched over my head. "I was trying to find out if you were in my house."

Pause. "I assume you mean San Carlos. Why?" He'd lowered his voice. I'd piqued his interest.

"Well, someone is, and it's not me."

I heard a woman's voice in the background.

"You gonna tell me where you are now?" I asked.

"Fiji, if you must know. Yes, darling," he whispered presumably to the woman. "Another would be lovely. Maybe another after that."

An old crook like him with an island princess. Way to be a stereotype. "Sorry to interrupt your little tryst."

"Oh it's no bother," he said, without hesitation. "And no, my companion is not my acrimonious wife. Question is, will you tell? Information, after all, is the most valuable commodity there is."

"I thought your wife left you. So problem solved, right?" What an evil thing to say. I didn't care.

"Quite so."

I'd heard all the conversation-as-currency shit while in the FBI's Intelligence Branch. None of that meant anything to me now. Sylvan Mendoza, distasteful as he was, could be a means to an end. I needed to know if he knew about the fireplace. I moved to the back of the property and sat on the ground on the other side of the brick wall, my bike ten steps behind me.

"There were two men in the house a little while ago," I lied. "I was watching from the back so I couldn't see. But I heard them."

"Heard what specifically?" he asked.

"Moving furniture, conversation. I heard it scraping the floors, and when I got into the room afterward, one of the living room chairs was pushed up against the fireplace." I paused there, wishing this was a video call so I could see his face. "Any idea what they could have been looking for?"

"In the fireplace? No idea," he answered, a little too quickly.

How could he not know? He was part of the whole Alice, TX investigation, and was probably the reason I got assigned to that case in the first place. Five, my secret contact, seemed to think Alice, TX was at the root of something, and Sylvan Mendoza was at the root of

Alice and whatever actually went down there. If Five was in contact with me today, I had to assume that whatever was going down here had something to do with that dusty little hick town.

"Go have a look around after they're gone."

I heard him slurping something through a straw, probably about to get laid. I should tell his wife. I just didn't care where he slept. But now Sylvan Mendoza thought he owed me something. And that made my day.

"I will." I waited, reading his thoughts through the phone line from five thousand miles away. He needed to know if I knew who had breached my house, and I needed to know if he knew about whatever secret my fireplace was holding. Our silence said everything. Oh, the games we play.

I drove off with the Lexus still parked out front. I wasn't getting anything today and I felt certain that whoever was inside didn't know what they were looking for. I could call the police and report a robbery, but that would just bring more police attention to me. There would be another time. I picked up 280 toward 92 and headed back to Half Moon Bay, hoping to see Officer Lopez before I met up with Dekker. Innocent or not, I didn't need another complication in my life right now, so my next meeting with Dekker needed to go well, or maybe just not be a disaster.

My phone rang as I crossed over the Crystal Springs Reservoir. I didn't use my handlebar mount for my phone anymore since it made it too easy to not watch the road, and one time it bounced off when I hit a pothole. So I did what I said I'd never do—picked up the call without viewing the caller first. I'd put earbuds on before I left and could answer with one button.

"Angus here."

"It's Nella. You on the road?"

Nigella. "Thank God." I exhaled. "Yeah, on my way home."

"Pull over and find someplace quiet," she said.

On the other side of Cañada Lake, Lifemark Road was coming up, which led to a funeral home further inland. I pulled off 92 and eased

CODEX

onto a shoulder where Lifemark intersected with Skylawn Drive. Motor off, I turned up the volume and exhaled again. "So glad to hear from you. Are you okay? Where are you?"

"Too many questions."

She was whispering. Bad sign.

"They're looking for a test lab."

I paused, making sure I'd heard her correctly. "A test lab? Where?"

"You were just there."

So Nigella knew I was in San Carlos monitoring the intruders. Jesus. "Did they find it?" I asked, stupidly, my thoughts spinning out of control.

"I don't think so. Not yet."

"Are you in danger?" Another stupid question. Of course she was, or why would she be whispering?

"In the trunk of a car. I can hear them talking, even right now."

All I could think of was Luther. God help me. "Are you crazy? Do you have air back there? Can you even breathe?" I tried to think of an intelligent line of questioning. "Do you have any idea whose car you're in, and any useful landmarks?"

"Michael Wise. It's not his car but he's here, a passenger. They're watching the guy who's in your house right now."

"Nella, can you get out of there?"

"Yeah, it's got a trunk release. I tried it when they stopped and I got out for a minute. I'll be fine."

I prayed I wouldn't have to answer to Luther about this.

Chapter 37

We agreed that I'd check back with Nella in an hour, via text, and that was only if she hadn't contacted me first. Was there actually any air in the back of a trunk, and for how long could an average human survive in that space? The thought made my breathing shallow and my heart race. My thoughts veered to the Half Moon Bay Brewery, not because of Jordan but because of the bar. Something in the core of my stomach lately had woken up from a long nap—that longing. For alcohol. Rudy had been my AA sponsor but that only worked if you actually went to meetings and consciously wanted to get well. I'd kept myself so busy, purposely frantic even, that I had no time to think about myself. Truth is, I felt like crap physically and looked even worse. Ignoring my needs all this time was taking its toll.

I checked my phone. It had been over an hour. I texted Nella, hoping she wasn't still in that trunk. *Just tell me yr breathing fresh air right now.*

I'm fine, stop worrying.

When I got back to the trailer, there was a text from Jordan inviting me to join her for a burger the next time I was in town. Why did I think there was some agenda attached to it? I pulled onto the gravel driveway and parked the bike under a few visible stars, sucking in a

CODEX

lungful of sea air, deciding whether I was more hungry or tired. Once my boots hit the gravel, my legs gave me their answer. I might even sleep in the bed again.

I stopped midway down Rudy's driveway to check for a text from Elaine, the person I most needed to hear from tonight. I copied my last text to her and re-sent it, knowing tomorrow would be enough time to file a missing person's report. What a thought.

"Hey."

The voice startled me. Officer Lopez. It was late and she was still in uniform, which shouldn't have surprised me. Almost too dark to see her, I made out the familiar shape of her face and her feet dangling off the platform where I slept. I don't know how I felt about that.

"Are you gonna tell me your first name now?" I asked, approaching slowly, though I already knew it was Regina. I guess it was more important to me for her to share it.

"Why do you care?"

The question had a tinge of irritation in it. "Louise," I ventured.

Her eyes closed. "I look like a Louise?"

"Madeleine."

"I like that name, but no."

"How about –"

"Regina. I go by Gina."

It suited her, too. Short, simple, no nonsense, with a nice ring to it.

"Before you go calling me Gina in front of Dekker, I'd advise you to –"

"Hold on," I said, my palms up. "Is this an official visit or unofficial?"

She crossed her arms, jaw set.

"I got your messages, or should I say threats, and I was planning to –"

"Threats?" Now she laughed for real. "I did not threaten you. They were warnings. Dekker wants to see you, and yes, if you must know, he did send me on this errand to make sure you were able to find your way to the station sometime tonight."

Tonight. It was already late. I wanted to invite her inside the trailer, my luxurious, shiny surfaces all going to waste. More than that, I wanted to sit down with her and repeat my million-dollar question about WP and see her face when I asked it. But that wasn't the vibe tonight. The vibe was us standing in the dark, barely able to see each other, posturing.

"Any chance you might tell me what was found in Wendell Peters' autopsy report?"

"No," she said, a little too quickly. "You know I can't do that."

"So an autopsy has been done then." I smiled, knowing I'd just trapped her. If I was truly still a suspect, she wasn't allowed to answer. I knew that.

"Look –"

"I asked you before, I left you two voicemails about it," I said.

"You know I can't share any details in an ongoing investigation. You, of all people should know."

"Okay." I stepped back, crossed my arms, and walked out to the edge of the dune overlooking the beach, remembering the man who was shot there two months ago.

"What I'm trying to figure out is why you care so much. I mean, of course if they found he wasn't a victim of homicide, that would exonerate you from any involvement. Is that the only reason?"

I walked back from the dune, a safe distance from her, still unsure of her motivations.

She moved toward me, sliding her hands into her pockets. The wind was up, always cold so close to the water. Stopping two feet away, she leaned her head down to scrutinize my face.

"What?"

"You don't think he's dead. Do you?" Her face lit up from her dubious epiphany, and I gave her nothing by way of confirmation. But I can't say I hadn't thought of it before. Maybe she was reading my thoughts. Maybe she was better at that than I was.

"I never said that."

"Mr. Mariner, it's cold and I was given a directive to bring you back to the station with me tonight. Let's go."

"I think I'm allowed an explanation of why you're bringing me in."

"Well, it's not because of Wendell Peters."

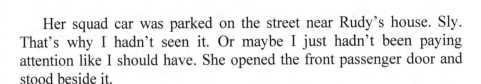

Her squad car was parked on the street near Rudy's house. Sly. That's why I hadn't seen it. Or maybe I just hadn't been paying attention like I should have. She opened the front passenger door and stood beside it.

"Front seat. Wouldn't a suspect usually be relegated to the back? Or should I just be happy you didn't cuff me?" I asked.

"Are you always this annoying?"

"Pretty much." My phone buzzed—Nella.

I'm out of the trunk and monitoring. Back to you soon.

Thank God. *Roger that.*

There was no talking as Officer Lopez took off down my street, driving past the Half Moon Bay police substation.

"What are you doing?"

"San Mateo," she clipped back in a controlled monotone, referring to the San Mateo Police Department.

It was on Franklin Street on the other side of Highway 92. If they were about to arrest me for the murder of Wendell Peters, Lopez would have been instructed and required to cuff me, Mirandize me, and chuck me in the back of her car. Besides, she'd told me it had nothing to do with him. I was in the front seat beside her, watching her stone face as she made her way over the reservoir. The water had been so blue today, the brush so green. This made no sense. I rolled down the window, startled by air too cool for mid-summer. She was getting off at Ralston Ave. Wait a minute. That was near Tower Road. Fuck.

Never any parking here, she managed to find one empty spot in the front lot just left of the main entrance to the San Mateo County Coroner's Office. Oh my God.

Coroner. I was here to identify a body. I curled my fingers over the door handle. I couldn't stop my mind from reverting back to Vera Madigan's shack and the look on Elaine's face when we heard someone else in the house. She'd known it was Miguel hunting her, I could feel it. She'd come back to the states supposedly for a family visit but was really running from her nemesis.

I half expected to see Dekker out front rubbing his palms together like an evil mastermind about to unleash terror upon the unsuspecting masses. But it wasn't Dekker waiting for us.

My stomach knotted when I saw Rudy, arms at his sides, face tight out front with the side of Dekker's head visible just inside the door. Were they smoking cigars together like Dekker said they did sometimes? Maybe, if not for the shaking in my core.

"What's the deal?" I asked Rudy, who held the door open for me and stood aside, leaving me facing Walt Dekker.

"Hey." Dekker looked at the floor. His hands were in his pockets. "Um, I asked Officer Lopez to bring you up here because we need you —" He paused and blinked a few times, drew in a breath. He honestly looked lost, like he'd forgotten where he started.

"What's going on here?" I asked, my gaze shooting from Dekker back to Rudy, then to Lopez who was just inside the doors avoiding my eyes.

"We need you to identify a body," Lopez said.

"Lopez! Really?" Dekker shot back, incensed. "Mr. Mariner, we received a report of a body found on the beach at the jetty early this afternoon. Mr. Richards, Rudy, came in to file a missing person's report, and he was there when we took the call." Dekker's voice was low and calm, no doubt from years of experience bringing tragic news to family members. I could hardly breathe. "As we haven't yet identified the body, Mr. Richards suggested you might be able to do so —specifically viewing two photographs."

Rudy? Why Rudy? My hands were sweating so much I had to wipe them on my pants. The viewing of bodies was nothing like what was depicted on TV, pathologists throwing back a sheet and family members wailing and fainting at the side of a gurney. It was all very clinical now, usually just photographs, and if the body itself was viewed, it was usually behind glass. While I watched their expressions, my chest heaved. I crouched and placed my palm flat on the cold, tile floor to steady myself, in some way comforted by the flecks of dirt and sand pressing into my skin.

"You think it's Elaine?" My voice cracked when I said her name. We'd talked about the missing person's report, Rudy and me. I just didn't think it was time yet, and I should have been the one to file it.

"Come on, buddy. We don't know anything yet." I felt Rudy's grip

CODEX

on the top of my shoulder. He wasn't pulling me up, but he didn't take his hand away either, like his care and support were not optional. "I'm right here."

Even if they didn't yet know anything conclusive, the body that was found must in some way meet the description of Elaine, or we wouldn't all be here right now. I shook off Rudy's grip and rose, standing away from him, from all of them, creating some breathing space. "I need information first."

"What do you need, Angus?" Dekker this time. For some reason, I liked him saying my first name.

"Where was the body found? In what condition, under what circumstances? Who called it in?" I watched Dekker and Lopez hold a tacit debate about confidentiality and compassion. No, not compassion —maybe just community service. That's what they were here for, right? No one answered my questions. I tried Rudy next. "Did you find her?" I asked him, my voice and knees still shaky.

Rudy shook his head and looked at Dekker. "Tell him," he said.

"Look, you know I can't reveal details on an open investiga—"

"Cut it out, Dekker!" Rudy snapped, the guttural boom of his voice echoing against the high ceiling. "How much loss do you think one man can take?"

"What are you all talking about?" The comment surprised me, a reminder of how close he and Elaine had become in recent years, and of the question always in the back of my mind—why?

Chapter 38

I nodded to Dekker and followed him and Lopez down the main hallway. We stopped at a set of glass doors. He went in first, turned on a light in the room, and opened one of the doors to invite me into the space.

"Does your sister have any identifying marks on her body?" he asked as he ushered me to a sofa, careful to use present tense.

"An angel tattoo behind her left ear. Small, you can barely see it."

He sat on the other end of the couch. "Could be helpful. Anything else?"

"Have you fingerprinted the body?" I asked.

"Of course. We're running them through the system, and you know as well as I do that can take a while. Any other means of identification you can think of?"

I closed my eyes to think back, regretting how I'd seen so little of her lately, scanning back over the years and decades for broken bones, surgeries. "Her ankle," I blurted, still deep in my head remembering the skateboard accident that left Elaine with a piece of rebar lodged in her lower calf. "She broke her ankle and was in a cast for like two months."

"How old was she, approximately?" Dekker asked, leaning

forward with his forearms on his knees, hands clasped in front of him.

"Eight or nine, I guess." Was. That was the only word my brain could process, almost like I was willing it to happen, the inevitable cycle coming around again, this time for another member of my family. He's coming. He might already be here.

Dekker stepped out and told me to wait. This substation seemed too small for a family viewing room like this, but nevertheless I was glad to sit on a comfortable couch. Soothing colors on the walls, pillows. Surprised they didn't have new-age music playing. I wondered, alone in that calming room, whether nice-Dekker was the real him, or if he really was the asshole he seemed and could be nice when needed. Jess used to say everyone had the potential for both. I resisted the urge to get up and find Rudy, knowing whatever happened to Elaine was her journey and her path and there was no sense blaming myself.

I checked my phone for another text from Nigella, but instead found a picture my new friend Five had sent with the text, *Do you feel pain or nausea when you see this photo?* The image was a close-up of a dark-haired businessman wearing a thick, metal band around his head with tiny screws in the sides. Taunting me, great timing. My God, it was happening again.

Dekker shuffled in quietly without his usual bluster and chose a seat on the very edge of the sofa. I could tell he wished there were a couple more chairs in here so he could keep his distance from me. I didn't mind; I'd feel that way too if I were him, if I were about to show me what his sweaty hands were gripping. He passed the folder to me without any words of instruction, caution, or apology. We both knew what this was about.

"Might not be her," Dekker said, his eyes on the floor. "She hasn't been missing for that long." Now he looked up. "I sure hope it isn't."

I managed a nod and fingered the edges of two photographs on slippery paper inside the closed file folder. I pulled the first one out, which showed a photograph of a blonde-haired woman with her head turned to the side. At some point I'd stopped breathing, or maybe stopped needing to breathe; I couldn't tell which. I knew that hair—the color, the highlight streaks she paid hundreds of dollars for and didn't need in the first place. I could see the hole where her pearl earring would have been, should have been. Where the fuck was it? The first of what would be a hundred little angers, I was sure. The next photo was as I suspected—a close-up of the spot behind her ear, showing the dark edges and wings of a dime-sized angel.

Some part of me was glad I wasn't in this room alone, yet I felt thoroughly disconnected from Dekker, from Rudy and Lopez waiting outside, and from any feelings about how my sister came to be here, in this station, in this condition. Here and now. It was surreal, even more so than the night I lost Jess. But our car had spun out of control and went off a cliff, and I was in and out of consciousness for the first day, with nothing more than a minor concussion. On that second day when I woke, I knew she was dead even behind closed eyes. Like the energy and vibration of the world, my world felt immediately altered and that was the only reasonable explanation.

"What time is it?" I asked, curiously.

Dekker stared at me, then wrinkled his brows to make sure he heard me correctly. He didn't answer, and I guess it didn't really matter, except that it was alarmingly quiet in here. I almost wanted to bang my shoe on the floor just to make sure I could hear something, anything. A person breathing, sneezing, a car's motor, dog barking. I started counting to keep track of the eerie silence. Maybe it was some kind of trick, or maybe I was the one who was dead, and Elaine was about to walk off that gurney, demand that someone deliver her clothes, ask for a cup of coffee and then tip her blonde head back and laugh, wide-mouthed, teeth showing, eyes squinted and looking up into the eyes of heaven.

"I'm gonna be sick."

"Right there." Dekker gestured to a door in the corner.

I managed to pull the door shut behind me and heaved into the toilet without even turning on the light. My reaction was as involuntary as sneezing, suddenly moving from that liquid stasis back to the raw ugliness of our profane world. Three more times I heaved into the toilet, hardly anything pulled from my stomach since I hadn't eaten in so long. How long? Had I even been paying attention lately to eating and drinking, sleeping? I brushed my teeth every day and took a shower every morning.

Still bent over the toilet, I thought back over the past two months,

CODEX

wiping my mouth with one of the three squares of toilet paper left on the almost empty roll. I'd been doing okay lately, post-accident. Making deliveries every few days for Rudy, volunteering with HMB Search and Rescue helping occasional hikers who got lost in the hills, daily rides on my bike, avoiding alcohol, smoking too many cigarettes, and avoiding thinking about it. On really bad days, Rudy let me sleep in one of the booths in the diner, the booth we were sitting in when I proposed to Jess. He called it my booth like he'd gifted it to me in honor of her. I hadn't done that in about six months, mostly sleeping in my sleeping bag on the ledge and more recently in the bed. I'd been sustaining—that's what I called it. Not necessarily dying inside anymore but not living either. I was sustaining myself while the stages of grief and loss bit thick chunks out of my soul.

Then, I met Wendell Peters one night in the parking lot of the brewery, the night I actually met Jordan Reid instead of just watching her, observing her from the patio. And my hapless but tolerable existence turned inside out. I felt Dekker's presence behind me. I flushed the toilet and washed my hands and face with some pump soap, unscented thank God, on the sink. I heard him pull four paper towels from the dispenser and he passed them to my right hand. I sopped up my face, then ran the water again to rinse out my mouth.

"You okay?" Dekker asked.

"Still standing."

Chapter 39

Dekker brought out two more sets of photographs, handed to him likely by a pathologist—white lab coat, booties, blue nitrile gloves. They all looked like different parts of Elaine, my confirmation of her identity still holding, even when we approached the gurney. No protective glass, a grief counselor stood beside me as a pathologist slowly lifted a small section of white sheet to show just the side of her head and face. My emotions were disengaged, like the detachment I used at crime scenes had automatically kicked in. Jessica hated this personality adaptation. She understood its usefulness to my career but didn't like when it made its way to our home and conflicts. My eyes were alert but my heart was unavailable. Elaine. Jesus.

After that, we sat in Dekker's office. Lopez brought me a cup of water, and next to it a mug of what smelled like fresh coffee. I knew I should drink both but doing anything normal right now seemed unthinkable, maybe even disrespectful. I was supposed to be broken right now, wasn't I?

Dekker sighed, open file in front of him, a pen and legal pad, ready to interrogate me.

"Let's get it over with," I said.

He shook his head. "I just need to ask when you last saw her."

I shrugged. "With you, the HMB PD, two days ago."

"Are you referring to—"

"Yeah, that," I cut in. "When you picked up Elaine and me from Rudy's diner under suspicion of breaking and entering. We didn't. The door was open."

"I know," he whispered. "It's still a breach, and I need to know what you were doing there, but for now, I want to ask you if you feel your sister was in any danger at that time."

I had two choices right now. I could tell him about Miguel and get him in their crosshairs as the prime suspect. The risk was that Miguel was slippery; he'd been in and out of jail since the age of twelve, and there was little chance Dekker with such a small, local police force would be able to track him down. I knew I could do it, maybe with the help of Michael Wise. I liked him, though I still didn't trust him yet. But right now I lacked the requisite mental fortitude needed for guile. Miguel showed up at Vera Madigan's house when Elaine and I were searching it. How had he known she'd be there, unless he followed her here from London? I knew I was the farthest thing from mission-readiness.

"You could say that, yes."

I honestly don't know what happened to time. The last thing I remembered was telling Dekker about Miguel—their tumultuous relationship, his history, the money he accused her of stealing. I woke up now and could see it was morning by how the sky looked, the position of the sun, the movement of the tides, the roar of rush hour traffic. I drank a cup, sometimes a pot, of coffee and then it was like somebody stole daylight. Low clouds huddled in the sky, hiding the sun, premature darkness covering the beach and the grassy dunes. What had I done all morning, all afternoon? Checked out is what. I had no memory of sleeping at night; I don't know where I went, or where I continued to go.

Rudy, in one of his moments of genius, had a lifesaving idea. He'd stay in the glitzy trailer and give me his house—for one week. I didn't even need to open the door if I didn't want to, and of course I didn't.

Complete seclusion. Absolute solitude, uninterrupted privacy from people – the pain on their faces and the way they looked for pain on mine. And he wouldn't tell anyone I was here.

For five days it worked. He didn't bother me, though for the life of me I couldn't imagine how a man his size could even move around that trailer, let alone sleep, shower, and cook. It was his gift to me. The gift of understanding. The gift of no questions and no demands. The first few nights he left a box of food outside the front door; I could smell it, but it stayed there untouched. I ate canned green beans at one point, always surprised by how a cook like him would have canned food in the house. God knows I wasn't expecting quality. A piece of toast, a browned, cut up apple in the fridge. Eventually I just gave up, not hungry anyway.

And then later came my gift to him: I rage-cleaned. Mornings were a blur, lying on top of the bed staring at a walnut dresser. But once that orange sun slipped into the horizon, some part of me—old, new, I don't know, woke up to a mission for tidiness. No joke—long, yellow rubber gloves, buckets of water, mops. I tried to be quiet about pulling the stove out from the wall, the dishwasher, cleaning the top of the fridge. Last night was all about grout. Toothbrush, baking soda, I was dripping with sweat. Maybe that was my way of grieving—letting it seep out of me one drop at a time.

One of the most freeing things about staying in Rudy's house was that I hadn't even looked at my phone. It was charged and available in case I needed help. My bike was gassed up outside. But I didn't want to feel like I was part of the world anymore, because the world would never feel the same way again, and that was what I couldn't bear. That was the old Jessica wound, but now, almost two years later, was even more painful. Not because I loved Elaine more than Jess but because I'd loved her longer. I'd loved my half-sister since the day I first met her.

Sometimes I'd check out for a while, then find myself fumbling with that tiny key still in the pocket of my wrinkled jeans—the key that opened a lock in our fireplace, a lock I hadn't installed. A lock that in my bones I knew had the potential to open something forbidden and answer every question I'd ever had.

I hadn't heard from Jordan, maybe because Rudy went to the

CODEX

brewery and told her. I think I'd gotten a text from Wise the day I identified Elaine's body, but I hadn't read it. The world would continue to spin even if I stepped off for a while.

Sometimes I heard Rudy on the phone in the trailer, at night when it was quiet with no traffic sounds, even over the roar of the surf. The word I heard him say over and over was *no*. I knew what it meant. Well-wishers wanting to see me, bring me cake, flowers, their company, share details of the memorial service that was inevitably being planned, or had it happened already? Yes, it's true. Rudy said I could stay a week, yet I'd been holed up here for more than two without setting foot outside. I was working through it in my own way. Sometimes I woke myself up talking or crying out in my sleep. In my head I was chasing Miguel around the storage area, like we'd found him, assuming he was the one who'd put a bullet in the side of Elaine's beautiful head, sullying her delicate, light blonde hair. Other nights it was about trying to find her missing earring. The brain, under duress like this, becomes fixated on odd things. A color, sound, for me that tiny pearl held on by sterling silver. The other one was still in her ear the day I came within an inch of her dead body.

Ear. I hadn't experienced that ear pain or sensation since I'd been holed up here, since Elaine's death, but that didn't mean I'd stopped thinking about it. I knew if I summoned the right image, like of someone wearing a metal head band, the sensation would return and some ancient part of my memory would reawaken.

Every few days a poisonous thought filled my head—an obsession with her autopsy. She was shot, a victim of a homicide, so of course they were uncovering all the forensic evidence they could to find her killer. Doing an autopsy would lead them to be able to conclusively determine her cause and manner of death from a legal perspective. I had the power, given my blood relationship to her, to demand an autopsy. What I couldn't stand about it was the way the medical examiner would cut her up—removing her organs, cracking her chest. It was nothing when watching it on TV, all the crime investigation shows deaden your sensitivity to it. But when it's a family member, it's barbaric and unthinkable, like the process would hurt and cause me physical pain.

All day today I could feel Jordan reaching out to me. Maybe she

203

was standing outside, crouching in the bushes and holding her hand on the window of Rudy's bedroom. We had some kind of shared destiny. I just didn't know what it meant yet. The cleaning started earlier than usual today – this morning right after coffee, this time tackling all the baseboards in the house. Wiping down walls, the fronts and backs of doors. My shoulders and upper back were killing me; I liked that. Pain was a familiar friend, maybe part of my karmic payback plan. Maybe the only thing keeping me alive right now.

At 2:30pm, I heard a knock at the front door. I knew the time because there was a clock on Rudy's stove. The black plastic and shiny glass sparkled. Ignoring the first few knocks, the next one came at the back door. God, people. No, I'm not ready. Rudy wouldn't do that, he'd just use his key. I moved to the back door and the floors creaked. Whoever was out there probably knew I was just inside the door, trying to disappear.

"Angus."

It wasn't a question, and I didn't recognize the voice. "Who are you?" I asked through the closed door.

"Five."

Chapter 40

July

Almost two weeks since my skin had touched fresh air.

I opened the door a crack and remembered, suddenly, the embezzlement case in Alice, Texas, putting away three guilty judges who simply vanished out of thin air. And I got blamed for that fact. The face that stared back at me wasn't the face of a federal judge, a legal pillar or even a fallen one. The gaunt, stubbled complexion had hollowed blue eyes and a wild mass of curly black hair that touched the collar of a faded jacket.

"What do you want?" I asked.

The man glanced behind him and kept his gaze on the water, almost like he hadn't noticed I lived on the sand dunes overlooking the bay. He turned finally, waiting for something. When I raised my brows, he raised his to challenge me, urging me to read his mind.

I nodded, found my leather jacket on one of the kitchen chairs, then paused to consider the vault key in my pocket. Not knowing where we were going, that key might not be safe. Rudy kept the key to his shed on a long string inside his back door. I left his shed key on the kitchen table and tied the vault key onto the string, then pulled it over my head. The metal felt cold on my bare chest. Here goes nothing.

Before I left, I texted Rudy that I was taking off and put the stove light on the way he kept it and another in the living room so it would feel welcoming when he got home from his ten-hour shift. Least I could do.

I wasn't sure if Five saw me get the key.

"No jacket," he said after I'd locked the door. What the hell? He jerked his head left and right. I checked his eyes for signs of drug use. He seemed twitchy.

"Seriously?"

"I brought you one," he said.

I re-opened Rudy's door and hung the jacket on his coat rack. The guy even drove a drug dealer's car parked on the shoulder. Tinted windows. Probably not a bad idea, all things considered. I climbed in the passenger side, Five monitoring the street and rear view.

"Put this on and climb into the backseat, passenger side."

He handed me a red baseball cap. I did what he asked, knowing somehow that whatever he had in mind was in the direction I most wanted to go—backwards. The past had answers. The future? Well, I'd already seen that, hadn't I? I watched him stick an Uber sign in the lower left of his windshield facing out, with an ID hanging from his rearview mirror, no doubt fake. I peered in to see the name—Jason Brixton. Yeah right. Good cover though.

"Thanks...Jason."

"Sensible precautions."

"Do I need to lay down on the seat or –"

He turned now and sighed, already showing signs of irritation. "Hat on, sit back there –" he pointed to my right– "strap in and look straight ahead. We're leaving."

The hat smelled like cigarette smoke, which reminded me that I'd managed to quit smoking. Maybe I wasn't dying inside after all. "Where are we going?"

"The source."

"Interesting piece of fiction on page eighteen," he said, pointing to

CODEX

a folded newspaper on the seat beside me. I opened the San Mateo Daily Journal and paged to the Obituaries.

"What do you know. Wendell Peters, scientist and businessman, died of a heart attack. Yeah right." I was sure that was the farthest thing from the truth.

I stayed quiet as he got on 280 South and exited at the San Jose Airport ramp. My eyes were half-open as we sped down the crowded freeway, the world passing in tiny fragments. The source? We were going to Texas. And there was no way Sylvan Mendoza wasn't behind this plan.

I said nothing but took notes on my phone—the time we left, even the license plate of this car, which I'd spotted walking out from Rudy's. Can never turn that shit off, can you? I checked the departing flights, assuming we were flying into either San Antonio or Corpus Christi. There was only one direct flight from San Jose, arriving in Houston. That had to be the plan. Well, maybe I had a plan, too.

I'd seen his eyes looking out the rearview three times in the past five minutes. "Are we being tailed?" I asked.

"Don't turn your head back."

I let out a heavy sigh.

"Sorry, didn't mean to insult your intelligence. Or maybe diminish your years of experience."

"Are you a tweaker?" I asked, staring at the large eyes in the mirror, uncaring of the disrespect I'd just shown and glad I woke him up. "I'd just maybe like to know that up front."

He scratched his right cheek and shook his head. More twitching. "Sleep."

"What about it?"

"I can't sleep. It makes me jumpy. Drugs are the last thing I need."

He veered into the San Jose Mineta International Airport long-term lot and, after parking, he turned back to hand me a ticket and a folded suit jacket.

I peered at the name on the ticket. "David Dunn." For God's sake. He handed me a California Driver's License that showed a guy with dark hair but no other resemblance to me, bearing the same name. "What are we doing?"

"Not we. You. I'll be there but we're not traveling together. I'll be

207

in the last row by the restroom."

I sat back and crossed my arms. "I don't think so."

"Look, you –"

"No, you look! I need an explanation of what the fuck is going on here. Now!"

He recoiled against the seat. We let the awkward silence envelop us.

"Who are you hiding from?" I asked.

I watched the man turn his head but only slightly. He seemed lost somewhere, but so was I. My mind returned to Vera Madigan's porch, the know-it-all look on her face, like of course I should know as much as she did. The Primes; she said there were four of them but one died or escaped. Why that word though? Why not say left or ran off? Escaped had a different connotation to it, like these primes were being kept against their will. One, five, seven, thirteen, and she said seven was gone. I kept one eye on Five as my brain sifted through the rubble, shaking out extraneous matter to see what truth was left.

Three primes, and something to do with Alice, Texas. Those three subjects, or patients, had to have something to do with the three judges I'd tried to take down in that embezzlement case.

Twelve years ago, I could still remember their names. Lockhart, Drumm, and Sykes. Drumm was African American, Lockhart was old, much older than the tweaker. Five, my mystery driver, was white and probably forty, forty-five at most. Could he be one of them? He certainly didn't present himself as a legislative pillar.

"Are you Sykes?" I asked. "Judge Sykes?"

I saw it, his head jerked to the right but he caught it, then shrugged and rubbed his chin.

"Come on man, cut it out. You're Judge Arlo Sykes of the Second District Court in Texas. I saw you. I saw your arrest. I watched the –"

The man's head jerked toward me now, his face streaked with tears. "Let's go."

I hadn't noticed that the ticket was first class. Seemed so wasteful, I almost felt ashamed nestling into row three next to what looked like

CODEX

an eighteen-year-old guy. Who had the money at that age, okay any age, for a first-class ticket? Trust fund baby, celebrity, professional athlete? The speculation felt like a mental rest from the heavy background programs that had been running in my head. Sure, sweating from obsessive cleaning was great exercise, but it was still avoidance. I missed Rudy's house. The ordered universe of its walled structure, the silence, the image of his jackets hanging on the coat rack inside the door.

Five told me not to look toward the back of the plane at all; he was very specific. The whole routine felt ridiculous, but I complied because of the tacit promise of an answer somewhere, sometime. Strapped into my seat, there was no going back now. Since the accident, I'd committed to nothing. No routine, no relationships or community ties, not even a commitment to myself. My body felt exhausted, malnourished and underslept. If I was ever going to commit to something, it had to be now. This was my opportunity to connect the past with the future.

I pulled the laptop out of the backpack Sykes gave me, held it on my lap while I crammed the bag under the seat in front of me. He'd texted a link to my phone, which he instructed me to email to myself and open it when we got high enough to turn on Wi-Fi, which was usually about ten thousand feet. No one took the seat to my left so I stored the laptop there after we took off and I zoned out. The punk to my right pulled the shade all the way down so there was no view of the clouds, which to me was the best part about flying. The drone of the engine and the clink of silverware in the row in front of me were the white noise I needed. The announcement came—electronic devices could be used and free Wi-Fi was now available. Time for some answers.

Chapter 41

The link he sent was to a site called Telegram. I'd used it before—a chat app like Google Hangouts. We used it at the Bureau during investigations processing. It offered end-to-end encryption, which provided another layer of security to prevent unlawful intrusion by third parties. What made it a favorite among the intelligence community, though, was the auto-delete of conversations after a designated period of time. I'd emailed myself the link from my phone before we took off and double-clicked the icon on the desktop. The app opened quickly, which meant a fast processor—nice. My opinion of Sykes was a little higher now. I used the login credentials he instructed, then searched through his list of Telegram contacts and selected one called Bridgit96, which was presumably his alias. Funny. I opened the contact, scrolled down to the default silhouette image and clicked Start Secret Chat.

Hey, I wrote to start us off.

Took you long enough.

I didn't care that he was an asshole. He was a means to an end. *I have about a hundred questions.*

We've got just under three hours, he wrote.

You're Arlo Sykes, former federal district judge. Confirm or deny?

CODEX

I counted to ten, twenty, of course it was him. *Confirm.*
Where are the others? Drumm and Lockhart?
Another pause. *Irrelevant.*
Where's number four?
Not four. Seven.
I meant the fourth prime, but he anticipated my next question. Let's say Drumm was one, Sykes I knew was five, Lockhart had to be thirteen, and there was a missing number seven somewhere. *Where's Seven?*
Longer pause this time. *They told us dead, but we don't think so.* *What do you think?*
How the fuck should I know? I liked how he used the word we. That implied that he was still in contact with Drumm and Lockhart, which might be why he wouldn't tell me their locations. For some reason, this made the whole odyssey feel a tiny bit safer. So he, Drumm, and Lockhart were working together, and the mysterious number seven escaped. That's a start.

The strange feeling I'd been getting in my ear started again, maybe because of the change in air pressure in the cabin. I sat back and stretched my neck and rotated my jaw. It didn't help. The guy next to me was snoring so I raised the window shade and at least had that as a diversion. Now the pain seemed like it started in my head but radiated into my ear. Was that even possible? I'd never had issues flying before. When the flight attendant approached, I ordered a Coke and opened the tray table on the empty seat beside me, then returned to the screen. The missing number seven. I scanned through our conversation so far to make sure I hadn't missed anything.

The plane jolted hard in an up down motion, and then a few times left and right, like someone was shaking it like a ragdoll. The laptop slid down to my ankles and half of the Coke shot out of the plastic cup onto the aisle. I knew what was coming.

"Ladies and gentlemen, we've hit a patch of rough air and until we can get around it I'm gonna put the seatbelt sign back on and ask you to stow tray tables and electronics for the next few minutes. Flight attendants will be by shortly to pick up any cups. Appreciate your cooperation."

211

So much for my hundred questions. He'd answered three or four, but at least now I knew who I was traveling with.

I checked the time—two hours left. I wasn't waiting that long.

The plane was still shaking in the same unsettling movements. I unclicked my seat belt and moved to the back of the plane, toward one of the three restrooms. A smile crept across my lips as I saw an empty seat beside Sykes. That meant the occupant was either in the restroom or the seat was empty. I caught his toxic glare as I approached, breaking whatever code he'd tried to bind me to, and stood before the two restrooms—both empty. I hovered in the aisle looking down at Sykes and a flight attendant approached.

"Sir, I'm sorry but you'll have to—"

"Apologies," I said. "I've just noticed that my brother's on this flight and has an empty seat next to him. Any issues with my sitting back here for a while?"

She eyed both of us and apparently we passed her initial scrutiny. "That's fine. Please put your seat belt on."

By now the plane had assumed a jagged up and down motion like we were caught in some sort of amusement park ride. I scanned the tense faces around us, white knuckles gripping the armrests, two babies crying, heads turned and eyes wide looking for comfort and reassurance. Sykes' mouth had contracted into a tiny dot, eyes staring straight ahead, and he didn't offer to move to let me in. Fine. I stepped over his legs and strapped into the window seat beside him.

"Who's they?" I asked in a normal voice, keeping the momentum of our conversation.

While waiting for him to answer, I watched two practiced flight attendants walk down the aisle with white, plastic bags looking for drink glasses. Their faces looked calm and friendly, hoping to de-escalate the terrified vibe in the cabin a few clicks. It wasn't working. Sykes closed his eyes and crossed his arms. I needed a Plan B.

Rapport-building 101: mirroring, also called matching. Now, there's casual rapport-building anyone can use to avoid looking awkward at cocktail parties. The bureau's and CIA's version is based on behavioral science all for the ultimate goal of extracting information from an interrogation witness. Sykes was, essentially, my interrogation subject and I had very little time left to get vital

CODEX

information from him—about me, about WP, and about Jess.

The matching technique, as I'd been taught by Sylvan Mendoza, only worked until the subject made you. Once they noticed the matching body language, words, or synchronous movements, it was all over and hopefully by then you'd gotten what you needed and it didn't matter. I sat back, crossed my arms, and turned my head to the left.

"The way I see it," I said, "if by some miracle this plane stays in the air, we need to entertain each other somehow."

I don't know what Sykes inferred from that comment, but his eyes popped open. "We can't talk here, it's not safe."

"My dad—"

"What?"

"My dad," I said, "used to take us on camping trips every summer to Yosemite and every single time, one of us came back with the strangest injury." I was talking too loud on purpose.

Sykes closed his eyes and sighed.

"A bat bit me on the scalp while I was sleeping one time. I didn't even realize I was bleeding until the next morning—"

"Fine."

"Wait, I haven't gotten to the story about my friend who wasn't allowed in our tent so he peed around the entire perimeter—"

Now he turned and stared, begging me with his eyes to shut the fuck up. The plane's movements stabilized as suddenly as the turbulence had appeared. So odd. The seatbelt sign turned off. I rose, waiting for Sykes to move and hovered there in his way, waiting.

"Take your laptop out," I said.

Back in my seat, I opened the loaner he'd given me and waited.

I'd just like to remind you that you came to me, I wrote.

Noted.

What do you want from me?

Not want—need, he wrote. That word added a layer of complexity I hadn't considered—leverage.

I'm listening.

You're gonna help us find something.

Ignoring the assumption of my cooperation for now, I started from the bottom. *Who's us?*

You know who. We've been talking about them.

He meant The Primes. *You and the other two?*

Three. There were four of us, remember?

I remembered. I guess I just wasn't sure I believed any of this yet. I knew he wouldn't tell me, not here, why they needed my help. But how was I supposed to have any knowledge that three federal judges didn't have themselves? I turned the conversation in a different direction.

What do you remember?

About what? he asked.

All of it. What I wanted to know was the truth about why they were held, where it happened, what they endured and the purpose behind it. As to the question of its connection with the embezzlement case, that would have to wait. *If it's too hard to talk about,* I wrote, *forget it.*

I can't tell you.

I suspected as much.

Another quake of shifting air rattled the plane left to right, then again two seconds later. I looked at my watch. We should be preparing for our descent soon. I kept an eye on the chat thread and had the sense Sykes was deciding something.

I can't tell you what I can't remember.

Chapter 42

I don't know if it was the sudden jolts on our descent or something else, but a nauseous dizziness flooded through me. I was ten steps from the first-class restroom in the front of the plane but there was no way I could walk right now. I heard a high-pitched pinging in my ear —faint but I could still hear it, and a sensation of pressure covered the back of my head. I reached up to touch it and it felt normal. My stomach gurgled the whole way down, the plane twisting and shaking through high winds and dark clouds. The final bounce when we hit the ground came with a loud roar from the reverse engines. It made my ear throb, the same ear as the high-pitched sound. I told Sykes about it when he got up to my row.

"Well, there's no hospital here so we'd better move."

I could tell he was trying to sound snide, standoffish even, but his eyes showed empathy. He knew what I was experiencing and why. I wish I did. We followed the mass to baggage claim, then to the rental car corridor. We stopped at Hertz, where I collapsed in a chair in the corner of the large space. Sykes stopped to appraise me.

"Go get the car, I'm staying here." More staring, or maybe he was waiting to see if I'd pass out. "Look man, I don't feel well."

"I heard you the first time," he said, and moved toward the

counter.

I willed myself to get up so I could get some fresh air, playing on Sykes' separation anxiety. It was warm out – humid. A muscle car with a broken muffler drove past. What was I doing here?

We didn't speak on the way to the car, out of the airport, or for the next thirty minutes. A sign showed that Alice was fourteen miles away.

"You gonna tell me where we're going?" I asked, finally.

"No."

"So it's a secret?"

"You're gonna tell me."

I suppressed the urge to laugh when a low, intermittent pressure started in the lower left side of my head. I wondered if it was jaw or tooth related. I hadn't been to the dentist in two years. "What the fuck does that mean?"

Sykes turned to me, glared for a second, then looked back at the dark, empty road.

"Hey, I want some answers," I said, a little too loud, my voice gritty, all out of composure. "You said 'the source' at my house. What does that mean?"

He turned right at a light where we were greeted by a "Welcome to Alice" sign that I recognized. Sykes watched me every few seconds, turning to look at my face, my eyes, for a sign. Yes, I recognized the wide streets, and knew we should turn left at the next light. How could this be? He got in the left lane, clicked on his turn signal, and looked back at me for confirmation. I nodded. Another two miles down this road and I knew he would turn right at a stop sign, which took us over the railroad tracks to the other side of town, the industrial side. I rolled down the window and let the night air fill the car. A deep breath did nothing for my ear pain but it did calm my stomach.

"Where?" he asked.

"Look, I don't know where we're going. I was here twelve years ago for like three days and –"

That garnered a frantic glance, his eyes were wide, bushy eyebrows rising toward his hairline.

"What, now you're gonna tell me I wasn't here for three days?"

"Not three days, no."

CODEX

"For fuck's sake. Well, you tell me, then. Where the fuck are we going, and why was I –" Something caught in my throat, emotion maybe. My chest felt warm and my nose started running. I sniffed and wiped it on my sleeve, fucking Sykes nodding beside me in his scruffy hair and dirty jacket. I cleared my throat and would have done anything for a cold bottle of water right now. Deep breath. "Left here, then two rights, and we'll go down a long dirt road for two miles. I don't remember being here before but yet tonight, in the dark, I seem to know the way."

I asked him why a few more times, but I could tell he'd told me everything he was going to for now.

The dirt road forked, with one side edging some thick woods. "Left," I said. "I know how to get there but not where we're going. How do you explain that?"

"That's the way it works," he said.

"What? The way what works?"

His mouth was closed, jaw set, eyes on the path with nothing but more dirt on each side of us. The sky was at that eerie precipice of dawn, the darkest part of night lined in stillness, almost stasis. Not even crickets.

Sykes slowed the engine and parked down the street from a wooden shack that looked surprisingly like Vera Madigan's house— the one I'd visited with Jordan and again with Elaine. That felt like another lifetime. Our headlights illuminated the front porch, with rough cut posts exactly like Vera's, positioned in exactly the same way. This had to be WP's secret laboratory. But how could it be? He developed highly sophisticated technological equipment, which meant he'd need a larger space than this, not to mention climate control, an IT network and sophisticated infrastructure. I wasn't sure we were even in Alice anymore; it was so off the grid. So, it had to be air-gapped without internet access, yet my phone showed a full signal, with three different networks available. Why would there be cell phone towers when there were no homes out here?

"What are you doing?" Sykes asked, annoyed.

I went through the list of available networks, all named by a

217

random collection of numbers and lett – Wait a minute. I looked up at him.

"What?" Sykes leaned in toward my phone.

I recognized the name of one of the networks: Ba-Vi. This was one of the codes Michael Wise reported to me, and something I'd found in Jessica's paperwork at the San Carlos house. I assumed that might be the name of WP's hearing aid device. This had to be the lab. But where was it?

I set my phone on the dash and took off my seat belt. "Why was I able to find this place and you weren't? Aren't you from here? From Texas? You were a judge in this county."

He turned on the motor to roll down the window, then turned it off again and sat silently staring at the odometer in a silent vigil. He exhaled slowly. "It works as a sort of homing device."

"What does?"

Now he turned in the seat to face me, his eyes peering over my left ear. It didn't seem possible, but when he looked at my ear, it started hurting again, slow at first, a dull ache that felt more like it came from deep inside my skull than the ear itself.

"Do you hear the noise, too?" he asked, his voice low and careful. "The tinny sound that sometimes turns into a high pitched *eee*?"

Oh my God, I felt sick. I thrust open the door and aimed my mouth toward the dirt but nothing came out except saliva. My eyes teared up the way they do when you throw up. The tears filled my eyes when I sat straight again, one foot still on the ground. It seemed fitting in a way—half inside, half outside of this car, of my life, the universe. "Oh God." This time I turned and got fully out and vomited on a pile of leaves, which made the most horrific splatter sound. Yes, I'd experienced that noise he described. The pain, the metal sound. What the fuck was going on?

"You've started remembering things too. Haven't you?"

The guy on the hill outside the police station with some kind of metal band on his head made me sick to look at him. Not sure if it had been a dream now, I also remembered something about being in a room with three other people, three men all at different stations, chairs connected to some kind of medical infrastructure.

I stood outside the car on some matted pine needles, my hand

CODEX

gripping the edge of the hood for balance. Sykes got out and walked to the rear of the car, then circled to the driver's side. He did this same litany three times, then went back further toward the road we'd driven from.

"Dude, what's the matter with you?"

He lowered his head. "No more," he said. "We need to shut it down. No more!"

"No more what?" I asked. "You're not –"

"There's no time left. We could've made it out of here but not now. They're coming."

His forehead was slick with sweat. "Who?"

He smiled with his mouth closed, eyes looking up, finger pointed at the top of the house. "Cameras. An elaborate recording system, audio and visual for anyone who comes on the compound."

This was a compound? I tried not to laugh.

"What," he seemed to read my thoughts. "You think this is just some abandoned shack in the middle of the woods?"

I watched Sykes' thick brows knit together as I considered his question. It did look like he described, abandoned, unassuming, the final vestige of someone's broken dream. It would have to be, wouldn't it? I nodded and moved to the front of the car, my eyes scanning for cameras positioned up high, but nothing was in immediate view.

"Don't forget the elaborate alarm system," he said.

"You're joking, right?"

His eyes were wild, his head bobbed out of a thrust of sudden energy or emotion. Something was happening to him here, just like something had been happening to me.

"How did you see this alarm system?" I asked, intending to keep his mind occupied on questions while I scoped out the place.

More blinking, like he was fighting some inner negotiation. "Same as you. When we were here before."

"I told you, I've never been here." My voice sounded more insistent now, a truth as solid as my own name, but now in this moment feeling somehow flimsy, like maybe I had been here before and just couldn't remember. Was that possible? "Are you saying –"

"I'm not saying anything. I don't need to." His long, curly hair had folded over his left eye. The other bore through my last inch of composure.

I felt a shaking start in my chest and hands. Was I having a heart attack?

"You already know."

CODEX

Chapter 43

I still had no conscious memory of this place but I was assuming, for argument's sake, that Sykes' unspoken theory was that I had actually been here, possibly several times, and at the same times as him. Was this theory likely? No. Was it possible?

"How many times have you been here?" I asked, emphasis on the you.

"Dozens. I don't know exactly. They memory-wipe us after each session and drug us in transit. That's why I never knew how to get here."

I ignored the word they for the moment. "You've tried?"

He nodded once. "You can find it, though," he argued.

"Why would I even know how to get here, let alone be able to find it if you can't?"

His eyes were wet now, and not from the sweat dripping from his forehead. This man was grieving, as if the secret poison of a caged truth had been released and was coursing through his veins, emerging through his pores.

"Because you escaped, didn't you?"

He reached up and wiped his eyes with the side of his hand, took a moment to steady himself. "It was just the three of us at first," he explained, in a more composed voice. He'd moved to the porch and collapsed on the bottom step, uncaring it seemed for the recording devices on the premises, if they actually existed. "They kept us here, somewhere," he added roving his finger around, "for three months during a recess in the court schedules. None of us were married. Nobody noticed our absences."

"All single. Maybe that's why they chose you," I said.

"You came later, and only a few times. They always had trouble sedating you. You had a lot of questions, even after being injected."

"Why the fuck can't I remember?"

It was a rhetorical question fueled by frustration. I understood about memory wipe drugs. We'd been trained at the bureau, and they were used and sanctioned in specific circumstances. Even so, it was like listening to him talk about somebody else. Half of me thought he was deranged and paranoid, the other half growing more certain every minute of the truth my mind was failing to reject.

"You found a way out. And you left us here, like lab rats."

Everything started spinning, like waking up too fast with a bad hangover. True or not, I felt an instantaneous stab in the center of my gut like I'd been pierced with something sharp. Then the vibration started again as if on some sort of timer. I held my warm palm over my ear, like that could somehow salve the wound these people had inflicted upon me.

He stood up on wobbly legs and took three steps toward me, both of us flanking each side of the rental car about twelve feet from the rickety porch. "You found this place, this compound, because of their homing device. Now you're gonna find the secret lab, Seven." There was an edge to his tone now; something had changed. "And together we're gonna shut it all down."

I had no specific reaction to hearing him call me Seven, though at this point in our surreal conversation, I had already surmised his theory. One was Judge Drumm. Sykes was Five. I was Seven, and Judge Lockhart had to be Thirteen. It was a theory so far that lacked any evidence so I would treat it as such.

CODEX

We moved around the left side of the house; he led, I followed. There were a few cars parked on the shoulder of the unpaved road, no landscaping, only dry mesquite native to the South Texas plains. It must have rained recently because the air smelled sweet, like sage. The back porch on the property had four steps and a regular, wooden door with a flimsy screen on the outside, just like you'd expect in this part of Texas, or any other backwoods hick town. Sykes stood aside and tipped his head toward the door. I tried the handle, locked.

"Is there a secret chant or something you suggest? An Elvish riddle?" I had no idea if Sykes liked *Lord of the Rings* or even had the capacity to process a quip like that right now.

"Don't be an ass, I didn't choose this. And neither did you."

"Fine." I took a step back, leaned on my left leg, bent low and kicked the doorjamb. Again. And on the third time the door separated from the frame, wood shards all over the porch.

We scrambled into the house, starting with the kitchen and turned left down a hallway. I remembered the layout from Vera Madigan's shack, set up exactly the same way. We moved to the back bedroom. Something in the center of my heart felt warm, a pain, a new pain, as I remembered being there with Elaine. And now, because of this…this place whatever it was, she was dead. Maybe for the same reason as Jessica. But there was no time to indulge in guilt right now. Whatever inclination Sykes had that they were coming had been transferred to me. I knew it like a tickle in my bones.

"Help me," I said.

We pulled the four-poster bed over toward the dresser. I crawled on the floor, lifting the rug and the rug pad, placing my palm on it to gauge the temperature. Same as Vera's house. The floor under the bed was cold.

"What?" he asked.

"Feel it."

He did. "It's cold. It must be under here, because it was always cold in there. I do remember that."

"I'll check here for an access point. Go outside and see if there's a crawl space. Text me if you see anything."

He paused at the door because he didn't want to be out there alone. How did I know that? I was reading his thoughts, though I hadn't been able to do that before. Were our minds connected because of some invisible force running through this house, or via technology we somehow shared? What kind of fucking sci-fi movie had I stumbled into? If I was indeed the missing number Seven of WP's control group, and if we had both been embedded with his cochlear implant, could our proximity to each other in this place allow us to read each other's thoughts? I willed myself to stay focused on something concrete and attainable. WP maintained a secret laboratory in Alice, Texas and in his mother's house outside of Half Moon Bay, obviously to test his device on unwilling subjects. Like Sykes, and myself. My God.

I heard Sykes fumbling around under the house; my job was finding access up here. Still, I couldn't help but wonder if I could communicate something to him and make him respond without speaking. I closed my eyes, placed both palms on the cold floor, and thought, *Can you hear me?*

Right away my phone buzzed in my pocket. Jesus, seriously? *Yes*, he texted back.

I froze, dropping the phone on the floor like it was on fire. I exhaled slowly, taking a moment to process this. The logical part of my brain concluded that if what just happened really did happen, it could only be possible if my brain was in some way linked to Sykes' brain by way of the technology buried under the floor of this room.

And inside our heads.

I had to get to that lab.

My iPhone flashlight lit up the floor so I could move the bed further away from the wall. I held it out in front of me, gliding the beam across the wood in long lines right to left. My well-trained eyes squinted for any sign of a mismatched wood grain pattern, scuff, chip, or any other sign that this wasn't just a forgotten patch of flooring under a guest room bed. But my mind was somewhere else.

The vault key.

I could almost hear the words emerging from deep inside my head. The fireplace backsplash in the San Carlos house was tile—expensive Talavera tile, and some of the most beautiful ceramic I'd ever seen. This was wood and looked like red oak as opposed to laminate

CODEX

flooring. Come on Angus, think! Could WP have been the one to install the secret vault in San Carlos and, if so, could he have constructed the same access here?

I still heard movement beneath me, but there was no time to inform Sykes of my new plan—not even via telepathy. They were coming. Now I felt it too, though I had no idea who 'they' could be yet. With the flashlight on, I balanced the phone against one of the legs of the bed, where I crouched on hands and knees. Using the same method as the fireplace in my house, I pressed down on the floor with both hands every twelve inches, then decided that was too large an area and tried every six inches. No anomalies so far. I kept going in long rows, then remembered what I'd seen in San Carlos—a separation in the mantel backsplash when I looked down on it.

I rose and aimed the flashlight straight down to check for any gaps that might shine through to the lower level, then I moved to the outer edge by the wall. With my left cheek on the wood and my body stretched out, I looked across to the other end. Something. I couldn't tell if it was darker or lighter than the rest of the wood, but something only visible from that angle didn't match up. I crawled in front of the bed to the halfway mark, confirmed the cool temperature of the floor, and started pressing again, this time inch by inch. Nothing. Dammit!

There's a car pulling up, Sykes typed as a text message.

I wasn't moving. I know my eyes hadn't deceived me. But the pressure on the wood wasn't working. How was—wait. When I raised my gaze a few inches from the floor up to the wall at the head of the bed, a part of the tacky, vintage wallpaper was torn in one spot—and only one spot—just above the baseboard. The rest of it looked fine, so that probably wasn't by accident. I shined the flashlight beam from my phone into the hole and saw a metal disc inside that resembled a small watch or coin battery. A button.

I pressed it and held it a moment like on the fireplace mantel. Suddenly a spring popped in a section of wood floor, pushing up, raising it an inch above the rest of the surface. I pressed the raised wood and, like in my fireplace, the top angled down, revealing a tiny…silver…lock.

Chapter 44

"Are you in here?" It was Sykes talking through the open window. Talking with his own voice, I smiled to myself at the distinction.

"Down here," I said.

"What the fuck are you doing? The car has driven past the house twice now."

"I found it," I mumbled, my fingers grasping the tiny key Jessica and I had found hidden beneath a chair in our San Carlos house. I saw her now, the moment slowed to half speed, me blinking my eyes, scrolling through an image of her sultry hair, the laughing eyes that could switch from hot to cold in an instant. I feared those eyes many times, feared I'd say the wrong thing and chill her heart, or accidentally push her away like I'd done so many times before. I leaned up and looked at Sykes.

His eyes were glued to my hands. "Do it," he said.

I leaned low to line up the key with the lock, still not certain it would even fit. I wiggled it up and down a few times. Finally, the teeth caught the metal so I pushed and twisted it to the left, waiting. It was the sound I heard before any movement, a low-pitched bonggggg that reverberated against whatever lay below. Sykes had climbed in through the window and was standing behind me.

CODEX

"Holy shit, look out!" He pointed to the floor. It was moving, sliding back toward the dresser at the foot of the bed, revealing a bluish light from the floor below. I stepped two paces to the left, gazing down into a cavernous space where a ladder led to the bottom fifteen steps.

I rose and stood beside Sykes, who was death-gripping the windowsill. "Are you okay?" I asked him, pulling the key out of the lock and pulling the twine back over my head.

"You fucking found it," he whispered. "I knew you would."

"But you're too late, Angus, aren't you?" The voice came from the hallway as Sylvan Mendoza's bald head and tall forehead emerged into view. "Well," he said. "You saved me from getting my favorite pants dirty at least." His right hand rose, holding what looked like a Sig P320 compact pistol, resting on his chest. "Let's go, gentlemen."

Sykes sniffed behind me, his face wet with sudden tears, his face reddened with rage. His hands were shaking. "You," he said, moving away from me and toward Mendoza.

"Dude, chill. Stay over here, right next to me."

"Yes, Mr. Sykes, do as Angus says. He's always so sensible."

I wasn't buying into Mendoza's bullshit. Needling remarks like that were his trademark, a way of feigning confidence and showing superiority over his adversaries. He'd tried to teach me that trick, but it wasn't in my nature to be so theatrical, and frankly it just wasted time. My ear was ringing and throbbing. I reached up to touch it and actually felt a vibration coming from inside my head. Poor Sykes was unglued from the sight of Mendoza. Despite my compromised state, I'd need to act fast. Not sure if it was even possible to get us out of here now, my goal was to not die in this forsaken place.

"Let's go, Mr. Sykes, nice and easy now. You first, please." Mendoza flicked the wrist of his gunned hand, watching us closely.

"So you can use us like lab rats again, performing your secret experiments?" Sykes had lost it, eyes wild and his voice a high, raspy shriek. "You've got one of the side effects." Sykes pointed to my ear. He was right. I nodded. "What about the other ones?"

No one moved. I had no idea what he meant.

"Oh, you didn't know about those?" Sykes moved ahead of me toward the stairs with Mendoza behind me.

Mendoza shook his head. "Wendell Peters has assured me and the entire medical community that there are no side effects from the use of his device."

"The others had them," Sykes said just to me. "Drumm, Lockhart, they both did. Hallucinations, auditory hallucinations, panic attacks, pinging, aching pain."

Mendoza's head moved left and right. "That's obviously some artifact of your specific physiology. It's got nothing to do with –"

I watched as Sykes' composure unraveled, hands formed into fists. Mendoza stood stone-cold frozen with his gun still in hand like an extension of his body. How many lives had he ended with that thing? I was standing on the threshold of the subterranean lab but with easy access to the open window. I could do it—I could jump through, fall onto the porch, and have a twenty-percent chance of escaping. I didn't move though, stuck in the sudden realization that this was what Jessica found in her research into WP's company. It all came into perfect view. She discovered, probably accidentally, the harmful side effects that WP tried to cover up by faking clinical trials, all grounds for losing his medical license, any chance of FDA approval for his device and the official partnership and funding from Mendoza's company.

"Mind control," I said. "Is that what this is about?"

"Isn't everything?" Mendoza's lips stretched, but not into a smile. It was more like a snake opening its mouth preparing to feed. "Manipulation, coercion techniques, social conditioning. It's all the same at the end of the day."

"Why, though?" I kept my eyes on Sykes, who was closest to the opening in the floor.

"Gaining strategic advantage, of course." Mendoza said it like it was obvious.

"Why is that so important?" I asked. I was stalling and Mendoza knew it. I wasn't sure how much longer he'd indulge me. Sykes and I were still close enough to the window for one of us to make it out of here alive.

"You can make people do things by either indirect influence or force. But the trick, the real coup, you see, is creating the illusion that they're deciding it for themselves."

"Sinister."

CODEX

"It's hardly new," he answered me. "The CIA's MK Ultra, DARPA, Project Pandora. There are many government-funded projects still in use today that not only read but write to the brain."

"Through implants like, like –" I struggled with the word, until Mendoza pointed at my head, and then Sykes.

"Like what's inside your head?" Single nod. "AR, VR, well it's just a matter of time." Mendoza was in lecture mode now.

"To what end, though? To use an oculus to implant commands into someone's brain?"

He put up his palm. "Look, it's not directly under my purview so I'm just speculating here but let me just say that there's extraordinary government interest in BCI technologies."

BCI had to be Brain Computer Interface. "I still don't understand why," I said. "To make more Jason Bournes to kill terrorists? Why destroy a human brain and manufacture one when it's cheaper to just pay an assassin?"

Long sigh, yet his hand hadn't moved from the gun he still clutched to his chest. "Intelligence assets on the payroll are risky business." He almost whined as he said it. "It might look seamless on TV but believe me it's messy and resource-intensive."

I was rapt listening to his claims, while Sykes changed positions every five seconds. He was about to lose it.

"So, when Dr. Peters came to us with a proposal to –"

"Wait. What?" I asked.

Mendoza shrugged. "Remote control. That's the safest way to control someone's thoughts and behavior. You no longer risk the exposure of labs and headsets and monitoring equipment with an implant."

"You bastard!" Sykes shrieked and lunged across the open threshold in the floor at Mendoza, who stepped backward two paces allowing Sykes to fall onto the stairs. He tumbled down and landed in a heap at the bottom.

Mendoza flicked his wrist. "Let's go. Now."

Mendoza closed up the stairs so we were trapped down there. But the vault key was around my neck under my shirt, and if it opened the lab once, I had to believe it could do it again.

Time passed at a different speed than normal. He must have injected us with something because my limbs felt like lead. Sykes and I were seated in two different stations in the lab. Pretending to still be out, I slitted my eyes to see Sykes' wrists clamped to the chair. Mine weren't. I heard Mendoza's shoes on the tiled floor walking around, preparing something, talking all the while about mind control. Who the fuck was he talking to?

"You're awake. Good," he said to me, peering cautiously at Sykes, whose eyes were closed.

"You said the words *expanding global interests*. Whose?"

"Well, ours of course. The government is always looking for new technologies and things to invest in, to boost our global defensive posture."

"By cultivating an army of counterintelligence assets?"

He shook his head. "You're thinking too small, Angus. Can't you see the potential here? You're smart, you could help us, join the mission." The snake-smile again. I maintained my blank stare. "Reading thoughts can be useful in criminal profiling, interrogating foreign adversaries; it's a fortuitous channel open to program people to do whatever you need them to do to advance a certain cause. Change the program, change the behavior."

"I think what you mean is you're weaponizing Wendell Peters' cochlear implants to use against enemies, or to sell to the highest bidder. Leverage, right?"

"Leverage indeed."

He wore no lab coat, no gloves. The Mendozas of the world weren't attending physicians; they were the security squad forcing commands with a single nod, the holding up of one finger, like a king deciding with his thumb whether someone lived or died. He typed on a laptop on the other side of the room.

"Sykes," I whispered.

He didn't answer. I was able to pull my phone from my pants pocket and balance it on my right knee. It didn't seem like Mendoza could see that from where he sat but I wouldn't assume anything at

CODEX

this point. After turning off the volume, I texted *SOS* to Michael Wise. Ridiculous, asking him for backup from thousands of miles away. But I couldn't bear to worry Rudy.

Roger that, Wise wrote back after ten seconds. Thank God. Typing no more than five words at a time to avoid detection, I told him the rough location of the house and its proximity to the Corpus Christi airport. The longer I stayed in this lab, the vibration and buzzing my ear seemed to increase in intensity, but the pain from the device itself seemed barely noticeable now. Maybe I was getting used to it. Or maybe I was getting better at numbing myself. Was this a good thing?

Mendoza got up to check on Sykes. I moved my phone under my right thigh and leaned my head on the edge of the chair back, eyes half shut. Why weren't my wrists clamped? He didn't even glance at me as he walked past, and not because he was preoccupied with his plans for Sykes. I suspected he knew I was plotting my escape. He was letting me do it, letting me dig my own grave. I thought he'd planned to use me again. Otherwise, why not just kill me? Moving to the laptop, he carried it to a console behind Sykes' station, took a long sip of water, and cleared his throat.

"Gate," he said in an affected voice, a louder, clearer voice. He had his back to me now, so I typed that word to Wise, asking if it meant anything to him.

Gate? Mean anything?

I've seen that referenced in the journal. Looking...

He said it as a command, I typed.

Keep going, transcribe what he says. I have the journal in front of me.

The irony - how I hated his access to Jessica's journal and how that might save my life.

"Freesia," Mendoza said. I texted it to Wise.

"Yes sir, good morning sir," Sykes replied in a mechanical voice, suddenly wide awake. I saw his eyes open, and fluttering. Oh my God, this was it. My heart rate tripled. Jesus.

"Are you ready to work today?" Mendoza asked him.

"Ready sir."

"Good. Let's begin." Mendoza sat back and rubbed his palms on his pants. He was about to command Sykes to kill me.

Chapter 45

While Mendoza managed the details of my assassination, I captured most of the exchange for Michael Wise. I wanted to take still photos and a video of the room, but they'd necessitate lifting my phone and Mendoza glanced back intermittently. When the time came to defend myself, I'd identified my weapon of choice: a large, hard-bound, metal binder from which he'd been reading the commands. Sure enough, I saw the letters Ba-Vi on the front cover. Fitting, wasn't it, that this would be the object I'd grasp to ram into the back of Mendoza's skull? Poetic, almost. I'd counted on the fact that he was six-foot-three and about three-hundred pounds. If I hit him at the correct angle using the binder's hard spine, that would help enhance the collision when his weight hit the floor. It all seemed too easy though. I'd been able to time my texting and movements to only when his back was turned, and so far I hadn't made any noise. If he knew what I was doing, there had to be a reason why he was letting it happen. It had to be a trap, but I had little time. Minutes now, maybe seconds.

He was still seated at the control station behind Sykes's chair, his gun holstered on his left hip now. Unsnapped, which was noteworthy because guys like him didn't make careless errors. Gun first seemed

CODEX

the best approach. I waited till he spoke commands again into the microphone, then I stood, took two steps forward and reached with my right hand. I grabbed the gun from his holster and jammed it into the back of my waist, and leaned right to pick up the binder from the table. I didn't turn towards Mendoza because I didn't have to. He was looming behind me about to attack. I raised the binder, and with a half-turn rammed the spine of it onto the left side of his head. The thrust of the blow shoved him into Sykes, where he bounced awkwardly then slid to the floor. Sykes hadn't moved, still staring at the wall in front of him. I checked Mendoza, unmoved on the floor, no blood visible so far.

I dialed Wise's number and ran around Mendoza's body to get to Sykes. "Sykes, can you hear me? It's Angus."

His eyes fluttered. He angled his head up and looked toward my face but wasn't able to meet my gaze. I looked down at his wrist restraints. They'd been taken off, no doubt so he could get up from the chair and kill me. When had those restraints come off?

"Hey," Wise picked up finally. "What's your status?"

"I've incapacitated Mendoza."

"Permanently I hope?" he asked.

I checked him again, body pressed to the floor, head down, still no visible blood, breathing shallow. "Temporarily, I guess."

"His gun?"

"Got it."

"Well what are you waiting for?" he asked.

"I'm not a goddamned killer!"

"Fine, but he might leave you no choice."

Now it was me wearing the snake-smile. "I'm gonna have Sykes do it instead."

"Hopefully it works. And for the record, I think that means you *are* a killer."

I moved to Mendoza's laptop. Thank God the machine hadn't gone into sleep mode, so it didn't require a password to access it, for the moment. I held the phone with one hand, the other used the mouse to scan through the folders on the computer desktop. He already had the file open and positioned to the right place. Mendoza was immobile but

I wasn't stupid. I moved quickly around the room looking for something to bind his hands. This wasn't the type of lab that would have things like rope or twine, and no closets. I checked drawers searching for anything that looked like Plasticuffs, even shipping tape. Nothing. I had on a leather belt but that wouldn't work. Shit.

"Okay, you still there?" I asked Wise.

"Closer than you think."

No idea what that meant, but somehow it felt comforting. "I'm gonna speak into the mic and use the exact sequence Mendoza used but end it with a new directive. Any suggestions?"

"Yeah, have a contingency plan if it doesn't work."

It was a good idea, but I was fresh out of plans.

"Sykes, can you hear me?" I said into the mic. No response. Time to use the script. "Freesia," I said.

"Yes, sir. Good morning, sir," Sykes replied. Chilling.

"Are you ready to work today?"

"Ready, sir."

"Good. Let's begin." I paused but I shouldn't have. Deep breath. "Viral effect."

"Yes, sir."

It worked. "Mr. Sykes, I'd like you to kill Mr. Mendoza using his gun, then come back to your station and be seated." I pulled the gun out of my pants and held it in my left hand. "I'm holding the gun in my left hand. Turn your head please. Do you see it?"

Sykes turned his head and looked at my hand. "Yes, sir."

"Can you do that?" It felt surreal to be asking, but I knew it was the only way to arouse Sykes from his controlled state.

"Yes, sir."

I watched Sykes rise from the chair with the energy of a teenager. He moved back toward me and picked up the gun from my hand. Without making eye contact with me, he held the gun at his side then walked away from me and back to Mendoza on the floor. Wait. Mendoza's body was in a different position now. Fuck. And his pant leg was pulled up, showing an empty ankle holster.

"Sykes! Look out –"

Mendoza rolled to one side and shot twice. One bullet rocketed over Sykes' head and the other hit him in the middle of his forehead.

Mendoza struggled to a standing position and wobbled on his feet. Sykes fell back onto the floor. I watched his blood and brains instantly pool under his head. I wanted to throw up.

"Hey, what happened?"

The phone, I'd forgotten about it. I reported the events to Wise.

"Dude, get out of there, now."

"I'm not leaving him here to use more people as lab rats and ruin more lives."

Mendoza's eyes were bloodshot, mouth open and panting like a crazed animal.

I bent low and rammed my head into Mendoza's waist, toppling him to the ground where his head hit the leg of a file cabinet. Perfect, that was two head injuries now. One of the overhead lights buzzed; something smelled like chemicals. Mendoza's eyes were closed. I was able to kick his sidearm out of his hand, then ran to Sykes and picked up Mendoza's pistol.

"Okay, I've got both guns," I said into the phone, out of breath.

"Killing him seem more palatable now?" Wise asked.

"I've got a better idea." I hung up.

I kicked the soles of Mendoza's shoes, enjoying how he flinched each time I did it. Ram. Ram. Left. Right. His cavernous eyes fluttered. He grunted out a moan, the moan of a man too old for getting his ass kicked but never too old for the kicking itself.

"Get up," I said, his own gun aimed down at his belly. No one wanted to die of a gut shot. It was a painful, slow, terrible death. He deserved nothing less.

I watched him raise his head an inch and gaze at the gun, then start to move. With two hands on the file cabinet that had injured him, he hoisted himself up again.

"Over there." I motioned him with the gun to Sykes' station, positioned him in the chair with his arms under the metal straps, then I clamped them down. My initial plan for him included injecting him with the same serum he'd used on Sykes, then administering an identical verbal protocol to prepare his mind for a command of my choosing. But that process could only work with the cochlear implant installed. Right now, he was barely awake and not going anywhere. Then again, I'd made that mistake once before.

I found a wooden panel over the keypad in the corner of the room that looked just like the wood panel concealed within my fireplace surround in San Carlos. I pressed and it rose up to reveal a small lock. I inserted the vault key and the floor opened up. I climbed the stairs, pretending for a moment that my new friend, Judge Arlo Sykes, wasn't lying dead in a pool of his own blood below me. Sykes, Jesus.

I remembered, only now, the image of red gasoline cans under the porch. The dirt road was quiet, no sounds, no traffic. The cans felt like they were about one quarter full—would probably be enough. I hoisted them up and carried them in both hands back through the house, into the bedroom, and back down the metal stairs into Mendoza's den of despair. Now his own.

What's happening? Wise texted. He'd sent me images from Jessica's journal while I was out getting the gasoline. I put the phone back in my pocket without responding, and moved to where Mendoza's wrists were strapped to the chair. I released the clamps and he pulled them up, rubbing them thoughtfully, cradling them. He seemed more alert now, probably wondering where I'd gone. Blood had dripped down one side of his head.

"Pour gasoline around the perimeter, then on yourself," I said calmly, looking straight into the eyes of the man I knew was responsible for Jessica's death, probably WP's, and untold other deaths, no telling how many of them happened in this very room. I felt no joy, no remorse, no nothing. A means to an end. I couldn't let anyone else be harmed by this weaponized technology. I set the gas cans at his feet and held the gun up to his belly again. "Do it."

He rose from the chair and snatched the gasoline can from my fingers, jabbing me in the waist with the metal spout. I recoiled, losing a step but quickly recovered. His hands tried to grip the gun but it kept slipping and fell to the floor. I grabbed it, watching his eyes widen to large, bloodshot globes. He reached his hands toward my neck, but I thrust my shoulders down and escaped. He wasn't going down easy. I knew one more blow to the head and that would be it. The gun wouldn't be heavy enough to do it.

CODEX

But the gas can would.

He got the idea even before I did, his arms folding around the bottom of the can. The gasoline sloshed inside it. The smell burned my eyes but I kept my attention on the gun still in my hand, the other gun tucked into the back of my jeans, and the open staircase leading out of this goddamn tomb. I wanted to move Sykes body out of the lab, but I'd never be able to pull him up the stairs. I could order Mendoza to drag him, but I wanted Mendoza down here. Besides, at this point I'd never get him back in that chair without shooting him first. I watched his face, barely recognizable now, contorted into a shape of desperation, knowing it seemed that these were his last moments on earth. With the gun trained on him, I let him shuffle to the other side of the lab trying to get to a cabinet where he no doubt kept emergency armaments. Probably for situations like this. Meanwhile I emptied gasoline over the perimeter of the room.

"Angus," he moaned, his hands fumbling with something inside a dark cabinet. "Angus! You never understood the bigger picture." His voice was strange. He obviously still had some of his faculties. "Don't —you—realize –"

"What I realize," I cut in while dumping gasoline closer and closer to where he was standing, "is that there's a lot of paper in this room."

I lit a match, dropped it and ran, a gun in each hand. I heard a whoosh as the gasoline pattern erupted in flames. I tore through the space speeding to the stairs, my heart aching at the image of Sykes and his crumpled body. A soldier, a casualty of war. All I heard was Mendoza's wail of "No!" behind me as my vault key plunged into the tiny lock in the bedroom upstairs, the lab doors closing under my feet. No escape this time.

One lab down, one to go.

Chapter 46

While I drove the rental car away from the smoldering house, Wise texted me a photo of a Welcome to Corpus Christi freeway sign. So that's what he meant. He must have been leaving Dallas at the time. What was he doing here?

I thought about booking two flights from Corpus Christi to San Francisco. No. It was too traceable. No doubt Mendoza's team would come looking for him and would tail us back west. Unless of course he'd alienated all his allies and had no more favors to cash in. Then he'd just die down there alone, the stain of his dark soul vanishing by the second. One could only hope.

I agreed to meet Wise at the Coastal Bend Bar and Grill. Typing the address on Waze while keeping Sykes' car on the road properly gave my traumatized brain something to do, distracting me from shock. It was at the Corpus Christi airport, which wasn't a great idea other than the plain sight advantage. I did short-term parking and followed the directions on my phone, then ordered food before Wise got there. I hadn't eaten in a few days so anything would taste like prime rib right now. I did my best to keep my mind focused on concrete things like that – food, hydration, and breathing while another part of me struggled to keep my hands from shaking. I thought about texting Rudy, or maybe Nella, but they'd no doubt ask me what happened and I wasn't ready for that question yet. Could it have all really gone down like that within the span of two or three hours? I'd walked into that house with one man, we were both attacked by another man, and I was the only one who walked out. It still seemed too fantastic a story.

"You're bleeding."
I looked up from my half-eaten burger and saw Michael Wise, hands dug low in his pockets, a deep groove between his eyebrows.
"Either that or you have ketchup on your face."
"Probably both," I said. "Is it smart to be visible here?"
"A burger joint," he said. "Who'd look for us here?"
"Have a seat." I downed a few more sips of soda. "Are you eating?"
"No, we're driving."
"You can't eat and drive in Texas?" I asked.
"Do you have a car?"
"Yeah, Sykes' car…in the lot." Obviously, my instincts about flying were on point. "Waze shows a 27-hour trip. That's what you had in mind? I'm exhausted just thinking about it."
He leaned in. "Eleven hours to Albuquerque. We can fly from there to LA, and then drive north."
Drive, fly, drive. Not a bad plan, really.

He got food to go and ate while I drove the first leg north to San Antonio, reciting the timeline of what happened in the lab. I was talking fast, and nonstop since we got in the car. Must be a coping mechanism.
"How'd you get in the lab?" he asked, again locking me in a moment of human trust. I hadn't yet shared with him anything about the vault key. He'd flown all the way here. So, he'd earned my trust, at least some of it.
"A key," I said. "The same key Jessica and I found in our house in San Carlos."

"Where?" he stopped chewing. "Like hidden somewhere?"

I felt wary of his question, finally slowing down long enough to ask myself why he was conveniently in the area. Was it to save me? Or did he have another motive?

"It fit the lock," I said, without answering him.

"Amazing."

"Why?"

"Well, there's no mention of it anywhere in the journals." He watched my face. "I brought them for you, by the way. All of them."

"How many are there?"

"A stack. They're yours," he said, with his hands in surrender-pose, like that would somehow appease me.

"I can't help but wonder what you're really doing here, and how you even knew about this place. Alice, I supposed that was in Jess's journal too?"

He took another bite of food and let my question hang in the air.

"Look, I appreciate seeing a friendly face, especially now, but you flew a long way across the country."

"Always gotta have an ulterior motive, eh? How do you know I wasn't already here?" He wiped his mouth, stowed the food bag on the floor and reached into the interior pocket of his jacket, bringing out two folded documents.

"What's that?" I asked.

"Been tracking Mendoza for a long time."

"Tracking?" I laughed. "He's a goddamned spy. You don't track guys like him."

"I'd been studying his past, his career path so to speak. I wanted to see the connection between him and Wendell Peters."

"Okay. And?"

"Peters published a paper fifteen years ago about his revolutionary new cochlear implant device." He unfolded one of the sheets.

I swear the mere mention of it made my left ear throb. I suppressed the urge to touch it.

"He wrote about the benefits, the applications of it, the specific technology because he's an ear nose and throat doctor –"

"Was."

"The paper mentioned he submitted the idea to the patent office for

CODEX

a patent filing." He paused and grabbed the food bag from the floor again.

I let out a heavy sigh. "Look, we've got a long drive ahead of us. Is that supposed to mean something? A patent filing for a technological invention. What about it?"

"The CIA is very interested in patent filings because they profit from safeguarding intellectual property. But they also recruit potential new technology investment projects through patent filings."

I exhaled. "The CIA owns the US Patent Office? That's a new one to me. Let me guess, this is all in Jess' journal," I said, not caring how it sounded either.

"Not owns, not officially. But there are channels open there certainly. She had a whole journal devoted just to Mendoza."

"Jesus." I felt like stopping the car. "How did she know him? I mean, her firm was conducting pre-merger due diligence investigating Mendoza's firm. But I think it's probably more than that."

He nodded, fumbling with the crumpled bag in his hands. "She outlined the turn of events. Mendoza's company, Jaspar Holdings, read WP's paper. Mendoza's team arranged an opportunity for them to meet accidentally at a cocktail party. WP mentioned he was looking for funders, and Mendoza said his firm was seeking high-tech cutting-edge investment opportunities. They agreed to a funding plan in exchange for Mendoza getting to control a portion of the strategic direction of the device's development."

"I know what that sounds like."

"Exactly," he went on. "And you'll read this in the journals. She believed Mendoza demanded they take the technology in a different direction, broadening it beyond just the hearing impaired. And not just applying it to mind control either."

"Weaponized mind control." I felt sick hearing the words come out of my mouth, the image of Sykes' body on the floor of that lab.

We each zoned out for a while on the brown flatness surrounding us, the drone of the engine, and a striking blue sky.

"What's the other document?" I asked, breaking the silence.

"Well, like I said, I'd been studying Mendoza for a while, long before Jessica ever came to me to publicize what she'd found about the side effects of WP's implant."

"Why?"

He looked out the side window. "I needed proof for a theory I've had. The CIA's been involved in mind control research and experimentation since they were first formed in 1947."

"Even before that," I added, having read about it while I was with the Bureau. "The preceding organization, OSS." The Office of Strategic Services during World War II. "So, what's your theory?"

"My unproven theory was that the MK Ultra mind control program run by the CIA," he paused, "was never shut down."

"Well, it would have had to be underground, and then where did their funding come from?"

"Mendoza's company…well, his other company, is called BA-Vi, spelled BA –"

"That's not the name I thought. But yeah, I've seen it on documents. I wondered if maybe it was the name of WP's implant. How many principles are in that company?"

"Not many," he said, "a handful maybe. But you're right, they'll no doubt come looking for him, and when they don't find him, they'll be looking for you."

"Okay," I said, following along. "Now I know your theory. What's the document? Is that your proof, and where did you get it?"

Wise unfolded the sheet. "It's his ROTC application."

"ROTC? Whose—Mendoza's? That's a long time ago."

"Irrelevant."

"Are you sure it's his?" I suspected these details came from the Freedom of Information Act website, which made all kinds of juicy nuggets publicly available.

"Got it from a friend of a friend, a favor. It's his." He paused to let me catch up.

"I'm guessing the name Sylvan Mendoza isn't on that form."

He grinned. "That's the most interesting part. Sylvan Gottlieb. Mendoza was his Basque mother's name. He took that to keep his famous, or I should say infamous, family name detached from his work."

"Who's Gottlieb?"

"Sidney Gottlieb ran the MK Ultra Project."

Oh my God. "And Mendoza was his son."

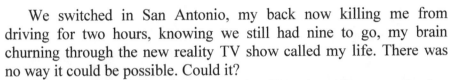

We switched in San Antonio, my back now killing me from driving for two hours, knowing we still had nine to go, my brain churning through the new reality TV show called my life. There was no way it could be possible. Could it?

We talked about all the reasons the CIA, the military, and other government agencies were so interested in mind control as a means of expanding global interests and superiority over foreign adversaries. The government was always seeking out new technologies, and mind control had always been a hot area of research, interest, and investment. The military looked at everything as a means to boost our defensive posture, probably with the hope of cultivating an army of secret counterintelligence assets.

I was still deciding whether I thought Wendell Peters was blameless in all this, inventing a new type of hearing aid that, through his collaboration, turned into a weaponized form of mind control. Did WP have a sinister agenda when he started, and was Mendoza simply the highest bidder? The more I thought about it, the more I felt WP was an entrepreneur who wanted to make money and get his name in print as an innovator and technological leader. Maybe he didn't intend, originally anyway, to harm anyone. But what about the horrendous side effects Jessica uncovered? He didn't stop producing his devices. What happened to those control group subjects? How many casualties were there, how many fatalities?

Wise was a fast driver but knew how to keep control of the car. I liked being a passenger finally, letting the trauma of the day drain into the heartland landscape sliding past my periphery. I breathed in, breathed out, and took stock of my broken body. I'd survived the death of my wife, and the death of my sister. But I'd survived Sylvan Mendoza and made it through this horrendous day. Maybe I could make it through another.

But I still had that fucking implant in my brain. One thing at a time, right?

Chapter 47

"What?" Wise asked out of nowhere, his voice jarring in the silence. "I didn't say anything." I'd been dozing in the passenger seat. I opened my eyes to a dry, flat landscape. Brownfield, Texas, the sign said. I looked it up on my phone, southeast of Lubbock and due east Roswell, New Mexico.

"You mumbled something about a helicopter."

I didn't think I'd mumbled anything, but I had been thinking about the helicopter. "I've been wondering about the relevance of the helicopter in this whole mess."

"Why he gave it to you, you mean?" he asked.

"Maybe he was trying to draw me in and that was the safest way to do it. He knew what they'd done to me, to all of us, and probably presumed I had no memory of it."

"Assuming he never wanted his implant to be weaponized."

"Right, and by then he was already in too deep with Mendoza and knew they were gonna dispose of him at some point. Knowledge makes you a liability."

"The helicopter's an interesting part of their operation," he said.

I rubbed my face and sat tall, willing my brain to wake up.

"Mendoza's company, as well as the slice of the intelligence community interested in mind control, has a historical challenge of finding available subjects. Typically, expendables are the safest bet because they won't be easily missed. The mentally ill, drug abusers, prostitutes."

I considered this. "Hence the strategic importance of Alice's proximity to the border."

"Exactly," he said. "It's about thirty miles."

"And you took my last turn driving."

"You were sleeping. Slacker."

He didn't grin when he said it but I caught the friendly vibe. "So the Mexican border is an hour's drive from Alice, even less in a helicopter."

He nodded. "Keep going."

"Well, I was just thinking if Mendoza's team was using immigrants at the border, that would be one way to have a steady stream of available experimentation subjects."

I knew Wise probably understood the scam they were running. I tried to pull all the strings together, despite the fact that my body hurt literally everywhere right now. I'd been a trained investigator, a sworn law enforcement officer with the FBI. Was I still that same person, with those same investigative capabilities? Maybe enough time had passed. Maybe necessity had woken it up.

"Good theory," he said.

"I don't think that's it. ICE," I said out of nowhere. Of course.

"Very good, detective."

"I think Mendoza – son of a bitch I can't believe I'm even saying this out loud, was grabbing detainees from ICE detention centers and using them as experimentation subjects." I took out my phone and brought up the map I'd been looking at earlier. "There are two detention centers on the way down to Reynosa." I watched his face. "Getting warm?"

"I've suspected Mendoza might have an office somewhere down there, maybe at or near the detention facility. Maybe his team, as you call them, is pretending to have some law enforcement jurisdiction down there, or maybe he's just formed an alliance with some of the ICE ERO guys."

"ERO?" I asked.

Wise shook his head. "Enforcement and Removal Operations."

"Makes it sound like pest control. 1945 all over again."

"Think about it," he said. "If Mendoza's a spy, and I know nowadays that's become a pretty broad term, alliance-building is really their most important skill. Maybe he's befriended a deportation officer with the ERO who believes Mendoza's team is providing some sort of punishment or negative conditioning that could help with ICE's interrogations."

I leaned into the passenger door with my head on the window, trying to disappear into the monotonous plains. "Why us?" I asked, not expecting a real answer. "The three judges and me?"

Wise shrugged. "Who knows? You were down there, you specifically, and you were available, plus you had a connection to Mendoza, so he knew you."

"Yeah, maybe. But what about the three judges? Not exactly the same demographic as ICE detainees." I realized it after I said it. "Maybe that was the point?"

"That's what I was thinking," he nodded. "Maybe they wanted to try their experiments on different types of people with different levels of intelligence, education, not to mention psychological profiles and personality types. The more diverse their experiments, the more chance of getting accurate data on which to make predictions. You said those judges were embezzlers. So, despite their career success, that gave them more interesting character traits to study, and exploit."

Even if we could confirm what Mendoza was doing at the border, it still didn't directly answer the question of why WP had given me his helicopter. Was it to bring me into the fold; was he seeking my help to get out from under Mendoza's control?

En route to the Albuquerque International Airport Hertz location, I'd used my phone to book us two tickets on Southwest to LA, where we'd pick up another rental car to drive north to San Francisco.

Wise turned every so often to keep an eye on me. When I caught him, he'd quickly look out the front passenger window like he was viewing scenery. He was hiding something; I could feel it. We were five miles from the airport rental car drop-off location now.

"What are you not telling me?" I asked finally. "It's something important."

CODEX

He nodded. "I'm sorry. Trying to find the right words."

"The truth, that's all I want. That's all I ever want from anyone. And so rarely get it."

We'd arrived at the rental car drop-off. Wise angled the sedan in the designated lane and snaked around a maze of cars and SUVs in an underground lot. He followed the hand movements of a uniformed woman, who directed us to park in spot 5C. I stared at him after clicking out of my seat belt.

"We'll talk when we get to the gate."

I watched him get out, grab a small pack from the backseat and start walking toward the Terminal A elevators. I couldn't tell if he was stalling or if my question was just bad timing, but my nerves were shot to hell. Anticipation buzzed in my palms in the elevator. Once we got to the main terminal, it was ten minutes of walking, twenty minutes in the security line and another ten minutes towards the gate. Wise seemed to be almost running, though we had plenty of time to kill before even pre-boarding.

I'd read about this airport in an airline magazine article once. It really did look like an art museum, with glass displays of Native American artifacts every twenty steps and amazing murals. But the beauty of RC Gorman paintings or native Kachina dolls didn't quell the shadows in my heart.

I kept my eyes on the back of Wise's head, about five travelers in front of me, a head that kept turning back every minute or so. Funny that we were walking all this time before I realized it wasn't me he was looking back at, and there was a reason he was walking so fast. Would it be too obvious for me to look back now to see if we were being tailed? I needed a reflection point, glass, clear plastic, something to see behind me without turning my head. My phone buzzed with an odd vibration pattern. I pulled it from my pocket and saw it was a text and a voicemail—from Rudy. Damn, I'd do anything to hear his voice right now. Keeping step, I checked the text first, almost afraid to listen to his message. *I've left you five voicemails and now your mailbox is full. What's the deal?*

When I looked up, there was no sign of Michael Wise. Great. I decided to keep moving to the next gate, then circle back around if I couldn't find him.

"Angus." It was Wise's voice coming from somewhere ahead of me on the right. I veered onto the blue carpet of the gate and did a quick scan with no sign of him. I kept walking closer to the boarding entrance and stopped at the row facing the windows. Sneaky. At the very end of it was a pillar that concealed a mini-row of four seats. I sat beside Wise and caught my breath.

"Did you see someone following us?" I asked.

He half-shrugged. "Not specifically but think about it. There would have to be someone tailing us, if you were them, wouldn't you think?"

"And who's them?"

"Mendoza's goons, I assume."

"I'm tired." I stretched out my legs and slid low in the seat, arms crossed, and closed my eyes for a second, hoping I didn't fall asleep. "Exhausted, to be honest."

"I can't imagine going through what you did in that lab," he said, staring out the window but turned slightly toward me. "Don't you want to know why?"

"The big why, you mean? Why this is all happening, why Jessica, why Elaine, why me, why all of it? Fuck, yeah. You found something."

That sheepish look again. "It's not really new. I've known for a while, but I think it's the last piece."

"Piece of what?"

"We can go to the authorities and claim whatever we want about who's done what to whom. But—"

"Cut to the chase, Wise. You have evidence? Is that what you're saying?"

"Keep your voice down. And yes."

I checked my watch. Thirty-five minutes till pre-boarding, which meant thirty-five minutes of relative quiet before the loud speaker announcements every two minutes. "You have her journals with you, right? You brought them?"

"Yes, but –"

"No no no, don't do that. There's no 'yes, but'. I'm her fucking husband. You will turn her journals over to me. Now." I crossed my arms. "Let me see them."

"Fine, I told you I brought them." He bent down to grab the handle

CODEX

on his backpack, picked it up and chucked it six inches to his right. "They're in there."

I stared at it before touching the zipper. I knew I needed to be ready for what I saw in there, like her handwriting for one thing, her words, and I was in no condition for more emotional turmoil right now. I slid it back to him and turned toward him. "Alright. I'm sorry, I'll look at them later. What's the 'yes, but' mean?"

"Keep looking out the window. It'll be harder to spot us if they can't see us walking or can't see our faces."

"Roger that." I returned to my sleeping pose.

"There's another journal that's not in here," he said.

I instinctively turned my head toward him, then checked myself before he could say anything. "Do you –"

"Shut up and listen, and I'll tell you everything. I don't know where it is, but she says in one of the journals in there –" he pointed to the pack – "that there's only one place she would have hidden it, and you're the only one who knows."

Chapter 48

I did know. Of course I knew. The vault. San Carlos. I reached my fingers up to my chest, I slid one finger in between the buttonholes of my shirt, which smelled like sweat and gasoline, to make sure I felt the cold metal of that key on the leather twine around my neck. Thank God, my single touchstone of sanity and hope. Oh, Jess. God help me, what I would do to see you one more time.

Wise suggested we both move over one seat to the left, which would mean I would be completely shielded by the pillar, and him partially. It was a good plan, which also allowed us to face each other.

"Evidence?" I asked. "Of what exactly?"

"All of it," he whispered, and raised a brow.

"What, like copied files and shit?"

Single nod.

I gulped hard.

"Yeah, there's a tiny jump drive she burrowed down into the hollow spine of the journal. But that's not even the most important part of it." Wise leaned back, pulled out his phone, turned on the reverse camera, and used it as a mirror to look behind us. "She hand-documented all the details of the gates for each of the four Primes." He paused and scrutinized my face.

"She knew, at that point, that I was one of them?"

"I assume so."

I thought about the word. "Gates. You mean the command scripts the doctors spoke into the microphone for each subject, like what I saw Mendoza do to Sykes?"

"Yes. There's an exact sequence WP used to access each subject so he could control them. They're post-hypnotic trigger phrases, customized to each person individually, and get this—he didn't write them down in any electronic file or hand-written notes."

"So how did she find them?"

"He made a video of it, and I honestly don't know how she got hold of it. Maybe she downloaded it from his phone, if she had access to it."

I felt sick hearing this, that Jess could have been that close to him.

"She hand-wrote a transcript of the video." He paused and took a long breath. "Including each of the four gate sequences, including the trigger phrase for each Prime." Wise sat back to catch his breath. I did the same. "She called it the Codex, and appropriately so. It's the key to everything anyone would ever need to successfully replicate these experiments and create their own, well...scenario. Exact positioning of the implants, tests they performed on potential subjects, drugs they used to prepare subjects, and the exact wording of commands they gave them to carry out testing tasks."

Wise stopped talking.

"I'm afraid to ask," I said.

"They made Sykes kill a cab driver, plus three other people."

"Christ. You could fund a six-month ground offensive for what this would be worth in the intelligence community. Can you imagine? No wonder. Fucking Mendoza." I wanted to ask him if there was anything about me in the journal; there must be. I was one of them, one of the four primes, the one who escaped. Why didn't I have any memory of escaping? What else had I done that I couldn't remember? I leaned down and prayed I wouldn't throw up on an airport carpet. Another text came in from Rudy, this time just, W_T_F??

I'm fine, I wrote back. *On my way home. Didn't mean to worry you.*

TG, he wrote back.

Thank God is right.

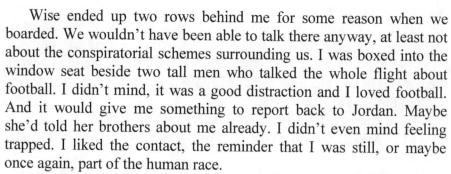

Wise ended up two rows behind me for some reason when we boarded. We wouldn't have been able to talk there anyway, at least not about the conspiratorial schemes surrounding us. I was boxed into the window seat beside two tall men who talked the whole flight about football. I didn't mind, it was a good distraction and I loved football. And it would give me something to report back to Jordan. Maybe she'd told her brothers about me already. I didn't even mind feeling trapped. I liked the contact, the reminder that I was still, or maybe once again, part of the human race.

Yet all I could think about, staring out at the cloud forest, was how brave she'd been, my wife the whistleblower, acting alone on a treacherous mission. How did she find the strength to do it, and how had she kept it from me? Wouldn't the strain have changed her? I didn't see those changes. She hadn't turned to me, and as far as I knew she'd only contacted Wise as a channel of publicity at the very end and as a last resort. And ultimately that was why she died, wasn't it? She'd compiled all the details of WP's mind control experiment into a well-documented volume, complete with the digital storage drive. She could have done whatever she wanted with it, sold it to the highest bidder, sold it on the dark web, or brought it to CNN. Just the story without the evidence in the Codex would be laughed out the door. Jess knew this. But what I knew was that even with the evidence, it was essentially unusable. How could she, how could I, or anyone for that matter, bring this out into the world and live to see the light of day?

A shadow in the aisle caught my eye. Wise, holding one of Jess' journals. Jesus, my heart jumped at the sight of it. "I think you might have dropped this. Is this yours?" he asked.

"Yes, thank you," I said.

Great cover but it was still risky if one of Mendoza's minions was on this flight. I had to assume he had someone following us, though we'd both looked and hadn't seen anyone. A text vibrated the phone. Wise from back in his seat. *Something especially interesting on p20. Any idea who she's talking about?*

How could we have only fifteen minutes left on this flight? It felt like there should be over an hour left. I kept reminding myself that this wasn't the journal, the Codex, as she'd called it. Just one in the stack of journals Wise had brought me. The guy beside me was rearranging things in his carry-on under the seat in front of him.

I opened the journal and felt my jaw set tight as I saw her slanted southpaw handwriting. *I sent someone today to warn Angus. I paid a man to do it, a stranger to tell him not to trust his CIA contact. I can't tell him myself, I still can't tell him anything about all this. I know they're watching me and I'm scared. Even so, I know I'm doing the right thing. Angus' safety is worth any risk.*

The plane started its descent through the clouds, me still stuck in a sort of memory-stasis staring at the journal. Remembering.

The day of the accident had been the weirdest of days, the kind of composite clusterfuck that makes you think I should have known disaster would touch me. It began with coffee spilled all over the floor, dropping my keys into the space between the two front seats, misplacing my cell phone. By 9am, I was ready to give up. The worst part was that I hadn't seen Jessica, in person anyway, in almost seventy-two hours. When she started working on the merger of ADS, WP's company, with Mendoza's Jasper Holdings, her previous eight to six schedule quickly turned to eight to ten or eleven.

When I'd eaten dinner alone for a week, I showed up at her office at 9pm honestly not sure what I expected to find. She was asleep on her back on the sofa in her office, her calves and bare feet hanging off the end, reading glasses on the floor, a file folder on her chest. I hadn't meant to startle her.

"Knock knock," I said, from the doorway, clacking my knuckles on the polished mahogany millwork.

"Oh." She shook her head.

When she half-rolled to her left side, the file folder threatened to slip onto the floor. Her hands caught it in time, eyes wide in shock, glancing left and right like she expected a garroting wire to slip over her head any second. I'd seen this reaction dozens of times before but never told her, never mentioned it to anyone, almost as if she'd had superhero training in some parallel universe.

"Baby, I'm sorry." She looked up at me finally, then quickly down again. "Did you—were you ..." Her voice trailed as she closed up the papers in the file folder with the precision of open-heart surgery, folding certain pages into one pocket, clasping others to the brads at the top of the file, pen affixed to the front cover and properly secured.

"What have you got there? Compromising pictures of congressmen or something?" My jovial tone made light of her frantic movements, but my heart knew, or should have known in that moment that she was in up to her eyeballs and taking the biggest risk of her life.

Like an expert, she used my cue and turned on her impish smile before dropping the closed file into her briefcase and walking over to greet me. A kiss, half-hug, then she nudged my hand to join her on the couch. We were the only ones in the entire building. We could have made love on that couch right then, and believe me, I'd thought of it. Even her face seemed to invite that energy, but I saw a darkness behind her eyes that night, that I don't even think I'd acknowledged to myself until now.

The landing gear touched down to the hot tarmac in Los Angeles, now late July, but my head was still on that couch with Jessica in her office. I insisted she follow me home, where I forced her to eat the dinner I'd set aside for her, with no questions about the file folder or whatever she'd been doing till all hours for the past month. I sometimes rationalized it as space, respect even, that I wouldn't push my way into a part of her life or work where I wasn't welcome. The thought made me shake my head in disgust now, nearly two years later. I should have pushed, should have demanded to be let into the dangerous circle from which she never escaped. Maybe I could have protected her. Maybe she'd still be alive now.

CODEX

Chapter 49

Wise texted me right before we disembarked from the plane. *Turn your head toward the left side windows, and from there look WITH ONLY YOUR EYES to the front of the plane.* A dark-haired man wearing a white polo shirt and dark jacket stood outside the bathrooms. He was looking in my direction.

Mendoza's team? I asked Wise via text. Had to be if he was waiting for us.

I'm assuming so. What's the plan?

I didn't have time to answer because the plane had emptied out to my row. Phone in hand, I got an idea. With five people ahead of me, I turned my phone landscape, pressed the front-facing camera option, and held it out in front of me. The guy backed up a few paces as I approached, with a tall flight attendant right beside him. Josette.

"Josette," I said with my widest feigned smile. I held out the camera and pointed to the man. "Would you mind?" I asked. "My brother. We haven't seen each other forever."

"Just a real quick shot right here. Sure." She grabbed the camera and switched places with me so I could stand beside what was no doubt a trained killer on Sylvan Mendoza's payroll. I slid my arm around his waist; he recoiled when he felt it. There was a gun on his

255

belt. How the fuck had he gotten that on the plane?

"One, two, three," the woman said.

I angled my head toward the man and smiled at the fact that I'd now have photographic evidence of him to use with facial recognition. Wise pushed past us toward the terminal. He would be proud of my ingenuity.

"Thank you so much," I said to the flight attendant, grabbed the phone and patted the man on the chest. "See you later, right?"

I walked out ahead of the man, hoping, no, praying that Wise waited up for me so I could tell him about the gun. I could see the top of his head ten people in front of me. I fake-sneezed, hoping the noise would make him look back. He did and I formed my hand into a gun. He nodded. We worked well together, he and I. Maybe in a parallel universe we would have been partners. Into the terminal, past the restrooms, three eateries, Wise was still about ten people ahead of me, no idea where our pursuer was. But running wasn't an option with him directly behind us. Too many people could get hurt here.

In a game-time decision, Wise ducked into the men's room. I stopped in the store beside it. *I'll go buy some hoodies in the adjacent shop,* I typed. *Leave your jacket in a stall.*

??? he wrote back.

The poor guy. Now I'd have to buy him a new one. *Just do it.*

Roger that. Pay for the sweatshirt ahead of time so I can just walk in and put it on.

I'd already done that, my eyes glued to the entry. No sign of my fake-brother from the plane. I chose a dark blue hoodie with LA in giant letters for me, and I selected a very special one for Wise. There he was, walking toward me. I held out a women's XXL light pink pullover hoodie.

"You're kidding me, right?"

"Do you want to stay alive?"

"Give it to me. Motherfucker."

Geez. I might need to buy him two leather jackets. He wrestled the hoodie on over his gray t-shirt and we watched a throng of teenaged girls exit the store. Their flashy outfits and rhinestone-studded suitcases would make for good cover. The rental car arrow was up ahead. There was no way to safely look back. I tried to slow my

CODEX

heartrate with a deep breath.

"Glass." Wise pointed ahead of us.

"Perfect. See him?" I asked.

"Nope. I recommend a cab. Will get us out of here faster."

"Good idea," I said. "Sorry about your jacket, but I think it worked."

"It's fine. Clothes are replaceable. That was a nice gag with the photograph. Well done."

"Thought you'd appreciate it."

This running thing was tiring. We took a cab up to Santa Barbara leaving our ridiculous hoodies in the backseat. From there we stopped at a coffee shop and ate in the front windows so we could keep an eye out for what I assumed was Mendoza's foot soldier. I didn't think they'd had time to clone my phone, so I booked us an Uber from Santa Barbara to Monterey, three and a half hours to let someone else drive so we could watch for a tail...maybe even sleep. Wise slept first; I took the first watch, alternating my gaze outside for the eyes of our driver, paranoid now that everybody we met was after us. He looked like a kid barely old enough for a license.

By the time we got up to Monterey, I'd slept for almost an hour, and we had to decide on the most strategic way to make it through the night alive.

"Harder to track someone at night certainly," Wise said.

I looked around and knew where we were, near the far end of Cannery Row a short trek to the boardwalk where Jessica and I ate at Paluca Trattoria, the best Italian food we'd ever had. Wise and I had things to talk about, I had journals to read, and we both desperately needed rest.

"Hey, can you drop us at the Monterey Bay Inn?" I asked the driver. "Do you know where that is?"

"Punching it in now."

I called the hotel and they had two rooms available.

"Book one room," Wise said, "or maybe an adjoining. Safer under the circumstances."

We ended up in adjoining rooms and got dinner delivered in from

257

Caviar. I was on one bed in my room holding Jessica's journals, unable to bring myself to read them just yet. It still felt good holding something that she had touched, an unspeakable romantic moment between us across time and space. He saw this and walked away, leaving me to keep vigil in my own way.

He took out our food and dove into a large salad, eating on the other bed. I heard him, sensed his presence, and saw him in my periphery, but I felt myself checking out, again.

"You don't have to read those, you know," he said between bites.

I shook my head, not at that statement but at the war I was losing with myself. I had to trust him. I had no one else available who knew as much as I did about what we were up against.

"What?" he asked, pushing me.

"The passage you had me read."

"Do you know what it means, the guy she sent to you?"

"Notice there's no date on that entry, or that page, or anywhere in the journal? Are all the journals like that?" I asked him.

"No dates, but some of the timeframes are obvious because of their relation to the merger of the two companies."

I considered this; it could be true. "Okay, and that merger happened when exactly?"

He stopped chewing and wiped his mouth. "A month before the accident," he said carefully. "Is that significant?"

"I'll tell you what's significant to me. There's no date on the journal or the passage I read, and there was a guy running on the beach half a football field from my trailer, not jogging but running from someone, yelling something. I heard him get shot, killed actually."

"When was this?" he asked, eyes wide.

"A few months ago. It happened early in the morning the same day I met WP. I was originally considered a suspect in that homicide, had Detective Dekker breathing down my neck."

Wise climbed off the bed and walked around the room. "You said a few months ago. Months?" he asked, brows raised.

I stayed quiet for a long time, neither of us talking, stuck in this sort of limbo.

"If she was the one who sent that guy to me, the guy who died on the beach, that would mean two things: Mendoza or one of his goons

CODEX

probably killed him…and Jessica could still be alive."

He heard me but didn't respond. No follow up questions, no long looks. He was being respectful, knowing this epiphany, this possibility, was life changing. And not just for me.

I laid on top of the quilt, a pillow at the foot of the bed, staring at the ceiling, then on my stomach staring at the dark TV screen. I think I was waiting for something, maybe for Jess to send me a sign, some kind of message. I didn't dare let myself even consider the possibility at this point. We were dealing with evidence, Wise and I, drawing logical conclusions. But not a single detail of this nightmare fit any traditional definition of logic.

The whole ride north from Monterey to the Bay Area the next morning, I couldn't stop thinking about Jessica's quick reaction to me the night I surprised her at work. And there was another time she almost got mugged outside a movie theater. Her best friend Gretchen told me she reacted like she'd been in training for it her whole life. The guy barely got away in one piece, yet she claimed to have never learned how to fight. Funny I'd never thought about this until now, like the pieces of a puzzle scattered all over the world, across time, now gravitating towards each other starting to form a vague shape.

Chapter 50

August

Wise and I parted ways when we got to Half Moon Bay. He was staying at Le Meridien Hotel in San Francisco, where Nigella had first tracked him. I still didn't know where he actually lived. He hadn't told me and I wasn't asking, because I suspected with the types of whistleblower stories he publicized, he might not tell me anyway. Besides, his residence might change every few months. Secrets are dangerous things, sometimes the undoing of you, and sometimes they're your lifeline.

We had business to take care of at the San Carlos house, as I was the only one who knew where to look for Jessica's secret volume of life-changing evidence. I honestly couldn't imagine what I'd do with it once I got it. I told Wise I'd text him when I was ready and he'd meet me there. The guy on the plane had to know where we were going. Both of us would be armed this time.

Rudy's car was parked on the street when I got dropped off. I walked up to the dunes at first, climbing to the top and looking out, squinting into the waves as if I might catch a glimpse of Jessica's light skin and purple swimsuit bobbing in and out of the water. I knew thinking about it was another form of self-abuse at this point.

I knocked on Rudy's door, deciding that procrastinating the inevitable suffering would only cause more suffering. I hadn't texted him first but I could tell he knew it would be me. He opened the door wearing the wounded look he used when he wanted to manipulate me to do something I didn't want to do.

"Hey," I said. "I'm sorry you were worried. There was no way I could call you without putting you in danger." It was kinda-sorta true, and the timing was perfect. I watched his large eyes, invisible brows and cheeks soften as he held open the door. No hug, not even one of our half-mans, as he called the one-arm slapping bro man variety.

"Hungry?" he asked, stone-faced. This could take some time.

"Starved," I lied and sat at his table.

I slept like a baby that night in the actual bed in my trailer. With Elaine gone, I could no longer ignore the forty-thousand-dollar gift she'd given me with her ridiculously lavish furnishings, most likely funded by her drug dealer boyfriend Miguel, most likely the man who killed her.

I bought a bouquet of flowers at New Leaf Market and brought them to a makeshift plot I'd designed with rocks at the end of our street with her name and picture. It would be okay until her plot was ready in the HMB Cemetery.

Next order of business was Nigella. I called her while riding to the brewery. She didn't answer so I left her a long voicemail saying I'd try her again tonight.

I found Jordan's car in the lot, the only one there, and I remembered how the whole nightmare started in this very parking lot, my bike parked in the same place, when drunken Wendell Peters stopped me with his manipulative song and dance.

I knew why I didn't remember him at the time, but the reality still stung right now that he had violated my mind and my body, along with Sykes and the two others, and countless strangers from the border, to further his research, appease Mendoza's demands, and feed millions of dollars into a cycle of human oppression.

I felt it in there sometimes, my implant, late at night when the mind was idle. But I wasn't taking any steps to remove it just yet. Michael Wise had an agenda to find Jessica's codex. In that journal will be pages of text that define how WP, Mendoza, and their vile medical team programmed me to carry out their commands. I was going to find that codex, use it, input a command to see if it actually worked. And Wise was going to help me.

I sat there, on the same rock WP was perched on that fateful night, just staring into the blue sky with the waves rolling into shore below. The roar was loud as the tide was high this morning. So much to think about. Nothing helped me do that better than the sea.

Was it really possible Jess was still alive? Had she been watching me all this time, watching me grieve all those months, holed up alone, or riding off into the hills and sleeping on the hard ground at the top of Pillar Point? Was she there then, hiding in the trees, waiting for the right time to tell me all her secrets? No. She'd consciously chosen to hide them from me, all of them, so many that they swallowed her whole. I could've helped her. She didn't give me the chance because she didn't trust me with her secret. She trusted Michael Wise instead. I wondered if I'd ever be able to get past that betrayal.

Where would we even go, now, if she really was alive and we could be together? Was there any *together* left for us, or did that trail run out a long time ago? The outline of Jordan Reid standing in the doorway, watching me, complicated an already complicated question.

"I heard you were back," she said.

Rudy. Had to be. The eternal matchmaker. Her voice sounded friendly but her face was tight.

I got up off the railroad tie and came toward her, realizing we still hadn't established our relationship status. Was there even one? Friends, potentially more than friends? "I came by to say I'm sorry."

"Why – are you leaving again?" she asked, emphasis on the last word and a tinge of strain in her face.

"No, no, I'm here now, I'm back. But you helped me, and we were starting to, I don't know, get to know each other a bit, then I vanished for weeks with no word."

CODEX

No response but she was listening.

"I got your messages," I said. "It's not that I didn't want to talk to you. I was involved, am still involved, in something dangerous. It wasn't safe to make contact with anyone. Anyone I cared about." Only a terrible person would use that excuse twice in a row. I was certainly going to hell.

"Come on inside. I'm making eggs and toast."

And that's how it went for the first few days I was back home. No car chases, no hitmen lurking behind doorways, no sign of the man from the plane. No of course it wasn't over, not even close. But I had a short reprieve, visiting people who apparently cared about me and missed me. And kept making me food.

I texted Wise about San Carlos. *Hey,* I wrote, *I'll call you from a new burner phone tomorrow morning with the exact address. You good to meet me there around ten?*

That works. Send me that photo you took from the plane. Wanna run it through my facial recognition tool.

Will do.

Chapter 51

I woke up early the next morning and got down to San Carlos before six. Parking on the next street over seemed like a smart idea, all things considered, especially while it was still mostly dark. My whole life in stealth mode now, I'd pretty much turned into a ghost.

I fell asleep on the carpet in the living room in front of the fireplace in my empty house. Lying there with my eyes closed seemed to calm the wild theories running through my head. Then I woke at seven and was mad that the long-vacant house had no coffee. I called Wise from a Starbucks drive-thru.

"Hey."

"Hey." Wise picked up my burner phone call on the first ring. "You're earlier than I thought."

It was 7:05am. "Just texted you the address."

"Thanks. Can I go back to sleep now?"

"Can his highness still be in San Carlos by ten?"

"Fuck off," he hung up. Omg hilarious.

Back in the living room, I sat on the floor in front of the fireplace leaning against the vault key chair, sipping coffee, remembering. Wondering, questioning. Had my wife faked her death and, if so, where the fuck had she been all this time? If I let that thought take

CODEX

root, I might never need coffee again. A lobotomy would be more like it. But there was another, scarier thought: was my wife a spy and, if so, has she been working for Mendoza all along? I grabbed the side of the chair to steady myself, sipping the hot frothy liquid, always too goddamn sweet for my spartan taste.

I could easily use my key, grab the journal and read the whole thing before Wise got here. But I felt like he'd been on this path far longer than me, so he deserved the moment of truth. I liked the idea of him thinking I was clueless about him. Fact is, I'd googled him a long time ago and had even listened to an episode of his subversive podcast, Spy101 about conspiracies, whistleblowing, and live case studies of anonymous speakers who talk about the risks of exposure. I wanted to learn more about his operation, see his studio, get access to all his research. And though I was loathe to admit it, some part of me was dying to see if there were pictures of Jessica plastered all over his walls. I knew they weren't having an affair, it wasn't that. Maybe I just wanted confirmation.

The doorbell rang as I was reheating my coffee in the microwave, pretty much the only appliance I trusted after two years of no use. I walked the length of the house and opened the front door. "Not much of a morning person, are you?"

He held up a Starbucks coffee cup and smiled, eyes still barely open, wearing a brand-new lambskin nearly identical leather jacket. Wait, it was identical. "Seriously?" I chuckled at his vanity. "You went back to the airport, didn't you, skulking around the men's room and the lost and found?"

"It was still on the back of the door."

"Am I forgiven then for the pink hoodie?"

He sipped the coffee and came inside. I closed the door behind him and we sat on the sheet-covered chairs next to the fireplace. Three sips later, he flashed his phone showing the picture of our airline assailant.

"Ah. You get anything on that?"

He cleared his throat. "Alex Banovic, Croatian, arrested last year for aggravated assault, no conviction, and he was carrying ID on him, sort of."

"Fake ID?"

"Jan Miske, who died in 2009."

265

LISA TOWLES

"I'm assuming he works for Mendoza's company. Did you see anything to the contrary?"

Brow raise.

"CIA?" I asked. "Is he an asset?"

"Formerly, yes."

"What does that mean? You don't exactly retire from that line of work. And how the fuck did he get a gun on the plane?"

"Maybe you just felt the holster and not the actual gun. I don't know. But let's assume yes he does work for Mendoza. And what he wants is probably right in front of us."

I got up and checked all the windows in the house from behind the closed curtains. I'd been careful, ultra careful. Would it ever be enough?

When I got back to the living room, I pulled the key from around my neck and stood on a kitchen chair, which I'd dragged in from under the butcherblock island. It was not only easier to move than the gigantic club chair but also taller. Wise rose to watch me.

"This is how you did it in Alice?"

"No, that was different. It was a lock the size of a light switch on the wall behind the bed."

"You've tried this before?" he asked.

"Not yet. Not here."

"Why'd you wait? Weren't you here for hours before I got here?"

I sighed and lowered the key, turning to face him. "We'll find it together. And in return you're gonna partner with me to find out the truth behind it."

"Truth's what I do, man. All in."

I got up high enough and pressed the wooden panel. When the lock emerged, I stuck the tiny key in, recalling how the floor moved out from under me in Alice. I jumped down from the chair, pulled it away from the fireplace and waited. Unbelievable. The segment of wall on the left side of the fireplace was actually a pocket door that slid open revealing a space the size of a small closet. White walls, no windows. This room, if you could call it that, was unlike WP's secret lab. It had no keypad or panel on the wall, and it occurred to me how easily you could entomb yourself in here. I backed away.

"What are you doing? You're not going in?" he asked.

266

CODEX

"I wanna make sure I can get out. Look for a dowel of some kind."

"Kitchen chair legs usually work, or a broom handle."

"Too long," I said, looking down at the chair where I was standing. The legs would be too short. I went to the kitchen to check out the other chairs. Amazing how unfamiliar this space felt after all this time, like it was somebody else's house. I was able to unscrew one leg from a tall, kitchen stool, which might be too long. Even so, it could be a spacer. I tried it in the doorway and it was about a foot too long, but leaning it between the two walls would be sufficient. I stepped through the threshold into the empty space, adorned with nothing but a long table in the middle and a large, wooden box on top. It felt silent and eerie, like a little chapel. I looked back at Wise. "You said this was the journal she was bringing me the night of the accident?"

"I did say that, yes."

I turned back toward him. "What the hell does that mean? Did she or didn't she?"

"She said she was bringing you the key to everything," he said, quietly. "I had no idea what that meant at the time."

I nodded at his answer, good enough. I lifted the lid on the box. The journal's black cover had the word Codex etched into its soft leather by a black pen, only visible from a certain angle. I picked it up, lowered the lid and flipped through to see how many pages were inked. About half of the thin volume contained Jessica's slanted handwriting. No time for reading it now. I stepped outside of the room and pulled out the chair leg. Nothing happened of course, I was just being paranoid. I used the vault key in the lock again and the door slowly glided closed, without any evidence it had ever been there. Amazing.

We closed up the house, left my bike on the back street, and took Wise's car to a Fedex store to make copies. "I have a favor to ask you," I said.

"Did you know that anytime someone announces they have a favor to ask you, there's a hundred-percent chance the favor will be something they don't want to do?"

I strapped on my seatbelt. "I bet you were the annoying smart kid who always had his hand raised."

"And I bet you were perpetually in trouble. What's your favor?"

"I need you to use the codex to read the commands, the ones for me specifically. I want to see if it works and I want to be awake if it does."

His face contracted and he looked back in the rearview.

"See something?" I asked.

"No. We're clear. And do what exactly? Give you a command to walk out in the middle of traffic or something? What is the point of –"

"Because I need to know how compromised I am with this fucking device embedded in me, that's why. I need to know if it still works, or if it only works in a lab under specific conditions after I'm injected with the drugs they gave me."

"No."

"What do you mean no?"

He pulled into the Fedex parking lot. "It's barbaric what they did to you and all the others. No, not even to test your theory. But I'll gladly drive you to the hospital to get the device removed."

And that was that, with no further discussion. We checked the codex to make sure the content was what Jessica described. It appeared to be a key or legend for each participant. There were forty-seven. I was number seven, corresponding to WP's code name for me—I was one of the four primes, his original control group. We made seven copies of the journal – one as a master; the other six would be mailed to each of us in a sealed envelope with a date stamp, to be opened only in an emergency. The Fedex office also had a mail station, so we were able to send them from the store, walking out with just the original and one copy.

While driving us back to my house I got a text from an unfamiliar number. *Under the box* was all it said.

I showed him the text.

We used the same kitchen chair and got into the vault the same way as before. I replaced the book in the box, lifting it off the wooden table. Not a thing under it. Now I felt stupid for believing in that text. *Under the box.* Could it mean something else? My face must have betrayed my irritation. But who could have sent this? Who else could

CODEX

know about this if it wasn't Wise?

"Flip it over," Wise said.

Taped to the bottom was a white business card with an address handwritten on the back. A Santa Barbara address.

He dropped his backpack, half unzipped, on the living room chair. The journals spilled out.

"Do you have copies of these?" I asked.

"No. The number ten journal—I numbered them," he explained, "has a note to me about publicizing them." He paused to make sure I heard him. "That's what she intended, after all."

"Right. With specific directions of how to do it or something?"

Wise gripped the handle on the entry door. "It was a message to give to you, just in case they got to her first."

Why hadn't he told me this before now? I shook my head, incredulous of what felt like another betrayal. Without another word, he left through the front. I took my motorcycle around from the back street to the garage where I sat alone in the dark on the cold concrete floor with journal number ten, door open to a sea of stars. My phone flashlight illuminated the pages as I flipped through a series of lists, summaries; she was always organized to a fault. Making it easy for Michael Wise, or whoever else, to understand her story and her claim. Then, on the last page, she wrote, *Michael, please show this to Angus in case they find me before I can tell him. Thank you for being a gentle ally in an impossible situation. And I'm sorry for the danger I'm putting you in. I hope you can forgive me.*

Chapter 52

Angus, My God, as I sit here I'm flooded with all the things I haven't been able to say all these months, these years, after being assigned the case from hell. And I'm sorry, that's what I want to say first. If you're reading this, you now know why I couldn't go to you right away. I found not only evidence of The Primes in Wendell Peters' control group notes...but your name was in them. Based on the work they were doing, on what they did to you, I knew you didn't yet know about this. The horror of seeing your name on those pages and remembering that you'd spent time in Alice made it all the more real. I didn't know what to do. The partners in my firm are as corrupt as Mendoza and probably on his payroll. That's why I was assigned to this case. They needed me to do the research and then get out of the way. I was trapped. I needed a path forward but I couldn't share any of it with you. You'll never know the pain that caused me. It wasn't my fault, it was nobody's fault. Even so, I'm sorry.

You know how I listened to podcasts when I went running in the mornings? Someone at work told me about Spy101, said the guy was a wonderful writer, and took on some heavy topics. He was doing a whistleblower story about some senator and something inside me just clicked. I knew I'd found my way out, the only way out.

I know I've put myself in a dangerous situation, and they'll stop at nothing to stop me. So, I wanted to warn you. The San Mateo Police Department has two moles from Mendoza's company—a woman whom I think you've met, and an ex-biker. Watch your back.
Love you, Jess

Wasn't my fault, she wrote. I knocked around the idea and it wasn't working for me. She could have taken a number of alternative actions, like saying no to the assignment early on, reporting it to the Bar Association, going to the police or the medical board.

A neighborhood cat wandered into the garage as I read; a dark tabby with pretty blue eyes sat beside me on the concrete. I'd never seen it before, but nothing surprised me anymore. Maybe Jess was a shapeshifter now. All I knew was that before the accident, I'd never had any connection to the San Mateo Police Department. I didn't move to Half Moon Bay from San Carlos until after the accident. Since the Half Moon Bay Auxiliary Police Substation was part of the San Mateo Police Department, I suspected the two moles were likely Officer Lopez and Carl Deakins. It's almost like I saw it in Lopez' eyes when she showed up at my trailer the night Elaine's body was found.

None of the journals were dated so there was no way to verify my claim, but the only way Jessica would have known of my connection to the SMPD was if she never died in that accident.

I suspected the only way she'd know about the moles was because she was also one of them, on Mendoza's payroll.

I told myself I was following a lead.
I told myself I was once part of a family.
But that all vanished the night of an event I didn't even want to go to.

It was financed by a third-party recruitment firm the bureau had used for some recent hiring. The banquet was intended to welcome the new blood, putting on a grandiose show of hospitality, support, and collaboration that didn't otherwise exist. Not in the least. Like any other social system, the federal law enforcement community was cutthroat, political, running on a secret currency of favors, which created an intricate landscape of power and corruption. Eat or be eaten. So, when Mendoza came to me in the early days and said some higher ups had noticed I had my shit together more than most of the newer guys, I actually believed he was going to mentor me and help my career. I felt sick just thinking about it. I found myself fumbling with the business card from Jessica's secret box, folding it in my pocket and taking it out, looking at the address. I had a decision to make, but it had already been made.

The ride to Santa Barbara was a beautiful stretch of coastline that embodied the whole reason for owning a motorcycle. Breathe the air, hear the motor, feel the contour of the road. Sadly, heavy rains from winter storms closed down the most scenic parts of Highway 1 around Big Sur, which meant my ride would be shorter.

I thought of Elaine lately every time I got on my bike, remembering my first bicycle and her always wanting to ride on the handlebars. Aside from the safety issue, it prevented me from seeing in front of me. But the danger-factor was at the core of how she lived in the world. Stretching, pushing, skating the ragged edge of acceptability. She felt it was her job to wake people up. I wondered what I'd learned from her.

I always envisioned keeping the San Carlos house and asking Elaine to be the interior designer and renovation lead, because it was the type of work she loved. She was also damned good at it.

The ride went by quickly after San Luis Obispo, bouncing off of Pismo Beach on the coast and then a straight shot south to Santa Barbara. Sometimes on the way to LA, Jess and I stopped off in Solvang to buy books or wine. We only had four years together. With all that's happened, with all that I now know, I wasn't sure how I felt about her or any of it. Anger and betrayal, like grief and loss, was still cyclical. Over time, there's more space between the cycles and the highs and lows aren't as pronounced. But I still felt the change, the presence every time it slid into my chest and head. You were played. You were used. You were abused in the worst way possible. Their damage wasn't permanent, and I probably would take Wise up on his offer and get the device removed at some point. The prospect right now felt even scarier than having it in there between my ear and brain.

CODEX

Was it out of sight, out of mind? Without testing, I might never know. And Wise was the only one I could trust with that process. So be it.

He offered to come with me, to drive me even, arguing that I needed backup now more than ever, and my bike made me too conspicuous. We talked about trying to identify my mysterious texter, knowing it could be from one of Mendoza's minions. "I need to do this alone," I told him, still now unsure why and even more unsure of my certainty.

In someone else's handwriting, 1331 Santa Barbara Street had been scrawled on a white business card and taped to the bottom of the vault box. I could see Santa Barbara Street was a quiet, stable neighborhood with mature landscaping. Weren't they all here? The property, if it was the right one, bordered Alice Keck Park and Memorial Garden, in particular something called Kids World with a playground.

I parked there, on the edge of the playground, walled in a heavy, black wrought iron gate with a yellow innertube winding slide and an aluminum, straight slide with a Tudor roof on top. A small child sat at the head of the slide, her face about to burst into tears while a woman held her hand and had the other hand on her back, gently gliding her down the slope under her comforting grip. The woman saw me watching her and immediately grabbed the child off the slide, enveloping her in a tight clutch like I might come charging up to attack her or something. She kept her large, dark eyes glued to me, while I felt glued to my spot on the sidewalk, unable to move or breathe, or even back away, like the woman obviously wanted me to do.

But why wasn't she moving, either?

The little girl, a toddler in pigtails…

I squinted to get a better look at those pigtails. They were a distinctive shade of strawberry blonde…a shade of strawberry blonde I'd only ever seen on one other person.

I stopped breathing.

We circled each other like wolves, slowly stepping left and right— me so I could get a good look at them and try to understand why she was looking like she'd seen a ghost. The baby, no doubt sensing the tension, started crying. The woman, obviously not her mother I could see now, had salt and pepper hair pulled back off her oval face, mid-fifties, a short and wiry frame. There was no street traffic and we were nearly close enough now to speak, but neither of us did.

We stayed there in that awkward bubble staring, wondering. Did she think I was going to steal her baby? She acted like it, but I'd never seen either of them in my life. A sick fear spread through my innards wondering if I'd been programmed by Mendoza's experiments, to do something to this woman. Was that why she recognized me?

I got my answer in a single movement, as I watched the baby stop crying and look at her caregiver: she reached out her chubby hand, tipped her head slightly to the right and smiled, the same way Jess used to.

The same way Jess used to.

Oh. My. God.

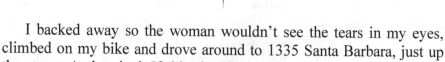

I backed away so the woman wouldn't see the tears in my eyes, climbed on my bike and drove around to 1335 Santa Barbara, just up the street. And waited. If this situation was as I expected, in the next few minutes, I'd see the woman pushing that toddler in a stroller.

I calmed myself as best I could by regulated breathing, slowly in, slowly out. Stay calm, Angus. Keep breathing. I couldn't keep my eyes from watering, but I wasn't actively crying. Maybe this was part of the grieving I never did, or not properly, I'd been told, after the accident that left Jessica dead on arrival. Now, on top of that, I was grieving that it was all a goddamned lie. Could this child be mine... and Jessica's? Could Mendoza's men have pulled her out of the car at the bottom of that ditch near Pescadero and brought her to some protected facility? The doctors told me the impact broke her arm, ribs, caused a head wound and she hadn't survived. No one ever said anything about a baby, certainly not Jess. Was it possible to rescue a baby in vitro if the mother didn't survive? All this swarmed around my head as I sat on my bike at the end of the driveway.

It was a two-story single-family home with a nicely protected front porch and what looked to be a sizeable piece of property. I wondered

CODEX

whose house this was. Had to be the woman's, the baby's caretaker. But who was she? Again, my eyes dropped long lines of tears; I stopped wiping them away. Maybe it was finally time to grieve. Or maybe it was time to live.

Chapter 53

I heard the wheels of the stroller before I saw them. Deciding to stay on my bike at the very end of the driveway seemed the safest course. The woman pushed toward me mumbling something to the baby. There was still no confirmation of my theory—just this essential knowing deep in my chest.

The woman stopped when they were six feet away. She and the baby stared in silence.

"Do you...know me?" I asked. Time seemed slower, clicking by one dot at a time.

She closed her eyes. "I knew you were coming."

I tried to place the accent. New York. Jessica's family was from New York, but this woman looked nothing like her mother.

More tears, and I saw the same on her face, the baby oddly quiet, watching in this tense moment. "Do you know who this is?" she asked me, then nodded. "This is Ava. Your daughter."

I didn't—couldn't—believe the words, didn't believe the ability of my ears to process sound, thinking trickery or sorcery had fooled me somehow. My weight wobbled from one foot to the other. Everything got blurry at that point. I parked my bike and followed the woman down the long driveway where she left the stroller at the bottom of a short set of stairs, and picked up the baby, who'd fallen asleep. "Come with me."

The house smelled like apples and cinnamon, and not from some artificially scented candle. There was an apple pie, homemade, on the counter of a modern kitchen. The house was nice, well appointed. There was money here. This child was cared for. *This child. Who's?*

It was so hard to suppress the thousand questions in my head as I experienced the most uncontrollable urge to hold the baby, hold her in my arms, to see, again, to test the theory that she came from Jessica and me, like I'd know somehow by her smell or her energy that she was umbilically connected to Jess.

The woman carried the baby upstairs to the nursery, where she set her in her crib. She must have seen my face. "You can hold her if you want, if you're ready."

"I—wait—won't she wake up?"

"She's a good sleeper. But you're not ready yet."

I turned to the woman, who was a foot shorter than me. "Can I ask your name?"

"Millie. I was Jessica's mother's best friend."

That's right, I had a vague memory of Jessica mentioning her name, usually related to relationship squabbles, Millie trying to parent Jessica. "I don't know what to say."

"We've been waiting a long time for you."

I spent the next two days with them, Millie and Ava. I didn't want to pick up the baby at first, but at one point Millie brought her to me and sat her on my lap. She was strangely calm in my arms and kept touching my face with her chubby hands, using her fingertips to dab my tears, almost as though she knew my heart was breaking open. I couldn't find words for the flood of emotions. My daughter.

Millie had baby monitors in every room in the house. She said she was trained as an ER nurse and took care of Jess after the accident. Ava was three months premature and stayed in the neonatal ICU, NICU, to help her gain enough weight so she could breathe on her own and go home. Home to a stranger's house, home to Santa Barbara.

Millie gave me plenty of time to adjust, and seemed understanding of the fact that every word out of my mouth was *why*. Why this, why that, why didn't anyone contact me, why was I kept in the dark? And the answer she gave to almost every question was that it was Jessica's wish.

"I know that man tried to kill her the night it happened, and there was nothing accidental about your car getting shoved off a cliff. And if anyone knew she was still alive, and especially about the baby, they'd use that as leverage."

"But wasn't it Mendoza's men who took Jessica away after the accident? I mean, so everyone else could perpetuate the lie of her death?"

Millie shook her head. "I don't know."

"Who pulled her out of the car, and how could they remove her body from the scene? The place was swarming with law enforcement."

"Someone with a lot of influence." Millie stared like I should know who she was talking about. I didn't. "It's the same person who texted you about the address taped to the underside of that box."

"Not you?" I asked, feeling clueless and overwhelmed with these details, and still struggling to fit this new reality into the confines of my head. "Look Millie, I don't care who it was right now. Is Jess still alive, like right now, today?"

It felt like an hour passed in the ten seconds she prepared her answer. My palms were sweating from an overabundance of adrenaline, my body preparing me for any answer. "She's alive."

"Well, where the fuck is she? Does she live here with you and Ava? Or did she go off and leave her daughter the same way she left me?"

Millie dropped her head in her hands and ran her fingers through her hair. "She didn't leave you. She stayed away to protect you."

I glared at her, waiting.

"We don't know where she is. She surfaces from time to time. I'll catch a glimpse of her looking in Ava's window from outside the

CODEX

house. Sometimes she'll wave, other times she'll wait till I come out and say hello, thank me for the hundredth time for taking care of Ava." She looked at the ground. "Then vanish again."

"For how long?"

"I never know. A week. Two months. It's how it has to be right now."

"Does she know…that I know? That I know everything now?"

She shook her head. "I can't contact her if that's what you mean. I'm sorry. I know that's not what you want to hear."

Both nights, after Millie went to bed, I went out walking down the length of Santa Barbara Street all the way to Stearns Wharf, my eyes always peeled for Jessica's hair, or the familiar shape of her hips, delicate hands, so much I still remembered. The wharf was open year-round and all night, a place where I could be alone with my tangled thoughts, alternating my gaze from the ocean to the stars. Just like the patio at the brewery back home. I tried to believe it all.

Ava had Jessica's temperament. She was a serious child, focused, studying people, watching them. It was strange—I could almost hear Jess's thoughts right now, curious how I was managing the shock, wondering how I was holding up. I could almost feel her—or someone's—presence.

Tonight at the far end of the pier near the water's edge, alone in the dark under a half-moon, I felt someone but saw no one. Then something moved behind me and I heard a sort of whoosh. I didn't dare turn my head in response to the creaking pier under the weight of steps, the miracle of matter where only energy should exist. Was it the promise of light and dark, or my unthinkable second chance?

"Angus?"

Chapter 54

"Hey," I said without turning around, my eyes filled with… something. Not sadness. Something else. "Don't come any closer."

"You think I'm a ghost?"

The reaction I thought I might have to the sound of her voice again wasn't what I expected. It didn't open an old wound. It's like the vibration of it flowed in and out of me, then it was gone. "No, Millie told me you come around. Told me you're…." I had trouble saying the word alive, her betrayal lodged in my throat like a piece of hard candy.

The pier creaked again. She'd taken a step toward me even though I asked her not to.

"How could you do it? To me I mean."

She sniffed. Two more steps, this time in the other direction. "Tonight it's a dark blue SUV. Two nights ago a black Toyota. They're not done."

"But Michael Wise never produced his podcast episode on them. You never actually revealed anything, not publicly. They didn't give you the chance."

"You did, Angus. You exposed them. People know who they are now, what they've been doing. Their project's exposed."

"Who's they? It's not Mendoza anymore. I took care of that

problem." It felt so strange to be talking like this, my back to her, emblematic of my inability to face her. But I knew if I saw her face again, held her in my arms, I'd never be able to let her stay away—from me and from our daughter.

"It's bigger than Mendoza. It goes much higher than that."

"Ava? How can you..."

"She's why I stay away. As long as they don't know where I am, they won't touch her."

I imagined I was standing on the patio of the brewery now, looking up at the sky, still barely believing my wife was standing behind me in the flesh, the living and breathing her, the version who'd let me die inside alone for the past two years. Even still, I couldn't help but turn toward her, my anguished eyes so hungry for the image of that face.

"What if..."

A noise from the trees cut off my voice. I turned back and stared into the empty spot on the pier where I knew she'd been standing. If I concentrated hard I was certain I could smell her Jo Malone perfume.

The next six months were a twist of tangled emotions. The new me trying to win the war against old me and a lifetime of baggage I was no longer willing to carry. The truth of Jessica alive in the world and me not able to see her went down hard. My apathy was followed by bitterness, occasionally rage, and then every time I looked in my daughter's green eyes, her tiny face buried in the bend of my neck, more of the icicles in my heart melted. The part of me that had died the night of our accident was never coming back. And it's like I didn't want it to, no longer needed it to. It created space. I was free.

The first time Dekker invited me to join his team at the SMPD, as a detective, he'd stated a mandatory two-month training period that was non-negotiable according to the CSLEA union stipulations. The second time, he arbitrarily reduced it to one-month as an enticement, and I suspected he'd eventually do away with the training altogether. I didn't mind being asked, considering what our relationship had been like for the past year. But even though Jessica never actually died in that ditch in Pescadero, *Detective* Angus Mariner did, and he no longer existed.

My alternate plan was something Michael Wise and I started discussing at the same time, during dinner at the Hyatt Embarcadero, like it was meant to be all along.

"So where's Jordan?" he'd asked me when we sat down. I'd barely told him a thing about her. I guess I didn't have to.

"I don't know. The bar I guess, working."

He was trying to control a grin. "You're blushing."

"I don't blush. Shut the fuck up."

"Fine. But for the record, you're blushing."

We ordered two appetizers - chicken potstickers and charcuterie board, while I knocked around his comments about Jordan.

"How's Ava doing?" he asked, though I knew what he was really asking.

"She's great." My chest felt warm just thinking about her. "Kinda shy around me still, but she seems to understand our connection now."

He nodded. "How are you gonna see her, like ongoing?"

"I don't know man, honestly. I don't know where Jess is at this very moment, but Millie's a nurse and Ava loves her and I'm gonna make it work somehow. There's no way I'd learn I have a daughter and turn my back on her, even if it is safer."

He picked up some chopsticks and dove into the potstickers. "Mendoza's gone. I know he has underlings, but the podcast is gonna expose them." He watched my eyes as he said it. "Have you decided? About the interview?"

"No interview," I shook my head. "You can expose any part of this saga with my blessing, but no interview. Not from me."

We didn't talk at all while we ate, not verbally anyway. When we were finished, the server cleared off our plates and we were left there at our empty table.

"What would you think about—"

And at the same time, I started saying, "Why don't we—"

We both stopped midway and laughed, somehow knowing we'd arrived at the same truth: we were a good team, and we both cared

CODEX

about the same thing. Justice.

"I know nothing about podcasts," I said. "But I think we're both good investigators."

"Private investigations? Is that what we're talking about? Mariner & Wise?"

I nodded, smiling at the fact that he'd put my name first, chewing on this idea. I liked how this sounded, liked how it felt. The possibilities were endless.

Chapter 55

Despite what Millie said about not being able to contact Jess, I knew she had to have some sort of secret spycraft method. I'd seen so many in movies. I sent her a text saying I needed to talk to Jess and that I'd meet her in the trees behind the same pier where we'd talked before, when she proved to me she wasn't actually dead. Eight hours later Millie sent a reply: *High Noon.* Funny, it had always been one of our favorite weekend westerns.

I liked how Jess seemed to be adapting to her new life on the run. Thinking like an operative, she knew that lunchtime under the bright sun would not be one of the surveillance periods. I got there first, an hour early, claiming a perfect vantage point under a huge elm tree hidden by a nest of shrubs about three feet tall. Perfect.

At 12:07 I heard a car door, then footsteps. Her fragrance was different today, Coco Chanel. She'd taught me all about fragrances early on, how the initial scent of citrus and jasmine could be very different from the *finish,* in this case patchouli. She'd dyed her hair a medium toned and uniform brown, which I thought made her even more conspicuous. She found a spot similar to mine on the other side of the walkway but close enough for us to talk.

"Hey," I said keeping my eyes on the deep blue water. Her long sigh told me how she was doing. "Thanks for meeting me," I added. "I know that complicates things."

"I don't have much time."

She was playing it cool, that's okay. I'd prepared myself for this. "I need some answers, Jess. You're not obligated to give me anything of course. But I'm still asking because I need to make sense of the world, such as it is now."

She pushed her lower lip out, the way she did when she was deliberating. "I understand." She looked right at me now.

"Did you intend all along to fake your own death? To deceive me?"

"Of course not. Obviously I didn't die in the crash like they'd hoped and shooting me would have been too obvious."

"What happened? Where the hell were you all this time?"

Long sigh. "They took me to a safehouse. North, I think up near Redding according to the driving time. And the smell of pines. They let Millie take care of me after the accident."

"You were a prisoner?" I asked. "Did they hurt you?"

She nodded. "I escaped, three times. They found me and the last time I was too weak to resist them. I had the baby up there, in that house. They let me give her to Millie." She snickered and shook her head. "They said I should be grateful."

I couldn't think about the baby right now. Focus. "Elaine? I assume they told you?" My voice cracked. The pain was still raw in my chest.

She was sobbing now. I heard the air coming in and out quickly. "I'm so...I can't..."

"I'm not gonna comfort you, Jess, much as I want to."

"It's okay."

"The truth is, I don't know you anymore."

After wiping her eyes with the sleeve of her shirt cuff, she turned to face me directly, but still camouflaged by shrubs. "I was gonna to tell you what I found, at work I mean, about Wendell Peters and his company. But then I found this secret drive with the data from his medical experiments. Your name was in those files."

"You still should have told me."

"By then, it was too long and convoluted a story and there wasn't enough time to tell you all of it. Besides, you wouldn't have believed me anyway because you didn't remember any of it until much later."

"So Mendoza's men are still after you for the journals."

She nodded. "They need the codex with the data on the gates in order to replicate the experiments." She'd lowered her voice and started looking around. "Don't tell me where the journals are but get rid of them somehow. Make copies, take photos of the pages and hide them in a password protected file, but make sure you get rid of the originals."

"Okay." Wise had already helped me do that.

We both turned back toward the water, a safer, more serene place to rest our eyes. We'd both lost so much.

"I can't even..." she started.

"What about Ava? I didn't even know you were pregnant."

"I knew but it was too early, and I'd only taken one test so far. I wanted to take a second to be sure, before I told you, before I let myself get excited."

I turned again to her, feeling a sudden urge to go to her. "I don't know how yet, but I'm gonna be a father to that child. I'll find a way to keep her safe."

"What about, never mind."

I knew what she was asking, of course. Examining the wispy threads of our former life, wondering if time might repair what was irrevocably broken. I shook my head but my whole body vibrated. "I don't trust you. Too much has happened. I can't go backwards and believe me I'd do anything if I could."

"Can you ever forgive me or at least believe that I was trying to protect you?"

"Maybe. Someday."

CODEX

Epilogue

[Podcast Transcript]

Say What?! A Podcast about Truth, Lies, and Everything in Between
Producer: Spy101 Enterprises
Host: Michael Wise

Welcome back to Spy101. You're about to get surprised, shocked, and a lot more cynical as we dive into a new series called Say What?!

As you know if you've been here before, Spy101 exposes schemes of corruption, fraud, and espionage among our country's corporations, lawmakers, and even average citizens. So strap in because this one's gonna be quite a ride.

Say What?! will be a multi part series tracking ongoing developments in a case folks from Northern California might remember. A little over two years ago, a car went off a cliff on the Pacific Coast Highway near a small beach south of San Francisco called Pescadero. The driver survived and the passenger, a 28-year-old lawyer, died instantly. What's most interesting is that there's considerable evidence now showing that the passenger, Jessica Mariner, was about to reveal information that would expose fraud, corruption, and medical malfeasance in the activities and transactions of ADS and Jasper Holdings. Jessica Mariner was a whistleblower preparing a courageous story, and someone stopped her before she got the chance to expose them.

Wendall Peters, a doctor, scientist, and entrepreneur, was an ear, nose and throat specialist who developed a new kind of cochlear implant to revolutionize the experience and quality of life for the hearing impaired. Sounds great, right? It was, at least until a CIA-funded venture capital firm called Jasper Holdings found out about it...and thought of a more nefarious application. What are we talking about? Mind control, which has been one of the most provocative concepts in military and government funded technologies since before World War Two. Jasper Holdings is, or I should say was led by CIA Assistant Director Sylvan Mendoza. And remember that name, folks, because you're gonna be hearing a lot more about him.

Ultimately this story is about science, public health, betrayal, and human oppression. Here's the thing: almost any technology can be weaponized. Technologies can be leveraged and monetized to gain advantage over a company, a government, even a country. Then you take that model to the world stage and see countless examples of this in foreign policy.

So the question is who would have been threatened by Jessica Mariner's report and who needed her to die? Sylvan Mendoza of Jasper Holdings acquired Wendell Peters' company ADS and immediately sank $50M into turning his innovative cochlear implant into a weapon for mind control. How did it work, who was in their control group and, more importantly, how did something like this stay off the radar until now? I'm a long-time journalist so I've got a file eight inches thick full of names, dates, witness statements. So in these following episodes we'll be laying it all out for you.

Subscribe to this channel so you'll be updated when Episode Two is

CODEX

dropped. Until then, keep your doors locked and clear your browsing history. You never know who's watching.

Until next time, I'm Michael Wise. Thanks for tuning in."

About the Author

Lisa Towles is an Amazon bestselling and award-winning crime novelist, and a passionate speaker on the topics of fiction writing, creativity, and self-care. She has twelve crime thrillers in print with a new thriller, *Specimen*, forthcoming in December of 2024. Her 2023 thriller, *Terror Bay*, won a NYC Big Book Award, Literary Titan Award, and is a Crimson Quill Awardee from Book Viral. Her 2022 thriller *Salt Island* won five literary awards and is the second book in her E&A Investigations Series. Lisa's deep commitment to helping other authors led her to develop her Author Spotlight blog and her new YouTube author interview series, Story Impact, which gives authors a powerful medium for promoting themselves as speakers and discussing the meaning and impact of their books to readers. Lisa has an MBA in IT Management, is a communications and marketing advisor, and is a member of Mystery Writers of America, Sisters in Crime, and International Thriller Writers.

Follow Lisa at LinkTree and subscribe to her monthly newsletter

LINKTREE   NEWSLETTER

Acknowledgments

Writing a book is an extraordinary experience. Every book is not only different in storyline but also its execution and process. Each one requires endless research, tireless energy, and takes a team of kind souls to keep you on track and sufficiently inspired to reach the final page. Then the real work begins. I owe a debt of gratitude to the people who made this book possible:

To my husband Lee, whose energy, passion, insight and verve are a constant inspiration. Your love and devotion bring me the greatest happiness of my life.

To my inspiring parents, who continue to surprise me with their grit, resilience, agility, and wisdom. You are my foundation and guiding light.

To my sister - a wise soul, inspiring role model, and insightful reader. You always show me the things I can't see myself.

To my precious nieces, Olivia and Cassidy – watching you grow up is an amazing experience. I'm forever in awe of you.

To my publisher, Lisa Orban, for her extraordinary vision in creating such a supportive community for authors, for her amazing expertise, patience, and support.

Without my amazing editor, Cindy Davis, this book would not have been publishable in the first place. Thank you for your expertise, support, guidance, and encouragement, and for pushing me to the next level.

Warmest thanks to my kind and tireless beta readers – Lee, Missy, Kat, George, Max, Natalka, Leo, and Ana. Your helpful feedback was so critical to improving this book.

To my graphic designer, Tatiana – you're a genius and incredibly skilled. Thank you for your talent and expertise, and for designing such a beautiful cover.

To my cherished Mystery Writers of America and Sisters in Crime writing companions - thank you for your inspiration, guidance, and companionship. I'm a better and happier writer because of you.

And to the wonderfully supportive readers of this book and my other books – THANK YOU from the bottom of my heart for your honest reviews, comments, support, and feedback.

Terror Bay
Psychological Thriller
Indies United Publishing House (2023)

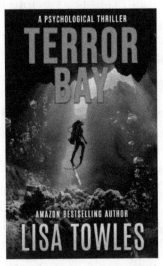

A woman. A ghostly summons. In a coma, no one can hear you scream. Detective Kurt Farin, shot in the line of duty, is haunted by a woman he sees in a coma. Come, she says. I'll show you things. Like the missing piece of your soul. His unshakable quest to find her leads him to northern Canada, where he discovers a shipwreck and a shocking family secret that can't possibly be true. As he digs deeper, he realizes his fate is inextricably tied to the enigmatic woman…and a long-lost treasure that's been submerged for centuries. His shooter, his nemesis, knows what he found and is coming to finish the job he started. Alone and exposed, Kurt's the only one who can bring down this notorious killer and expose an international scandal. But is the cost of justice - to him and everyone he loves, too high? Terror Bay is filled with intrigue and action, with surprises at every turn. Fans of John Sandford and Christine Kling will love Lisa Towles' new psychological thriller. Join Kurt's quest for the truth and Buy Terror Bay today.

Chapter One

I can see things in here, things the human *living* mind wasn't ever intended to see. I know how it sounds, how it makes me sound. I'm just reporting from this strange place.

I don't know exactly where here is right now, but I also don't think I'm dead. I seem to be waiting for something, but I don't know what. I feel it, my body preparing me. Making plans – shoving things in corners, finishing less significant tasks before the insistent takeover. I can't move forward until I find it, or it finds me. I can't move at all for that matter, or breathe, or remember the *before*. This thing in my future, an intangible presence, will clutch onto my spine, feast on my innards till it's eaten the whole of my vitality. And when it clicks into place, God help me. It's happened before, I can't see it yet but I feel its warm breath on the crown of my skull, descending like a promise of its inexorable coup.

Inside the deepest me there is this knowing, a knowing of another knowing. It could be music, or a name, even a person.

Genevieve Lucas. Yes, my bones vibrate inside as I say those five syllables in my head. Somehow, I know that Genevieve Lucas is my nemesis and my destiny.

Water has this smell deep beneath the surface. I recognize it from my scuba exploits so many years ago. A scent that's simultaneously fresh and rank, laden with hope and death. More than that, though, the inky-blue unlit terrain is a secret cosmos unto its own. The lack of light brings about a different kind of perception down here, the way sensory deprivation in one way boosts awareness - and capabilities - in others.

My arms are floating, and my body's anchored to something soft, but with more form than a mound of sea vegetation or sand. More like a bed. But if I'm under water, how could that be? The brain in this state is capable of mysterious magic, though I can't say exactly what state I'm in. I have pure awareness without the burdens of physicality. No, please, I can't be dead. Can I? But then what is this watery grave? I say the name again to myself because it feels good and real and home to say it. Genevieve…Genevieve Lucas. It echoes, distorted by the water. I am submerged. Separate, but close.

All the Zombie apocalypse movies I've watched aren't helping. I try opening my eyes wider but only see the same bubbly nothing all around me. What's odd is that my arms and legs can move. I try kicking and punching, but my torso and pelvis are anchored. I feel anger moving through me. What is going on? I'm a detective, dammit. So detect.

Okay, what's the last thing I remember? A case, a young girl at a club shot at close range on the dance floor and nobody heard a thing. We found our suspect, Jimmy Breslin, who'd been drinking at the same club every night since, as if paying vigil to his victim. We followed him, cornered him, we had him. And now I'm here in this floating nightmare, a house without windows. Something must have happened after that, happened to me, and that's the reason for this transcendent in-between. Coma? It must be, because nothing else makes sense. I admit it's not completely unpleasant, either. Peaceful, serene almost, but with no way out. It's a quiet jail that comes with a dull ache in my heart. I'm getting used to the pain now, the pain of knowing.

Wait, now I'm diving again, maybe part of this same dream, if that's what this place is. The frigid water seeps into tiny holes in my wetsuit. My body's shivering and I'm eyeing the surface, or at least the direction I think is the surface. Then I look down and see something. A dark outline of some structure. On one side there's seaweed, brown and fine. No, it's...hair. Brownish red, the color of seaweed half flowing with the water's current, the other half held down under its head. I use my fins to move toward it.

Something yanks against my waist. Dammit, my partner pulling my cord, a sign that we're heading back up. *I see you*, I say to the figure down there. You're not dead, I can save you. I see her. Please, one more minute. She's just—

Two tugs this time, harder, more insistent, a reminder of life and death. Turn back now or else.

A hand pushes outward from the body, a woman. Oh my God, she's alive. She's...there's no...how could she be down here without any breathing apparatus, how could she possibly be...? But she's moving. She sees me. I can feel her presence *inside me.*

One final tug and the cord's pulling me backwards now against my will.

Genevieve Lucas.

The name feels right. I see her head and shoulders now, buried under the two-hundred-year-old ship. Of course she's dead. She'd have to be, right? Who are you and why are you haunting me? What do you want? Did you bring me here to this liquid jail?

The cord pulls me away from her and I feel myself sobbing. I see light from the surface. I'm rising with the pull from the cord, my partner three feet ahead looking back to make sure I don't escape, knowing full well that is my intention.

Terror.

Terror.

I've seen it. It's coming.

REVIEWS
"A brainy, dazzling read" - *The Prairies Book Review*

"Gripping and twisty—a propulsive psychological thriller" - *Reader Views 5-Star Review*

"A rollercoaster ride of suspense, intrigue, and psychological tension" - *Readers Favorite*

AWARDS
NYC Big Book Award (Distinguished Favorite)
Readers Favorite Crimson Quill Awardee
Literary Titan (Gold)

The Ridders
Political Thriller
Indies United Publishing House (2022)

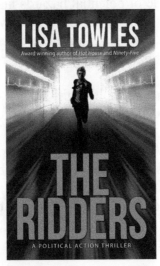

Young PI, BJ Janoff is randomly approached by a stranger with a proposition he can't refuse – a million dollars to deliver an envelope to a hotel lobby. The pusher forces him to accept the money upfront and threatens to kill him if he doesn't deliver the envelope in three days. BJ's growing obsession leads him down a treacherous path toward the orchestrators of the game, where he discovers a large-scale political controversy, a treasure hunt for a priceless sword, and a global crime ring linked to a WWII-era secret society. When an act of brilliance changes the balance of power, the safety of everyone he loves is in jeopardy. And the more he digs, the closer he comes to truths he can't bear to face – about his missing father and the elusive Bilderberg Group.

Chapter One

What would you do if someone offered you a million dollars to bring an envelope to the reception desk of a luxury hotel? That's it. Sure, a no-brainer. A relatively inconsequential risk, easy money, right? Trouble is, anything involving a million dollars might not be what it seems. So many questions. Namely why me, BJ Janoff, should be offered this seemingly innocuous task. There were no answers available, no consultants waiting with details or clarifications. One million dollars in cash to perform this social experiment. Right now. Yes or no?

I know what my older brother Jonas would do. He'd say no because of the multitude of potential hazards his paranoid mind would concoct, keeping him tied to the past, still wearing the same ugly khakis from ten years ago, stuck in the protective bubble of his big house in Ladera Heights and his geriatric Mercedes. So, of course I didn't tell him. Yet.

Then there was Lacy Diaz, the girl-next-door-turned-lawyer, who drives a car flashy enough to get a speeding ticket if she goes over fifty on the freeway.

"Hell, yeah, I'd take it," she said, with about a hundred caveats. What do you expect; she's a lawyer. "Wear rubber gloves," she said. "Ask to see the contents of the envelope first. If it's money, fan it out so you can see the bill denominations. Take photos of the payor."

"Photos of the payor?" I laughed and closed my eyes, a response Lacy inspired by pretty much everything she did. "Excuse me sir, would you mind if—"

"I'm just trying to protect you from potential—"

"Potential. Now you sound like Jonas. His whole world is so much potential there's no room for now."

"He's your brother. You can't choose your family so get over it."

So be it. A million dollars? Hell yeah, of course I said yes, I'm not stupid. Luckily, the task was intended for not only the most beautiful hotel in LA but the one I went to almost every morning. Sure, the cappuccinos were okay at the Peets counter, but the staff was even more noteworthy.

"Good morning," I said, loping up to the counter.

"Is it?"

"Pretty sure." I didn't let my eyes fall below Raquel's neck, given her choice of a low-cut blouse.

"Usual?"

"Yeah." I watched the Westin Bonaventure Hotel staff moving wordlessly through their tasks today. A keen observer of human behavior, I knew something was going down when Mario the bellhop pushed an empty cart past me and lowered his eyes to the floor. No banter, humming, rapping, high fiving me. No smile. "Hey?" I called after him. "What am I, invisible?" Alena, who managed the daytime housekeeping staff, hurried after him toward the elevators. Her face looked like she'd been crying all morning. No makeup and she was buttoning her uniform top while she walked. Maybe I'm paranoid.

Raquel was moving slowly and clearly not interested in talking. So I took three steps to the left to get a view of the reception desk. The typical chorus line of coiffed, perky concierges today included a confused, twenty-year-old in a wrinkled t-shirt. Something, no doubt related to the FedEx envelope I'd tucked into the back of my pants, was afoot. Out of coffee sleeves, I burned my fingers on Raquel's cappuccino and hunkered low on a lobby sofa watching and sipping. A cadre of men in identical black suits marched to the reception desk. Here we go.

I calculated my distance to be roughly fifty feet from the polished, walnut counter, maybe forty-five. Lucky for me, the acoustics in here rivaled the Guggenheim and I could hear everything. One suited man in front, nine underlings huddled behind awaiting instructions. I heard the word envelope posed as a question. The misplaced pothead behind the counter looked like he might start crying any moment. He gazed through the suits into the cavernous lobby space. Don't look at me, buddy, I don't exist right now. I took three more sips of coffee then back to my morning theater.

My phone buzzed with an incoming call. Jonas, who I suppose qualified as my business partner even though I wasn't paid an equal salary, and there was no legal agreement in place that formalized our working arrangement. "Hey, bro," I whispered.

"Hey, bro?" Repeating was one of his annoying traits. He had so many.

"What?"

"Where the fuck are you?"

"On a job," I lied. "Where are you?" I laughed inside, knowing this would unglue him. He hated the idea of my taking side jobs because he felt I was unqualified to be a private investigator. When our partner Archie Dax was still around, we used to laugh about this. He and I were so similar. He understood me almost better than anyone. I'd only had my investigator's license for less than a year when he died, but he never thought that mattered. Said I had the right head for PI work. Aww, Arch. My world's not the same without you.

"Job? What job?"

Poor Jonas. I still hadn't told him.

"Okay look, we've got the Bergman family coming in at nine tomorrow morning and I need the…" He exhaled long and hard, specifically to relay his frustration and inspire guilt. That ploy never worked with me.

"What, Jonas—WiFi? Maybe you've heard of something called the internet. Yes, I know, and we're good."

"Router, that's it."

Lord. "It's not the router, it's the modem speed and the unit will be upgraded within the hour. We're fine. Just let them in when they arrive."

No response.

"Are you crying?" I asked. "Pacing? Take your pill, Jonas."

"Fuck off. Say hi to Raquel for me."

I hung up and the phone rang again. "Dude, what?"

"And please don't wear your stupid backwards baseball hat. Please? I beg you. The Bergmans have money, a lot of it. We need that right now."

"Okay Jonas, no hat. Happy now?"

"We'll see."

Okay, so about the Bergmans. Jonas had been talking with them, Sten and Estelle, for the past two days about their vanished eighteen-year-old daughter, Anastasia, heir to their multi-billion-dollar estate, and how her net worth made her an especially enticing ransom target to what they described as "the underworld". LA's not utopia but not sure I'd call it an underworld.

Just two more errands today. First, I put a five-dollar bill in Raquel's tip vase even though she didn't see me. She still deserved it for being open at 6 a.m. and for looking so goddamn beautiful first thing in the morning. Then I held a small, black plastic ball in my hands and set it on a side table with a perfect view of the hotel's reception area. The table was on the other side of the seating area so that meant roughly thirty feet from the front desk. The plastic ball, a nanny cam designed to look like an air filter, was partially concealed by the fat leaves on a fake rubber tree plant. Unless someone moved that plant, or the filter for that matter, I'd be able to see the front desk of the Bonaventure Hotel for the next twenty-four hours via an iPhone app, which I suspect would be time enough to see why someone would pay a stranger a million bucks to deliver a stupid envelope.

REVIEWS

"A fast-paced, tense and gripping murder mystery" - *Readers' Choice*

"A captivating tale that engrosses on many levels" - *Midwest Book Review*

"A must-read for fans of suspense thrillers" - *Book Viral Reviews*

AWARDS

BookFest Award (1st Place)
American Fiction Award (1st Place)
Millennium Book Award (Longlisted)
Literary Titan Award (Gold)

Ninety-Five
Techno Thriller
Indies United Publishing House (2021)

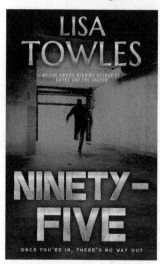

Troubled University of Chicago student, Zak Skinner, accidentally uncovers evidence of an on-campus, organized crime scam involving drugging students, getting them to commit crimes on camera, and blackmailing them to continue under the threat of expulsion. Digging deeper, Zak discovers that the university scam is just the tip of the iceberg, as it's connected to a broader ring of crimes linked to a dark web underworld. Following clues, Zak is led to a compound within Chicago's abandoned Steelworker Park, only to discover that he's being hunted. While trying to find his way out alive, Zak discovers there's something much more personal he's been running from – his past. And now there's nowhere to hide.

Prologue

"Ten dollars…each."

I reached for my wallet. Riley put up his palm. "We're guests of a member."

The bouncer eyerolled. "Who?"

"David Wade," Riley said.

"We're both students here. Asshole." I held out my ID.

"Wade's not here and I'm not going looking for him. Twenty dollars or leave."

I handed the guy two tens, then he stamped both our wrists. The entry doors opened with David Wade on the other side, hair styled like a teen magazine cover. Typical.

"Hope you didn't pay," he laughed. "You're my guests."

"Wade." I had a feeling I'd be doing that a lot this year. We followed him back to a booth by the pool tables.

"I've set up two meetings," Wade explained. "For each of you, and they'll be conducted separately."

"Why? Divide and conquer?" Riley asked.

"I shouldn't even be here," I said eyeing the door. "Riley's way more desirable to a fraternity. He graduated third in our high school class." I was in the top thirty percent, if that.

"Dude, you are not leaving me here alone. This was your idea," Riley reminded me.

"Listen up. Sigma Chi's first, then Phi Gamma Delta." Wade with his frat salesman flair. Fine, I'd give them five minutes.

"What's your finder's fee?" Riley asked the most important question of the night.

A pitcher and three glasses appeared on the table. Funny how I never knew what I was drinking in this place. Just beer. Not IPA, Pilsner, Belgian. We were college students; we'd drink anything, right?

"You mean if you're selected? Less than forty-percent of frat recruits actually make it in." Wade lowered his head. "Even lower for enlistees."

I repeated Riley's valid question. "What do you get out of this? For some of these elitist Republican machines, the dues are like three hundred bucks a month."

"What?" Riley snapped his head toward me. "You're right. What are we doing here?"

"We're socializing, remember?" I said. "We just transferred two months ago. We hardly know anyone." I could barely remember NYU at this point. Chicago's a long way from home.

Wade smiled his smooth, snaky grin, enjoying the logic of my statement. He raised his glass. "Well, here's to new beginnings."

"Choke on it." Riley clocked Wade's glass. He glared at me while he guzzled the entire contents.

Wade refilled Riley's glass and disappeared with the empty pitcher. Now that the pool tables were filled, the noise had doubled, probably because we were getting drunker. Riley hated to drink. In fact, I was surprised he agreed to come in the first place. But it was on campus, just a short walk from Granville West, our home away from home.

"Hey." A new guy shoved into Wade's side of the empty booth. "Sigma Chi, how's it going? Which one of you is Zak?"

Riley and I pointed to each other. The guy had a peach fuzz crew cut. His face looked like it was scrubbed every thirty minutes.

"I can't imagine why you'd be even remotely interested in me," I admitted. "Riley's got a 4.0 GPA and a way better pedigree."

"Yeah, but you have lawyers in your family," Riley shouted in his bar voice. He leaned in and smiled in a way that revealed rising blood alcohol level. "More likely you'd be able to afford the fees."

The frat salesman shifted on the bench, sizing us up. He turned his head back toward the bar, probably looking for Wade, the eternal icebreaker.

"Fees are optional," he said in a bitchy tone.

I peeked one eye at the door, making sure we had a path of egress. Wade was naturally nowhere in sight.

How could Riley bring up my family like that? So crude and indifferent. He never could hold his liquor. I didn't mind paying to get in here, or even sitting through this ridiculous formality. It beat the monotony of hanging out in our dorm waiting for life to happen. But Wade had showed up at the door, vanished, and now I just felt played.

"Oh, I see," Riley broke in. "You only charge them to offset your legal fees resulting from discrimination, rape, and aggravated assault lawsuits? I get it. That must be really expensive. You know, hard to plan when all your Daddy's money's going to—"

"Riley," I clipped. "Shut it. Let's get out of here."

I scanned the interior. Pool tables, dart boards, wood paneled walls; I remembered reading that The Pub in the basement of University of Chicago's Ida Noyes' Hall had been run by descendants of the Medici's. The only thing missing in here was Sherlock Holmes. Raised voices caught my attention from the opposite corner, then the sound of a beer bottle breaking. Ah, the perfect diversion.

I yanked Riley's elbow and we headed for the entrance. Five seconds later, I looked back still plowing through the crowd.

"Where are they?" Riley asked.

I pulled open the door and we slipped out.

Two guys followed. One from Sigma Chi and another I didn't recognize. They were all the same to me.

"Walk faster," I said. "Follow the path, straight ahead." Sure, we needed to get away from these people, but the more important question nagging me was why we would be of interest in the first place. New to campus, barely social, not wealthy. What attributes would be of value to them?

"The Fountain of Time's up ahead," Riley said, speeding up. "Are they behind us?"

As I was about to answer him, two different guys cut through the evergreens to our left and blocked us.

"Hey guys," one of them said, palms up, toothy grin. "Look, Damen got us off to a bad start. Let's start over. I'm from Sigma Chi."

"And I'm from Phi Gamma," the other said. "Please, come with us so we can talk. That's all we want."

"We're not interested in you frat clowns, the world's fucked up enough already."

Riley drunk always cracked me up.

"We're all here because you think we might have the money to pay your dues so you can maintain your alcohol supply," he added.

The thugs squared off in front of us. Riley stepped back. When he crossed his arms, he lost his balance and fell back on the grass. Nice.

Phi Gamma dragged him off with an arm around his shoulders. Sigma Chi stayed with me, waiting. Watching. He sat on the grass and pulled out a flask. I kept my eyes on Riley, now twenty feet away.

"Liquid courage?" I crouched on the ground across from him, knowing at this point we'd need to listen to the pitch before they let us go. If.

Riley and Phi Gamma were no longer visible. Fine. I'd give this freak five minutes of my life, then I'd go find him. I had no fear of him at this point, just irritation. I watched the guy pour something into two little silver cups—one the lid of the shiny flask, the other from his pocket. What else had been in that pocket?

"Absinthe," the guy said with conspiratorial pride.

I raised an eyebrow. More impressive than Budweiser.

"With or without *thujone*?" I asked of the historical wormwood hallucinogenic constituent.

"You know your poisons," he replied. "Without." He handed me a cup and tapped it, then swigged his down in one gulp.

Where was Riley? What the fuck were we doing out here? I came to this school for a fresh start, as my mother put it, and somehow I didn't think this was what she, or even I, had in mind. Sigma Chi, my salesman, held out the shiny silver cup with a wet smirk on his lips. Was I about to end up in Mexico or as somebody's bitch in Danville Prison?

"Riley, you alright?" I shouted behind me.

No answer. Sigma Chi stared, wiggling the cup. At this point I was more annoyed than afraid. I wasn't happy at this place yet, at this University. Riley wasn't either. But I wasn't ready to throw it all in either. Had anyone ever died from absinthe? I grabbed the cup, swiveled it around a bit, smelled it, then chucked it back in my throat. Like sophisticated licorice. God help me.

REVIEWS

"A dazzling trip into a dystopian techno-nightmare" – *David Prestidge*

"A riveting thriller" – *San Francisco Book Review*

"Marked by its striking execution and razor-sharp dialogue, this places Towles among the best of the genre" – *Prairies Book Review*

AWARDS
Readers Favorite Award (Winner)
Literary Titan Award (Silver)
Clue Award (Finalist)
Indies Today Award (Semi-Finalist)

Printed in the USA
CPSIA information can be obtained
at www.ICGtesting.com
LVHW052328250524
781225LV00017B/55/J